DEADLY

The Undersecretary pointed to the holographic close-up of Jupiter. "This is the original predicted configuration of the moons at the time of the comet's passage."

Suddenly, the four moons were in different positions. "This, however, is the current predicted configuration. According to the monks, the moons have moved. And the new trajectory of the comet . . ."

A glowing trail showed where the comet would pass. As it sped past Jupiter, it came within a hairsbreadth of hitting Ganymede and Europa. Its exit trajectory continued to extend until suddenly it terminated—midway between Sumatra and Sri Lanka.

The Undersecretary's face was grim. "It's coming straight at us, over a distance of half a billion miles, at ten times its normal speed! It is an act of war. . . . The Buddhists have renamed the comet Death."

"Well imagined and inventive, by two writers who harbor wild imaginations beneath their sober academic roles. I enjoyed every moment."

—Gregory Benford,
Nebula Award-winning author of *The Martian Race*

"Weaves an astounding array of threads into a tapestry remarkable for its scope, richness of detail, cleverness, and imagination."

—Stanley Schmidt, editor of *Analog*

wheelers

ian stewart
and jack cohen

ASPECT®

WARNER BOOKS

An AOL Time Warner Company

WARNER BOOKS EDITION

Copyright © 2000 by Joat Enterprises and Jack Cohen

Cover design by Don Puckey
Cover illustration by Bob Eggleton

Aspect® name and logo are registered trademarks of Warner Books, Inc.

Warner Books, Inc., 1271 Avenue of the Americas, NY, NY 10020

Visit our Web site at www.twbookmark.com.

For information on Time Warner Trade Publishing's online publishing program, visit www.ipublish.com.

 An AOL Time Warner Company

Printed in the United States of America

Originally published in hardcover by Warner Books
First Paperback Printing: October 2001

10 9 8 7 6 5 4 3 2 1

wheelers

1

Giza, 2194

. . . and in the fifth month of the fifth year of the reign of the child-king Anshethrat, in the city of Gÿzer . . . a spear of fire pierced the northern sky, harbinger of the wrath of Ysiriz the Sky Goddess. And fire and flame rose from the ocean, which became as molten brass. And the spear of flame sped like a hurled javelin toward the heart of the Sun. It became as a fiery chariot, drawn by four winged horses, with manes of burnished copper, pursued by a trail of shining dust. One horse had the face of a hawk, and one the face of a wolf, and one the face of a snake . . . the face of the fourth was devoid of form . . . Ysiriz the Sky Goddess had the face of a lion and the claws of a leopard, and her tail was the tail of a lion . . .

And Y-ra'i the gods-that-dwell-beneath-the-Sun awoke, and saw Ysiriz riding the shaft of flame. And Y-ra'i began to stir, and seethe. And they frightened the horses of Ysiriz. And dust and stones fell upon the Earth, and the ground shook with the thunder of their hooves, and the mountains cracked and the Earth shook . . . and the child-king Anshethrat called his Priests to him, and he demanded of them what could be done to appease Ysiriz the Sky Goddess. And the priests ordered the sacrifice of five thousand bulls, and five thousand rams, that their blood be shed for the appeasement of Ysiriz.

And so it was.

And still the chariot drew nearer, for the gods were displeased.

And Lofchepsit the Moon Goddess awoke, and shivered with fear . . . And the Sun trembled and shook, and . . . Y-ra'i flung a spear of flame at the heart of Ysiriz.

And the horse with the face of a hawk stumbled, and fell, and was crushed to dust. And the horse with the face of a wolf stumbled, and fell, and was crushed to dust. And the horse with the face of a snake stumbled, and fell, and was crushed to dust. And the horse with no manner of face stumbled, and fell, and it was as if it had never been . . .

And the fiery chariot of Ysiriz plunged into Lofchepsit the Moon Goddess, striking at her very heart, and the chariot vanished in flame . . . And Lofchepsit fell in a terrible swoon, as if dead.

And the whole sky shone as a sheet of beaten gold, and the Sun's heart blackened and seethed. And the Priests of the child-king Anshethrat were much afraid, and they cried out for forgiveness from their king, for all were fearful of the wrath of Ysiriz and the slaying of Lofchepsit. And the king in his great wisdom denounced the Priesthood, and sent them out of the city into the sands of the desert, there to build a monument to Y-ra'i.

But now the gods-that-dwell-beneath-the-Sun arose, and their wrath was as the wrath of a raging torrent, and they spread great wings of burning flame. And their breath became a breath of fire, and they spat at Anshethrat. And the Moon was aflame, and the sky was aflame, and the Earth was aflame, and every tree in the city of Gÿzer turned to blackened ashes, and every house in the city became as a pillar of flame . . .

But the Priests of the child-king Anshethrat hid themselves, and the flames passed them by. And they proclaimed the miracle to be a sign from Ysiriz the Sky Goddess, who had protected them from the fiery wrath of Y-ra'i. And the High Priest Shephatsut-Mir ordered that the monument to Y-ra'i be

*torn down and built anew in the image of Ysiriz, multiplied
twelvefold, to seal forever the devotion of her people to the
Sky Goddess.*

And it was so.

Charlie Dunsmoore brushed sand from his rolled-up shirt-
sleeves, opened another can of beer, and sighed. He focused
a small pocket lens on the chipped clay tablet, comparing the
incised hieroglyphs with Prudence Odingo's transcriptions as
they floated holographically before his eyes, and nodded.
Then his rubber-gloved finger slid through the air to where
she had translated the text into English, and he shook his head
slowly from side to side with a fleeting, wry smile.

Prudence was eager, he had to admit. *And* she was intelligent. She had the kind of luck that could make an archaeologist's career . . . Sexy, too, as he had discovered to his
surprise the night after her astonishing find. Not that he considered it ethical for academics to have sexual relationships
with their students—he knew that just stored up potential
trouble and his department head wouldn't be at all happy if
she found out—but it had all happened so fast, and so spontaneously, that he'd never even thought about all that until far
too late.

Anyway, there were criteria other than ethics. That said, he
wasn't sure what their relationship was anymore—or even if
they still *had* one—because they had both been so tired after
working flat out on the tablets for three solid days, snatching
a few hours' sleep whenever they could no longer keep themselves awake, that there had been no opportunity for a repeat
engagement, and no point in hinting at the possibility of one.

He could hear deep breathing and the occasional snore
from Prudence's partitioned-off corner of the big tent that the
two of them shared. Administratively straightforward, and

cheaper than *two* big tents, but—he now saw—asking for trouble.

If only the funding agency had taken the ethical position into account . . .

His thoughts returned to Prudence. Motivated, bright, lucky, sexy . . . If only she could stop being in such a *rush*. Her translation was wonderful, it told a fascinating story from an unknown pre-Egyptian mythology: Y-ra'i *the gods-that-dwell-beneath-the-Sun* . . . Brilliant.

The only problem was, she'd woven the tale from whole cloth. Where a more cautious scholar would have flagged a word as dubious or a sentence as conjectural, Prudence simply jumped right in with what looked like a claim of a definitive text.

She had excellent intuition; he'd seen it in action on conventional Egyptian hieroglyphics. That was why he'd agreed to take her on as a graduate student, and why he'd put her in charge of the most significant part of the dig.

Dig. He laughed under his breath—the term was a reflex, and not at all appropriate. "Disassembly of the Sphinx," that was closer.

He put the notebook down on the small, rickety table, stripped off the gloves, and stepped over to the open flap of the tent. He loved the feel of the desert air, cool and dry on his skin. Fine sand dust gave the air a faint but unforgettable smell, bringing back vivid memories of previous expeditions . . . Silhouetted against the starry sky he could see the flat triangles of pyramids and the slight swell of desert dunes. To his right, less than half a mile away, was the Great Pyramid, the most famous of all the ancient monuments at Giza. He had seen it so often that he had lost count; he had climbed its crumbling stones, sat at its tip, and stared for hours across the desert, trying to visualize what life must have been like when the stones were newly quarried . . . and still it possessed the power to move him. There was something elemental about the ancient rock pile—even now, nearly five thousand years after it had been built. The Great Pyramid was a symbol of power, the awesome power of Khufu, founder of the Old Kingdom. It was awesome now; just think how effective a reminder it must have been at the peak of the fourth dynasty. And it was just one monument out of many, evidence of a vanished civilization that he would give *anything* to bring back to life. The three much smaller queen's pyramids were scattered almost as an afterthought along its near right flank. Ahead, diminished by the distance, was the pyramid of Khafre, in reality only marginally smaller and just as impressive. To his left, Menkaure's Pyramid, its base a mere hundred yards square, dwarfed by its gigantic companions. And looming above him, still glowing like embers in the dying sunset, was the haunting, battered face of the Great Sphinx. Restored by the eighteenth dynasty in AD 1500, its nose chiseled off, but no one knew when or why. Pockmarked by windblown sand and, more recently, acid rain, it bore a face so similar to that of Khafre that there could be little doubt that it had been fashioned in his image.

The pitted eyes stared blindly at the desert, serene and enigmatic. Carved in the stylized image of a lion, the monument was most probably a symbol of the Sun—human head on a lion's body, a guarantor of cosmic order with a scarf for a mane.

Or so the scholars believed. Charlie had his doubts.

Whatever its original purpose, the Sphinx was in trouble. Its base was hidden by an ugly skeleton of steel scaffolding, wooden planks, ladders, and walls of yellow netting. Three large cranes were lined up along its left flank, spindly by comparison. Although he couldn't see anything from where he stood, the Sphinx's hindquarters and most of its body were gone, sliced into rough cubes of rock fifteen feet across, lifted by the massive cranes onto enormous low-loaders with huge soft tires, driven slowly away across the open desert to the higher ground of Jabal Abū Shāmon, some thirty miles to the east.

Not for the first time, Charlie shook his head in disbelief. It was a tragedy. The collapse of the Aswan Dam, some sixty years earlier, was to blame. An ecological and archaeological disaster from the moment of its conception two and a half centuries before, it had slowly crumbled under its own weight, victim of shoddy workmanship and worse planning. Its inevitable destruction was hastened by climate change, which dumped huge amounts of rainwater into the catchment area around Lake Victoria, the source of the Nile. The dam had burst under the strain and the silt that had previously been deposited on the bed of the vast artificial lake had flowed downstream like molasses; now it was clogging up the Nile delta to the north of Cairo, in Al-qalyubiyah governorate. Charlie had seen the devastation for himself while flying his tiny Deronda into the Cairo airport. He was an avid pilot, and wherever he went in Europe or Africa he took the lovingly re-stored propeller-engined four-seater along. From the air, it was evident that much of Cairo was slowly disappearing under the floodwaters—there had been heroic efforts to divert the river and dredge new channels, but Egypt was not a rich country. The Giza complex was slowly succumbing to rising levels of groundwater, and the best that an international rescue effort could offer—as for the fabled Temple of Abu Simbel two and a half centuries earlier—was a belated and rather panicky project to cut the Sphinx up into transportable chunks and re-erect it on higher ground.

The pyramids would have to fend for themselves.

Charlie found it all quite incredible, but the disassembly of the Sphinx created an unprecedented opportunity to try to re-solve some of its mysteries, and the prospect had lured him to Giza like a glowworm to a female's seductive lantern.

How old *was* the Sphinx? That was the big question. According to Egyptologists, the monument had been built in Khafre's reign, at the same time as his pyramid. Why else would it have borne his face? Charlie knew that Khafre, son of Khufu, had flourished around 2400 BC. But geologists who had studied the natural bedrock that formed the Sphinx's paws and body had found evidence of substantial weathering by rain. It *could* have been caused by wind, assisted by unstable minerals in the stone—but on balance, rain seemed more plausible. There hadn't been much rain in Egypt around the time of Khafre, but there had been plenty two thousand years earlier. The head could have been added later, or remodeled—it was too small in proportion to the body, suggesting that it had once been larger. Perhaps the original had been a lion in all particulars, and Khafre had stolen its face. So geology placed the Sphinx somewhere prior to 4400 BC, a date that would force a complete rethink of Egyptian and pre-Egyptian chronology, while impeccable Egyptology placed it two thousand years later.

Thanks to Prudence's discovery, it was beginning to look as though those geologists who favored rain might be right. Before the giant diamond-toothed saws were permitted to slice into any new bit of Sphinx, Prudence had to use gravimetric equipment to test for concealed chambers. She had found several, but all were natural cavities in the bedrock—until three days ago, when she had discovered a priceless treasure. The workforce had opened up a cavity, *very* carefully as always, and within it she had found a cache of several hundred clay tablets, inscribed with symbols that looked like hieroglyphs but seemed to be some earlier form of script out of which hieroglyphs had evolved, and some rather odd clay figurines of crouching naked women with lionlike features. A first stab at isotope distribution dating had placed them somewhere between 6600 BC and 3800 BC, with 5500 BC as the maximum-likelihood estimate.

They *could* date from a period before the base of the Sphinx had been carved from bedrock. Both Charlie and Prudence doubted this—the figurines had a Sphinxlike quality that was distinctly unnerving. So now they were translating the tablets in the hope that the text would settle the matter once and for all. They were having to do it on the spot because the Egyptian authorities, with justification, refused to allow the tablets to be removed from the site. Charlie and Prudence were permitted to look at them in small batches, and because Charlie had made the scientific case eloquently, they'd been given access to the actual tablets. Holograms were all very well for archiving, but a hologram wasn't accurate enough for serious archaeological study.

Charlie yawned, walked back to the table, and sat down again. He told his wristnode to check the weather forecast, wondered whether it would be any more accurate than usual, and pulled the thin rubber gloves back over his fingers to protect the precious tablet. He put his 'node back into word processing mode, told it to open a new file, and began editing Prudence's efforts into something publishable.

". . . and in the fifth month of the fifth year"—that was okay, though it needed a footnote to the effect that the rudimentary hieroglyph for "month" bore no resemblance to that of the Late Predynastic period—which, however, was only to be expected since the clay tablet had been dated to a period some fifteen hundred years earlier—and its meaning was amply confirmed by other texts found in the same location and with similar dates. "Of the reign of the child-king Anshethrat"—oh, dear. The glyphs that Prudence had read as "reign" might equally well refer to "stewardship," and "child-king" was almost certainly "viceroy"—"king *in place of* a child," not "king *who is* a child." As for "Anshethrat," the clay was so flaky at that spot that there could have been a dozen readings. His eyes flicked onward and he mumbled to his wristnode sotto voce, as was his habit when dictating. He rather liked "harbinger of the wrath of Ysiriz the Sky Goddess"—it was a defensible reading, though a reference to the theories of Gutzmann and Monteleone was definitely in order . . . but there was no way he could justify "fiery chariot," and as for the alleged winged horses . . .

He mumbled on, and a tortured, laborious text, full of brackets indicating lacunae, footnotes to alternative readings, and labored arguments regarding the unorthodox grammatical structure began to assemble itself in midair in faintly glowing letters.

He was just starting to get it into an acceptable shape when Prudence came in. "God, I feel like I haven't slept for a week." She saw the text a moment before Charlie told his wristnode to kill it. "What are you doing, Charlie? That looked like the text you gave me to translate!"

Charlie looked sheepish. "Um . . . yes, it was. I was—er—licking it into shape. For publication."

"Oh, god. Are you messing up my work *again*?"

Charlie considered this unfair. "Now, look here, Pru, don't forget that I'm the supervisor and you're the student." The look that she gave him was far from happy. "Damn it, you know I'm not the type to pull rank. But I *do* know what the journals will let us publish, okay?"

She shrugged. Charlie was clever, Charlie was kind of cute—short blond hair, blue eyes, tall, strong without being musclebound—but Charlie was also an unimaginative stick-in-the-mud. *He* called it scholarship, *she* called it chickenshit.

However, he was right, which made it all the worse.

"Oh, come *on*, Charlie! Give me a break, hey? I *slaved* over that translation most of the night! Sure, I filled in a few gaps, but it *feels* right. Better to tell a clear story, even if a few pedantic details turn out to be wrong later, than end up with unreadable trash that commits us to nothing."

They'd had this argument before, though at that time he hadn't been sleeping with her. Assuming he still *was*, which was not exactly clear. "Mmm, yeah, in a world where everyone who reads your work can intuit the intended context instead of deliberately looking for possible ways to misunderstand your intentions and label you an idiot, that's right. Unfortunately, most academics don't *live* in such a world—they'd all love to run the whole show, but they don't have the guts to take responsibility for their own decisions, so it's much more comforting to sit on the sidelines and carp. And

Egyptologists are the worst of the lot, believe me. Which is why, in my professional role as your research supervisor, I'm telling you that we write the paper *my* way, even if the result lacks your journalistic flair."

Prudence's face softened a bit . . . a hint of a smile? "Okay, Charlie, you can call the shots on the paper. But you leave the press release to me."

If he'd been less tired he might have seen the trap yawning and managed not to jump into it feet first. "*Press release?*"

"Charlie, dear, we have just made the biggest Egyptological discovery since Snuckpot the Great stuck a small rock on top of a larger one and thought that a big version would keep the rain off his corpse after he was dead! We have *got* to go to the media before the story leaks."

Typical Prudence, belying her name as always. "What story, Pru?"

"Proof that the Sphinx is *aeons* older than everyone thought! Evidence of a flourishing civilization two millennia before the first dynasty! Ancient writings by the trucklo—"

He spoke slowly and distinctly. It wasn't intended to sound patronizing, but that's how it came out. "Prudence, we don't *know* any of that. The dating is only preliminary, it could be wrong. All we have is a stack of clay tablets, which for all we know record nothing more interesting than how many people turned up at the annual spitting contest. And the tablets could have been shut up in a cavity in the bedrock, and the Sphinx built around them later."

Charlie's affectations of pedantry raised Prudence's mental temperature close to the boiling point. "*Come* on, Charlie! You don't believe a word of that! You know damned well that I prepared those dating specimens properly! I spent *hours* making absolutely sure! And what about those figurines? *They're* a lot earlier than first dynasty! And they look amazingly Sphinxlike, you *know* that. What *else* can it all mean?"

He didn't know how to respond. He felt confused, bewildered . . . and more than a little scared. Prudence was right, really—this discovery could make both of their reputations, secure them fellowships with the International Archaeological Society at an unprecedentedly young age . . . *But* if they went to the news media prematurely, their best career prospects would be drilling into asteroids for a neo-Zen mining combine. Charlie was not a natural risk-taker; Prudence knew no other way.

"We can't trust intuition here, Prudence. There will be *no* press release." He was intending to add the word "yet," but he never got the chance.

"You brainless, chicken-livered *idiot!*" He half expected her to go for his throat, the way her fingers were shaping themselves into claws . . .

"Don't be childish. This is *my* project and *my* grant—"

"And *my* discovery, which *you* are trying to take credit for—"

"And *you* will do what I tell you. Don't forget what it says in your contract."

Prudence froze—then glared at him. In a voice vibrant with the effort of control, she told him exactly what he could do with her contract.

It is difficult to storm out of a tent, but she managed it with something to spare.

Finally waking up to what he'd done, Charlie swore, briefly and scatologically; then slumped into a chair and stared morosely at the sandy floor. *Smart. Really smart.* He thought about rushing out after her. It wouldn't do any good; he knew what Prudence was like when she'd blown her fuses. Best to wait, give her a chance to cool off . . .

He spent half an hour feeling miserable, and twice he nearly set off in pursuit, but reason prevailed. Finally, to try to break the foul mood, he carefully lifted a tablet from the box, at random, and peeled back the layers of bubblewrap. He didn't feel like accessing his 'node, so this would have to be an informal, preliminary scan.

In the artificial light he ran his pocket lens along the wavering rows of symbols, trying to translate them on the fly.

He was about six sentences into the text before he consciously realized what he was looking at.

He felt the hairs rise on the nape of his neck—legacy of ten million years of ape ancestry, a primal signal straight from the limbic brain. With exaggerated care he set the tablet back amid its plastic wrappers before his shaking hands dropped it. "Bloody hell," he muttered. "Bloody hell, bloody hell, bloody hell." Inventiveness failed him.

He rushed from the tent shouting for Prudence, to tell her what they had found. The noise woke up his collaborators from the Cairo Museum and the entire workforce of forty-eight local men and women. But Prudence was long gone. He tried calling her wristnode, but it was locked off. By the time he traced the taxi that had taken her to the airport, her plane was crossing the Italian Alps.

2

Nyamwezi Condominium, 2210

Moses had disappeared. There was nothing unusual about that, but so had a week's supply of goat cheese. Charity Odingo knew what that meant. Cursing under her breath, she set off at a run for the cheetah pens. Dried yellow mud puffed about her bare feet as she scurried through the makeshift farmyard, bright skirts flying. Hens scattered, squawking their protests. A pig raised its snout in surprise, grunted, and went back to sleep.

She ducked under the dead thorns of a stunted acacia and swung herself past the corner of the giraffe house by grabbing the rain gutter from the roof. Twenty yards away, a small brown figure stared at her, frozen by surprise. In its hand was the missing cheese.

"Moses!"

Silence.

"Moses Odingo, you stay out of that cage, you hear?" She slowed down and swept the child into her arms. The cheese flew from his hands into the dirt.

"Nice pussycat," said Moses, grinning.

"Yes. But keep your hands out of the nice pussycat's cage. And stop stealing cheese from the refrigerator!"

"But the pussycat likes sheese," said Moses, as if that settled the issue.

"No, *cheese*. With a 'ch.' "

"Sheese."

"Not quite, but better. Chuh-chuh-chuh cheese."

"Chuh-chuh-chuh sheese."

"Have it your own way. Just don't steal it."

"Sheese makes the pussycat go buzz," said Moses, as if to justify the theft. Charity set him back on his feet and knelt beside him. The cheetahs loved cheese, they purred their heads off whenever they got it. As a special treat, Moses was allowed to feed a small amount to the baby once a week. Charity didn't think it was good to indulge either of them more often than that.

"Mo, you mustn't put your hand in the cheetahs' cage. I know they seem friendly—they *are* friendly—but you can never be sure with wild animals. They could bite or scratch." *And Mbawa could take your arm off at the shoulder in an instant.*

"Can I feed the pussycat some sheese now you're here?" asked Moses hopefully. "Please?" he added after a moment's thought. That often tilted the balance in his favor.

"Not today." The boy's mouth turned down in a half sulk. Charity looked at the dirt-covered slab as it lay on the ground. Already the ants had discovered it. "Well, maybe later, okay?"

"Okay," said Moses, but he still looked downcast.

"Look, tell you what: I'm going to need some help with Zemba. You can help me take her over to the house if you want."

A huge grin split his face. "Can I carry Zemby, Ma?"

"Yes. Now you just wait outside while I go and get her." Charity sat him on a tree stump, unlocked the door to the service accessway, and ducked inside. The air was hot and heavy, sharp with the pungency of dried blood and stale urine.

She loved it.

Her wristnode's hardware link was a bit temperamental,

but eventually she persuaded it to activate a movable partition and separate mother from cub. Predictably, Mbawa didn't like this much, and when Charity opened up a small trapdoor and pulled the cub out, the big cat made her dislike known half a mile away.

"Calm down, you great furry lump—she'll be right back." The adult cheetah just snarled at her—as Charity would have done had their positions been reversed. The baby wriggled in her hands and mewed piteously. "Only a moment, Zemba," she said, juggling it uncomfortably with one arm while shutting the door behind her with the other. With the cub clutching at her shoulder for balance, Charity carried the baby cheetah out into the sunlight.

Moses was jumping up and down with excitement. "Can I carry Zemby? Please? She likes it when I carry her."

"Yes, you can carry Zemby." With care, Charity lifted the cub from her shoulder and placed her into Moses' arms. Lacking proper claws, Zemba clung to him as if her life depended on it. It looked like a very top-heavy arrangement as the four-year-old staggered along under the weight of the fast-growing cub, like some kind of giant mobile spotted mushroom. Only six weeks earlier, Zemba had been a fuzzy ball that an adult could carry in one hand; now she was the size of a decent dog. But Moses didn't seem bothered; he cooed at the cat and stroked the long smoky fur that ran down her back.

Charity picked up the cheese, now liberally coated with sand and ants. She could salvage a lot of it, and Moses could feed the rest to Zemba. As they walked toward the house, she shook the ants off and brushed away most of the dirt.

Tucked between two ancient acacias, it was a simple house, corrugated recycled plastic nailed to a timber framework, roofed with slate-colored solar cell arrays. A faded sign nailed to the door said, GOOMA ZOODIVERSITY FACILITY. The furniture was sparse, and all of it was old—some bought in the local market, some trucked in from Dar es Salaam. From the front window she could just see Lake Eyasi; from the back, the teeming plains of the Serengeti and the distant crater of Ngorongoro. Not far away was the Olduvai Gorge, one of the best-known sources of fossil hominids. Charity felt as if she was at the center of the universe.

Naturally, she thought. *The horizon is equally far in every direction*. Charity considered herself a realist. But it was a dramatic location. A hundred and fifty miles northwest was Lake Victoria, and a hundred and twenty-five miles to the north, a short hop across what used to be the border into Kenya, was Nairobi. The Swahili name for the land was still Jamhuri ya Muungano wa Tanzania—but its English version, the United Republic of Tanzania, was no longer in use. In 2170, what used to be Tanzania and Kenya had become the Nyamwezi Condominium.

"Okay, Mo, put Zemby down on the table." With difficulty the boy separated himself from the fur-covered jumble of what appeared to be rubber springs, and sat the cub down. She looked nervous, but relaxed when Moses scratched her head. He had an instinctive rapport with animals—always had, even before he could crawl or talk. Sometimes Charity found his empathy with the animal kingdom uncanny. Mosquitoes never bit him, bees never stung him . . . and normally shy birds would sit and sing to him if no one else was nearby.

A pity that he was so hopeless when it came to *people*. He could become moody and withdrawn for no apparent reason. He was a strange child, and she loved him desperately. His father had died before he was born—she never talked about it, tried never to think about it . . . Moses and her sister were all the family she had.

Charity cut off the outside of the cheese and handed it over to her son. "Give her this to keep her happy. No, that's too big, Mo: one *little* piece at a time, okay? That's better." Zemba began to purr. Moses grinned and fed the cat another bit of sandy goat cheese.

Charity opened her instrument case and pulled out a small bulbous unit with a stocky handle. Moses recognized it as a razor. Ma was going to shave off a tiny piece of Zemby's fur, so that she could be tattooed. It wouldn't hurt.

"You've seen this before, Moses. Can you remember why I'm doing it?"

Moses nodded, looking very serious now. "So's we can find out where she goes when we set her free."

I may just be a foolish proud mother, Charity thought, *but Moses is* very *quick to remember the things that interest him.* "That's right!" she said, in the overenthusiastic manner that parents of small children use for positive reinforcement. "That's *very* clever of you, Moses!" The buzz from the razor merged with the purr from the cheetah cub. Expertly Charity bared a rectangular patch of skin an inch or so across.

At that moment her wristnode indicated an urgent incoming call. She put the razor down. "Hello?"

There was a split second's hesitation. Then, voice-only: "Chatty? That you? It's your big sister. Hope I'm not interrupting anything, but I've only got a few minutes to make this call."

"Pru?" *Big sister, indeed.* It was a family joke, though one that had long ago worn thin. Prudence Odingo outranked her twin by all of two minutes.

Charity rummaged in a cupboard. "I'm in the middle of getting a new cheetah cub registered, Pru."

"Carry on, I can talk while you work. Reason I called is, I'll be landing shortly at Kisangani and I thought I'd drop by and see you. How's young Moses? I can't *wait* to see him at last. How old is he now?"

"Four. He's fine, feeding cheese to Zemba. Oh, you won't know, that's the new baby cheetah, she's absolutely adorable, and a total pest as you'd expect. Like Moses. Mo, it's your auntie Pru." Moses perked up. He had never seen Prudence, but some of his friends had aunties, and when they visited, they always brought presents. "Kisangani? You can get a shuttle to Nairobi and Moses and I'll pick you up from the airport. Pru, I can't believe this, it's been absolutely *ages*. Where are you right now?"

"Can't you tell?"

"How could I— Oh, *wait* a moment. I noticed you were a bit slow responding, but I thought you were just tired, or maybe one of the relay nodes was slow." Charity clipped the handle onto the tattoo unit, placed it on the shaven patch on Zemba's side to be sure it would fit. "It's communication lag, isn't it?"

"Zero point four seconds and falling even as we speak. *Tiglath-Pileser* is one hundred and twenty kilomiles from orbital insertion, and my crew are preparing an OWL for touchdown at the Kisangani spaceport in the early hours of tomorrow morning."

Prudence was a businesswoman; she owned an old but very well equipped deep-space cruiser. Charity had always wondered how her impulsive sister had acquired anything so expensive. A night landing? That was unusual . . . Belatedly Charity remembered her sister's line of business. "Did you have a successful trip?" she said carefully.

"Mmm, so-so."

How to say this? It's an open channel. "Any—er—problems? Need any help when you land? Specialist independent advice?"

Prudence laughed. "No need to call the lawyers, sis—the police aren't hot on my tail this time. I'm a legitimate entrepreneuse, if that's the word. Speaking of which, this call is costing a small fortune. Pick me up at Nairobi National, *not* Intercontinental, at"—the carrier wave hummed on its own for a few seconds while Prudence diverted to the travel-page—"twelve-forty local time tomorrow. Love to Moses, see ya. Bye."

"Bye, Pru." Charity looked down at her wrist. "Phone off." The subminiature computer/communicator's neural net searched for a few picoseconds, recognized the command, looked it up in its master table, and put its eXtraNet link into standby mode.

"Is Auntie Pru coming to stay with us, Ma?"

"For a little while, Mo. Tomorrow." Charity thought she was looking forward to it. Well, she knew she was; that is, she knew she was *mostly* looking forward to seeing Prudence. Her only reservation was that Prudence was synonymous with trouble—take the last time she'd turned up. But to be fair, the police had been overzealous, it hadn't actually been Prudence's fault. And the lawyers did straighten it all out, and *Tiglath-Pileser* hadn't been forfeited after all. But it had cost Prudence most of the profi—

"Is she going to bring a present?"

Moses jerked her attention back to reality. "Uh, yes, I'm sure Auntie Pru will bring you something nice." *Nuts. It'll be something totally unsuitable, if I know my sister.*

Zemba wriggled, but Charity got a good grip on her neck while Moses popped the final lump of cheese into the animal's mouth. Making sure she was holding the tattoo unit in the right position for the wristnode's infrared beam, she spoke more commands. "New database entry. Name: Zemba. Sex: female. ERO code: g-z-f-slash-chee-slash-f-slash whatever the next free number is. Parentage: merge from Mbawa's file, you know which. Statistics and health record: merge from zemba-slash-stats. Moses, you do know what I was doing, don't you?"

The boy nodded solemnly; he'd observed the procedure before. The most recent time had been the piglets, but before that there had been a goat, a zebra, some young giraffes . . . oh, yes, and the snakes. *Hundreds* of snakes; that had been *real* fun. Of course, you don't shave snakes. "Uploading Zemby's stats, Ma."

Charity nodded in encouragement. "And why are we doing that?"

The child pursed his lips in thought. " 'Cos then Zemby goes into the register." Charity smiled her encouragement, but he could see she wanted more. "And then she gets set alight protection."

"*Satellite*."

"Uh—*sat* alight."

It'll do. "Good boy!" Charity pressed the bulb of the tattoo unit to the cub's shaven flank and squeezed the handle. In an instant the device made a tiny slit in a fold of skin, impressed a transponder circuit into the animal's flesh using indelible metallic ink, implanted fine wires to pick up tiny but adequate electrical power from the cub's own electrolytes, and glued the slit together again. Zemba, her tiny horizons more than occupied by Moses and goat cheese, didn't even notice.

"Tested and working," said the wristnode. From now on, the satellite network of the Ecotopian Register of Organisms would monitor Zemba's health and track her every move via its interface with an extensive but still incomplete network of dedicated ground-based nodes. On this occasion, mother and baby would be released back into the wild immediately. Through the Xnet, and the survsats that the Ecotopian authorities had finally started launching, the Diversity Police would do their best to guard them against illegal poachers, hunters, souvenir manufacturers, and purveyors of folk remedies.

Not that there were many of those anymore—but the few that still operated were tough, mean, and *very* well organized.

In the old university town of Coventry, on a medium-sized island just off the edge of continental Europe, it was getting ready to rain. You could tell, because slatted covers made from recycled plastic were unrolling to protect the unstable material of the ancient brickwork. Nursing a glass of brandy, Bailey Barnum lounged on a couch watching reruns of his first vidivid series, *Rose Red Cities*. He hadn't been born a Barnum, it was a professional pseudonym: "Ironbottom" hadn't been vidivisual enough. Jonas Kempe and Cashew Tintoretto, the other two members of his production team, conversed quietly in a corner.

"Call for you, Mr. Barnum," said a sexy female voice. His wristnode had woken up.

"If it's a fan, promise the usual package and disconnect. I'm busy."

"The caller is Ruth Bowser, your agent."

Bailey rolled lazily upright. "Accept. Oh, Ruthie, *hi*. Wonderful to hear—" He fell silent. "Hmmm. Yeah, sure, I get the picture. Okay, so *you* come up with a new idea you're the— Do I *what*? Did I really sign *that*? Why didn't you protect— Oh, you mean it's in my agreement with *you*. Okay, okay, you don't need to rub it in. I'll get the team on to it straightaway. Call you back." He canceled the connection.

Jonas and Cashew had stopped talking and were staring at him.

"Okay, no need to look like a flatworm's swallowed your socks. The Lumleys on *Ends of the Earth* are down a little. Nothing to worry about." Without warning he hurled the glass against the nearest wall. It bounced and dropped to the floor intact. But there was a dent in the wall and the wallpaper was splashed. "*Shit!*" Tears welled into his eyes.

Cashew sat down beside him and took his hand. "They're down more than a little, then."

"Falling like a barometer in a frigging hurricane. Not even in the top hundred. My god, six years I've been in this business and never been out of the top fifty." He didn't have to point out that there was more to it than just a few figures. Production costs for *Ends of the Earth* had been astronomical, and their cash flow was very sensitive to the Lumley ratings. "Nobody's interested in this planet's unexplored regions anymore."

Jonas chose his words with care. "That's because—well, frankly, it's because there aren't any, Bailey. Even when we did the northern ice cap, we had to inject suspense by sending you *under* it in a one-man sub. Face it, there are no un-explored frontiers left. Unless you go offplanet."

"Yeah, sure," said Barnum. "Damn right. Do you realize that less than two centuries ago there were still whole *tribes* undiscovered in the jungle? Now you can't get ten yards into the underbrush without getting a ticket from the Diversity Police. Amazonia, Papuguinea, Chukotskii Hrebet—same everywhere. Not a thing moves without some snoopy computer logging its entire family history. How the dump can you be a trailblazing explorer when the navsats have your position pinned down to the nearest inch?"

Cashew picked up the fallen glass and placed it on the table. Bailey *did* exaggerate; they were only accurate to a foot or so. "What we need is something that doesn't use navsats."

Barnum laughed. What an idea. "Cash, how else would we find out where we were?"

She reddened. "Sorry, it was a dumb idea. Just thinking aloud."

"No, it wasn't," said Jonas. He activated his wristnode.

Cashew craned her neck to see. "History?" she said with incredulity. "Jonas, we'll *never* get even a *toehold* in history. The Xnet's got nothing but—"

"Shhh. I'm getting a new angle. History is just the entry point." Cashew shut up. Jonas's flair for the vidivisual was legendary throughout the industry.

He muttered some commands to his wristnode, then looked up. "Simple idea, but lots of potential. We re-create historical voyages. Using the same kind of gear, the same technology. Crossing the Antarctic in a dog sled, like that Scott Amundsen guy in nineteen-whatev—"

Cashew was quick to point out the flaw. "ERO wouldn't give us a dog license, not for VV. 'Gratuitous involvement of animals.' And ecovisas for the Antarctic are as rare as pandas' thumbs."

"You're right," said Jonas. "A managed ecosystem is all very well, but there are times when this one is *too* managed.

But I didn't mean the dog thing literally." He reactivated his wristnode. "Plenty of alternatives . . . Yeah, *this* one looks tasty . . ."

Bailey glanced at Cashew, who shrugged. Jonas liked a little drama; it was in his blood. "Okay, genius, let's have it. But remember, it'd better work or we're *all* out of a job."

"You cross the Atlantic," said Jonas.

Bailey gritted his teeth in exasperation. "Jonas, a three-year-old child could cross the Atlantic blindfolded on a rubber duck."

"Using the navsats, yes. But *you're* going to do it using only pretech navigational aids. Let me give you the rundown on a primitive Italian geezer called"—he glanced at his wrist—"Galileo."

If ever a child had been ineptly named, it had to be Prudence, thought Charity, as she waited impatiently near the arrivals gate. And if ever anyone needed evidence that the phrase "identical twins" was a misnomer, the Odingo girls were living proof. As children, first in the foothills around Gulu and later in the bustle of Kampala, they had been almost indistinguishable—physically. But mentally they were not so much opposites as orthogonal—their thoughts ran at right angles to each other. It had made them a powerful team on the rare occasions when they had joined forces. Orthogonal vectors span the largest dimensional subspaces.

As they'd grown older, they'd changed. Charity was now distinctly on the plump side, heavy around the hips like most middle-aged African women. The unforgiving equatorial sun had tanned her face like old parchment, but her hair was still dark, not even a few gray curls, which was unusual. People lived longer now than two centuries ago; a hundred years was common, a hundred and twenty not unheard-of. They were fertile longer, active *much* longer, and usually kept their faculties right up till the day they died. But the medical advances hadn't affected the timing of gray hair, and there were just as many bald men under forty as there had ever been. Charity was just thinking how strange it was that medicine could cure Alzheimer's but not hair loss, when she saw her sister, accompanied by a robocart bearing a pile of exceedingly scruffy suitcases.

Prudence was tall, slender, lightly clad for hot weather, long legs and a riot of multicolored hair held together with a huge wooden pin and an orange sweatband. She emanated drive and *energy*. Charity considered her sister to be something of a fidget. Right now, though, Charity was the energetic one, jumping up and down and yelling. Prudence spoke a few words to the cart and it negotiated its way through the crowds toward her overexcited sister.

"Pru, you haven't changed a *bit*! How do you keep so slim?" *And how do you keep looking so young?* But Charity knew the answer to that: years cooped up in the low light of a cramped spacecraft, years of low gravity. There was a downside, too, of course. Low gravity could also cause physical deterioration, if you didn't exercise. Bone damage, muscular atrophy. And it took a very special kind of person to survive years of trying to stay sane in the company of the same few companions. She'd always wondered how the spacers handled it, but whenever she'd asked Pru about it, her sister had changed the subject. She did know that some people didn't handle it at all—insanity, obesity, and addiction were just three of the failure routes, and every so often some autodestructively inventive spacer came up with a new one.

What were the routes to *success*? The spacers knew, but they weren't telling.

"You're looking well yourself, little sister."

"Moses makes me feel younger than I am." She stopped. "Mostly. The rest of the time he makes me feel a great deal older. By several million years."

"But you're glad you had him? Yes, you are. Motherhood suits you."

"Maybe you ought to try it."

Prudence laughed, a dry laugh with no hint of malice, and changed the subject.

"Galileo? Wasn't he that French guy that dropped a cannonball off the Leaning Tower of Pisa to prove that gravity existed?"

Jonas took a deep breath. Bailey had talent, but his talent came at a price. "Italian. Legend has it that he dropped two cannonballs of different weights to show they both fell at the same speed, Bailey."

"So did they?" asked Cashew.

"Well, there's no actual evidence that he *did* it—it was more of a thought experiment. But that's not the point. What I'm thinking about is one of his astronomical discoveries. 'The Cosmian stars,' he called it."

"And what does that gibberish mean?"

"The moons of Jupiter. The four biggest ones—Io, Europa, Ganymede, and Callisto, numbers five to eight out of sixteen, but the rest are *tiny*. Galileo observed them through his telescope, realized that some bodies didn't go 'round the Earth, and got himself into hot water with the Inquisition."

Cashew chuckled. "Smart career move. He ought to have hired Ruthie Bowser; she'd have set him straight."

"Yeah. Anyhow, Galileo was kind of obsessed with time. In those days there were no accurate clocks, which was a nuisance because Galileo wanted to work out the laws of motion and it's difficult to do that if all you've got to measure time is a pig-fat candle marked into hour-long lengths. He tried all sorts of tricks, including humming tunes to himself. Then he discovered the principle of the pendulum clock. In fact the development of clocks and astronomy went hand in hand: Better clocks let the astronomers time celestial happenings more accurately, and a better understanding of astronomy helped to improve the design and testing of clocks. With me so far, Bailey?"

"Galileo was a nut for clocks and moons. Sure. Jonas, is there anything vidivisual in this deluge of factoids?"

"Uh-huh. Burnings at the stake, harmony of the spheres . . . But most of this is deep background, just for us, okay? Main thing to realize is that the big deal in those days was ships—for trade—and the big problem with ships was navigation. No navsats then, okay? Finding longitude, that was the nasty one. Latitude was easy: Measure the altitude of the sun at noon, or the pole star at night. But longitude—basically, what was needed was a clock. Every fifteen degrees west, the sun rises and sets an hour later."

"So Galileo's pendulum clock solved everything, right?"

"Wrong. It wasn't anything like accurate enough. Instead, Galileo found a huge clock in the sky."

"Oh, I get it. The Cosmian stars."

"Precisely. What you see when you look at Jupiter through a telescope depends on whereabouts on the Earth you are. The moons move pretty damn fast, and they cross each other or the edges of Jupiter practically every day. Galileo drew up tables of the positions of Jupiter's moons and worked out how to use them to tell local time. There was a big prize on offer, and in 1616 he sent his idea to King Philip III of Spain. But Philip was so besieged by cranks that he wasn't interested. Galileo tried to sell him the idea on and off for sixteen years, but—"

Cashew's marketing antennae flickered into life. "Hell, if the network execs won't buy, there's no point asking twice. Didn't Galileo know that?"

"I guess life was slower in those days, Cash."

"He could have tried another network," said Bailey.

"He did. After twenty years he offered the idea to the Dutch."

"Wow," said Cashew. "Rapid response time."

"The Dutch gave him a gold chain as a retainer, and they were going to send a marketroid to Italy to negotiate terms when the Pope got wind of it and they had to cancel his ticket.

Galileo wasn't exactly flavor of the month with the Pope, on account of theological differences about whether the Earth went 'round the Sun or vice versa. By the time the Dutch plucked up enough courage to send someone, Galileo had snuffed it."

"That," said Bailey, "is about the least vidivisual story I have ever heard. Jonas, you're a genius. The kind of genius that dies of poverty in a garret."

Jonas shrugged. "Still deep background, Bailey. It gets better, trust me." Bailey found an unopened bottle and poured a round of drinks. Jonas was a great guy; it just took him a while to get to the goddamned point.

"Another Italian guy took up the same idea. Gian Domenico Cassini."

"Right *on*! The womanizer, right?"

"No, that was Casanova."

"Oh. Don't we get *any* breaks?"

Jonas tried to keep calm. "These guys were scientists."

"We don't."

"Cassini made lots of new observations, drew up new tables, and in 1668 he revived the whole Jovian moons scam. This time, a lot of people pointed their telescopes into the night sky and tried it."

Despite himself, Bailey was starting to get interested. If only Jonas would explain how any of this would revive their flagging fortunes. He poured himself another glass, offered one to Cashew.

"Did it work?" she said.

"Sort of. With the equipment they had in those days, you couldn't actually make the observations from a moving ship. Imagine trying to keep a telescope steady on the deck of an old sailing ship! But land-based telescopes were okay. In the 1670s hundreds of cities and towns used Jupiter's moons to work out their longitude. Cassini even made a map of the whole goddamned *world* that way, called it the planisphere. Twenty-four feet across, it was, on the third floor of the west tower of the Paris observatory. King Louis XIV came to see it—brought the whole of his court—"

Bailey sat up in his chair. "Now, *that* fucking well *is* vidivisual! I can see it now. Lots of pomp and circumstan—"

"Yeah. Bailey, shut up, huh? We'd never get a license for the horses, the History Channel always grabs the whole allocation."

"Thanks, Cashew. Now, Louis was *really* impressed, and he invested big bucks in the whole deal. Then in 1682—"

Bailey groaned. "For God's sake, Jonas, what's the bottom line? What's the program idea?"

It would ruin the careful buildup, but Jonas could see that his boss was about to explode, so he relented. "Okay, Bailey. The bottom line is: we re-create the expedition of 1682 made by a couple of guys named Varin and des Hayes—two of King Louis' engineers. Just like them, we set out from Gorée and end up in Martinique."

"Huh?"

"Across the Atlantic from east to west, filling in the biggest navigational gap of them all—the longitude of the New World."

"Eh? What new—"

"The goddamned Caribbean, Bailey—outpost of the American continent. It was new *then*. Thanks to Varin and des Hayes, people found out, for the first time, exactly where it was on the face of the globe."

The idea seeped in slowly. "Hmm. Yeah, maybe. *Normerica: Its Place in the World*. Not your best program concept, but—hmm. Needs a bit mo—"

"We don't just re-create the appearance of the voyage, Bailey. We do it using only the navigational methods available in 1682. A sextant to find latitude, a pendulum clock, a nineteen-foot telescope, and an ephemeris of Jupiter's moons to calculate longitude."

There was a stunned silence. Cashew was the first to break it. "You mean we don't use the *navsats*?"

"Yeah."

"But how would we know where we were?"

Jonas took her gently by the hand. "Cashew, haven't you listened to a single word I've been saying?"

The thought was awesome. "You mean that ridiculous old method actually *works*?"

"Think of it as a kind of God-given system of navsats. But they're going 'round Jupiter, not the Earth, and the only signals they broadcast are light."

"*God's Navsats!* That's what we'll call it! Jonas, it's brilliant!" Bailey leaped to his feet, stopped, sat down again. "Provided we can actually pull the scam off. I thought you said nobody could observe Jupiter's moons from a ship."

"Not then. Easy enough now. Quick snap with a charge-coupled device and a photomultiplier tube, all over before the ship can move."

Cashew wasn't buying that. "You said 're-create.' "

"In spirit. You said yourself we'll never get the horses, probably have to use wire-frame simulacra and postproduction graphic drapes. So we fuzz out history a bit on the telescopes. Nineteen feet long, yeah: old-fashioned optics—nah. Likewise we set the calculations up on a wristnode, rather than doing them freehand with pen and paper. Safer that way." Jonas's eyes were wide, his heart racing.

"Yeah." Bailey's vidivisual antennae were pulsating, glowing—*melting*. He could see exactly how it would go. And it would, indeed, *go*. Ballistic to big One, please God. Provided—"But we do one thing *right*, and this I insist."

"What?"

"We don't take any navsat gear."

Cashew was reluctant. "Not even as failsafe?"

"Nope. We want it fail*un*safe. For the Lumleys."

Ah, yes, the sacred Lumleys. The others nodded.

"And we don't take any transponders."

That was even harder to take. Not even passive observations by outside observers. "Hell, Bailey, that's genuinely *dangerous*. The insurers will throw a fit."

Bailey dropped his final bombshell. "No insurers."

Hot shit. "You mean we take the responsibility *ourselves*?" Cashew's voice had gone up an octave. This was totally new intellectual territory.

"Tranq yourself down, Cashew, then hear what I say. The way to get the Lumleys is to grab the audience by their collective balls and squeeze them so hard their eyes pop out on stalks. No navsats, no transponders, and no insurance. Just a trio of intrepid explorers against the raging ocean."

Cashew shuddered. "You're mad, Bailey. Stark staring crazy." She tossed back her drink. "It's brilliant."

"Yeah."

"Provided our master navigator here can hack it with the gear."

Jonas rose to the bait. "Are you doubting the abilities of the best vidi-engineer in the known universe?"

"No, Jonas. I'm doubting *your* abilities."

"Crap. Bet you a week's pay our final landfall is accurate to within a hundred yards."

Cashew nodded like a woodpecker on speed, and Bailey entered the bet into his wristnode's notary.

Charity had been unusually quiet during the drive back to the house, but as soon as they reached it, her pent-up curiosity could no longer be contained. As she bustled about the tiny kitchen fixing food and drink, she dropped ever heavier hints. She knew Prudence had made some kind of discovery, otherwise she wouldn't have returned to Earth. Last time it had been giant Ionian sulfur flowers, worth a fortune to any private collector and therefore beyond the reach of any legitimate scientist—which is what had caused all the trouble.

What was it this time? Charity desperately wanted to know, and it showed.

Prudence sighed. Soon she'd have to put her sister out of

her misery or there would be some kind of meltdown. She hesitated, knowing how difficult Charity found it to keep her mouth shut. When she was a kid they'd called her Chatty; Prudence still used it as a pet name. But in a sense the damage was already done. The moment Prudence had set foot on Earth, her sister would guess there must be a very good reason indeed for her return. That thought would not be lost upon others, either.

Anyway, the story would soon be public domain.

"Chatty?" Charity put down the potato peeler and looked up. "Promise you won't breathe a word of what I'm about to tell you? Not to anyone? Not your confessor, not your lover, not even your personal disorganizer." Charity blushed: only one of the three was even a remote possibility. She nodded, then said, "Yes, I understand," to show she was serious, even though she had no idea what her sister was talking about.

"Soon—very soon, but I can't yet say when—you'll be free to tell everybody. But not till I give the word, okay?"

"Okay."

Prudence unpeeled her flight bag and pulled out a box sealed with tape. Setting it on the table, she pulled off the tape and pried the lid off the box. Inside was an irregular lump, about the size and shape of a squashed cat, wrapped loosely in bubblewrap to absorb shocks. She removed it from the box, placed it on the rough kitchen table, and unwrapped it.

The object was metallic, bent, and corroded. Its shape was hard to describe—sort of lumpy and lopsided, curiously organic yet technological . . . Its most recognizable features were three wheels set deep into the body, one at each corner, except that where the fourth should have been there was just a circular hole. It had a row of what looked like lights at one end, of several different sizes and shapes, and two short stumpy tailpipes at the other. The corroded parts were off-white and looked crumbly. Here and there flecks of metallic silver reflected the afternoon sunlight.

Moses looked disappointed. Prudence suddenly twigged.

"No, Moses, it's not a present. Here's your present." She rummaged in the bag and handed over something soft in bright wrappings. Charity dispatched the boy to a corner of the room while he struggled with the garish paper. Then she picked up the strange object.

"Careful!" said Prudence sharply. She forced herself to relax. "Sorry, Charity, but I get nervous when anyone touches it. It's very old, and I'd be hard-pressed to put an upper limit on its value, so don't damage it."

Charity turned it over in her hands. The underneath bore a faint pattern, like the tread of a tire. "What is it?"

Prudence took a deep breath. "An artifact."

"I can see that. A pretty badly preserved one, too." The corrosion *wasn't* crumbly—it just looked that way. It was rock-hard.

"Archaeological," said Prudence.

Charity touched a wheel, but it didn't turn. Axles rusted solid, no doubt. "How old?"

Prudence shrugged. "Haven't had it dated accurately yet, but we did a particle impact estimate which should be right to within a few percent." Moses had succeeded in opening the package, to find a shapeless furry lump.

"Pru, you *shouldn't* have. Memimals cost a fortune."

"Present?" asked Moses plaintively. He was obviously unimpressed.

Charity remembered her question. "Like I asked, how old?"

"Before I answer that, maybe I'd better..." Prudence reached over, took the artifact from her sister's grasp and cradled it in her hand. "Safer that way, Chatty, sorry. Roughly . . . roughly a hundred thousand years."

Charity was having none of it. "Nonsense. They didn't have wheeled toys a hundred thousand years ago. Uh—Mo, it's a memimal, you *squeeze* it, okay? And then say 'doggie.' "

"They? Who's 'they'? *Somebody* did."

"Doggie!" shouted Moses. The lump pulsated, then

sprouted protuberances here, shrank there. It wagged its tiny tail and barked. Moses giggled.

"Memofoam," said Prudence. "This one has a database of over a hundred animals. Moses, say 'piggy.' " The memofoam reshaped itself and oinked soulfully.

"Archaeology? And here's me thinking you've been in deep space these last ten years," Charity mused. "Out near Jupiter, grubbing around on its moons, looking for exotic extraterrestrial mineral specimens to sell to the highest bidder."

Prudence's face was unreadable. "I have," she said. "And that's where I found this."

3

The Oort Cloud, 997,642 BC

The Oort cloud danced a stately saraband, dripping the occasional comet sunward in a timeless cosmic drizzle.

The human mind is a metaphor machine, but its metaphors are those of a creature that evolved on the savanna and the seashore, not in the unimaginably vast realms of space. The "asteroid belt," for instance, is not a belt. When the first space probe made the daunting journey to Jupiter, passing through the Belt along the way, many of the mission's managers were seriously worried that it would collide with an asteroid—unaware that an encounter between two bacteria released at random into the Pacific Ocean would be far more probable. If you count rocks, then indeed you find unusually high numbers of them in between the orbits of Mars and Jupiter, and if you draw pictures of their orbits, you see a broad belt of ink. If you draw dots to represent their positions, you see a fuzzy ring in the same position. But those dots, proportionately, are larger than planets—larger even than awe-inspiring Jupiter. If you drew them to scale, no printer in existence could lay down such a minuscule speck of ink.

So if you go to the Belt and stare hopefully out of your spaceship expecting to see a floating sea of rock, you will actually see . . . nothing. Unless, like the neo-Zen monks, you go in for some careful, deliberate, and very well-equipped rock hunting.

Yes, there are lots of rocks out there. But there is also an incredible amount of *space* out there to put them in.

In the same metaphorical manner, the Oort cloud is not a cloud. It is a huge region of space, a hollow sphere whose inner surface lies about a thousand astronomical units from the sun—twenty-five times as far away as the orbit of Pluto—and whose outermost reaches are at least thirty times as distant. Possibly even a hundred times—nearly one-third of the way to the nearest star. Within that hollow sphere are a hundred million big lumps of ice and snow—made from hydrogen, methane, ammonia, and water intermingled with dust particles, pebbles, irregular lumps of more solid matter—the debris of alien solar systems overwhelmed when their suns exploded—or, more prosaically, leftover lumps of matter that accreted too far from a major center to form bodies of any size.

These dirty snowballs are comets-in-waiting, and it would be as futile to try to count them as it would be to enumerate the grains of sand in all the Earth's deserts.

Despite their numbers, the space that surrounds them is even emptier than the asteroid belt. The nested surfaces of the Oort's thick but tenuous rind exist only in astronomers' imaginations: there is no cloud of proto-comets, no fuzzy blizzard of interstellar snowflakes. There is only emptiness piled upon emptiness, just marginally less empty than hard vacuum.

Most of the lumps of ice in the Oort noncloud pursue roughly circular orbits under the influence of the near-invisible Sun, tugged tentatively this way and that by Jupiter and Saturn, brushed by the faint gravitational feathers of Uranus and Neptune, all but oblivious to the feeble attraction of the remaining planets, responding about as much as a human ear to a whispered word on the far side of the globe.

Occasionally, however, the random dynamic of chaos places two proto-comets in closer proximity than usual. They seldom collide, but for a fleeting moment they may become locked in a mutual gravitational embrace. Like dancing lovers they whirl each other around, swaying in time to the harmonies of the cosmos . . . then they part, their union unconsummated, retaining only memories of what might have been . . .

The Oort noncloud trembles. Imperceptible density waves ripple through its filmy medium.

Sometimes the star-crossed lovers pass so close that they fling each other away in radically new directions. Even more rarely, one may experience a series of brief encounters, so that the disturbances reinforce each other. And sometimes the result is to redirect a proto-comet's orbit sunward, changing it from a fat circle to a thin ellipse, initiating a million-year plunge from the cold of the Oort noncloud to the inferno of the sun's photosphere.

Now, at last, it has become a true comet. It will fall faster and faster, slicing across the sedate orbits of the major worlds like a fox darting across a desert highway . . . It will see the sun grow larger, brighter, warmer . . . As the comet approaches the orbit of Mars, its lighter gases will melt, then boil. Nearing the orbit of the Earth, its water-ice will start to liquefy, then turn to steam . . . An outpouring of vaporized molecules will trail behind it in a splayed arc as its icy heart melts in the heat of the ever-looming Sun: the dust tail. Often a second trail of ionized particles will stream away from it in the solar wind, straight as a die: the ion tail.

Now the excitement will reach its climax. Speeding close to the sun's seething photosphere, boiling and exploding in a percussion of superheated steam, spitting droplets of molten rock, the comet will turn in the parent star's fierce gravity like a motorcyclist on a wall of death. Rounding the tip of its elliptical path at breakneck speed, the comet will begin its long plunge back toward the far void, slowing imperceptibly with every passing second. Its rocks will cool, its boiling waters will once more freeze . . .

No longer in a hurry, the comet will continue its languid journey back toward the Oort noncloud, the first of many such cycles of interminable slumber and violent awakening, until so much of its material has boiled away that it breaks up into a loose cluster of snow and gravel. Parts of it may then go out in a blaze of glory as brilliant meteor showers in the Earth's atmosphere. Some fragments may be captured by the asteroid belt. Most will merely join the unnamed ranks of orbital junk that smear themselves thinly over the entire Solar System.

While Prudence ate breakfast and Moses fed the jerboas, Charity Odingo browsed the eXtraNet, and a short filler item caught her eye. The caption shouted: BOLIVIAN BAKER BAGS BARMY BUDDHIST BELTER BOOTY.

"Pru, have you ever been involved with Belters?"

Prudence swallowed a mouthful of cereal. "Ran into a few, yeah." *Why is little sister raising that issue* now?

"Why do they keep giving away fortunes to random people?"

Oh. Prudence's brow furrowed. "That's a long story, Chatty. Belters are generally a tight-fisted bunch, but sometimes they can be very generous. That's how I got the title to *Tiglath-Pileser*, as a matter of fact—though technically that was for services rendered."

Charity pounced. "I always wondered how you came by that ship! What services?"

Prudence was dismissive. "Oh, I translated an old tablet for some Belters . . . Anyway, the Belt's a great place for peaceful meditation, but it's an even greater place for making money, and they make so much that sometimes they give it away. Why do you ask?"

"The Xnet says that a baker in Cochabamba woke up this morning to find a yard cube of tungsten on his doorstep."

"Yes, they do that kind of thing. All the time. Usually tungsten, but it could be almost any metal. I heard tell that some Paraguayan farmer woke up to find a cube of osmium in his pigpen."

"Just think what a grapefruit-sized lump of osmium would do for the facility," Charity said. "Let alone a yard cube. Who are these mysterious benefactors?"

"Weird neo-Zen sect, calls itself the Way of the Wholesome."

Charity spoke to her 'node and for once it obeyed her: the dim holoscreen blossomed into a commentary box. She peered at it in the bright light. "Right, here it is. The Tibetan word *bde-ba*, often rendered as 'good' but more accurately as 'wholesome' in the sense of 'bringing merit.' As such it possesses an overtone of *action* as opposed to merely passive— who *writes* this stuff?"

"If you access an obscure etymological commentary, Chatty, you shouldn't expect great literature." Prudence poured some more cereal. "God, you can't imagine what it's like to taste fresh food."

"Help yourself. Fatten yourself up a bit."

"Don't have the metabolism, Chatty. To prove it: I'm thin. Spacers who *can* get fat, *do* get fat. *Very* fat. I prefer less metabolic perversions to keep myself marginally sane. But I'll have another slice of mango, since you're offering. Spacers call it the Cuckoo's Nest."

"What? Mango?"

"Mmmmph, no, the Way of the Wholesome Orbital Monastery. An inhabited asteroid in the Hilda Group. I'm surprised you haven't heard of them, they're notorious—I guess Moses and the animals keep you pretty busy, though. They struck it rich early last century with a series of heavy-metal asteroid claims; now they own most of the Belt. They can afford to spread their wealth around, and they do. Totally at random."

Charity's eyes returned to the main item. "Says here there was a poem engraved on the metal cube."

"Yup, they do that, too."

Another tap, another commentary:

One must be aware that hoarded wealth must be dissipated.

One must be aware that gifts now given are stored up for the future.

One must be aware that a state of unhappiness is the harvest of evil deeds.

One must be aware that all happiness is the harvest of good deeds.

Prudence nodded. "Right, the King of the Vultures. That's why we call it the Cuckoo's Nest."

Charity put down her fork with a clatter, and stared at her sister. "Prudence, I haven't the faintest idea what you're talking about. You call it the Cuckoo's Nest because of something to do with vultures?"

"Oh, no, sorry. That bit of the poem is said by the King of the—no, I'd better start over. Let me show you." Prudence got up, walked around the table, and studied the Xnet screen layout. "I *wish* you'd invest in a flatfilm screen, Chatty—they're dirt cheap. Um—yup, here." She jabbed with a finger, and the head and shoulders of a man appeared: an Oriental, with the traditional triple pigtail and pale blue robes of a neo-Zen monk. Behind him was an enlarged projection of an ancient manuscript.

Another touch called up a caption. THE BUDDHA'S LAW AMONG THE BIRDS. The face became mobile, the lips moving in speech. "This curious but charming old book bears marked traces of the *Bka'-brgyud-pa* sect, and is believed to have been written by an anonymous lama some time in the seventeenth century. It was published in Tibetan in 1904 under the title *Bya chos rinchen 'phren-ba*, which means *The Dharma Among the Birds: A Precious Garland*."

"I see," said Charity. She obviously didn't.

Prudence pulled up a commentary box. "Dharma: the righteousness that underlies the law of the Buddha. Freely paraphrased: the Buddhist worldview."

The monk continued. "The book is a highly simplified exposition of the basic tenets of Buddhism, cast in the form of a debate between different birds: the parrot, the vulture, the white grouse, the pigeon . . . The debate is led by the King of the Birds, the cuckoo."

"Oh!" cried Charity.

"Shhh, little sister. Let the monk speak."

"On the border between India and Tibet, so the *Bya chos* tells us, there lay a wooded mountain named Pleasant Jewel, where dwelt the great magician Saraha and numerous other saints. And on this mountain lived innumerable birds and animals. It was a paradise on Earth. Lord Avalokita, an Indian prince, son of the King of Varanasi, was accidentally transformed into a cuckoo; and he became the spokesman for the council of the birds, and taught them the Dharma."

Charity froze the vidiclip.

"The Way of the Wholesome," she said, "like all orbital monasteries, was set up in order to mine the asteroid belt. It's a harsh environment out there, and quite unsuited to the kind of gold-rush mentality that historically opened up the great mining areas on Earth. Aggressive personalities would just get themselves killed. So, as you know, nearly all of the mining is performed by monks. Originally many different religions owned orbital mining monasteries, but only the neo-Zen Buddhists could hack it commercially. They soon had the Belt pretty much sewn up.

"The Way of the Wholesome was founded by a sect that takes its teachings from the *Bya chos*, or *The Dharma Among the Birds*. Its chief functionaries are all named after the various birds, according to their status in the book—so that in place of what in a Christian monastery would be the abbot, they have the Cuckoo."

"Which is why you call it the Cuckoo's Nest," said Charity.

"That's one reason. They're a very strange sect. Apparently Lord Avalokita, in his avian incarnation, preached the wholesomeness of giving wealth to the poor. The Cuckoo's Nest has the best record ever of multiple hits on payrock: it's rich beyond belief. It invests most of its profits in Belter technology. It built the New Tibet Habitat, which manfactures the biggest and most powerful mass-drivers in the Solar System. It's *the* major distributor of asteroidal minerals, and it handles the products of most of the smaller monasteries.

"But of course it consists of humble, peaceable monks, so it generally maintains a very low profile. Except for its habit of dumping big chunks of valuable metal in the backyards of the terrestrial poor, which it considers to be in the best tradition of its spiritual founder.

"So the second reason we call it the Cuckoo's Nest is, the neo-Zen monks are crazy."

Nāgārjuna, a Thrush—very junior monk—in the Celestial Lamasery of the Way of the Wholesome, reflected on the advice that the Council of Birds had to offer and found it wanting.

Not to say contradictory.

One must know that laziness and sloth hinder the performance of good, the Great Crane had said. He had no quarrels with that—after all, laziness and sloth hinder the doing of *anything* much. Except sleeping. But what was one to make of the words of the King Vulture, only a page earlier: *One must observe the folly of this ceaseless busyness?*

And to cap it all, it was an *uposatha* day.

Probably.

The Buddhist calendar is a lunar one. Indeed, the Buddha was born into the Gotama clan on the full-moon day of the month of Vesākha, exactly ten lunar months after his mother Mahāmāyā dreamed that she was visited by a silvery white elephant of extraordinary beauty which entered her womb by passing through the side of her body—a portent that was interpreted either as the coming birth of a world king or, as it turned out, a Buddha. Even on Earth, the combination of a calendar system based on the Moon with seasons that follow the Sun had caused no end of historical headaches, and the rotation of the Earth, incommensurate with both lunar month and solar year, piled complication on complication. When the religious home of one's sect was an asteroid in the Hilda Group, spinning on an oblique axis every three hours twenty-nine minutes and some irrational number of seconds, the calendric complexities became ridiculous.

The brand of Celestial Zen Buddhism practiced by the monks of the Way of the Wholesome was a syncretic one, taking its teachings from many sources. Along with all the Theravāda followers—those that trace their lineage back to the Pāli Elders of the first Buddhist *sangha,* the assembly of monks that studies and preserves the teachings of the Buddha—the orbital monastery observed four holy days every lunar month. These were the full moon, the new moon, and the eighth day following each of those. And it was there that the confusion of celestial periodicities intruded into the inconsistent precedents of holy law, and Nāgārjuna's headaches began.

Unfortunately, the ancient writings had failed to specify clearly whether the phase of the Moon should be observed from the Earth or from one's lamasery. The fact that Nāgārjuna was currently at neither, but sitting on about seventy thousand tons of rock liberally veined with the oxides of rare-earth metals, was irrelevant. Various passages in the sacred writings, in particular the *Bhikkhu-pātimokkha,* suggested either one location or the other, and at least one source, the *Patisambhdā-magga,* was absolutely clear that it was both. In the days when monasteries were immobile, the distinction of course had no force, but as soon as the Solar System began to be developed, and it became clear that the monastic lifestyle was particularly suitable for those whose work required them to live offplanet for years at a stretch . . . Well, it was a mess.

It had been especially confusing at the Way of the Wholesome's first lunar base, a hastily erected conglomeration of plastic domes and metal tubes near the Moon's south pole. The phases of the Moon make sense from any observation point . . . other than the Moon itself. Even to a neo-Zen monk, the Moon observing the Moon was a shade *too* self-referential. It was much more in the spirit of Zen to leave the question unresolved, and from its earliest inception the lunar base had found ways to live with the ambiguity. From the Cuckoo's Nest, on the other hand, the phase of the Moon was a perfectly well defined concept, and could easily be observed on any local node by logging into the telescope that was situated two miles outside the lamasery's perimeter . . . And when they did, they found that the phase of the Moon as seen from the Cuckoo's Nest seldom agreed with its phase as seen from the Earth.

So Nāgārjuna sat on his rock in his pale blue spacesuit, next to his temporarily discarded gas-jet harness, and pondered. He knew that today was definitely not an *uposatha* day in monastery-based coordinates, because he had observed the Moon on a local-node holoscreen in the Cuckoo's Nest the previous day, and from long experience he could tell that it was nowhere near one day short of a perfect bright circle. But what if the day's status was determined from Earth? Unfortunately, he couldn't remember what the rule was. He could easily radio over and ask the local node to tell him, along with whether it happened to be an *uposatha* day in Earth-based coordinates, but the nature of his dilemma was that possibly this was forbidden.

To be precise, it was definitely *not* forbidden if the answer was no, but it might be forbidden if the answer was yes.

The nub of the dilemma was that on *uposatha* days, monks and laity alike must observe the five precepts—to refrain from murder, theft, falsehoods, drugs, and sexual perversions. The monks, male and female, had to observe several more: no sex of any kind, no eating after midday, no watching entertainments, no jewelry or body paint, and absolutely no sleeping in a comfortable bed. Of course, it being a low-gravity environment, *any* bed was comfortable, so the final precept was normally interpreted as no sleeping in a bed, period. But just to lie stretched out on the floor would still be fairly comfortable . . . no matter.

By the curious accounting of tradition, this made eight precepts in all.

Seven of those—well, eight less one, which was seven as long as you didn't start asking what eight less eight was—caused him no heart-searching, provided he quashed the urge to kill whichever fool was still insisting on basing religious rituals on an ill-defined lunar calendar. However, accessing the Xnet was traditionally interpreted as entertainment, even when one's intentions were scholarly or a matter of duty. And if he was to *do* his duty, he would shortly be required to link up with the neo-Zen Buddhists' deep-space telescope array on the Moon, thereby accessing an entertainment medium.

Of course, he could do the whole job electronically and look at the results later, but according to the rules this would be the same as looking *now*. Otherwise the monks would all record entertainments that were forbidden on *uposatha* days in order to watch them later, which the Green Parakeets, senior monks, deemed to be inconsistent with the spirit of self-denial that was, after all, the very essence of *uposatha*.

Nor could he consult his superiors for advice, since to do so would again require accessing the local node.

To compound the problem, the contrary advice from *The Dharma Among the Birds* meant that he wasn't sure whether he ought to carry out his duties, thereby earning the condemnation of the King Vulture, or shirk them, meriting the wrath of the Great Crane. Either might raise the ire of the Cuckoo himself—the High Lama of the entire orbital lamasery.

Nāgārjuna swore, which as far as he knew was acceptable on any kind of day, holy or not . . . provided none of the Parakeets heard you. He'd made sure the microphone was temporarily switched off.

Basically, the best he could manage was to make *some* decision, and live with the consequences. The Birds would just have to decide for him. With clumsy gestures his gloved hands opened the leg pocket of his suit and extracted a copy of the sacred text, printed like a scroll on a long strip of vacuum-proof paper. He shut his eyes, twiddled the wing nut attached to a rotating device that rolled the paper sideways, continued for a random period of time, and then opened his eyes again.

The idea was to obey whichever line first met his gaze. *Honey stored by bees for themselves alone can serve no other.* It was the Cuckoo's summing-up speech, the one that always brought tears to his eyes. He instructed his suit to suck up the moisture before it clouded his visor.

Now all he had to do was figure out what the oracular phrase *meant*.

It took half an hour, but then it came to him in a rush. There was no inconsistency after all. The three quotations were not about actions, but about motives. *Laziness and sloth hinder the performance of good* meant that you should not *intend* to be indolent. The *folly of ceaseless busyness* was not that it was wrong to be busy, but it was wrong to create *unnecessary* work *deliberately*. The warning about storing honey was what gave it all away: it meant that you should not set out to serve your own sole ends.

All of which meant two things. First, that he should indeed carry out his assigned duties, and second, that if by misfortune it turned out to be an *uposatha* day after all, then he could trot the whole story out to explain his decision to the White Grouse—the senior lama to whom he was assigned.

Taking a deep breath, he activated the suit's node and asked to be logged on to LADSOCS.

"Sun*block*: grade ten, one carton. Sun*dew* electrolytic sports soda—um, twenty crates." Cashew Tintoretto was checking a huge pile of equipment and provisions against an interminable list displayed on her wristnode. She was beaded with sweat, streaked with dust, and looked distinctly harassed. "Sun*glasses*, anti-UV: twelve pairs—Jonas, do you think four each is enough? We'll probably drop them over the side or sit on them or—"

"Cashew, stop fussing." Jonas opened up a camera case and began sorting through its innards. "Four pairs each is more than enough—but don't forget the crew. Bailey, are you ready for the press conference yet? We've only got ten minutes."

"No rush," said Bailey. "The longer you keep 'em waiting, the more excited they get; the more excited they get, the more publicity they give you."

Cashew pouted and returned to her list. "Tables: five hundred. *What?* Surely we only need—"

"Let me look at that." Jonas peered at the tiny screen. "No, Cash, that's not 'table' as in 'dining'—it's 'table' as in 'look up where the Moons of Jupiter will be.' And it's five hundred *pages*, not items. It's a hard-copy backup for the wristnode programs."

"Hey, there isn't a table in the dining sense at all. We've forgotten the damned—"

"Cashew," said Bailey gently, "ask for a search under 'boat.' Subreference 'galley.' "

"Huh?"

"Just do it."

"Okay. Mmm. Oh, *right*. There's a table built in."

Bailey nodded. "Along with seats, sails, an engine for calm weather, and a hull to keep the sea—"

"All right, no need to be sarcastic. Tacks: five pounds.

What the devil do we—oh, never mind. Tack, hard: six packs. Tack, soft— Jonas, what the devil are hard and soft tack? Never mind, I'll look it up. Oh. Aren't we taking this ancient nautical business a bit seriously here?"

"Authenticity," said Bailey. "Authenticity is *everything* on this trip, Cashew."

"Weevils, ten million. Scurvy, one case per crew member." She flipped her wristnode to standby and sat down on the crumbled wall of the old prison, long derelict. "Well, this volcanic derelict is certainly authentic. It's an authentic hellhole."

Bailey shrugged, stood, looked once more at the barren tufa that formed the tiny island. "Gorée *village* is okay. Kind of picturesque, in a decayed sort of way. And Fort Nassau is definitely vidivisual. Pity Fort St. Michel collapsed."

Jonas slapped some fresh memory into one of the cameras. It was a handheld Suzuki-73, and the cameraman fussed over it like an emperor penguin tending its egg.

"I don't know why you bother with that lump of old junk," said Bailey.

"Junk? This is pre-Pause technology! Worth a fortune! They don't make them like this anymore."

"I thought the Pause happened because the technology then didn't work," said Cashew.

"Yes and no," said Jonas. "It *worked* fine. Just got too smart."

"Oh, right." In the twenty-third century everyone knew the dangers of smart technology. The main one was that it wasn't, smart, that is. Any manager knew that the main problem wasn't machines, but people. People are smart, they have ideas of their own. Unfortunately, they aren't always the ideas that the managers would like them to have. So making machines more like people was *dumb*.

This had become obvious in 2072.

The Pause had been building for a long time. As standards of living rose, the anti-technology movement rose with them—a simple lifestyle always looks more attractive when you've got time on your hands and little work to do. Meanwhile, every item of machinery from can openers to buildings was becoming more and more proactive, anticipating its user's needs. This was wonderful except on the innumerable irritating occasions when the smart machinery goofed. Anything might have triggered the backlash, but in this case it was the destruction of the fledgling Mars Colony. The smart computer that discovered a fire inside the colony's main dome tried to turn on the sprinklers—but it was overruled by the smart computer in charge of health, which had just discovered legionella bacteria in the water supply. Warmth, the medical computer reasoned, was just what those bacteria needed to multiply, so the water had to be kept away from the fire. Since medical priorities overruled all others, the colonists never stood a chance.

The needless disaster triggered a Luddite revolution on Earth. All over the globe, smart machinery was smashed, piled high in the streets and set on fire, or shoved off cliffs . . .

"Jonas, if the camera comes from an age when everything was too smart, why do you use it?"

"Remember what the Pause led to? Dumb smart machines are better than *no* machines. To be honest, I *like* its proactive features. It sets the light level very intelligently and the fuzzy logic anti-shake system is a dream. Mind you," he added sheepishly, "I did have to dumb down the autofocus. The stupid thing always made the foreground sharp. Bloody useless when you're trying to shoot a distant herd of elephants with an artistically out-of-focus thornbush in the foreground."

Cashew was running through a list of questions that the press were likely to ask. "Do you know this place was a major port for the Atlantic slave trade back in the eighteenth century?"

"No," said Bailey. "Hmm, hope we can keep that under

wraps, might put some viewers off. Maybe we ought to revise our point of depar—no, we've *got* to start from here."

Cashew waved vaguely toward the mainland. "Why? Dakar has a better harbor, an infinitely more exciting night-life, ten times the territory, and air-conditioning."

"Authenticity," Bailey reiterated. He headed for the conference room. Cashew checked in a pocket mirror to make sure her dishevelment looked sufficiently vidivisual, rubbed a bit more dust on her face until she was satisfied with the effect, and followed. Jonas brought up the rear, carrying his precious Suzuki-73.

The neo-Zen monks of the Way of the Wholesome had originally developed an installation on the Moon as a step-ping-stone to the asteroid belt, a celestial way station that freed them from Earth's stifling gravity well. An inevitable consequence of that strategy was to develop an industrial infrastructure on the Moon, and the key resource was water. There were only two places on the Moon where you could find water: the north and south poles. There, huge deposits of ice survived in endless shadow, forever hidden from the hot rays of the Sun by steep crater walls. Everywhere else the Moon was drier than the most extreme desert. Nearly all of the water in the Moon's rocks had turned to superheated steam in the first few minutes of the worldlet's existence, three and a half billion years earlier, when it had been splashed from the Earth's mantle by an impact with a body the size of Mars. Sunlight had decomposed the water molecules into hydrogen and oxygen; then the hydrogen, being the lightest gas of all, had escaped the Moon's low gravity. By now most of the other gases had gone, too. Only at the Moon's poles had water survived; presumably some of the vaporized water molecules had pooled there as the worldlet cooled, and then had frozen. Everywhere else, the heat of the Sun would have prevented any vapor from becoming liquid.

The Buddhists, great believers in the belt-and-braces approach, had built bases at both of the Moon's poles. And there, as expected, they had found an abundance of water, enabling them to construct thousands of crude spacecraft using metal smelted from lunar ores by solar-powered machines. There were vague rumors that these early neo-Zen Moon bases had found *too much* water—that is, far more than could be explained by the standard theories—but there was nothing on record to confirm or deny this.

As the orbital mines—and their attendant monasteries—in the asteroid belt became productive, the Buddhists expanded their lunar operations to match. Even with a moderately high-powered telescope, none of this activity was visible from the Earth, and when the ultra-green anti-technology movement now known as the Pause cast its long, deceitful shadow over humanity, the people of Earth lost any interest in the Moon. The Belters pulled in their horns and waited patiently for the groundhogs to regain their sanity. The Pause halved Earth's population, then halved it again—mostly the nasty way.

As the ultra-green policies came spectacularly to pieces, the survivors split into two political camps. China went one way, the rest of the world renamed itself the Community of Ecologically Responsible Nations, Ecotopia for short, and went the other. Ecotopia rebuilt selected technologies in order to manage its environment effectively; as a result, post-Pause Ecotopian technology was a weird mixture of hi-tech and low-tech. Computers did what they were told and not much more, but they did it with blistering speed. Machine designers did all they could to keep people in the loop, either in control or with the semblance of control: human psychology was considered a major design factor. A suitably qualified human could always overrule a machine. Earth's technologies turned inward, with an emphasis on everyday life: basic science languished, and anything outside the thin layer of the planet that was inhabited by people was left to its own devices. So by the time the neo-Zen presence was once more acknowledged, the Buddhists had laid claim to the entire lunar surface and all attendant mineral rights. Earth, belatedly realizing that it was heavily dependent on the flow of minerals from the Belt, had no choice but to accept that claim.

As the Buddhists' operations grew ever larger, they began to realize that the greatest danger to their thriving business would be a cosmic collision. An inbound asteroid or comet could hit a monastery, the Moon—or, worse, the Earth, their spiritual home (and, it hardly need be said, their main customer base). Even a near miss could cause unwanted perturbations, throw orbital mining gear out of position, and generally create havoc. Precisely what remedy the monks had in mind if such a body were ever sighted was far from clear, but the general plan seemed to be to send out a massive fleet of rockhounds who would *mine* it into dust. Or, perhaps, push it into a safer orbit, but that wouldn't be as profitable.

Of course it was also in the Earth's interests to have advance warning of any dangerous incoming bodies, so the monks set up LADSOCS—the Lunar Automatic Deep Space Optical Comparison System. This employed sophisticated optical interferometers to combine the observations of several hundred telescopes, using the electronic wizardry of charge-coupled devices to collect incoming photons. The system watched for changes in the position of distant bodies, possibly indicative of an inbound comet from the Oort cloud and beyond, or a wayward asteroid.

Nāgārjuna had been assigned a duty by White Grouse—more a character-building exercise than anything else, since the same job could easily have been automated. But the Way of the Wholesome had also learned from the Pause—and what led up to it—and it encouraged its devotees to undertake as many burdens as possible themselves. So each local monastery has assigned several junior monks to a rotation, and their job was to keep an eye on LADSOCS and try to get visual identification of any inbound lump of cosmic junk.

The system had been running for half a century and so far the worst that had ever been seen was a small comet that missed a medium-sized mining complex by two million miles. So when Nāgārjuna hesitantly logged on to LAD-SOCS's main computer and downloaded its latest scans, it took him several seconds to register that one sighting actually required attention. From the look of it, LADSOCS had spotted a new comet. That was hardly unprecedented—it usually found about three a year. But this one was heading for the inner Solar System.

Or was it?

The Solar System is fortunate in having its own celestial vacuum cleaner, a planet so massive that its tremendous gravitational field sucks in many incoming comets, keeping them away from the more fragile planets inside its protective circle. This is the gas giant Jupiter, and it is likely that without it, life would never have gained a foothold on the Earth. Even Jupiter is fallible, of course: sometimes it has an appointment in the wrong part of its orbit, and the inbound impactor escapes its clutches. Sixty-five million years ago, one such intruder had exterminated the dinosaurs.

Nāgārjuna instructed the computer to make the best prediction of the comet's orbit, based on all available data.

There was room for error—the comet was still a long way off and accurate observations were difficult at that distance—but in ten to fifteen years' time the intruder might well be swept up by Jupiter. Or possibly miss, swing past, and make one or more further attempts at self-immolation in the gas giant's thick atmosphere. Even though the impact would be equivalent to that of millions of hydrogen bombs, there were some ancient records of cometary impacts on Jupiter—a complete impact sequence of comet Shoemaker–Levy 9 from the twentieth century, and a series of sketches of what might be the remains of an impact, drawn over an eighteen-day period by Cassini in 1690. This showed that the planet would gobble up the comet with little more reaction than a few huge ripples scarring its upper atmosphere for a week or two. The gas Goliath would be more than a match for the slung pebble.

Nāgārjuna copied the data summary to his suitnode. When he got back to the monastery, he would have two things to report: a rare-earth-rich asteroid, and an inbound dinokiller— probable prognosis Jupiter-bound. The first, he knew, would win him a commendation. His superior's reaction to the second would depend on whether, in fact, today was an *uposatha* day. He could check on the 'node, of course—as well be hung for a sheep as for a lamb. But he didn't dare. If it *was* an *uposatha* day, the news would be just *too* depressing.

Bailey leaned over the mezzanine balcony and surveyed the pandemonium in the hotel lobby, while Jonas took a few shots. "This should please the manager. It'll really put this place on the map."

Cashew always felt uneasy in crowds. "Maybe he's worried it'll wipe it off the map altogether."

"Rioting and mayhem are the lifeblood of journalism, Cash. This is our party: let's enjoy it." They took the rear elevator down to the gathering.

While the press filmed the expedition, Jonas filmed the press, infraredding the choicer images to the room's giant screen. Every wristnode had a tiny built-in screen, but this was useless for anything beyond a brief message or for displaying operational icons. There was also a holographic facility that projected an illusion of a flat screen in front of the user's face, about where you would hold an antique book. However, the screen resolution was barely acceptable and the picture tended to fade in bright light, so the usual way to display wristnode information was on flatfilm screens, slaved by infrared signals. Flatfilm technology was cheap, and public screens were stuck up everywhere—literally, for they came in huge rolls of flexible plastic with self-adhesive backing. You could cut them to shape with scissors and put them up anywhere, powered by ambient lighting. Enthusiasts often carried rolled-up screens disguised as umbrellas or walking-sticks, or stuck stretchable ones onto their travel bags, their clothes, their companions' clothes . . . or sometimes just onto their companions. A broad back made a highly effective display, and a stomach or a thigh wasn't so bad, either. Most users, however, were happy to select a temporary personal window on a public screen. The method lacked privacy, but what with the hackers and the snoops it was crazy to imagine nobody else was reading your Xmail. Anyway, if you really wanted to access a private message, you did so in private.

The questions came thick and fast. The reporter from *Wicked* predictably focused on the wisdom of two men and one woman being confined together on a small boat for two weeks. With malice aforethought, Jonas pointed out that there would also be an all-male crew of six, because someone had to be able to sail the boat. The *Wicked* reporter nodded knowingly and spoke rapidly into her 'node. "No problem," said Cashew. "I'm sure the boys will be capable of protecting themselves."

"Jemima Reynolds, *Xclaim*," said a tall blonde in the front row. "Is it really true that you're not using navsats?" Next to her what looked like a bodybuilder in a khaki T-shirt hoisted a huge wide-angle VV camera on his shoulders and zoomed in for a close-up. Bailey paused until he judged that his face would fill the frame.

"Yes. That's the whole point of the expedition. We intend to validate a pretech navigational technique, so we are deliberately cutting ourselves off from the navsats." A shudder of excitement went around the room. "And there'll be no cheating. To prove the navigational concept, we will lock ourselves off from most of the Xnet, leaving only a mathematical processing facility. The lockout will be independently verified and enforced by Xop." Several people in the audience nodded. "And to anticipate the next question:

no, we are *not* carrying any insurance, we are taking responsibility *ourselves.*" That really got to them.

It didn't all go as smoothly. An overweight reporter from XBC was clearly having problems with the heat, and he sounded irritable. "Bailey, why did you have to start out on a godforsaken lump of rock like this?"

"To make life difficult for you guys." There were a few wry laughs. The ferry from Dakar had been unable to cope, and local fishermen had quickly spotted the chance for a profit. Only problem was, their boats were inches deep in water and the smell of fish took days to wear off. Bailey chuckled. "Just kidding. No, Varin and des Hayes began their voyage at Gorée Island, and therefore so shall we."

"*Why* did they start from here?" asked another, whom Bailey recognized as the anchorperson for *Xworld.*

"It's all on the X, Vladimir—you can pull it up anytime."

"There's too goddamned *much* on the X, Bailey. And too many media trying to access too few feeds. The information parking lot. Let's have it in your own words. Gimme a quote I can *use,* willya?"

"Mmm, okay, but I'll keep it short; most of these guys don't have your attention span. Netbite: *we will remake history.* In-depth, or what counts for that nowadays: Varin and des Hayes were carrying out a commission from King Louis XIV of France. Gorée Island is on the extreme western edge of Africa, and the French had just established a colony here, so it was a logical choice."

"It was a science jaunt, right?"

"Yes. They took lots of astronomical instruments, including two telescopes. We've got copies of them both."

"We haven't seen your boat yet. Why not?"

"Ship. It's being readied in Dakar harbor. The crew will sail it over here tomorrow for a prevoyage shakedown."

"What sort of boat is it?"

"The *ship* is a reconstruction of a late second millennium seagoing sailing vessel, which has generously been supplied by the Senegalese Nautical History Association, at their own expense." The strangely named *Tanzrouft* was from a period about two hundred years too late, but an old boat was an old boat, right? "It is required by law to have an engine, for emergencies, but we intend to make the entire journey using only sail. There are six crew members, all volunteers from the association's membership." There had been more than two hundred volunteers, and to avoid arguments the crew had been chosen by ballot.

"Where do you plan to make landfall?"

"Guadeloupe," said Bailey, putting up a map of the eastern Caribbean.

Jonas set his wristnode for local information exchange. "To be precise: right there, where the red arrow is."

"How confident are you that you can navigate by the moons of Jupiter?"

"Jonas," said Cashew sweetly, "tell everyone about the bet."

The press's collective antennae pricked up. Here was a human interest angle; even the dumbest viewer would understand what a bet was. Jonas was reluctant, but he didn't have much choice.

"A week's pay if my navigation is out by more than a hundred yards," he confirmed, admiring the way he had been maneuvered into a public admission. He wouldn't be able to back down now.

Cashew glanced up at the screen. "You all heard him. Jonas, I've got independent witnesses." She flourished her wristnode. "I'll just take a copy of those coordinates, so that there won't be any argument when I come to collect my winnings."

4

Secondhome, 1936th Continuity

The cities were feeding.

Deep beneath Secondhome's multicolored canopy they cruised, sucking up aeroplankton by the billions.

Other creatures grazed on the aeroplankton, and those attracted predators.

In the skies above, a terrified blimp larva was metamorphosing, spilling precious liftgas into the thin air, sinking toward the cloud layer. Though it had not yet achieved full intelligence, the adolescent's instincts were smart enough to keep it scanning the gaps in the clouds, frantically searching for a city—for only a city could save it from the gathering predators in the lower cloud layers . . . *There!*

Miles below, Serene Balladeer of the Humid Luster picked up the public announcement from the babywatchers and instantly scratched his plan to spend the morning parading the lending malls. Suddenly in an upbeat mood, he grabbed his second-best knapsack and headed downflow. Merry crowds thronged the city's cushioned floatways, all with the same objective, and he joined the impromptu street party, chanting an ancient and mildly racy life-poem in an overconfident baritone.

He hoped he wouldn't be late, for such an opportunity was quite uncommon.

Toward every city's prow, off-center either to port or star-board, was the birthing arena—an amphitheater in the shape of an inverted truncated cone—and there the crowds were now assembling. The flat central court was ringed by hun-dreds of concentric circles of tethering rails, and Balladeer secured himself to one by a few of his secondary (that is, non-manipulative) trunks. There he could float in serene comfort while enjoying a clear view of the court—and, especially, the trimming pond.

In a society in which each individual possessed extreme longevity, the arrival of a potential new citizen was a com-paratively rare event and a highly significant occasion. So as soon as the babywatchers who scanned the overhead cloud layers became aware of an impending arrival, a general alert went out for wakeful citizens to throng to the birthing arena. It was this that had attracted Balladeer and his fellows. Along with thousands of other citizens he bobbed gently in the local swirl of air, as the city coasted along at the mean speed of its incident winds. Like them, he did his best to sway away from the vertical, in the hope of catching the first glimpse of the approaching larva.

Miles above, in the thin air of the troposphere, the larval blimp whirled aimlessly along in an interzonal jet stream, a spongy mass of gas-sacs that resembled a cross between a bunch of grapes and bladderwrack seaweed. The larva was nearing the end of its third-instar stage, and its rudimentary consciousness had awakened to a crisis. Billions of tiny pores in its lift-sacs had spontaneously opened in response to an age-old imperative, triggered by subtle changes in the weather, bleeding away precious hydrogen. Slowly but re-lentlessly the adolescent was sinking back into the depths where its life had first come into being . . .

The life cycle of a blimp was complex and poorly under-stood, even by the blimps themselves after a billion years of speculation and research. The main reason for their ignorance was that several early stages of development took place two thousand miles down in the high-pressure abyss of Second-home's oceans, at the upper phase boundary where a gaseous mixture of hydrogen and helium gave way to liquid hydrogen and the pressure was unbelievable. Here neither blimp nor symbiaut artifact could penetrate. So what little they knew about these stages of their own life cycle was inferred from larval and adult genetics and physiology—and they were well aware of the limitations of such inferences.

Reproductively, blimps were *r*-strategists—they produced huge numbers of potential offspring and totally ignored them until a drastically reduced subset neared adolescence. Although blimps had approximate analogues of sexes, these denoted cultural roles rather than reproductive ones; there was no separation of genetic material into sperm and ovum. Instead, when a blimp came into season—typically an interval of six days in every eight hundred, except when collectively excited—it produced trillions of submicroscopic nanogametes, tiny packages of genetic material, each containing perhaps one-tenth of a complete blimp genome. Oddly enough, each such fragment contained about twice as much "information" as was actually expressed in the phenotype of an adult blimp—but blimp development proceeded along lines very different from most terrestrial lineages, and even in principle no single nanogamete could ever give rise to a complete adult.

Every city trailed behind it a cloud of nanogametes, small enough to blow away on the local winds like spores of earthly fungus or orchid, dense enough to sink once they had been left behind in the city's wake, and compressible enough to *continue* sinking until—if they survived—they finally regained neutral buoyancy at the upper phase boundary. As the nanogametes made their perilous descent toward Union, they were winnowed by innumerable species of aeroplankton—along with countless numbers of nanogametes of other species—those indigenous to Secondhome and the many imports from Firsthome.

Every organism's new generation began its existence as food for everyone else's larvae.

At the phase boundary, the miracle of Union was enacted. Drawn together by Van der Waals forces, fitting snugly into place through molecular geometry, nanogametes linked themselves into Fibonacci chains—first in twos; then in threes as single nanogametes attached themselves to a pair; then fives, as pairs and triples conjoined; then chains of eight, thirteen, twenty-one, thirty-four, and finally the Sacred Number of the Lifesoul Cherisher, fifty-five. Temporary molecular markers, stripped off later by specialist enzymes, tagged each chain to ensure that the sequence of Fibonacci lengths was maintained . . . but in the seething sea of organics at the phase boundary, many mistakes were made. None of these were viable, but they provided nourishment for the perfect fifty-five-link chains.

Each completed chain of nanogametes closed into a ring, an act of fertilization that created a cyclozygote, newly capable of growth and development under the orchestration of its fifty-five-fold genome. Across the nanogametic ring there grew two thin, soft membranes, and in the space between there was room to trap molecules of both nonviable *and* viable but incomplete chains of nanogametes, sucked in like spaghetti through osmotic pores. Once inside, they were stripped back to simpler components and rebuilt into the growing body of the cyclozygote. These strange molecular machines, little bigger than an earthly virus, constituted the first instar of a blimp's metamorphic existence. Each cyclozygote incorporated parts of the genetic codes of fifty-five separate adults.

The cyclozygote's double membrane also constituted the first step toward a lift-sac. Molecular machinery sucked liquid hydrogen from the surrounding ocean into the gap between these tough, thin membranes. Exothermic chemical reactions in the cyclozygote's digestive system could heat the hydrogen, causing it to expand, and in this manner the cyclozygote could make itself rise through Secondhome's dense atmospheric ocean. By releasing excess hydrogen through its valvelike feeding pores, the cyclozygote could—if necessary—sink.

Mostly, it rose. There was a long way to go.

The beauty of the system was this: *it worked in any medium*. The adult blimps in the upper atmosphere could float on hydrogen-filled gas bags, because there hydrogen was gaseous, and because at that height the air had twice the density of hydrogen (one-sixth of it being helium). Cyclozygotes, immersed in hydrogen, could find no lighter medium to create buoyancy, so they turned themselves into hot-air balloons rising through colder, hence denser, air. Except that the "air" at the phase boundary was a hydrogen sea. Evolution's physics were simple and elegant: as the tiny organism floated up into less dense layers, exactly the same buoyancy system still worked.

How had such complex genetics evolved in the first place? Blimp scientists believed that back in the lost histories of Deep Time the process had been far simpler, with diminutive molecular machines competing for resources and driving each other into more sophisticated strategies. The evolution of the nanogametic ring, and much later its attendant double membrane, had sparked an explosion of diversity as the molecular gadgetry acquired the ability to explore the upper reaches of their planet's atmosphere. In a new environment, evolution played a new game. A game that had enormous implications for the old environment. A game that could change its own rules . . .

Whatever the reason, the bizarre chemistry of blimp genetics was undeniable, even though it could not be observed directly. It left numerous traces that *could* be observed.

From the almost crystalline numerology of the cyclozygote, blimp development headed toward its second instar, in which entire colonies of cyclozygotes merged together and grew into an endless variety of bizarre aeroplanktonic forms. There were no species here—creatures of the same species took on many distinct forms, while those from different species often converged on the same weird strategies for survival. Gone was the neat mathematical symmetry of Fibonacci chains, for now blimp molecular structure was deep in the domain of emergent complexity, where every process, functional or not, appeared to be entirely random unless contemplated in its totality. Intricately patterned clusters of tiny lift-sacs fought incomprehensible battles in the crushing dark, sensing each other through the chemistry of pheromones and excreta. Only a few of any species, however, had enough usable heredity to build their predator bodies. Those that didn't were food. A few became ephemeral parasites. Only a tiny fraction "worked." In the interplay of the laws of physics and the lawlessness of chance, the fundamental body plans of the organisms of Secondhome were cryptically laid down.

The aeroplankton formed a rich soup of competing/computing molecules, and it sustained endless higher forms of Secondhome life. Indeed, the largest organisms on the planet—the cities—kept themselves vibrantly alive by grazing the aeroplankton. The blimps thus inhabited the converted bodies of countless trillions of their own dead children—a fact that they suspected, but did not *know,* and were completely unmoved by in any case. This is the way of the *r*-strategist, which has evolved *not* to care for its offspring . . . for there are too many.

Out of a million nanogametes spawned by a mature adult, perhaps ten would survive to reach the phase boundary. Out of a million cyclozygotes, perhaps one would make it into the aeroplankton. Out of a billion blimp aeroplanktonic instars, an average of just two might reach the next stage—a huge, high-floating preadolescent larva, a colony of fully developed gas-sacs. For every five preadolescents, only one would sur-

vive to begin the transformation into fourth-instar adulthood . . . at which point its real trials would begin.

Early, small preadolescents, third-instar metamorphs, generated copious quantities of liftgas and rose in a mere forty
days from the crushing pressures of the abyssal oceans to the
thin air of the troposphere, hugging the upper levels of Secondhome's cloud layer but remaining above them. By the
time they got there, their lift-sacs had metamorphosed into
regular hydrogen-filled gas-sacs. Up in the weak daylight, the
preadolescent colony creatures could begin to extract energy
from the sun, grow, and change. Borne this way and that on
the alternating jets that separated the atmospheric bands, now
soaring, now plunging on convection currents and storm
surges, assailed by turbulent swirls, they were relatively safe
from predation—for although they would have provided a
rich source of protein for any hungry predator, the troposphere was suitable only for a semi-vegetative existence.
Nevertheless, the occasional raid by a desperate snark pack,
gasping for breath in the thin air, disturbed their otherwise
tranquil existence. And many accidents could happen during
the lengthy childhood of a preadolescent.

The audience (eager, attentive) could see it now, an increasingly panic-stricken adolescent dropping toward the
city, desperate in its search for protection from the predators
cruising hungrily below. Instinct, honed by evolution, drew
the pathetic creature toward the comforting bulk of the city,
and wafted pheromones from the congregation of sexually
excited adults attracted it to the birthing arena and the trimming pond. A squadron of midwives rose to meet it, in a glorious display of massed aerobatics, guiding the youngster
down to the waiting sculptor-surgeons, calming it with sooth-
ing grunts and chanted birth-poems. Already they were assessing its hugely redundant mass of gas-sac-riddled tissues
in the hope of determining the True Adult that according to
mythology and custom was supposed to be buried within.

   The adolescent was chivied into position, tied down with
thick fleshy ropes, and half submerged in the anesthetic balm
of the trimming pond. The sculptor-surgeons readied their
trimming knives—sharp blades of symbiautic metal mounted
on long, slender poles, some joined in pairs to pivot like scissors, others bearing ugly, serrated edges.

   The midwives splashed liquid from the pond onto the adolescent's quivering exterior, to ensure that there would be as
little pain as possible. Balladeer winced as a sympathetic
ache shot through his trunk tips.

   Satisfied, the midwives drew back . . . and the surgeons
advanced. Symbiaut assistants sampled genetic imprints from
the outermost sacs, comparing them to the city's records,
seeking profiles that were most needed or that hinted at unusual gifts. Unwanted sacs were sculpted away by the skilled
surgeons, who took care to maintain the structural integrity of
the sacs that remained. The carving of a True Adult was a
matter for experience and compromise: the adolescent must
be left with a sustainable harvest of sacs, as well as an approved genetic makeup and a functional procerebral organ.
More than one promising citizen had been ruined because the
sculptor-surgeons had placed too much value on genetically
pleasing combinations, choosing sacs that lacked adequate
physiological cohesion. Most juveniles would be edited clean
away in the search for acceptable combinations, a strategy
that helped keep the population of near-immortals within
bounds.

   Balladeer felt his body trembling with emotion as the
trimming pool became discolored by seeping body fluids.
Discarded gas-sacs were towed away by the midwives, and
teams of symbiauts distributed small morsels of afterbirth to
the audience, who ate them. Balladeer's hide rippled with joy
as he gulped down a dripping gobbet of flesh. As the adolescent's unwanted fluids dribbled down their hides and ran
back down the conical sides of the amphitheater to pool at the
edges of the birthing arena, the audience convulsed in a col-

lective orgy of sexual secretion. A blizzard of nanogametes filled the amphitheater, so dense that for a time it all but obscured the view. It was a scene of extreme beauty and emotional significance, and it left the audience sated and drained of energy, trembling as they rode the bars of the tethering ring and surged from side to side in great moaning waves of crowd-sway. Balladeer found it hard not to swoon into firststage estivation, and he was by no means alone.

As the blizzard began to clear, the dozy postclimactic audience could see the outline of a recognizable adolescent emerging from the carnage, drenched in anesthetic liquid and its own body fluids, dripping thick yellow gore.

The surgeon-in-chief sliced away a few remaining strands of unwanted flesh, ate them, discussed the genetic and physiological indicators with its retinue of symbiauts, and pronounced the infant blimp to be both viable and socially desirable. Two vital questions now had to be answered. Was the infant sane? Was it competent at offcasting? To find out, the midwives bore the infant away to a specially prepared blisterpond. Now the healing would begin, and the Fourth Change . . . and the Life Trials.

In its specially cultivated nursery blisterpond, the juvenile blimp's consciousness seeped into being. At first it could sense nothing except an all-embracing dampness. As the days passed, other sensations began to impress themselves upon the rapidly developing young mind, pruning the overcrowded network of neural pathways to those that gave the mind its texture of awareness and its computational/processing abilities . . . The juvenile's sense of touch became many times more sensitive as pathways began to specialize for temperature, roughness, stickiness, gelidity, and the detection of edges, corners, sharp spikes . . . textural boundaries and orientation gradients . . . gradually a new world of *feel* took coherent spatial order ("shape" is the wrong word).

The juvenile's sense of molecular vibrations also began to tailor itself to key features of important compounds—both micromolecules and macromolecules, for this was an adaptive learning process and it could learn complex patterns as readily as simple ones. Indeed, to the incipient neural network there was no distinction . . . for all were just input/ouput reinforcement associations. The watching psychodacts made sure that the infant was subjected to a steady stream of culturally significant molecules, from liftgas in trace amounts to social pheromone suites that were likely to be encountered during focal occasions—group nanogametogenesis, conclave bureaubonding, and the nine levels of estivation.

Only now did the psychodacts begin to initialize the infant's longer-range senses. First hearing, as nerve-laden membranes dried out and began to detect the airborne vibrations that filtered through the blisterpond's insulating rind . . . Then vision, as the photochemistry of the blisterpond's interior was altered by the psychodacts so that the damp surfaces began to glow in all the colors of the mistbow. The lenses of blimp eyes were made from a rare substance: water ice. They were therefore receptive only to wavelengths to which water was transparent.

There was one further sense to be initialized, but not yet. First, the juvenile had to prove itself fit for adulthood. It had to offcast.

The juvenile's newly established sense of molecular "taste" informed it that the mix of liquids seeping through the blisterpond's membranous walls had suddenly changed, becoming far richer in metallic salts. Now its metabolism had to kick into a new gear to deal with compounds that were essential for life, yet, if they overaccumulated in normal bodily tissues, were fatal poisons.

Possibly . . . *Yes!* This juvenile was functional! Its tissues had created a sealed cavity near a weak section of hide! Within, electrolytic reactions were bleeding off liftgas and sequestering metal atoms into a burgeoning crystalline matrix. The atoms were segregated according to atomic number, and unwanted elements were excreted as small flakes. In the nor-

mal world of the city, roving cyclers would collect any flakes
that they encountered, store them if they had any intrinsic
value, and unceremoniously dump them over the side if not.
As unwanted flakes fluttered down into the darkness, acids
and alkalis would convert them back into salts, to be selectively ingested by aeroplankton and cyclozygotes ... or to
fall for hundreds of thousands of years, all the way to the
core.

The psychodacts rejoiced as the juvenile's metabolism
laid down its metal atoms layer by layer, creating macroscopic
monocrystalline forms that meshed with hair-thin tolerances
to form a complex three-dimensional structure. When that
first reflex-engineered symbiaut was complete, the thin skin
of the juvenile's body cavity split, peeled back ... A muscular spasm ejected the symbiotic mechano-chemical construct/
growth, and it tumbled to the bed of the blisterpond. Worry-
ingly, it was a poor construct, and at first they doubted it
could be functional; but perhaps it would suffice after all ...
Lying in warm damp slush, it began to absorb electromagnetic energy from the photoactive walls.

When its stored energy was adequate, the symbiaut self-
activated. Awkwardly and with much grinding of gears, it
struggled over to a sensitized area of the blisterpond's wall
and began to burrow a ragged tunnel through the rind.

Outside, a small crowd of blimps had gathered, the juvenile's prospective squod, or socioeconomic bonding group.
They listened in to the young mind's strong but uncontrolled
squark emissions, tapping directly into its untrained senso-
rium, their excitement growing as the new citizen successfully surmounted each of the fifty-five traditional stages of
awareness and the thirty-four cusps of sentience.

A small region of the blisterpond's rind crumbled, and the
newly offcast construct emerged into the pale light of the Secondhome day ... and seized up.

Baby's first symbiaut.

There would be many more offcast mechanisms, and better ones—constructed to different "designs" determined by culturo-chemical feedback mediated by pheromone profiles. If a blimp did not excrete its ingested metals, it would die, so the ability to excrete had evolved along with the earliest proto-blimps. Subsequent evolution had refined the excretion process from simple expulsion to the tumorlike growth of rudimentary tools—needles, blades, pounders—and thence, with increasing rapidity as the production process became increasingly sophisticated and eventually self-referential, into a versatile range of symbiotic machines without which blimp culture could no longer function.

These were the symbiauts and their many variants. They had no genetics, since the blimps' genes, physiology, and culture ensured that the symbiaut adhered to mechanically viable "designs." Yet there had never been any designer. Were symbiauts a form of life, or not? It was pointless to debate, and the blimps had never given the question serious consideration. Symbiautic constructs were what they were: complex organizations of metallic matter that were adaptable, autonomous, and without doubt as conscious as the blimps themselves.

The blimps *knew* that symbiaut minds were the equal of their own because they could bureaubond with them by squark telepathy. A symbiaut's senses were different from those of a blimp—sharper and more "digital," discrete rather than continuous, combinatorial rather than topological/analytic. Philosophers from both macrotaxa—organic and symbiometallic—speculated that subtle overtones were lost in the "translation" from organic minds to selectronic ones. Many blimps were convinced, for example, that no symbiaut could truly appreciate the exquisite anguish of a deathsong. Symbiauts *knew* that the blimp mind was insensitive to the beauty of well-crafted algorithmic topography.

The symbiaut's tunneling allowed the outside air to flow into the blisterpond. This sudden influx had two effects. The blisterpond opened like a flower, its rind splitting into half a dozen segments that peeled back in tightening coils. And the juvenile's mind became aware of incoming squark wavepackets, as well as broadcast them wholesale. In a single timeless instant, the adolescent blimp imprinted on its squod-elect. Adult patterns of thinking downloaded into its receptive memory. Unlike the symbiauts, whose symbi-engineered digital minds could hard-download operational code, this was a soft download of approximate patterns, nuances of neural flow, fuzzy-edged templates that would have to be sharpened by subsequent experience. Yet, in that instant, the adolescent grew up. It ceased to be an animal and became a citizen.

The squod's group mind bonded, merged, and became one.

Tentatively, the group mind explored itself, accommodating the new member—its first for a quarter of a million years.

When the mind later separated, the juvenile/citizen would carry with it vague memories from long before its birth, soft-downloaded from others in its squod. Most importantly, it would register its own sense of identity, an indelible shared memory of its own Commencement—its emergence from the blisterpond as a true citizen with its symbiaut construct as proof. As its body metamorphosed into adult form, its mind would forever retain these powerful memories and be shaped by them.

The squod explored the newcomer and hoped that she would be an adequate replacement for Pungent Whimsy. Whimsy, sorely missed by them all, had been detonated by a freak stroke of lightning while illicitly observing the Forbidden Storms during a risky circumnavigation of the Whirl. This dangerous diversion had been occasioned by an unusually severe vortex season in the south fringe of the Equatorial Belt, but in retrospect the city had made a bad choice.

The squod explored, contemplated, and considered itself

moderately satisfied. Encouragingly, the newborn had a huge potential for unorthodoxy . . . a vice that this particular squod secretly relished, for they were subversives, every one.

They cemented her membership with a Ceremony of Nomination, dubbing her Bright Halfholder in recognition of her shining clarity of thought and her semi-competent grasp of offcasting.

Her squod was Violent Foam.

The city's thoroughfares were even more crowded than usual, yet most of the malls were deserted. There was an air of expectancy, especially among the younger blimps, and even Halfholder—whose ability to intuit mass consensus was still at a formative stage—was aware that something special must be happening.

She stopped to look at the crowds bubbling up from the lower levels, but the rest of her squod were in a hurry. They didn't want to miss the fun.

<<Where are we*bbb!bqqq!cpcp!cp*+++>> — she was still learning to direct her thoughts, too, and for a moment they tailed off into overspill from the nonlinguistic parts of her brain—<<going?>>

<<We are going to see the fireworks display, Halfholder.>>

Having access to a group mind is not the same as understanding it: juvenile blimps still had to learn to put the group knowledge into context. <<What is a fireworks display?>>

<<It is a surprise. You will enjoy it. Fireworks are a lot of fun. But you must hurry, or all the best tethering rods will be taken, and then you will not get such a good view.>>

That sounded promising, and Halfholder concentrated on staying with the rest of the squod. She had never seen so many blimps all going in the same direction, certainly not at night.

They found a good place to tether themselves, and Halfholder made sure she'd gotten a firm grip with several trunks. It would be embarrassing to start floating away in front of so many others.

The banks of tethering rods quickly filled up, and Halfholder was glad she'd hurried.

<<What is going to happen?>> If she had been more adept at bonding, she wouldn't have needed to ask—she could have called up the information from the memories of any member of the squod—but that was adolescents for you. She was quite advanced in most respects, and it was easy to forget that she was only a few hundred thousand years old.

<<You will see. Nothing important will happen until they have dimmed the city lights and given our night-eyes time to adjust, do not worry.>>

<<Why are there so many blimps?>>

<<Because they want to see the fireworks, too.>>

<<Why?>>

<<Because everybody likes watching fireworks.>>

<<Why?>>

<<They just *do*, Halfholder. Blimps are like that.>>

<<W—>> *Maybe not.* The squod often got irritated if she asked too many questions in a row.

The lighting began to dim, and the crowd took the hint and began to settle down. Overhead, skeins of lighter cloud ratcheted across the impenetrable darkness of the upper layers. At the city's own level, visibility was fairly clear: the city authorities had authorized a descent to a relatively cloud-free level.

<<Look into the sky, Halfholder. No, not straight up, all you will see there is clouds. Look forward, over the city's prow . . . yes, that is right. And get your chromatic-eyes ready, or you will miss the colors.>>

Obediently, the young blimp exposed the color-sensitive elements in her eye-ring. Ahead, the cloud layer began to glow, a warm rich orange. Then a brilliant yellow streak split the sky, slanting across her field of vision and disappearing beneath the bulk of the city. The crowd moaned with pleasure as the afterglow faded from violet to pale blue.

<<That was a firework, Halfholder. Keep looking, there will be a lot more.>>

The city's flight had been diverted months back to bring it close to the fireworks display, as soon as the Elders had passed on the information from the symbiautic watchers. The display would last for at least half an hour.

<<What is that?>>

<<That sound? Almost like somebody wailing? That is the sound from the fireworks. It takes it longer to get here than the light.>> This was new information, and Halfholder filed it away for later consideration. She hadn't realized that sound took time to go anywhere. In fact, she hadn't realized that it traveled at all—but of course it must; it was obvious once you thought about it.

Another streak sliced through the darkness, a third, a fourth. Then dozens, almost at the same time. One exploded into a brilliant green fireball right in front of them, followed seconds later by a loud bang. There was a sudden hiss of ejected liftgas, an instinctive reaction of the crowd. <<You are lucky, Halfholder. Those are rare. The last time I saw a banger was three million years ago.>>

<<Why did it go bang?>>

<<There must have been a gas bubble trapped inside the firework as it heated up. The bubble burst.>>

They watched the pyrotechnic display until all trace of the last firework was gone. Halfholder noticed that afterward the air smelled fresh and clean.

<<Yes. You may notice a lot more aeroplankton soon: keep your eye-ring open for them. New kinds, too. They seem to thrive on fireworks. The changes in the air must be good for them.>> Halfholder knew about aeroplankton—you could eat them, raw or cooked, and they were *delicious*.

It was time to go home. On the way, Halfholder started

asking all the other questions that she had suppressed while the display was happening.

<<Where do fireworks come from?>>

It was typical of Halfholder to want more than just the spectacle. Annoying though her attitude sometimes was, her squod valued it as a sign of an inquiring brain and did its best to satisfy her demands. <<They come from the sky, Half-holder.>>

<<The clouds make them?>>

<<No, they come from above the clouds. A long way above them.>>

<<Above the clouds?>> Halfholder had never heard about above-the-clouds. This was exciting. She'd noticed that grown-ups often told her exciting things on special occasions. <<What is above the clouds?>>

<<Space. Lots and lots of empty space. Nothing, not even air.>>

<<No clouds?>>

<<Well, there are some very big clouds of very thin gas a very long way away . . . but mostly what's up there is rocks.>>

<<You said it was empty.>>

<<Pedantic child. *Nearly* empty, then. Lots of space and a few bits that aren't.>>

<<What are rocks?>>

<<Lumps of very hard stuff, there is none of it here. The rocks . . . float in space, and sometimes they fall down. That's what the fireworks are—bunches of small rocks. When they encounter our world, the air makes them heat up and that makes all the colors. The watchers only let the little rocks through, the ones that just make pretty sparks and don't do any harm.>>

<<Are there *big* rocks in space, too?>>

<<Some. We don't usually think about them, Halfholder: that's the watchers' task, symbiauts are very good at that sort of thing. There is one very big, special rock . . . but it is not

really a rock, it is made of gas. Very hot gas. That one is even bigger than Secondhome. Other rocks go around it—Secondhome is one of them.>>

<<I did not know Secondhome was a rock.>>

<<Well . . . it is a *kind* of rock. A small solid rock inside a big gas . . . rock. That is why we can live on it—it has the right kind of gas. We call the gas <air>.>>

This was fascinating. *We live on a big rock . . . there are other big rocks* . . . <<Who lives on the other rocks?>>

What a question! <<Nobody. Blimps cannot live on them, they have the wrong kind of gas.>>

Halfholder's imagination was racing. <<But—could there not be . . . special kinds of blimps that breathe a different kind of gas and do not mind the cold?>> It seemed reasonable enough to her, and it all came out in a rush.

<<Do not be so foolish, Halfholder! How could there be different kinds of blimps? Blimps have lifesouls. The Lifesoul Cherisher could not cherish a creature without a lifesoul, and if you have a lifesoul, you have to be just like us. That is why animals have no lifesouls.>>

Halfholder digested this. It made sense of a lot of things she'd been hearing about as she grew. Which reminded her . . . <<Do plasmoids have lifesouls?>>

<<Who told you about plasmoids?>>

<<The Didact for the Distant Past. I have been learning about the Exodus.>>

What are *they teaching the young these days?* <<Plasmoids. Xxxx . . . >> *A tricky one.* <<Plasmoids have . . . their own kind of lifesoul, I suppose. I have never thought about it before.>>

<<The Didact said the Exodus happened because the plasmoids were upset by snowstrikes. But when I asked him what those were, he said I would have to wait until I was grown up. What's a snowstrike?>>

<<Xxxx—oh, look, Halfholder, there's a vendaut selling

ammoniated aeroplankton! Would you like some? They're *really* nice!>>

Humplet and Turbo were fine, but Halfholder was getting worried about Mopple. The three brightly colored gaspods had been gifted to her less than a thousand years ago; watching them growing up in the netting enclosure that fenced off one corner of her private nook, she had become fond of them. Halfholder had been aware for a while that Mopple was in some sort of trouble, so it wasn't a complete surprise when she came in one day and found the bulbous creature floating on its back. It seemed perfectly happy that way . . . but you couldn't have an upside-down gaspod in your vivarium: everyone who saw it would huffle. And she couldn't bear the thought of sending the poor thing to the terminator when it seemed entirely contented with an inverted lifestyle.

She cast around for an idea and spotted a disused flotation bladder. *Yes!* A bag or two of live levispheres, a spot of glue, and she'd be in business.

She was holding the levisphere-filled bladder down with two trunks and dabbing the glue onto it with a third when Phrasemonger bobbed in unannounced. Startled, Halfholder let go of the bladder and it popped up to the ceiling. Ample Phrasemonger of the Violent Foam's eyes popped out in involuntary shock, but he quickly recovered his poise. Glancing around the nook, he took in the inverted gaspod, the cocoon of quick-drying glue, and the flotation bladder.

<<It is an interesting idea, Halfholder, but it is *still* going to look very silly. We can get you another gaspod, and Mopple will be well treated by the terminator . . . There is no need to look at me like that, gaspods do not—xxxx, very well, have it your own way. Just do not expect anyone else to help out if it does not work.>>

<<It will work,>> said Halfholder, floating up to the roof to retrieve the bladder. <<But Mopple may not like it. If he

does not, we can have him terminated. I just want him to have a chance.>>

Phrasemonger could sympathize, but there was a problem. <<You know what is wrong with him, do you not? You know that whatever you do, he will slowly get worse?>> Clearly the adolescent had no idea. <<He must have a tumor, a nasty lump, on the top of his reservoir—it is quite common and I have seen it before. The lump has made him top-heavy, so he rolls over. It will just keep growing until it kills him. Better to have him terminated before it gets uncomfortable.>>

<<As soon as it gets uncomfortable, we will. Not yet; he is happy.>>

True. It could wait. In fact, it would be a salutory lesson. Phrasemonger helped hold the gaspod down while Half-holder pressed the bladder against its back and they waited for the glue to dry. *An adult would have done that with an empty bladder, and put the levispheres in last . . . oh, well.*

<<I like Mopple's colors. He reminds me of the fireworks . . . When are we going to see fireworks again, Phrasemonger?>>

Oh, dear. She had really liked those. This was going to be a big disappointment. <<Xxxx . . . I do not think there are going to be any fireworks for a while, Halfholder.>>

<<Why? Have the little rocks stopped falling down?>>

<<No . . . but we won't be able to go and see them anymore.>>

<<Why not?>>

If in doubt, tell the truth; it stores up less trouble for later. <<The Elders have forbidden it. Do not look at me like that, they had good reason to. They have decided it is dangerous to take a city that close to a fireworks display—a blimp got hurt recently when the city authorities made a mistake.>> *A chance in a trillion, but that is the Elders for you, reactive rather than proactive, and very cautious.* <<So now everybody has to stay well away from any fireworks.>>

<<But I *like* fireworks!>>

<<So do lots of blimps. Halfholder, we cannot always have what we—>>

<<I hate the Elders!>>

You are not the only one, youngling, but it is unwise to say so. <<Never squark that again, Halfholder. The Elders are acting in everyone's best interests.>>

Halfholder bobbed politely. <<Yes, Phrasemonger.>>

The glue had set: they popped Mopple back into the vivarium. It stayed upright, but . . . They watched as it drifted up to the ceiling, its flukes flapping ineffectually. <<Perhaps it would be a better idea to take some of the levispheres out, Halfholder. Then Mopple can float next to the others. Gaspods like to stay together.>>

And I like fireworks, thought Halfholder, *but I do not get what I want. I may not be allowed to squark it, but I can still think it . . .*

I hate the Elders!

5

Olambwe Valley, 2210

In the shade of a rocky outcrop, two men sat waiting for the sun to move away from the zenith. Their names were Carlesson and Kandinsky. They wore heavy boots, khaki trousers, and military-style camouflage jackets. Crossbows, of the kind used in international sporting competitions, were slung on their backs.

Carlesson passed the water bottle to his companion, who wiped the top and swallowed several mouthfuls, cursing the heat.

"Careful with that. It's all we've got and the next water hole is ten miles away."

Kandinsky grimaced. Carlesson was much too uptight. "Better inside us than inside the bottle." But it was understandable on his first run. Kandinsky remembered his own initiation—the taut nerves, the dry mouth, the sweat seeping from his skin.

"Us." The tone was accusatory.

"Okay, me. But I've taken no more than my fair share, Henrik. Early, that's all."

Carlesson nodded wearily. "Sure, Pyotr, sure. Sorry. It's the uncertainty; it's getting to me." He unsheathed the knife that hung from his belt. It was nearly a foot long, with a thick taped handle and a razor-sharp serrated edge. He touched the edge gingerly with a finger.

"Don't worry about the knife," said Kandinsky. Knives were for close-up work only; if the crossbow did its job, you wouldn't need a knife. "It's not how sharp your knife is, it's how sharp *you* are." He glanced toward the sandy ground, gauging how far the rock's shadow had moved. Carlesson's eyes followed his gaze. "Aim your bow accurately, and you can forget about the knife. When the shadow hits that patch of pebbles, we'll move on. Agreed?"

Carlesson grunted and returned to his knife. A lot was going to depend on that knife. And the training that went with it.

From the distance came an eerie wail.

Kandinsky shut his eyes and leaned back against the rock. "Hyena. Nasty little beasts. I hate 'em. Pity there's no market for hyena bones, we could clean up." He licked the corners of his mouth, which already was becoming dry again. "Must have found a lion kill, probably zebra." He pulled himself to the corner of the rock and peered round. "Yeah, there are vultures circling. Highly intelligent birds, vultures." Kandinsky fancied himself as a bush naturalist, although his information was occasionally wildly inaccurate. "You know, hyenas are often thought to be cowards. But I've seen 'em take a zebra carcass away from half a dozen hungry lionesses."

"More likely a wildebeest," said Carlesson. "More common."

"Not 'round here."

"If you say so." Carlesson sounded skeptical.

Kandinsky felt an irrational wash of anger. He checked his wristnode to see when the next survsat was due. There were still only a handful of surveillance satellites, but they could spot an unusual movement from two hundred miles up and photograph its smile. Assuming they were looking in the right direction, and Hunters were trained to make sure that they weren't.

Like all Hunters' wristnodes, Kandinsky's was shielded, and hooked up to the Xnet via an anonymous baffle. Provided they were careful with the survsats, they would have only the Diversity Police to fear.

There was a clear twenty-minute window. Knowing he was being childish, Kandinsky got to his feet, pulled a pair of collapsible binoculars from a pocket of his camouflage jacket, and began climbing the rough wall of the outcrop. "Let's take a look." There were easy footholds and he had no difficulty making his way to the flat top, some fifteen feet off the ground. Standing near the edge, he raised the binoculars and performed a series of slow scans. He could see where the vultures were swooping low, getting ready to land, gliding in with their clawed landing gear already lowered—but there was no sign of the hyenas or their prey. The grass was too thick.

A movement caught his peripheral vision. After a few seconds he gave a low whistle. "Henrik? I can't see what kind of kill it is, but we've hit paydirt. Scramble up here and take a look."

Carlesson joined him, took the binoculars. It took a few moments for his eyes to adjust. Then he saw them.

"Cheetahs."

"You said it, sunshine. A mother and her baby."

Carlesson felt his muscles tightening, part excitement, part apprehension. An adult cheetah was worth $250,000 in Shanghai—$220,000 for the bones and the rest for the skin. But a baby would be worth twice that. It wasn't the quantity, it was the special *quality* of infant cheetah bone that pushed the price up. Stripped of flesh, dried in the sun, and ground to powder. Cut every which way with talcum, flour, you name it . . . But with that elusive touch of ancient Oriental magic. The sellers of folk medicines must make a real killing, considering the price they were willing to pay; pinch for pinch, cheetah bone was worth far more than heroin or cocaine on the wholesale market. Guess what the retail value must be.

All because jaded Shanghainese merchants thought it would give them a hard-on. Crazy. There were drugs for that kind of thing, they actually *worked,* for god's sake. But Free China did not trade with Ecotopia, barbarian drugs were not the Old Ways, and some were so dissipated that they were beyond drugs. In the name of such ignorance, the world's rhinos, tigers, leopards, and other big cats had been brought to the brink of extinction. The elephants were just about holding on.

Carlesson wasn't hot on morality or political correctness, but every so often he became dimly unhappy about his chosen—and utterly illegal—trade. He quite liked animals. But he liked a big bank balance more. *Survival of the fittest,* he told himself. *If the big cats can't hack it against humans, tough.* In any case, the Hunt had rules that gave the animals a fighting chance; the rules had evolved to keep the populations viable, modeled on the international case law that two hundred years before had preserved what little was left of global fish stocks. The main rule was: *no guns.* Hunters were trained to use crossbows for long-distance work, knives close up, and bare hands in an emergency. Hunting cheetahs was a crossbow job: Carlesson hoped fervently never to get near enough to a living cheetah to need a knife.

A hyena wailed again. Concentrating on the scene through his binoculars, Kandinsky failed to notice that a slab of rock was splitting off from the top of the outcrop. He leaned his weight forward, and it tipped up. His arms flailed at the air, and he toppled off the edge. Carlesson barely had time to register what had happened before Kandinsky's anguished scream assailed his ears.

He scrambled down from the rocks. Close to panic, he maintained just enough presence of mind to check his 'node for survsats. Five minutes. He knelt beside Kandinsky.

Kandinsky moaned as a wave of pain swept over him. His left leg was shattered; a jagged end of fractured bone poked through the flesh, white smeared with red.

"Fuck you," said Kandinsky through gritted teeth.

"You're the one that fell off the goddamned rock."

"Yeah. And you're the one that—" he moaned again as Carlesson touched his broken leg. "It *was* a fucking zebra," he hissed, while part of his mind realized he was being ridiculous.

"Yeah, it was a zebra," said Carlesson. He looked blankly around him in search of inspiration. Kandinsky was the experienced one; how would he, Carlesson, survive on his own?

"Help me," pleaded Kandinsky.

Silence.

Carlesson came to a decision. He got to his feet.

"Henrik! Where are you going? You can't leave me like this!" Kandinsky levered himself half upright, ignoring the pain. "Call Base. Arrange a pickup."

Carlesson had remembered another rule. He stopped, turned. "Pyotr, you know I can't do that." No guns—and no outside help until after the kill. "Base will send a 'giro to pick up the cheetahs. But they won't pick me up, and they won't pick *you* up. Alive, dead, whole, injured—Hunters are always on their own."

Kandinsky was on the verge of tears. It wasn't *fair*. It was Carlesson, the rookie, who ought to have broken his leg. Suddenly the Hunt's rules, intended to preserve a macho image as well as keep animal stocks away from extinction, seemed pointless and stupid. *Not me! They don't apply to me!* Nearer now, a hyena's cackle split the air. The joke was on Kandinsky, and it was a sick joke. Fear welled up from his stomach. *Hyenas. Dear God, hyenas.* "Henrik! For pity's sake, Henrik!"

Suddenly Carlesson was back at his side, but before Kandinsky could register his relief, a knife was at his throat. "Kandinsky, if you move an *inch* while the survsat is overhead, I'll slit your miserable throat, you understand?"

"Hyenas," moaned Kandinsky. He felt ill, he felt dreadful. He felt afraid. "Teeth like bolt cutters. They slice through bones. They kill sleeping people, Henrik, and drag them away." Tears ran down his face. "They'll cut me into pieces, eat me alive."

"Shut up, and stay *very* still." This was where the camouflage jackets were worth their weight in gold. Carlesson and Kandinsky formed a frozen tableau, welded together by the knife. One minute . . . two. Then the survsat's footprint was transected by the rocky outcrop, and they were hidden again.

"You bastard."

"Nothing personal, Pyotr. You know the rules. I'll stay with you a few minutes longer." Carlesson's face softened. "I'll splint the leg."

"With what?"

"Your crossbow." He knew it was a waste of time, but somehow the gesture made him feel better.

"No. You're right." Kandinsky swallowed hard, felt lightheaded. "Hunt rules. But for the love of God, Henrik, *please* don't leave me for the hyenas."

Carlesson looked at his hand, then the knife. He placed it next to Kandinsky's throat. One quick slice . . .

His hand fell away. "Sorry, Pyotr. Truly sorry. I can't." He got to his feet.

"*Please.*"

Carlesson pulled Kandinsky's knife from its sheath and placed it in his hand. "You want it, you do it." The next survsat wouldn't clear the horizon for a couple of hours: plenty of time. He began crawling through the brush toward the big cats.

"*No!*" Kandinsky howled. He screamed obscenities at Carlesson as he crawled through the long grass, heading toward the cheetahs. His voice sank to a croak; then nothing.

Carlesson crawled on. He hoped Kandinsky would be dead before the next survsat passed overhead. Should have slit the bastard's throat, stupid, stupid. But he knew he never could have done it, not in cold blood.

He could leave Kandinsky to be eaten by hyenas, though. The mind is very strange.

*   *   *

Prudence had held high hopes for the return trip to Io, but she hadn't reckoned with Pele.

For millions of years Io had been locked in a gravitational resonance with Jupiter's other Galilean satellites—those that, along with Io, Galileo had named the "Cosmian stars": Europa, Ganymede, Callisto. Held fast in its inflexible orbit, the moon was repeatedly squeezed like a pat of butter, molded by forces beyond comprehension. Friction produced heat, which escaped too slowly; trapped heat created a sea of molten sulfur and sulfur dioxide, overlaid by two miles of hardening crust, the top mile frozen solid. The crust—gray, white, and pallid yellow to the naked eye, but a spectacular splatter of mustard, white, orange, red, purple, and black when enhanced in a ship's viewscreens—was brittle, riddled with cracks, and fragile. Plumes of molten sulfur and dioxide gas forced their way through flaws and spewed into space in vast fountains, with romantic names like Loki, Marduk, Pele.

Surrounding Io's orbit was a plasma torus of ionized sulfur, half a million miles in diameter. An electric current of five million amperes flowed perpetually between Io and Jupiter in a ring-shaped flux tube, at right angles to the moon's orbital plane. Io was wild, beautiful, harsh, inhospitable, deadly.

Io was ever-changing.

Io was treacherous.

Io was the home of huge, intricate, flowerlike sulfur formations, as bright as the moon's false-color images, worth millions to any wealthy rock collector. They were found only on Mafuike Patera, a few degrees due west from Pele. At least, that's where Prudence had found them on her first visit.

Between her first and second visit, Pele had become plugged with a solidified mix of sulfur and silicates. The pressure had built, until it became intolerable. In an explosion that would have dwarfed a hundred Krakatoas, Pele had exploded, becoming Pele Caldera.

She had known of the disaster from the data that streamed

from the ever-present monitor satellite. But she'd had an ir-rational hunch that the field of sulfur flowers had survived.

It had proved to be just that: an irrational hunch.

Thwarted, Tiglath-Pileser *had cast off from Io in an im-provised search for a substitute cargo. Europa had proved a dead loss. The region of Ganymede around Gilgamesh was littered with weird ice extrusions, but* Tiglath-Pileser *lacked the necessary refrigeration facilities, and there was no way to tow them outside the vessel without damaging them. They had made a halfhearted search for giant tektites, hurled from neighboring moons by meteor impacts aeons past, but with-out success.*

They moved on to Callisto, where once a lucky rockhound had dug up a dozen diamond-encrusted geodes, formed in a grazing impact with a fragment of carbonaceous asteroid.

Callisto is the least dense of the Galileans, and a large part of its bulk is water, some of it liquid—but water that lies buried beneath a thick layer of rock and ice. It is more heav-ily cratered than any other body in the solar system. At each destination they had left Tiglath-Pileser *in Jovian orbit, tracking the moon in its own path, and piloted an* OWL *down to the surface. Callisto's craters had made this particular de-scent especially tricky, and part of the landing gear had been damaged. Several days had gone by and nothing of value had been found. While Prudence was supervising the welding of a new strut for takeoff, Fat Sally had taken her teddy bear for a walk in a small meteorite crater nearby. A strange metallic glint had drawn her attention to a lump protruding from the crater wall. Slowly warming the ice around it, careful not to cause any damage, she had pulled the object free and popped it into a sample bag at her waist.*

Later, back inside the OWL, *a casual remark had caused her to remember what she had found, and she dug it out of the bag and placed it on the table for them all to look at. In the dim light outside the Orbit/World Lander she had thought it was some kind of mineral—metal, crystal, a chunk of mica . . .*

But minerals aren't shaped like a wheel.

They had half dismissed the resemblance as coincidence, a freak of blind nature . . . until Prudence went prospecting in the crater and dug up six wheeled objects.

Over the next two days, they found another hundred and thirty, in a variety of forms. Some had been damaged by the meteorite impact, but most were intact. All of them had wheellike protrusions, usually either four, six, or eight of them, arranged in pairs except where they had been damaged or broken off.

Fat Sally named the objects "wheelers," and the name stuck. They were not mineral specimens, but alien artifacts. Wheeled machines the size of a cat. Solid metal robots.

Wheeled robot vehicles, buried in the dead ice of crater-strewn Callisto . . .

It made no sense whatsoever.

Prudence paused to collect her thoughts, momentarily overwhelmed by memories.

"Aliens," said Charity in awe. "There were aliens on Callisto."

"Maybe. But there's no reason to suppose they lived there, and plenty of reasons not to. No atmosphere, bitterly cold—"

"Maybe the aliens didn't need an atmosphere. Maybe they liked it cold."

"Yeah, and maybe there are little green dancing men on Venus who happen to like singing in the sulfuric acid rain at eight hundred degrees Celsius. Yeah, sure, maybe. But I don't think so. I think somebody—some*thing*—came down in a landing craft, just like we did, and dumped some worn-out machinery."

"A hundred thousand years ago."

"Give or take a few thousand."

"But *why*?"

"Why was *I* there? Not for any reason that would make sense to an alien."

Charity nodded. Hunting minerals for money was hardly likely to be a universal feature of intelligent cultures. In fact, now that she came to think of it, money was a pretty weird thing in its own right. Its value depended solely on a shared delusion that because everybody else shared the same delusion, a few digits in a computer file were valuable.

"Did you find any traces of the aliens themselves? Apart from the wheelers, I mean?"

Prudence grimaced. "No. Didn't really expect to, but it would have been nice to find a six-legged skeleton frozen in the ice, or even the alien equivalent of a knife and fork. But all we ever found was wheelers. Dozens of them, just below the surface, frozen into the ice. Unless we got incredibly lucky and hit just the right spot, there must be thousands of the things."

"But why didn't anybody el—" Charity checked her mouth, which as usual had gotten ahead of her brain. "Sorry. Nobody else had had any reason to wander around melting the ice."

"No. But there have been mining expeditions, so I guess there are plenty of places on Callisto that don't have buried wheelers. We *did* get incredibly lucky."

Charity spread her cupped hands. "Of course you realize the value of this find to science. It will make your reputation."

Prudence shrugged. "I know that the value to rich collectors will make my *fortune*. Before we left, we took care to smooth away all traces of our excavations. It was real fun eliminating the marks we made on takeoff, I can tell you . . . Had to go get *Tiggy*, poise it just off the surface, use it like a blowtorch . . . So, sister dear, if the scientists want to get in on the act, they'll have to pay the going rate." She caught a glimpse of her sister's astonished face. "Chatty, I'm a businesswoman, not a benefactor to the human race. Don't look so prissy. I need the money to finance a real expedition, get back out there, find what else is buried."

"And sell that, too." There was no mistaking Charity's disapproval. "Damn it, Prudence, to think that I slave away in this godforsaken little station trying to save animals from extinction, and here you are turning the biggest scientific discovery of all time into some kind of auction. The media rights alone ought to satis—"

Prudence's mouth tightened. "Chatty, *leave it*. I know what I'm doing. I've been working for this all my life, and it's been hard. Bloody hard." Her pulse quickened. "You don't know how hard it is in space."

"The neo-Zen monks in the Cuckoo's Nest spend all their lives in space, but they give their wealth to the world."

"Huh. The neo-Zen monks in the Cuckoo's Nest give a tiny *part* of their wealth to the world. They're the richest bunch of bastards in creation . . . heck, they paid me a whole cruiser just for translating a single clay tablet! Let *them* buy the wheelers and give them to the world. They can afford it!" Eyes locked, Prudence and Charity held the tableau for long seconds. Then Charity put one elbow on the table and leaned her head against her hand, closing her eyes in defeat.

Prudence sighed. "Okay, Charity, the scientists can have a few specimens cheap after I've made my first fifty million. Does *that* satisfy your sense of higher obligation?"

But Charity just turned her head away, and stared out of the window at the animal pens.

"Basically, what we're doing," Jonas explained to Cashew, "is following the observational protocol worked out by Cassini. He gave Varin and des Hayes their instructions in writing, so we know exactly what he wanted them to do." He paused. "Of course, they could only use the system once they got to Guadeloupe, whereas we can put it to work any time Jupiter's moons are visible. With modern opto-electronics we can take an obervation in a fraction of a second, so the motion of the ship doesn't fuzz everything out."

They sat on crates on the *Tanzrouft*'s deck. Another crate

had a flatfilm screen slapped on its side. The ship bobbed erratically on the Atlantic waves. A few clouds scudded over, but through the gaps the stars shone brightly.

Sighting along the wooden tube, Jonas aligned their reconstructed and technologically enhanced nineteen-foot telescope with Jupiter. Deep inside, sophisticated circuitry automatically switched into action.

Cashew peered at the image captured in silicon by the telescope's charge-coupled device, bled off electron by electron into micron-sized bins, marshaled into the computer like diminutive rolling stock, then reassembled one by one into an array of pixels. Jonas spoke to his 'node and one limb of Jupiter expanded, filling the screen. To its left was a small disk of light.

"Ganymede," he said. "Just off the limb. Io's behind, and the other two satellites are off to the other side. Now, to use Cassini's method we have to make six observations—three now, as Ganymede passes behind Jupiter, and three more later on when it emerges at the opposite edge and comes 'round to the front. And we do that whenever any of the Galilean satellites passes across either limb."

Cashew could understand the reasoning easily enough. "He wanted three observations of each event to increase the accuracy, right?"

"Yeah. His equipment wasn't as well made as ours, but it's a sensible precaution anyway. One when the satellite is its own diameter away from Jupiter's limb, one when it just touches, and one just as it disappears. Average the three and you've got a pretty precise estimate of the instant at which it first touches the planet's edge. At the other limb you do much the same thing, but it's difficult to spot the moment when the moon first emerges from behind Jupiter. Cassini advocated recording the time whenever you think you first see anything, and discarding the result as soon as you realize it was premature."

They watched in silence as the tiny dot drew nearer to its

parent world. Jonas blew up the image until clear pixels were visible, counting how many were needed to traverse Ganymede's disk. Then he counted the number in the gap.

"Three more pixels to go," he said. "Woops, now it's two." He clicked the timer button on his wristnode, in readiness for the real thing, and grinned. "First clear night after we arrive, I'll carry out Cassini's protocol for the final time, and . . ." his voice trailed off meaningfully.

Cashew felt her stomach sinking. It looked awfully *precise*. She began to see just why Jonas had been so confident. And with four satellites to play with, perpetually cycling to and fro across Jupiter's limb . . .

A clock in the sky, accurate to a fraction of a second . . .

Maybe that bet wasn't as safe as she'd thought.

A discreet plaque at the entrance identified the building as the Berlin headquarters of the International Archaeological Society. The plaque was about the only thing that was discreet. The building was huge, with a neoclassical columned entrance and an atrium that rose twenty-three floors above ground level to a nest of rooftop balconies, bars, and restaurants. In a luxuriously appointed conference room on the floor below, an emergency seminar was getting under way.

"I've been in this business for most of my life." The face of Sir Charles Dunsmoore, president of the IAS, glowed red in the light of the holoprojector. Those who knew him could tell, by subliminal signs, that not all of the color derived from the holoslide stills that were ratcheting through the expensive nano-drive projector.

Sir Charles was distinctly peeved; you could tell from the way his fingers wrapped around his beloved laser pointer.

"During that time," he went on, "I've encountered just about every kind of lunatic nutcase you can imagine. And some"—he gave a short humorless laugh—"you can't. But *this* . . ." For a moment emotion overcame him. "*This* is the stupidest thing that I have ever come across in my entire career. A madwoman with a criminal record arrives back on Earth with a sackful of rusty Tinkertoys, and the silly bi—the woman has the gall to claim they're alien artifacts! Aliens who make toy trucks, with *wheels*! It's absurd."

"*We* make toy trucks with wheels," observed a bespectacled woman in the third row.

"Yes, but *we're* not aliens, are we, Dolores?"

"Well, to us, no," she said. "But to *them*?"

Sir Charles shook his head in pity. "*What* them? It's an evident hoax."

From a corner of the room, half hidden by draping ivy that had escaped its intended container, came another objection. Montgomery Jay had made his fortune with robotic machinery for removing fiberglass roof insulation. His company was about to go bust when the glass had turned out to cause some obscure lung disease in laboratory mice, and suddenly everyone wanted their insulation removed overnight. A year later the observations were disproved, but in the interim Jay had become a multimillionaire. As such, he wasn't scared of Sir Charles, his influence, or that of his many contacts. "Charles: I don't know why you're so bothered about fake alien artifacts—this organization's mandate is to help preserve terrestrial antiquities for science." A thought struck him. "Hey—wasn't the Odingo girl one of your students, on that Sphinx project? It wouldn't do for you to be seen to be harboring a grudge—"

"*Grudge?* Monty, you know damned well that she nearly wrecked my career! Tried to claim the credit for discovering the true date of the Sphinx!" He glared at Jay as if daring him to contradict, then lowered his voice in an effort to sound calm. "She was *registered* as a student, sure—but she didn't have what it takes. Just one of those wannabes that get used for grunt labor." It still rankled, clearly, but he tried to conceal how strongly he felt, and almost succeeded. "Not that any of that *past history* is relevant to this aff—business. Fake antiquities fall firmly within our remit—on the Earth and off it. This ridiculous 'discovery' will attract huge amounts of publicity, and it's our job to stop it in its tracks.

"Monty: are you advising me to ignore an obvious fraud merely because it is being perpetrated by somebody who once—briefly, and not very competently—worked for me?"

Jay found it all a bit distasteful, and he saw no reason to make waves over a triviality. "Charles, I'm sure that your motives are as pure as a newly formed snowdrift and as dispassionate as the Day of Judgment—but if you're going to go over the top, you'd best get some facts straight, otherwise the vidivids will crucify you. Firstly, there is no hoax, because there has not yet been any official announcement. All we have to go on is rumors."

"Not rumors. Intelligence. And there's *going* to be a hoax," said Sir Charles firmly. "I am a scientist, and I refuse to condone scientific fraud. We must nip this nonsense in the bud *before* it becomes public knowledge, not after."

"Maybe," said Jay, who had been discreetly consulting his 'node. "The fact is that Prudence Odingo does not have, and never has had, a criminal record. She was cleared of all charges in the affair of 2204—"

"Only because the judge was prejudiced," Sir Charles pointed out with mild indignation. "Odingo got off on a technicality." Jay noticed that Charles had not required Xnet assistance to recall the incident, but did not remark on it.

Dolores Johnston, who knew all the scandals by heart, hid a grin behind her hand. *On the technicality that she was innocent, yeah.* But there was no advantage in pointing anything out to Sir Charles if he didn't want to hear it, and she had long ago learned to keep quiet. After all, she had six ravenous Afghan hounds to feed, and unlike Jay, she needed to keep her job in order to feed them. And herself, for that matter. Instead, she said, "I think Monty's got a point, Sir Charles. What we need is facts. All we have right now is a piece of limited-circulation Xjunk that wasn't intended to come to IAS anyway."

"It came to us," said Sir Charles, "because *somebody* had the imagination to take out a subscription, under an assumed name, to every bulletin board likely to be accessed by dealers in pirated artifacts. Now, who might that person have been? Anyone recall?"

Several of them nodded. Sometimes Sir Charles's ideas really *were* bright.

"Which page was it on?" asked Jay. "Collectors' Items, something like that? That's a public page, Charles. It's just not very popular."

Jalid Mbaruk, the meeting's secretary, consulted his wrist-node. "Rare Collectibles. It's not a page, Monty, it's a limited-access billboard. Subscribers only, and the price is *high*."

Sir Charles treated them to a predatory smile. "We'll put a team on the case. I want everything we can dig up about Odingo—her past, her family, her career, her legal record, what color she likes to wear in bed, if anyth—whatever. We also want to search the criminal records archives to find out whether she has skeletons in the closet—expired and erased cautions, for example. Also get on drug enforcement to see if she's ever shown up on the narcnode—"

"There's never been any suggestion of drugs," said Jay.

Charles gave him a look of mild exasperation. "She owns a space vessel, we know she's carried semi-legal contraband in the past. She might be smuggling drugs to Belters."

"I suspect the abbots and whatever their equivalents are in Zen, Confucianism, and Tao take adequate steps to ensure that their orbital monasteries are free of illegal substances," Dolores muttered. Sir Charles glared at her, and in her mind's eye six psychically receptive Afghan hounds froze in horror. "Sorry, Sir Charles. I was jumping to conclusions. We can't make assumptions about hypotheticals." He acknowledged the apology with a brief tilt of his head and the hounds relaxed again.

"I agree," he said magnanimously. "Belters and drugs . . .

well, probably not—though I insist that we make sure. Better safe than sorry."

When the others had left, Sir Charles remained behind in the conference room. Bah. It had been his discovery anyway . . . And it was hardly *his* fault that she'd gone off in a huff and couldn't be contacted when the press got wind of the Find of the Century. The problem was, Odingo's record was unlikely to be anything like as bad as he'd just painted it. She'd had a lot of bad luck, even if some of it was self-inflicted. Too reckless, too impulsive . . . she'd never have made a good field archaeologist. It would, of course, be convenient if Odingo was involved in something shady . . . and *if* they could prove it.

If wasn't good enough.

If was going to need some help.

He sat for a long moment in front of the room's master node, thinking. There were dangers in becoming personally involved: he had a reputation to protect. But that, of course, was exactly *why* he had no real choice but to get involved. His early brush with Prudence Odingo was on record, and the vidivids would dig it out in seconds. The whole Sphinx question might get reopened if Odingo gained the kind of credibility that he could foresee. Especially given the usual credulous approach that the media adopted toward pseudoscience, mysticism, and the irrational.

So there was no question in his mind that Prudence's reputation had to be ruined; and if assiduous detective work couldn't find any skeletons in her closet, then he would just have to put one there.

"If my calculations are right," said Jonas—not for a moment doubting that they were—"then we'll soon be within sight of Guadeloupe. Half an hour or so, I'd guess." For the dozenth time he took a quick look at his camera to make sure it really was fully charged. He wanted plenty of footage of the landfall.

He and Cashew were leaning against the *Tanzrouft*'s rail, staring out to sea. Bailey Barnum was belowdeck, catching up on some sleep before the Big Moment, though it was about time he poked his head out. It had been a satisfyingly difficult voyage, extremely vidivisual, the climax being a major electrical storm creating waves that had tossed the tiny vessel about like the proverbial matchbox. Nobody had slept a wink that night, but they'd gotten some brilliant shots of waves breaking over the ship's prow, with Bailey prominent in the foreground doing his impression of Nelson at the Battle of the Nile . . .

He'd been violently sick immediately afterward, but that bit would be edited out.

Cashew looked up toward the crow's nest, where one of the crew was peering through a modern reconstruction of a telescope. He wore old denim cutoffs and a red bandanna. "Guess? The master navigator has to *guess*?"

"The seas are still quite high, Cash," Jonas protested. "I can't predict the height of the waves, though I *have* managed to factor the tides in. But it'll be at least twenty minutes before we have any chance of sighting land, and by then I'll be up the mast next to that bugger with the red headcloth that you're so fascinated by."

"Red headcloth? Oh, you mean Clifton." Cashew knew all of the crew by name, together with their life stories, family history, and career prospects; Jonas had never quite managed to sort out who was responsible for what. "He's the one whose father had those awful problems when he was working halfway up that power station chimney in Lesotho."

"Yeah, him," said Jonas, wondering what power station chimney she was referring to. He checked his Suzuki-73 again, then his watch, squared his shoulders, and set off for the rigging that led to the mast top.

Cashew watched while he climbed. Ordinarily, Jonas had a dislike for heights—not a phobia, just a preference to stay well behind a rail or a window when the ground was a long way down. But he'd do anything to get a good shot, and he scampered up the rigging without a qualm even though the ship was swaying lazily from side to side.

Clifton leaned down and gave Jonas a hand up into the crude basket of the crow's nest. Jonas sighted through the camera's long-range lens at the horizon.

"Anything yet?" Cashew yelled, her voice falling away on the breeze. Jonas guessed what she was trying to say and shook his head.

Ten minutes passed. Bailey stumbled up on to the deck from his cabin in the fo'c'sle, rubbing at his eyes. He'd set his 'node for a prelandfall wake-up call.

"Nothing yet," said Cashew. "You're calling it pretty close."

Bailey grunted noncommittally and shrugged. "No matter. We could always have faked my scene afterwards and edited it into sequen—"

"Land ahoy!" Clifton yelled. Jonas found Clifton's craggy face in the viewfinder and asked him to repeat the cry. With the camera lens on him, Clifton suddenly became self-conscious. He fluffed the first take, but Jonas had faced this particular problem many times in his career, and with quiet encouragement Clifton succeeded at the second attempt—in fact, the yell looked impressively spontaneous.

Jonas turned the camera toward the horizon. Separating sea and sky were two tiny dark triangles, wavering in the heat—the tops of Mount Sans Toucher and the slightly higher Soufrière, situated a few miles to the south. It took him a moment to find them, because they weren't quite where he'd expected. Were his calculations wrong? No, he hadn't looked at the compass for several minutes and he'd lost his bearings, that was all. Guadeloupe was shaped like a slightly asymmetric butterfly. Grande-Terre, the eastern wing, which on a map looked as though it belonged to a swallowtail, was relatively flat. The higher regions were on the oxymoronically named Basse-Terre, farther to the west, which more resembled the wing of a common cabbage white. The capital, unimaginatively also called Basse-Terre, was hidden from sight behind the southern end of the hills.

As the *Tanzrouft* sailed closer, more detail came into view, and soon Jonas could pick out the long thin shape of La Désirade in the foreground; then behind it the promontory of Pont Château, the tip of the swallowtail's wing. The coast of Grande-Terre swept away to the north, but fell back due west on the south side, until it swung south around Marin Bay. The separate islands of Marie-Galante and the tiny and totally un-oxymoronic Petite Terre peeped above the horizon.

Jonas grunted in satisfaction.

Tanzrouft turned south of Point Châteaux, following the coral coastline past the tiny resort of Sainte-Anne, heading for their agreed destination of Gozier. It probably wasn't where Varin and des Hayes had landed, but Cashew's sources hadn't been able to pin their landfall down any more precisely, and the town had the best facilities for the world's media, who were even now awaiting the climax of the historic reenaction of a key moment in the development of human civilization.

With its Senegalese crew scampering all over the deck in a remarkable display of synchronized chaos, the ship came about into the narrow navigable channel that cut across Gozier's shining coral reefs. Jonas borrowed Clifton's telescope and put it to his eye.

A moment later he removed it, shook his head as if to clear away cobwebs, and replaced the instrument against his eye. He whistled in surprise.

Bailey joined him at the rail. "A good crowd, I imagine."

"Well," said Jonas. "You could *imagine* a good crowd, yes." He passed the telescope to Bailey.

Bailey raised it, screwing up his eyes to bring the image into clear focus. Despite its deep tan, his face went pale. Jonas took the telescope before he dropped it.

"Trouble," said Cashew, reading the signs. "Deep trouble, right?" Jonas nodded. "Nobody there?"

"I can see three people, with two cameras between them," said Jonas. "I imagine two of them are the local newscaster and her assistant. I can't be absolutely sure, but the other one is carrying what looks suspiciously like a Sony microcam. Tourist gear," he explained.

"Goddamn it!" yelled Bailey. "We spent *millions* setting up this voyage. The publicity at the start was out of this world, never seen anything like it! Every night we've topped the Xnews in a hundred countries! And now, when we finally come to the main payoff—nothing. Where the blue bloody hell has everybody *gone*?"

6

Gozier, 2210

The two people with cameras turned out to be tourists as well.

Jonas's immediate reaction was a sickening feeling that was becoming all too familiar. They'd been kidding themselves all along. Once you're on the way out, you're on the way out, and it's stupid to think you can pull it back again. It was the first law of media survival. And they'd imagined they could break it.

Only Cashew seemed able to accept the reality. She had stared at the tiny group on the dock, shook her head in a baffled parody of denial. "It's not *where* they've gone that matters, Bailey," she said softly.

"Eh?"

"It's *why*." No, that wasn't right, either—she *knew* why. They all did. They'd been preempted. A really big story had broken.

The question they were all groping for was: *what?*

The *Tanzrouft* docked amid a stricken silence, the crew's voices hushed, all hopes of instant fame eradicated. Jonas noted with no satisfaction at all that the tourist camera was actually a Marcos B5; he'd failed to observe the wraparound wrist tag. Cashew asked one of the other two tourists if any major news story had broken recently. All he could say was:

"*Que?*" Nobody else on the dock spoke a word of English. There wasn't much chance of solving the mystery until they got properly hooked up again to the Xnet, and that would have to wait until they reached their hotel.

Bailey started arguing the fare with the solitary taxi driver. He didn't speak English either.

They marched into the hotel and got themselves reconnected via the public node in the foyer, only to find that the microwave link to Miami was down for maintenance until the morning. They made the most of it by ordering two bottles of Best Old Grouse and three glasses, and locked themselves in their suite.

Jonas turned on the VV and skipped channels, but the most exciting thing he could find was a baseball game between the Talinn Tigerlilies and the Kabul Freedoms.

Next he accessed the newsnet, pulled up the day's lead items.

Not a word about the stunning conclusion of the Tanzrouft's *epic voyage . . . and not much joy on anything else, either.*

"Mmmph . . . Tornadoes in Indonesia, nobody killed . . . Prince Rupert of the Mozambian Republic had abdicated in favor of his pet crocodile Rasputin . . . some vacuum-drunk spacer's come back with fake alien toys, probably knocked them up in the ship's machine room . . . the Pancontinental Weather Control Commission had failed to agree on the shape of the negotiating table again—bloody pointless when we don't have any functioning weather-control technology, but then, I suppose it's best to be prepared . . . No elections anywhere; now, that *is* unusual . . ."

He deactivated the node and sank back into the sofa, nursing his glass.

Somewhere around midnight a disheveled and very drunken Cashew Tintoretto remembered that she and Jonas had a bet. She shook him awake and pointed this out. She also pointed out that an emersion of Callisto was due within the hour.

They staggered back down to the dock and clambered aboard. A crewman was guarding the telescope, but he recognized them immediately and tactfully moved to the far side of the deck.

Jonas tapped into the navsats to pinpoint their position. Then he accessed his navigation programs from the Xnet, to work out the local timing for the anticipated emersion. Because they'd been able to *see* the dock, there was no point in testing whether they had arrived in the right place. Instead, Jonas would use Jupiter's moons and his navigational algorithms to calculate their position, and see how closely it agreed with where they actually were.

A hundred yards, that was the bet. Child's play.

Cashew sighed. It was hard, from this side of the Atlantic, to imagine how Jonas could possibly be wrong. He was such a whiz at coding math . . .

They waited. Finally Jonas began counting down the seconds. "Should be emerging round about . . . *now!*"

They stared at the CCD image.

"Don' see anythin'," said Cashew. The seconds passed. "Hey, whassat?" A bright speck had appeared against the black of space, growing visibly brighter.

"Callisto."

"Oh. So I've lost the bet?"

"What did you expect? I'll just work out where we are, to make sure." He talked urgently into the tiny microphone. "Mmm, something's screwy . . . According to my calculations we're not here—we're somewhere else."

"I'll prove you're not here," Cashew muttered under her breath.

"Huh?"

"Ancient joke. Straight guy an' funny guy. Funny guy says 'I'll prove you're not here.' Straight guy says, 'Whaddya mean, I'm not here? Course I'm here.' Funny guy says, 'No, you're not.' Straight guy says, 'Yes, I am.' Funny guy says, 'Are you in Paris?' 'No.' 'Are you in Ams'erdam?' 'No.' 'Are you in Ouagadougadougou?' 'No.' 'Well then,' says the funny guy, 'if you're not in Paris, Ams'erdam, or Ouagadougadougouwossit, you mus' be somewhere else.' 'Of *course* I'm somewhere bloody else,' says the straight guy. 'Right,' says the funny guy. 'And if you're somewhere else, then you're not here!' "

"Ha-ha."

"Hey, just trying to cheer the loser up!"

Jonas scratched his head, screwed up his nose, and made funny little noises. "No, Cash, there's something really screwy. Maybe the Xnet has the wrong coordinates for this place." A thought struck him. "Or maybe it's observational error. Don't forget the protocol. We've got to make two more measurements and then average. It'll all come righ—"

"Oh, come off it, Jonas!" Cashew clambered up on to the crate in triumph, caught her foot on some strapping, and toppled into a coil of rope. Jonas helped her out of the tangle. He knew that, drunk or not, he could run software, and this software was telling him that he wasn't within a hundred yards.

He was out by twenty miles. "I don't believe these figures."

"I've won the be-et, I've won the— How much *do* you get paid in a week, anyway?"

Jonas had to face up to facts. "Okay, Cash, you win." He entered the transaction into his wristnode. "I've cocked it up somewhere, God knows how. Must be the algorithms, though they worked fine in Gorée . . ."

Unless,

It was crazy, it was the drink talking.

Had to be.

"Unless," he said, staring at the sky.

"Unless what?"

He swallowed hard. "Unless . . . Jupiter's moon's aren't where they're supposed to be."

Cashew giggled. "Yeah, Jonas, sure. Either you've screwed up, or Jupiter's gaddamned moons have moved. So, naturally, it *must* be the moons. Forget the law of gravity, it's been torn up and thrown inna bin jus' to shave Jonas bloody Kempe's pathetic face. Ish a fucking mir'cle, the hand of God. Hallelujah, brothers! Jonas, you'll say anythin' rather'n admit you made a mishtake."

Jonas nodded glumly, and they struggled back to the hotel.

When Cashew woke up, an overhung Jonas had been re-running highlights from the previous day's news and had finally found out what story had preempted them.

"Aliens?" Bailey couldn't believe his ears. "*Aliens?*"

"Yeah," said Jonas. "Aliens. The vacuum-drunk spacer with the fake alien toys. We passed the story over last night because it didn't look strong enough."

"You're telling me that we sailed uninsured and without modern navigational aids across the entire goddamned shark-infested *Atlantic* and we've been upstaged by some goofball who claims to have encountered *aliens?*"

"Bailey, there are hardly any shar—oh, forget it."

Bailey was disgusted. "Hasn't anybody told the program controllers that aliens were done to death years ago? Haven't they watched all six hundred and ten episodes of *The U-Foes* along with the other seventy million dimwits?"

"It's a very popular series, Bailey—"

"I *know* it's a popular series, Cash! I'm just buggered if I can see why!"

"It's technically slick," said Jonas. "Excellent camera-work, very suspenseful storyboard . . . *atmosphere*. Big budget, that's the main factor. Not strong on common sense or logical coherence, I admit . . . Anyway, Bailey, this Odingo woman isn't claiming she's *seen* aliens, or that her cat has been abducted by them and come back as a chameleon. She just claims to have dug up some alien artifacts." Jonas switched the VV to memory mode.

"Same difference," said Barnum. "She's still goofy, and her popularity is riding on the back of years of *U-Foes* hype.

Those idiots out there"—he waved a hand in the general direction of the window—"are *receptive* to aliens in our backyard. They think it's *real!*"

"The story was stronger than we thought. Let me show you why." Jonas had broken into the middle of the program and had missed a few minutes of the early chat. He looked at the screen and stroked his beard. Cashew recognized the faraway look in his eyes. "Maybe the aliens *are* real this time."

"And maybe my Great-Aunt Matilda gave birth to a two-headed alligator," yelled Bailey. "Artifacts? Crap! One look and you can *see* they're phony!"

In a long shot, Prudence Odingo looked very alone in a vast studio with minimalist furnishings. When the producer switched to a close-up she seemed more self-possessed, but the interview clearly wasn't going her way and she was none too pleased about it.

"Who's that? Delia Ricardo?"

"Don't think so, Cash—wrong eye shadow. No, it's got to be Nathalie Courtney with a new hairdo. The woman being interviewed is a spacer named Prudence Odingo." He turned up the sound.

"A hundred thousand years old," Courtney said slowly. "How can you be sure of that? Got sell-by dates stamped on them, have they?"

Prudence was coming around to the opinion that going public had been a strategic error. Unfortunately, she'd had little choice. Her normal clients had been strangely subdued when she'd posted her epoch-making prospectus on the Rare Collectibles billboard, and nobody had seemed eager to bite—not even to *look*, which was decidedly strange . . . Any attempt to drum up business on the public-access sector of the Xnet, however discreet, would have brought the vultures down anyway: the media knew Pru had returned to Earth, and her notoriety was enough to keep them on her tail until they found out why. So she'd decided to be hung for a sheep, and had put out a general media release.

Trouble was, the wrong sector of the media had taken the bait. She gritted her teeth. *Why* did Nathalie Courtney have to be such a total scientific ignoramus? She drew a breath. "Well, Nathalie, there are dating techniques for objects found near the surface of airless bodies—"

Courtney interrupted her. "I know dating techniques for hairless bodies, too, honey, but not any I can tell on a family program."

Cute. "Ways of telling the age of the wheelers. Based on the effect of cosmic rays."

"No need to get technical, honey." Courtney picked up one of the wheelers, showed it to the camera, put it back down before anyone could get a good look. Nathalie Courtney was not about to be upstaged by a toy truck.

Pru nodded. "Uh-huh. The wheelers were buried under a thin layer of ice. The particles hit the ice and plow their way into it, decelerating rapidly. Like a bullet hitting a brick wall. The impact creates a shower of secondary particles that create characteristic conical cavities. So the longer the objects have been exposed to cosmic radiation, the more impact cavities you find. All you have to do is image the surface of the object and feed the results to a proprietary impact dating algorithm. That tells you how old the object is."

The image switched to a close-up of the alleged artifacts. There were four of them, each looking like a child's toy that had gotten too close to a fire. One was little more than a corroded gray lump with oddly shaped protuberances. The other three were about the size and shape of a cat, and curiously snubnosed. Their most striking feature was their wheels, mounted in pairs front and back, which seemed to flow into the bodywork. One, more battered than the others, had a wheel missing. The three better-preserved artifacts had an array of headlightlike blobs along one end.

"Obvious fakes," said Bailey. "Look, that one's even got a tailpipe!" He was overwhelmed with irritation at the stupidity of VV programmers. They didn't care about the truth; all they wanted was a good story line, even if it was all pseudo-scientific trash. *Aliens? Nuts.* "Why would aliens have toy trucks, anyway?"

Jonas leaned closer to the VV.

"They just *look* like toys, Bailey," said Cashew. "No reason to suppose that's what they really were."

Jonas slapped his hands despairingly to his cheeks. "Cash, are you *believing* all this rubbish?" He sighed elaborately. "You a lifelong *U-Foes* fan, by any chance?"

"Sure," said Cashew, her voice dripping sarcasm. "I even collect the screensavers." She sensed Bailey was on the brink of losing it, and her voice softened. "I dunno, Bailey, I really don't. But I do recognize a gratuitously aggressive interview technique when I see one. Very Emily Crooke. Adversarial."

"Pig-ignorant, too," said Jonas. His eyes were glued to the screen. What *was* it about those Tinkertoy constructs that sent shivers along his spine? If only the camera would stay on them for more than a few seconds . . .

"For chrissake!" yelled Bailey. "We're sitting here arguing about a stupid cow who ruined a year's planning, three weeks on location, and all our careers!"

"Bailey," said Jonas carefully, "shut the fuck up, okay? There's something very weird indeed about these funny-looking toys."

"Yeah. That woman, she's weird."

"No, Bailey, she's the only one on the show with any marbles at all. And I'm pretty damned certain that those things aren't toys."

The interviewer had now maneuvered Prudence Odingo into a dead end and scented blood. She leaned closer for the kill. "So your entire case for the age of these wheeler things is based upon an analysis of particle impact cavities?"

"At the moment. There are other meth—"

"Let's move on." Courtney turned toward the camera. "On our Xlink I have Dr. Emilio Battista from the Technical University of Milan. Dr. Battista: what I want to know—along with our zillion viewers—is just how easy it is to fake objects like this."

Battista cleared his throat. "Very easy. Any rapid proto-typing company could do it."

"But to fake the particle cavities? To counterfeit aging?"

"You would need access to an accelerator to simulate the effect of cosmic radiation."

Courtney pursed her lips. "An accelerator. Dr. Battista: thank you." His image faded.

Prudence sat rigid. There was no way to counter this non-sense without lending it credibility. Courtney continued. "Ms. Odingo: have you ever made use of a particle accelerator?"

"Of course not!"

"Hmmm." Courtney signaled to the mixer desk with her left hand, out of shot. A window opened in the VV image to show an enlargement of a document. "Do you recognize this?"

"I've never seen it before," said Prudence. "What are you—"

"All in good time." Courtney was keeping an eye on the studio clock. One minute to wrap. Enough. More than enough. "This, Ms. Odingo, is a notarized copy of a purchase order to a company called Etched Nanofilm." The camera fo-cused on the document's hologo for a moment, long enough for the name to be picked out. "Do you know what Etched Nanofilm's business is?"

"Never heard of it."

"They make masks for VHD chip manufacture. And they etch those masks using a particle beam, produced by an in-house accelerator. This document is a purchase order for five hundred hours' time on the accelerator." Prudence saw which way Courtney was heading. She would deny it, but nobody would believe her, and it might take weeks to regain credi-bility. "Do you know whose signature is on that order?"

"If it's mine, it's a fake."

"No, it's not yours. Let's see whose it is." The document

moved in its window, expanding until a signature was clearly visible.

Charity Odingo.

The shock was too much. "You rotten bitch!" Prudence shouted. "You leave my sister out of this! It's a setup! She's never—" *Oh, damn.* Prudence stopped, but the damage was done.

"Precisely. Your *sister* purchased time on an accelerator. Doesn't she normally work with animals? Does she use an accelerator to count monkeys?" She glanced again at the clock. The camera zoomed in until her face filled the screen. "Ms. Odingo, thank you for taking part in *Breakers* this evening." Cut to Prudence, also in close-up. "This is Nathalie Courtney for QVX/WashDC, signing off until the same time tomorrow night—and every night. Good night."

Roll credits, fade in ID jingle. The theme music swelled, the image of Prudence's horrified face froze, held for a little *too* long, fragmented, reassembled into the production company's hologo.

"Nine-hour wonder, just had to break during our crucial window." Bailey shook his head glumly.

Jonas swore.

Cashew turned to stare at him. "What's got into you?"

He was fiddling with his 'node. "I'm booking a flight."

"What, *now*? You haven't had breakfast."

He nodded. "Now."

"Where to?"

Jonas pointed to the VV. "There. DC. Odingo."

Bailey Barnum looked at his cameraman in astonishment. "Jonas, she's a nut!"

Jonas shook his head. "Oh, no. Not at all. A crook, maybe, but not *that* kind of a crook."

"How can you be so certain?"

"Occam's razor. You can counterfeit a purchase order an awful lot more easily than an alien artifact. That business with her sister's signature really shocked her rigid; I don't think she's a good enough actress to fake it. But I need to talk to her, see those wheelers myself, before I can be sure."

Cashew grabbed his ears and pulled his head to face her. "Sure of what, lunkhead?"

Jonas reached up, took her hands, and gently but firmly removed them from his earlobes. "Sure that those alien artifacts are genuine."

On the way to her very expensive hotel room—courtesy of QVX/WashDC—Prudence Xmailed her lawyer a succinct summary of events and some terse instructions. He'd listen to them in the morning. She checked in and flung herself full length on the bed.

That didn't go too well, she thought. *In fact, my dear, it was a total disaster.* It was ironic. Here she was, sitting on the greatest archaeological discovery of all time, and nobody— not her clients, and certainly not the media—would believe a word of it. And now Charity—poor, innocent, helpless Charity, happy in the tiny world of her animals—had been dragged into the spotlight. Scientific fraud. Charity's job depended on her scientific reputation; she would never survive separation from her beloved animals . . .

I hope she wasn't watching. Probably not: Prudence hadn't told her she'd be on, and Charity would rather tend her animals than watch VV . . . *Think, woman!* They would survive; any investigation would soon discover that the purchase order was a forgery. The prospect of being hauled over the academic coals for scientific fraud was just a minor distraction, though her past record wouldn't help . . . The authorities would take their time deciding she was innocent, but she could live with that . . .

No, the big problem was the very large hole that Nathalie Courtney had shot in Prudence's immediate credibility. And if she couldn't sell some wheelers *soon,* she wouldn't just lose out on a fortune; she'd lose *Tiglath-Pileser.* She'd had to mortgage the ship to finance her last voyage. She could almost *see* the triangular fins of her creditors, circling, circling . . .

She felt like bursting into tears. She'd been so *sure* that the world would beat a path to her door.

Like every moustrap merchant before her.

Idiot.

Time to start outthinking the opposition. Nathalie Courtney didn't have the smarts to come up with such a technical scam. Probably she'd received anonymous Xmail, then a package with the forged purchase order inside it—silly bitch probably thought she was a great investigative journalist . . . Hadn't double-checked her sources, just jumped in with both feet . . .

The worst thing was, most people wouldn't see it that way. *Great show, Nathalie—really stuck it to that Odingo con-woman!* And now the rest of the media would suck it up like giraffes round a watering hole. Pseudoscientific crap about strange lights in the sky, alien abductions—they believed that kind of thing implicitly. But show them signs of *real* aliens and it was just too much for their tiny imaginations. Stupid grounders thought they knew everything. Never felt the vacuum of space all around them, going on forever; had never known the vastness, the incomprehensible *otherness,* of the universe. Cocooned in their thin layer of atmosphere, how could they know the reality?

Of *course* there had been alien life-forms. Are now, somewhere out there in the godless emptiness. Inevitable as the Sun turning red giant . . . So why not here? Not *now,* that would be too great a coincidence, like two ants meeting in the Sahara . . . No, back when mammoths roamed the Siberian plains, when *Homo erectus* threw its first rock at a rabbit, when dinosaurs danced by the light of a spinning Moon, or when the first muddy amphibian crawled out onto dry land to set up a new home . . .

And if they had been here, they might have left a calling card.

She hauled one of the wheelers out of its padded bag and

put it on the bedside table. Its triple headlights—for that's just what they resembled—stared at her. She ran her fingers over the wheels, which were locked solid, probably by corrosion. She swore, quietly now, and swallowed a tear.

Not beaten yet.

She tried to give Charity a call, but there was no answer. She left a short explanatory message and a long apology for her sister to listen to whenever she got around to it. Then she pulled off her clothes, slid between the sheets. She was so exhausted that she fell asleep almost at once.

In the middle of the night she sat bolt upright in the bed. *Prudence Odingo, there are times when you are so slow that you amaze even me.*

If Courtney has received anonymous calls and packages, then somebody *must have sent them.*

It might be a smart move to try to find out who, and why.

She was just about to check out of the hotel when she looked out of the window and noticed the police car parking outside. Maybe it was just a guilty conscience, but she suddenly decided not to wait around to find out if she was right. It had dawned on her that as well as scientific fraud, she might be open to criminal charges, too.

She slung her overnight bag across her shoulder, picked up the padded one with the wheelers nestling inside it, and took the service elevator to the basement. From there she made her way to the underground loading bay where the hotel took delivery of everything that it needed to keep running. She dumped her 'node in a trash disposal unit. She hated being off-X, but wristnodes could be traced.

She peered around the end of the loading bay, but the only people in sight were two men supervising a forklift robot stacking boxes of soap. Presumably the police hadn't expected her to fly the coop.

Police! Prudence imagined more of them raiding Gooma Facility, carting her bewildered sister away to face questions that she couldn't possible answer. *Poor Charity . . . She didn't exactly approve of my plans to sell the artifacts, did she? What will she think of me now?*

At least Charity had no idea where the rest of the wheelers had been stashed. Not on *Tiglath-Pileser,* and not anywhere near Gooma Facility, that was for sure. She thought about calling her sister, but Xcalls were easily traced. This made her feel really guilty. But guilt wouldn't help anybody. What Prudence had to do was find out who had set her up, and why.

The trouble was, she had no idea how to start. The most constructive thing she could do right now was to go to ground. A cheap, disreputable motel—one that asked for no names, not real ones . . . She headed for the nearest pedway terminal, to take her out of downtown DC to where property values were lower. She had almost reached it before she realized that she was being followed.

All kinds of thoughts rushed through her head. Police? Was the stalker linked to whoever had set her up? Was he government? Neither seemed likely; he was much too unprofessional. Proof: she'd spotted him. Reaching the pedway entrance, where there were plenty of witnesses, she stopped suddenly and turned around; her pursuer all but bumped into her.

"Why have you been following me?"

The man seemed unperturbed by her directness. "I'm a VV journalist. I want to talk to you." He leaned up close, a sharp whisper: "Ms. Odingo: please come with me before the police find you. I assure you that you will be safe with me. Do I *look* as if I could do you harm?"

How could she trust him? "From some scandalbox, are you? Well, listen, buster, I've just about had it up to here with jour—"

"Yes, you would. Nathalie Courtney's a real weasel, isn't she? I saw your interview; she gave you a rough ride. Unprofessional, unprovoked, and unfair."

This wasn't what Prudence had expected. "Who *are* you?"

"Name's Jonas Kempe. I'm not really a journo, I'm a cameraman. I want to help."

"I don't need any—" She stopped. She *did* need help. But from a total stranger? "Why Kempe? What's in it for you?"

"Don't know. Not until you tell me a lot more than you said on *Breakers*."

"How did you track me down?"

"QVX gave me your hotel address. Got here just as the police arrived. On a hunch, went around the back, saw you making a getaway." He took her arm and propelled her onto the pedway, heading uptown. "Which we'd do well to continue. When we get close to South Fontenay, jump off and follow me. Um." He hesitated. "Do you have those alien artifacts in that sack?"

Prudence lost what little patience was left. "For God's sake, *why*?"

Jonas shrugged. He wasn't completely sure himself. "I want to look at them. Just a hunch." He grinned self-consciously. "I've learned to listen to my hunches."

Prudence acted on impulse. "So have I. Find us somewhere safe to talk, Mr. Kempe; convince me you're kosher . . . and if you can do that, maybe I'll tell you what you want to know."

He found them a small bar, the kind where the proprietor tips off clients if the police are going to show up. It was cleaner inside than it looked from outside. He ordered two coffees and had a whispered conversation with the bartender, who gave a quick nod and pocketed ten times the cost of the drinks. Jonas could hardly keep his eyes off Prudence's bag, but this was definitely *not* the place to open it up and see what was inside.

Thirty minutes later they were still there. They hadn't exactly become old friends, but Prudence had lost most of her suspicions when Jonas explained how her media release had upstaged Bailey Barnum's triumphal landing.

"The important thing to find out," said Jonas, "is who set

you up. I did a stint as a hacker before I turned to camera-work. I know ways to persuade the Xnet to spill useful information. What have we got to go on?"

"Etched Nanofilm."

"No, they'll turn out to be innocent bystanders. That purchase order is a fake."

"Battista, then."

"No, he was just hauled in as a talking egghead. Poorly informed, too."

"Sorry?"

"I worked for years making science features—picked up all sorts of stuff, I'm a regular walking scientific database, and it's all in my head. I'm good with gadgets, too, and I can hack software in my sleep. Anyway, I made features on accelerators, and on cosmic rays. So I know that you can't fake a hundred thousand years' worth of cosmic ray damage in three weeks, not on that kind of accelerator. You can't fake it in three years. Hell, you can't fake it in a hundred thousand years."

"*What?*"

"Nanomasking requires a beam of positrons. Those are the only particles that Etched Nanofilm's accelerator would be able to produce. But cosmic radiation is a mix of all kinds of particles, and positrons are somewhat rare."

"Shit. You'd get the wrong kinds of cavities! I should've thought of that. Damn."

"Back to basics, then. We *do* know you were set up. Someone wanted to discredit you, forged that purchase order. Who? Who would want to do that, Pru?"

She leaned on her elbow, face supported by one hand. "Has to be a private grudge. Somebody whose position would be threatened if my discovery was to be believed. A commercial competitor—no, that doesn't sound right, what would they stand to gain? An old enemy—Lord knows, I've got plenty of those, but this doesn't have their smell. No, it has to be—an *academic* competitor! Someone whose *reputa-*

tion would be threat—" She stopped, a terrible thought pushing itself into her mind. *Oh, shit.* "I'll tell you who it *might* be, Jonas. Charlie sodding Dunsmoore."

"Who?"

"Sir Charles Dunsmoore, president of the International Archaeological Society. We—we had a professional dispute, years ago . . . He got me kicked out of grad school . . . Nasty business, the bastard walked all over me and enjoyed every minute of it. Hate the swine, and it's mutual . . . Jonas, this is just the sort of dirty trick Dunsmoore would pull."

Jonas mulled the information over. It would be a mistake to leap to conclusions. "Pru, I know the X backwards. I could—"

"Waste of time if you're thinking of an Xsearch. If it's Dunsmoore, he'll have covered his back *very* thoroughly. You'll never connect him to anything. He's as slippery as a weasel dunked in castor oil."

"Yeah, but—okay, okay, I'm sure you're right. Confident bugger, then? Yes, I know the type—" A thought struck him. "Wait . . . Pru, listen! The story is going to fall apart when the police find out that the document is a forgery. Won't take them long. So Dunsmoore's aim must have been to discredit you *temporarily.* And that plan makes no sense unless . . ." He snapped his fingers. "Trouble. It has to be an improvised holding operation. Something quick-'n'-dirty to buy enough time to set up the *real* whammy."

Ohhhh. "That's *really* encouraging. Now I'll be looking over my shoulder all the time." She saw fear flood into his face. "Metaphorically. Dunsmoore never resorts to violence. It's too honest for him." *Stick to what's important, girl.* "Jonas, since you claim to know so much about the Xnet, maybe you can help me with a few other tiny problems. First, get me in contact with my sister in Africa—untraceably."

Jonas actually blushed. "Sorry, Pru. Untraceable communications over the X need special equipment. Mine is half a continent away."

"Too bad. The other one is, I can't get a buyer for the wheelers. I've tried my usual clients, but nobody's taking the bait. I need a different approach, something unorthodox."

Jonas tried to think. "Tricky, not really my line . . . Wait. *Wait* a minute. Angie Carver! Woman we interviewed for *Weird Xzine*. You will love this lady, Prudence, you really will. She owns a museum."

Prudence laughed without humor. "Jonas, in matters of archaeology you're an innocent abroad. Museums don't have the kind of money that I'm after."

Jonas shrugged elaborately, hands palm up, fingers spread. "This isn't the usual kind of museum."

7

Gooma Zoodiversity Facility, 2210

When the police car pulled to a halt outside Gooma Facility, Charity had been feeding the bonobos. These astonishingly humanlike chimpanzees were her special favorites, and she often stood and watched them socializing for hours. They were noticeably more lightly built—the jargon was "gracile," an elegant word that she rather liked—than the common chimp. The babies, of course, were cute and cuddly—*like* all *babies,* she reminded herself. *It's a universal evolutionary protection mechanism.* But the one that intrigued her the most was Pogo, an old male with wise eyes and an unsettlingly direct way of making his wishes felt.

She heard the whir of the electric engine, and the driver clambered out. Charity wondered what he had come for. There were a few local policemen who often dropped by the facility for a cup of coffee and a chat—or just to watch the animals, as she was doing. But this face was unfamiliar.

"Charity Odingo?"

She nodded. "How can I help you?"

"I am Jairus Mwanga, special constable." He looked distinctly embarrassed. "I am here to arrest you on charges of—"

"What?" Charity was on the edge of panic. "Surely there must be some mistake?" *My God, do they really want Pru-*

dence and somebody's got the names mixed up? Her mind raced, out of gear.

Stolidly the special constable tried again. "To arrest you on charges of fraud and handling counterfeit works of art." He fumbled in the pocket of his uniform shirt.

Charity slumped into the nearest chair, her mind awhirl. It *must* have something to do with Prudence. What had her sister gotten up to this time? But there were more urgent worries. "Moses! What will happen to Moses?"

Mwanga stared at her. "Moses? Who's Moses?"

"My son. Asleep in his room. He's only four years old!"

"Oh. Nobody told me about a child. Wait a moment." Mwanga found what he was looking for, pulled out a flat-form card printer, infraredded it to his wristnode, and printed out a copy of the standard caution, which he handed to her. Then he had to explain to her how to enter a certified notice of receipt into her own 'node to satisfy legal requirements. She tried several times to raise the question of Moses, but Mwanga seemed able to handle only one item at a time, saying merely, "We'll fix the child in a moment." By the time she had satisfied him, Charity was weeping in frustration and fear and Mwanga was becoming more and more flustered.

He spoke rapidly into his 'node, and after a few moments a reply from someone senior must have come through, because he grunted a couple of times and then said, "Moses, he comes along with you. We've got a court order. They'll look after him at the station."

She was too confused to think straight. "But he won't like sleeping in a cell!"

Mwanga shook his head. "He won't *stay* at the station, lady. The desk sergeant will sort him out good, don't you worry."

"Oh." She knew Milton Obote, and she wasn't sure that having him sort Moses out was much improvement on a night in a cell, but by then she had worked her way around to another worry. "The *animals*! Who's going to feed and water my animals?"

That set off another round of gabbling into the 'node. More grunts. "We'll take care of *that* at the station, too."

Mwanga waited patiently while she roused Moses and dressed him. The boy, bleary-eyed, stared at the policeman. Then his eyes opened wide, and without warning his face took on the unreadable mask that so baffled her.

"Who's that, Ma?"

"That's a nice gentleman who has come to take us both for a ride in his car," Charity said, not quite lying—or, at least, so she hoped. Moses gave her a funny look.

She turned to the constable. "I'll just call a few friends to sort out the anim—"

"No." Mwanga was adamant. "Wait till we get to the station, okay? Your animals'll be fine for a few hours."

True or not, she had little choice. She shepherded Moses into the rear of the police car and climbed in beside him. Only then did she notice that his shirt was all lumpy at the front.

She investigated as the car drove them away from Gooma Facility.

Oink!

Moses had brought the memimal.

Prudence wasn't impressed. The Carver Museum of Human History, in her opinion, looked pretty damned ordinary. All the usual exhibits, every one a hologram. A very large copy of the Rosetta stone dominated the entrance hall, revolving slowly. Just beyond was Sylvia, of course: the world's oldest fossilized human ancestor, a specimen generally held to be *Australopithecus afarensis,* though Prudence doubted it very much; the original had been dug up near Peninj, just to the north of the Olduvai Gorge, where so many of the early ancestors of humanity had been found over the last few centuries. In Prudence's opinion it was almost certainly a prehuman ape, probably a species of *Paranthropus,* very likely *P. ignavus.* The Goldin brothers always claimed that fragments of bone found nearby proved the creature to be a tool maker, but several apes used rudimentary tools—such as sticks or strands of grass to poke ants out of their nest and eat them—so she remained unconvinced.

She pointed out as much to Jonas, who laughed. "Trust me. I want you to meet my friend Angie." He peered around. "She's usually pottering about among the exhibits, talking to the customers—" He broke off and grabbed the attention of a passing assistant, who muttered vaguely and pointed toward a distant doorway. They made their way past the exhibits (*A reproduction of Mona Lisa, how crass,* thought Prudence) to the Mycenaean Hall, cutely decorated with a tiled maze and a fiberglass minotaur.

"There she is! Angie! Angie! Over here!"

A severe-looking and rather large woman carrying a plastic bucket looked up, frowned for a moment, then gave a brief smile of recognition. She put the bucket down and strode majestically over to them. She gave Jonas a piercing look. "Why, if it isn't Jonas Kempe! How's the vidivid business? Who's this, then? New girlfriend?" She gave Prudence a quick once-over. It was like being appraised at a market; Pru half expected the woman to lever her lips back to look at her teeth. "Looks a lot more sensible than that Cash woman hanging on your arm when you interviewed me."

"No, no, Angie. I told you then, Cashew is just a colleague. Always was, still is, okay?" Angie gave him a look that showed that she hadn't believed it then and she wasn't about to concede it now, but said nothing. "And Prudence here isn't a girlfriend, either—she's just somebody that I want you to help."

Angie scented intrigue. This was getting interesting.

"Angie owns the museum," Jonas told Prudence, trying to get the conversation back on course.

"Inherited it from Mikhail, my seventh husband," Angie told Prudence blithely, giving her a special "woman-to-woman" look. "Wore him out like all the others. The first one, Henry was his name . . . owned his own stable of Thoroughbreds. And the hotel chain, of course. The second, Jean-Louis, owned several airlines. Osborne, my third—well, he'd inherited some tourist complexes in Bali and Tahiti from an aunt. Yoshiki, number four—"

"Angie," said Jonas, "has more money than God."

"That," said Angie, "is because I haven't got much God, Jonas." It was clearly a standing joke between them.

"Seems to me," said Prudence bluntly, "that you haven't got much *taste,* either."

Angie seemed unperturbed. "Ah, a straight talker. Now, just what do you mean by that, young lady?"

Prudence gestured at the exhibits. "Holograms. Fiberglass junk. Plastic clichés. All the obvious stuff, and none of it *real.*"

"Oh, *that* old tat?" Angie laughed. "Honey, you are so right—so *very* right. But it's what brings the public in, you see, and by statute I can only keep the lease on this building if I haul at least twenty thousand of the buggers through my doors every year." Angie took her by the arm. "Jonas: *is she okay?*" He nodded. "You'd better be right, Jonas." She came to a decision. "Yeah, she's okay, she knows how to keep her mouth shut. Anyway, I can buy better lawyers than the government, any day . . . it's not a big risk." Angie turned to Prudence. "You want to see some real exhibits, my dear, you just come along with me. And you, too, Jonas." She winked at Prudence. "You and I will get along just fine, young lady, but I must ask you not to reveal what you are about to see to *anyone.* Now, let me tell you about Maddison, my *fifth* husband—a major league basketball player he was, and by heck, he . . ."

In response to a code punched in by Angie, the elevator went down several more levels than its panel showed. When the door opened, there was only darkness. Angie reached for the light switch. "You want something real? Then look at"— she flipped the switch—"this!"

It took a few seconds for Prudence's eyes to adjust.

No, it can't be.

The underground room was huge. Everywhere were benches and boxes, tables and glass-fronted cabinets. Facing her was a large slab of rock propped up against one wall. It was painted with what looked like animals, in blacks, browns, rust-reds, dull greens . . .

"Like it?" said Angie.

"It looks like a cave painting," said Prudence. She stepped closer. "*Just* like a cave painting. It's a remarkable reproduction, Angie, but I thought we were going to see something *real*."

"That ain't no reproduction, honey."

Prudence stared at her, eyes wide. "But private collectors aren't *allowed* to own real cave paintings! The IAS won't—"

Angie patted Prudence's shoulder. "What the International Archaeological Society don't see, its heart don't grieve over. Now you understand why you were sworn to secrecy. This old thing is one of my favorites—look at the way that bull's flank curves . . . It's from a tributary of the Dordogne, and I used some of Henry's money to rescue it before the cave got washed out by mudslides when some damn fool defied a court order and started chopping down the trees on the hillside."

Jonas gave Prudence a proud smile. "Angie may hoard illicit artifacts, Pru, but ecologically speaking she's as pure as the driven snow."

"It's a fetish of mine," said Angie. "Gotta do it *right,* girl. Otherwise I can't live with myself." She paused, then shrieked with laughter. "And I certainly can't live *without* myself!" It was clearly another old favorite.

Prudence was moving from one bench to another, almost at a run, eyes widening at every step. "An ichthyosaur! I've never seen one so big! My God, are those *really* stone chippings made by *Homo habilis*? Skulls! You've got—oh, no, I don't believe it, a whole skeleton!"

"Minus several toes and a kneecap," said Angie. "Maybe one day I'll get a complete specimen."

"Most of my customers would *kill* for— Angie, what the

devil is this?" Prudence held up a large fossilized bony structure. "Part of a dinosaur?"

"Customers?" Angie gave Prudence a much harder stare than before. "You're in the trade, aren't you? I *thought* I knew that face. Prudence . . . O'Donnell? No, no, wrong ethnic grouping—I know, Odingo! Ionian sulfur flowers! You're the one that got into all that bother with the police back in—"

"It was all a mistake," said Prudence defensively. "Never reached a jury."

"Sometime, not now, I want to talk to you about those sulfur flowers. Never quite approved of—"

"The area got wiped flat when Pele erupted a few years ago."

"Oh. That changes things, I guess. So the ones you brought back are the only specimens?"

"Yes."

"Good, I've got a dozen up at the far end in humidity-free containers. Should be worth a fortune now."

"My God, Angie, they were worth a fortune *then*!"

Angie nodded. "I think I sold Humphrey's meat-packing business in Argentina to get them. Husband number six, dear. Or was it one of his silver mines? Hard to remember, the old brain cells don't work so well as they once did." She snapped her fingers. "God, they don't! You were on the vidivid the other night, getting creamed by that Courtney bimbo." Prudence groaned. "You're in trouble, young lady, you know that? Police trouble. You—"

"Yes, I know," said Prudence wearily. "But you haven't answered my question." She pointed to the fossil.

"Oh, that. That's my thoat bone."

"Throat bone?" Jonas interrupted, confused. "Throats don't *have* a—"

"*Thoat* bone," said Angie. "It was found by the Second Mars Expedition. Pre-Pause."

"You're not serious," said Prudence. "Pulling our legs?

April Fools' joke? The thoat was a fictional invention of Edgar Rice Burroughs. There never were any *real* thoats."

Angie rubbed her neck with one hand. "That's what the Second Mars Expedition thought," she said. "Until one of them found this."

"Nuts."

"Maybe. It was found by Silas Shatner, a communications engineer, while he was setting up the long-range antenna. He knew nobody would believe him, so he kept it quiet and stashed the fossil away in a toolbox. He sold it to a dealer for a few hundred dollars. I picked it up for seventy thou about ten years ago. I've had it analyzed in strictest confidence, and it's perfectly genuine, some kind of fossilized bone, totally unknown to palaeontology." She shrugged. "Of course, Shatner might have been lying when he said he found it on Mars." Angie's face looked troubled for a moment. "But if so ... well, he took an awful lot of trouble to impregnate it with genuine Martian minerals. The molecular structure, you see. It's unmistakable, or so the archaeologists tell me. Anyhow, I decided to call it a thoat bone—just in case it was."

"Two million dollars?" Charity was aghast. "You know I can't raise that kind of money, William!"

William Jumbe, her lawyer, nodded sympathetically. Nyamwezi law wasn't very enlightened, and the accused didn't have as many rights as in some other countries. But even taking that into account, something wasn't right. Setting this ludicrous level for the bail bond proved it. Everybody knew that Charity Odingo was harmless, and with her beloved animals to look after there was no chance whatsoever that she would run away.

"What about Moses? I want him back!"

"Judge Peterson has signed a court order giving the state temporary responsibility for his welfare," Jumbe told her.

"Peterson? He's crazy as a coot."

"He's still a judge, and it's still a court order. I'll put in a challenge, but it all takes time. Obote has made arrangements for Moses to be packed off to stay at a residential care home run by the Mwinyi family. They're decent people and it's only a mile or two away."

"William, how can I explain that to Moses?"

"Tell him it's a special treat."

"He'll know I'm lying, he always does. And what about my animals?" Eventually three strapping young men from Gooma village, who often acted as casual labor for Charity and between them knew how to care for all the animals, were picked up in the police car and given a list of instructions that she had printed out on the police station's computer.

Obote's orders had come from very high up, in response to a request from the District of Columbia Police Department in Normerica. He told Charity that a Normerican attorney was already on his way aboard a Cape Airlines passenger jet. "When he arrives, I'm sure everything will be a lot clearer. In the meantime, I'm afraid you'll have to spend the night in our cell." Obote made it clear that he and his squad would do what they could to make her stay as brief and as comfortable as possible. No doubt it was all a mistake and would be sorted out once the attorney arrived from Normerica.

No doubt.

Charity tried to work out what Prudence would have done in the same circumstances—after all, her sister was more used to this kind of thing. Obviously, call her lawyer, which she'd already done—but what then?

No good, she had no idea what madcap thing Prudence would have done, and if she knew, she'd never be able to bring it off. Best just to relax until Jumbe had made some more inquiries.

She was just beginning to regain her composure when an embarrassed desk sergeant arrived at her cell door. Moses, he said, had absconded from the Mwinyi's home. Charity, frantic, did her best to pull the bars of her cell door out by their roots, while he did his best to calm her down, reassuring her that with his entire squad hot on the trail, the boy would soon be found.

Charity was too intelligent to be mollified—her imagination was in overdrive. But she *was* intelligent enough to realize that there was nothing she could do, and after some persuasion she stopped rattling the bars and sat on the bed, sobbing quietly. She tried to put on a brave face. It was absolutely typical of Moses to escape from the Mwinyis—he never stayed where you put him. But Moses was a clever child, very resourceful for one so young. He'd be fine. The police would soon pick up his trail and track him down.

Of course they would.

She got not a wink of sleep that night.

"You said Prudence needs my help," said Angie to Jonas. "With the police?"

Jonas reminded himself that Angie was a very shrewd operator and anybody who tried to put one over on her generally got short shrift. "Yes and no."

"Give me the yes first."

"The police tried to haul Pru in for questioning this morning, but she'd scooted before they arrived. We assume they're after her."

Angie gave a short laugh. "They certainly are, she's all over the X. There's a general alert for your arrest, honey. They already got your sister. Bail provisionally set at two million dollars—each."

Prudence's mouth opened wide. *Charity? What about Moses? What about—*

"You mean you didn't *know,* honey?"

Prudence shook her head, stunned by the news. "Four million—the only way I could raise that is to sell *Tiglath-Pileser*! And it's in hock already!"

"Your ship?" Prudence nodded. "Impounded pending your trial on counts of forging artworks—"

"*Artworks?*"

"Don't ask me. Lawyer-speak. Oh, and serious fraud. Your ship is liable to confiscation if it can be proved that you employed the vessel in commission of a felony."

"*What?*" Prudence was aghast.

"Don't worry, you're safe here—at least, until somebody traces your transport."

"We took a car that I hired from the airport," said Jonas.

"That could slow 'em down. Unless there are records connecting the two of you."

"None."

"Good. That gains us an hour or two. Now tell me the 'no' answer."

"Uh?"

"You want help with something else, too. Not just the police."

Prudence put her padded bag on a spare length of bench. It was show-and-tell time, and now it was *her* turn. "You saw *Breakers*?"

"Some of it."

"Oh. Then you didn't see *these*. I call them wheelers." Prudence pulled out one of the alien machines and unwrapped it. Angie stared at the corroded metallic form. Jonas's fingers developed a sudden itching. *Now* he'd get a chance to take a close look at the things.

"Hmmm. And you're going to tell me you found this thing on Callisto, right?"

"You *did* watch the program." Angie said nothing. Prudence launched into her sales pitch. "Angie, I need three things, and you can provide them—though I don't know how to make it worth your while. One: get my sister out of jail. Two: find a buyer for my wheelers."

"The program said they were fakes. That's why the police are after you. I'm not in the market for fakes."

"That's the third thing I need help with. Someone is trying to discredit me, and I'm becoming more and more convinced that I know exactly who, and why. If I'm right, it's a stupid personal grudge, that's all. The wheelers are genui—" But Angie had bustled away to a far corner, where she took something from a cabinet. She plonked it on the bench.

"Calm down, sweetie. *This* was found on Callisto. Always wondered what it was. Thought it was some funny mineral formation, but it never looked right."

It was a single alien wheel.

"I'd need to run some lab tests to be sure, but I reckon I can judge character. You're quite right, my dear, your wheelers are *not* fakes." She gave Prudence a sharp look. "Hmm, you seem worried, young lady. Don't fret. To my knowledge this was the only one of its kind until yours turned up. Bought it from a drunken lidar operator in Cairo, years ago—big blond man, muscles like a rhinoceros. Cost me two beers and an indecent proposal which I had to turn down." She looked wistful.

"I thought I was the first to find them," said Prudence in a worried tone. Jonas picked up one of the machines and stared at it. What *was* it that shouted "alien" at him so emphatically?

"First to find any *intact*," Angie confirmed. "So you want a buyer?"

"That's right."

"You've found one. Which is how you make it worth my while to help you. How many have you got?"

"A hundred and thirty-seven."

Angie showed no surprise. "More where those came from?"

Prudence started to relax just a little. With a buyer lined up, she could start to get the mess sorted out. Freedom for Charity and security for *Tiglath-Pileser* were a little closer.

"Lots more. We took what we could before we ran out of time."

"Leave any clues?"

"No. I torched the area on take-off, then hung around to make sure we hadn't left any signs once it froze."

"Cool." Angie scratched her head. "Release too many at once and the price goes down, you know."

Prudence was a professional and didn't need a lecture on supply and demand. "Yeah, yeah, sure. Only ten are for sale right now."

Angie's eyes glinted. "You just sold the lot, honey. Let's shake on it."

"I haven't told you the price yet!"

" 'If you've got to ask the price, you can't afford it.' I'm not asking. It will more than cover those bail bonds, that's for sure." She gestured vaguely with one diamond-studded hand. "But I want first option on the other hundred and twenty-seven, *plus* everything else you dig up from now on. Because that's the fourth thing you need help with, right?"

"Fourth thing?"

"I'm not fresh out of kiddygarten, young lady. You need finance for another expedition to go and get everything *else* the aliens left. Obviously."

Jonas had turned the wheeler over to get a good view of its underside, and now he felt the hairs on his neck prickle. "I *knew* those things were real as soon as I saw them, but I couldn't work out why! But if you look at them from underneath, it's obvious."

"What do you mean? *I* can't see anything obvious. They do look a bit weird."

"Yes!" Jonas almost shouted in triumph. "Too weird to be fakes. I—oh, just look at how the wheels are aligned!"

Angie turned the wheeler on its back and held it in front of her face. "Uh—they aren't."

"*Exactly!* They don't come in symmetric pairs. They're a bit offset. Not much, but enough."

"I'm not sure I follow you."

"Angie, humans have a very strong innate preference for symmetry. It comes from a sexual selection mechanism: women prefer to mate with men whose faces are nearly symmetric, they've evolved a tendency to have more intense orgasms—well, anyway, humans always design wheeled objects with the wheels in opposite pairs. These things have them offset in a very funny manner. Definitely alien."

"You seem very certain," said Prudence.

"Heck, there was even an airplane designed with a wing that slanted backwards one side, forwards the other. More fuel-efficient, and perfectly stable. Company called Epsilon Air built it. Went bust. You know why?"

"No."

"Passengers refused to fly in it because it wasn't symmetrical. Yeah, yeah, I know, a really good forger might think of making his alien machines asymmetric. But I back my hunches: he wouldn't, the instinct for symmetry is too strong."

Sir Charles poured himself a small glass of Armagnac. He had just flown himself back in his private jet from a meeting in The Hague. Normally he enjoyed flying—he was an excellent pilot and it took his mind off work for a few hours—but this evening the distraction hadn't worked and flying had been a real pain. He definitely needed a drink. He looked at the corroded object on his immaculate desk and for a moment his eyes glazed over and his mind wandered . . . After the heady excitement of the day's politicking and fixing, it was a tremendous relief to relax for a few minutes and be himself again.

He had almost forgotten how.

Charles Dunsmoore was not, deep down, a villain. He was a complex man who, by virtue of a retentive memory and an agile mind, had been propelled step by step into positions of authority that were marginally beyond his natural capabilities. Years of academic infighting and backbiting had honed his reflexes for self-preservation; by the time middle age approached he had evolved a conscious ruthlessness that his younger self would have despised. He remembered the humiliation of his first Egyptological conference presentation when the moderator had demolished his presentation, and even now he felt a warm flush of blood to his neck and cheeks. Foolish, after all these years, with Drittseck dead and

buried for half of them. How hard it is to excise the lizard in
our brains . . . Unconsciously he narrowed his eyes in a reptilian squint, directed at a small lump of corroded metal that
lay on the table at his side, resembling a broken coin.

Part of his extensive collection.

Prudence Odingo. He sighed. Clever, indubitably; talented, very probably; a woman of immense physical courage
but much too impulsive . . . and an ever-present danger. Such
a pity that it should be she who had stumbled across the first
definitive evidence of alien technology. Such a pity that it
was necessary to discredit her, silence her, destroy her. It was
such a magnificent discovery; such a shame to bury it—but
one day, when Odingo was forgotten, he would bring it to
light once more and then it would be his.

Memories . . . Some were painful. Poor Prudence . . .
she'd walked out on him at precisely the wrong moment. If
only he'd gone after her sooner . . . then he could have told
her that one of the tablets was going to rewrite pre-Egyptian
history. It recorded, in convincing detail, the construction of
the Sphinx—*with a huge lion's head instead of the familiar
face of Khafre.* But before they'd been able to look at that
particular tablet, she'd lost her temper and stomped out. He'd
tried to get in touch with her, to explain, to call her back—
nothing. He sipped at the brandy, but it didn't dull the pain.
Isotope distribution dating, the most accurate method available, had placed the tablet at $4560 + 25$ BC, and that had
knocked the whole thing on the head. Couldn't she *see* there
was no way he could have kept the discovery quiet after that?
After all, she'd told him as much herself. He'd *tried* to contact her, but because she wouldn't reply to his messages, he
couldn't get permission to use her name on the press release,
though he'd given her full credit in the text. But the media
had wanted a hero, a genius who had solved the Riddle of the
Sphinx—and there was only one choice. They'd *had* to leave
Prudence out, because she was a loose end and the media

couldn't handle loose ends. They needed neat, tidy, well-rounded *stories*. Pretty fairy tales.

The same problem had arisen when he was writing the discoveries up for scientific publication. His paper had contained lavish thanks to her for finding the tablets, for making the preliminary translations . . . but she couldn't be included as an *author*. There'd been no way even to get her signature on the copyright transfer. He'd tried, but all his Xmail had been bounced. He'd damned nearly begged. *Nothing*.

Then, of course, when it was far too late, she'd resurfaced. Anonymous flaming all over the X, accusing him of everything from piracy to rape. Fortunately it was so over-the-top that it hadn't been necessary to sue. Tempestuous, hotheaded . . . it was all so *unfair*. It hadn't been *his* fault that Prudence's contributions—which, he now found himself admitting, had gone far beyond the initial fortuitous discovery—had been overlooked.

What else could he have done?

He gave a wry shake of the head and sipped at his drink. He took no pleasure in doing what was necessary. He'd had no choice. Fate, he thought, was brutal and impersonal . . .

His wristnode emitted a sedate buzz. He cocked his wrist to bring up the holoscreen. The 'node's operating system noted the characteristic movement, and a husky female voice drew his attention to a new development. "Sir Charles—there is an urgent message for you. Confidential. Do you wish me to display it, voice it, file it for later recall, or trash it?"

"Voice."

"The message is from Marie Dellarmée at the Comité Européen des Instituts d'Archéologie. She has an important commission for you."

Sir Charles yawned. How tiresome these people were, how inextricably wedded to prestige. There were a dozen up-and-coming youngsters who could do all he could, and more, if they were given the opportunity. Except, of course, that they lacked his experience, influence, and network of contacts. So in point of fact there was no way they could be given any of the more sensitive—and lucrative—consultancies.

"Virginia"—that was his private name for his 'node's personality simulacrum—"confirm financial conditions."

"Scale A fees, Sir Charles." That meant elaborate expenses, all the best hotels and restaurants, plus five thousand dollars a day. Difficult to turn down when you had an expensive collector's appetite to feed. He hoped fervently that the commission would be an interesting one. He asked Virginia for details.

"It is to investigate Prudence Odingo's claims of finding alien artifacts," Virginia told him in sultry tones.

Sir Charles's antennae sensed a unique combination of opportunity and danger. He set the glass down. "Continue."

"CEIdA has authorized a public inquiry into her claim."

Damn. The idea was to bury it, not hype it across the entire global VV network.

"It will be hosted by the Public Interest Channel on prime-time VV."

This gets worse every moment.

"They have asked you to present the scientific background required for a dispassionate assessment, and to chair the inquiry in person to ensure that it is seen to be fair and unbiased—with particular regard to laboratory tests designed to authenticate the artifacts or reveal them as—"

Sir Charles spat a brief obscenity and shook Virginia into premature silence. He had assumed that the hostile reception on *Breakers* would sink Odingo without a trace, lost in unplumbed depths of legal paperwork and police investigations. That had been the game plan: derail her from a distance, remain behind the scenes; avoid personal involvement, because in that lay infinite dangers. Sir Charles had invested a lifetime's effort: he had a lofty position in society and an unparalleled reputation among his peers.

Unfortunately, he also had a few secrets which, should they come to light, would ruin both.

He would decline. Invent an excuse—field trip overseas, major address to prepare, grant committee to select . . .

He was about to instruct Virginia accordingly when he saw the trap.

He was the natural, obvious choice. It would be wildly out of character to say no. Reporters who knew him of old would ask awkward questions, for they knew that he would never turn down such a golden opportunity for publicity, nor would he ever decline such an important application of his expertise. Odingo's wheelers were potentially the find of the century, if not of the millennium; however unlikely her claims were, they had to be taken seriously. Seriously enough to dispose of them for good.

He should have thought it through more carefully. Too late, the damage was done. No excuse would ring true; indeed, there was a distinct chance that any refusal would stir up the very hornet's nest that he was trying to leave serene and undisturbed. The one thing he could salvage, though, was his reputation for independence. Someone *else* would have to chair the meeting. He could plead a hypothetical conflict of interest, emphasize the need for the inquiry to be seen to be absolutely fair.

Before this thought had crossed his mind it was followed by another. A genuinely independent investigation might very well *vindicate* Odingo's story. If it was carried out competently, it certainly ought to.

His eyes flicked back to the desktop. He picked up the corroded, broken disk and stared at it as if it held the key to the riddle of the universe.

Maybe it did.

He had known for a long time that it must be ridiculously ancient—120,000 years, the lab report had said.

He had been sure it was manufactured. There were no natural formations of quite that shape. In any case, the report said that it was a monocrystal, which argued high technology. So either there had once been an extremely advanced civilization on Earth—which was possible: few traces would have survived for 120,000 years—or the disk was of alien origin.

His instincts shouted "alien."

He had known that his colleagues would never be convinced on such flimsy evidence. He didn't even know where the disk had originally come from; it had been part of a job lot smuggled in from Turkey. For more than twenty years he had hoped to turn up something more tangible to confirm his surmise, to ensure not just a reputation but immortality. And every day he had feared that he would be beaten to the punch.

Now his fears had come true.

All of which led, inevitably, to the third thought. By accepting the commission and taking part in the inquiry he would be uniquely placed to ensure that its outcome was to discredit Prudence Odingo *irrevocably*. By declining the invitation to chair it, he would put himself in a far better position to arrange that outcome, because he could play a more active role. Chairs were supposed to behave as if they were dispassionate and disinterested.

He could even suggest one of his bitterest rivals as the chair . . . *Yes, that would be very neat.* He instructed Virginia to accept the contract and settled down to some long and careful planning.

The boy had run as hard as his young legs would carry him—along narrow footworn paths between rows of simple block-built houses, past small gardens, some overgrown with weeds, some carefully tended with neat rows of vegetables, some resembling a junkyard. An old man resting in a hammock waved to Moses as he dashed past. The child noticed none of these things—he was too busy running.

In his hand he clutched the memimal. At intervals it meowed.

He had no plan in his head. To a four-year-old the world is a confusing place at the best of times, and even the most familiar of surroundings are perpetually springing new sur-

prises, some pleasant, some not. And Moses was not an entirely normal four-year-old. He was wonderful with animals,
totally unpredictable with people. He could disappear into
himself for hours and ignore the rest of the world, and you
never knew what would trigger it.

He had enjoyed the ride in the car, but he had not enjoyed
being separated from his mother. Even very young humans
have a deep-seated instinct for emotional undercurrents, and
Moses had sensed that his mother was frightened. Even
though she had talked brightly; indeed because she had talked
too brightly, though Moses could not articulate such an analysis. Things just seemed *wrong*. He hated it when people said
one thing with their tongues and another with their body language. To him, the lie was glaring—the insincere smile
shouted its dishonesty. That was what he so loved about animals—they hardly ever told lies. Except for the bonobos, but
they were such charming liars.

Even though the Mwinyis were saying nice things and
pretending to act like parents, he'd known straightaway that
he had to get away from those horrid people with their fixed
smiles and hard eyes.

As usual, it had been easy. Grown-ups have such a simple-
minded view of the capabilities of the young. The screws securing the window had been loose, and his nimble fingers had
quickly teased them out using a paper clip that he had found
in the trash bin under the table.

He slowed down to catch his breath, and his eyes darted
this way and that, looking for a place to hide. He had learned
that trick long ago. If you run away and remain visible, they
soon catch you. Grown-ups are slow thinkers, but out in the
open they can move surprisingly fast.

He had come to the edge of the village, and now he was
trotting alongside fields of maize, twice his height and more,
cobs ripening in the African sunshine, their sheaves of surrounding leaves halfway to a dry brown—funny horsetaillike

tendrils hanging down from their tips as they nestled close to the thick upright stems.

He finally noticed that the memimal was meowing and silenced it with a sharp command.

Moses had a natural sense of direction. He had watched the many twists and turns of the police car as it made its way from Gooma Facility to the nearby town of Nambosa, and again when he had been taken to the Mwinyis' residence at the edge of the village. Now he stopped, caught his breath, found a suitable tree, and shinnied up it. Not far away, people were working in the fields, harvesting root crops. Away and to his right he saw a familiar shape, the outcrop of rock known locally as the Crocodile's Nose (after a tribal myth of some improbability with a highly amusing punch line). Ma sometimes took him there on one of their many walks. Ma was all right, she hardly ever told him lies. He didn't explicitly work out that he could find his way home from the Crocodile's Nose; it was more that he instinctively homed toward anything familiar. He scrambled down the tree, picked his direction, and began running again.

His instincts told him to hide. But *where*?

A side track led up a short cutting to an abandoned shed—some kind of farm building, maybe one that had been used for storage. The roof had fallen in and one wall was half collapsed. Weeds had grown into the gap, over and around the fallen rubble. Birds had made a scruffy nest atop one wall.

He wriggled between the bars of an old, broken gate, not noticing that he had dropped the memimal in the scramble. He knew from experience that hiding *inside* buildings didn't always work—grown-ups sometimes looked in such places. But up in the corner, where part of the collapsed roof jutted out over the top of the wall, that was the kind of place they never thought of searching. He scrambled up the sloping edge of the gap in the wall, using it as a staircase, and squeezed in beneath the jutting sheet of recycled plastic.

He was certain that nobody had seen him take refuge.

He was tired, hungry, and thirsty, but more than that, he was scared. Scared that those horrible people who had taken him away from Ma would find him and drag him back again; scared because his mother wasn't at home where she ought to be.

Bad people had taken Ma away.

He squinted and watched the sun climbing higher in the sky. Before the heat became too great, he ought to look for something to drink—

He heard voices.

Two policemen appeared on the path below, talking loudly, their heavy boots making slapping sounds against the sun-baked mud of the track.

"No sign of the little bastard," said one. Moses didn't understand the word, but he recognized the uniform and he didn't like the tone of voice. *Bad people.* He huddled in the shadows, trying to be as quiet as a mouse like the heroine in one of his favorite stories.

"Wombaga said he saw the child go past headin' in this direction," replied the second policeman.

"Old fool's drunk most of the time. You can't rely on his memory, or his sense. Probably made the whole story up."

"Maybe— No!" The policeman pounced and held up a lumpish foam shape. "This toy belonged to the child!" He shoved it in his belt: this was *evidence.* He looked around, saw the shed, pointed. The other nodded. They wrenched the gate open, snapping off several brittle staves in the process. Their feet crunched on the rubble.

"Looks deserted."

"Oh, yeah? See where those plants have been bent over?"

"Probably an animal."

Moses became aware of a faint slithering sound close by. Below, the two men rummaged in the ruins of the shed.

"Watch out for rats and snakes."

"Nothin' here 'cept beetles and spiders."

"Let's go, then. He must have dropped the toy as he ran past."

"No, I got kids of my own. You'd be amazed how clever they are at hidin' . . . I'll take a look up there." He began to climb the broken wall, heading straight for Moses' hideaway.

"Careful," his companion warned. "Could be scorpions!"

"Yeah. An' you watch out for stampeding rhinos, okay? Don't you tell *me* how to go abou—"

An instant before the man's head reached a position where he couldn't fail to notice the child, the source of the slithering noise made itself apparent. A huge python, six inches thick and at least twelve feet long, flowed past Moses and straight at the man. He yelled and fell off the wall to the ground beneath. He picked himself up, and both men ran off, stopping only when they had regained the main path.

"Like I said, scorpions I don't mind," said the man who had fallen. "*Snakes*—ugh!"

"No kid'd be up *there*," said the other.

"No," the first hurriedly agreed. "Where did that snake go?"

"No idea. Into the bushes somewhere."

"The kid must've gone farther along the path. Let's go after him. I hate snakes."

The sunset was spectacular. The whole western sky acquired an orange glow. Streaky wisps of cirrostratus hung across the horizon like wreathed trails of smoke, set in dark relief against the glowing backdrop of the sky. To the east, random clumps of cirrus shone salmon pink in the afterglow.

Skeins of geese straggled across the darkening heavens like the strings of a tattered fishing net. Lengthening shadows pointed skeletal fingers at the onrushing darkness.

Covered in dust, his face tear-streaked, his feet sore and blistering, Moses limped from isolated tree to isolated tree, skirting clumps of brushwood. He had been walking since midafternoon, and the village was far behind him.

The familiar silhouette of the Crocodile's Nose still seemed as far away as ever.

He was desperately thirsty. His lips were cracked and bleeding, his throat parched. He had no clear conception of "death," not as applied to himself, so he could not recognize that unless he found water within a few hours he would collapse and die . . . but he knew he had to *find* water, and quickly. He had seen dead animals in times of drought and he knew that without food and water, animals stopped working.

He just didn't know that the same applied to people.

Animals . . . The *animals* knew where there was water. Moses would follow the animals.

First, though, he had to *find* some animals to follow, and that wasn't so easy. There were birds, but they either sat immobile on tree branches or flashed past so quickly that his eyes could scarcely follow them. Snakes didn't help, either— mostly they lurked in slack coils in the central hollows of grass tussocks, or else they slithered away at his approach.

Distantly he heard the howling of a hyena pack.

He turned in that direction and began to pick his painful way toward them.

Hyenas, despite their loutish appearance, do not lack courage. A lone hyena will take on a single lioness; a pack will attack a pride of lionesses and dispossess them of their kill, no matter how hungry the big cats are. A human child poses no terrors for these tenacious beasts. It never occurred to Moses that hyenas were dangerous. It never occurred to him that *any* animals were dangerous. To him, they weren't, because he could virtually read their minds.

It did occur to him that where there were hyenas, there would be food animals for them. His mother had explained all about food animals, in terms that a four-year-old would comprehend. Although Charity's maternal instincts were strong, and her chief urge was to protect her son against the cruelties of the world until he became old enough to understand them, she was also a trained field zoologist with an old-fashioned distaste for pretty lies. The Disneyfied picture of happy, care-free animals at play in a perfect world was not one that she cared to put over on anybody, least of all her own offspring. So Moses had been given an extensive course in the true nature of animal existence, and he knew that some animals killed others and ate them, and that many animals stole the food that others had killed, ganging up on them if need be. That was how it *was,* and Charity had tried to explain how silly it was to endow animals with human characteristics. So although he didn't know the *words,* he knew that it was stupid to speak of the cowardly hyenas stealing food from the noble lions. The hyenas merely adopted their own, very effective tricks to get food—and if the lions couldn't compete, tough.

Hyenas, then, meant food animals—and food animals meant *water.* He knew that much.

The sun continued to set: soon darkness would fall. He limped on.

He could *smell* the water hole now. And the odor of departed animals—zebra, gazelle, rhinoceros . . . When the sun began to set, they had left the water hole—zebras and gazelles to their herds and rhinos to their solitary devices. The water hole was dangerous enough during the day. At night, the hyenas were king.

Moses staggered ankle-deep into viscous, liquid mud. It tripped him, and he splashed face down. Sobbing, he pushed himself into a kneeling position, scraped his eyes as clean as he could manage, and crawled a dozen yards toward the glint of the water's murky surface. He was almost there when the hyena stepped out of hiding. They both jumped, and stood nose to nose, barely a yard apart.

He could smell the animal's warm breath. It was foul.

The hyena opened its jaws and snarled, showing sharp teeth. It barked half a dozen times, the call-sign of its pack.

Moses took a deep breath—and barked back at it.

The hyena wasn't expecting that. It backed off a few feet, snarling.

Somehow Moses knew that it would be wrong to snarl back. Instead, he barked again, but he put a whine into his voice, the kind of whine he'd heard baby hyenas making. He instinctively made the whine sound a *bit* like the pack's call-sign—not too close, not too different.

Now the hyena was nonplussed. The prey wasn't *behaving* like prey. It was behaving more like a hyena, like a pup from his own pack. But it wasn't a pup. The hyena had never seen anything less like a pup.

And yet . . . there was something about the prey's body language, the way it held its pose for an instant, the way it moved its head . . .

The hyena backed away a little farther. Something was wrong . . . it felt distinctly uncomfortable.

Moses whined again and tossed his head from side to side, glancing sideways to avoid direct eye contact.

The hyena paused, growled uncertainly deep in its throat . . . then slunk away into the darkness.

Moses had known that it would. He didn't know *how* he'd known, but he *knew*. With animals, he *always* knew.

He bent his head and drank deep from the muddy, fouled water. He spat lumps of floating solid matter from his mouth.

At that moment, it tasted like nectar.

He coughed, staggered fully to his feet, and squelched through the mud away from the water, toward a solitary acacia tree. He scrambled up, ignoring scrapes and cuts, and made his way to a fork about fifteen feet above the ground. He wedged himself in as firmly as he could.

Within seconds, he was asleep.

A moment later, the veldt was lit only by starlight.

The Hunter packed up his gear, the work of a few minutes, and checked the action of his crossbow. It was getting light, and he couldn't afford to waste the daylight.

Testing the wind to make sure it hadn't changed direction

from the previous evening, he made his way carefully toward an outcrop of rocks that overlooked the water hole.

The zebras and gazelles held no interest for him. Their hides had some value, but it was traditional medicines that he was after. With a high-powered rifle he could have gone for rhino horn and made himself an easy fortune, but that was not the way of the Hunters. You can't down a rhino with a cross-bow. Carlesson was hoping for a leopard. Or, if he was really lucky, a cheetah. Even a lion cub would do . . . The bones of all the big cats were in short supply. The more difficult the Diversity Police made it to hunt them, the more their value soared. The economics made restrictions counterproductive. For a moment he let his mind wander, to all the good things he would be able to do and buy when he'd made a kill . . . to Kandinsky, left alone to die a miserable death . . . Then he shook his head, to drive the distracting thoughts away. He was a Hunter, and a Hunter always stayed focused on his target.

Out among the long grass, a quarter of a mile away, he saw three lionesses slinking through the grass, crouched low to the ground, shoulder blades and haunches prominent, tails swishing, their necks stretched out so that in profile you could see the funny little beards they wore beneath their chins. They were stalking a distant zebra herd. Then, more easily than he'd ever hoped, his target presented itself. From behind a line of nearby bushes came two cheetahs, an adult and a cub. Obviously the adult was a female, the cub's mother.

The female was being very cautious. She raised her head and sniffed the air, alert for any sign of danger. But the wind wafted the Hunter's scent away from her. And both she and her cub needed to drink. One step at a time, she edged toward the water hole, while the cub kept close to her side.

Moses opened his eyes, tried to stretch his painful limbs, and nearly fell from his perch. His head ached, his whole body ached, he felt terrible. He was plastered with dried mud.

He held on to a branch for a few seconds while memory

returned. He turned his head to look at the water hole and saw the cheetahs. He sucked in his breath.

It was Zemba and Mbawa.

He began to scramble down the tree. To his childish way of reasoning, Zemba and Mbawa equated with "home." It didn't occur to him that they had been released onto the plains, and home could be fifty miles away.

He didn't see the Hunter behind his rock pile, but he heard the snap of the crossbow release and the dull *twock* as the quarrel slammed into Mbawa's flank. The mother cheetah was knocked sideways into the dust, where for a few seconds she lay, kicking. Then she stopped moving. Blood trickled from her nostrils and the corner of her mouth.

Zemba padded over to her mother and sniffed at the corpse. She knew something was wrong. She nuzzled her mother's fur, but the big cat didn't move. She began to make curious chirping sounds.

Moses hit the ground running. *"Zembyyyyyy!"*

Startled, the Hunter leaped to his feet. He hadn't had time to reload the crossbow, so his hand dropped to the hilt of his knife. Then he relaxed.

It was just a kid.

Moses noticed the Hunter, gasped, and skidded to a halt.

"Don't be frightened, kid. I won't harm you." The Hunter's smile was predatory. Moses turned and ran for his life. There was a tight clump of thorny bushes where he might scramble through at ground level . . .

The Hunter caught up with him before he'd gotten halfway. Moses kicked and bit and screamed, but the Hunter merely tucked him under one arm, then sat on him and tied the child's hands and feet with a length of rope from his pack. Then he walked casually over to where the cub was whining at its dead mother and slit the baby chetah's throat.

Dollar signs danced in his head. *Three-quarters of a million!* This was some initiation, and no mistake. It would go down in the Hunters' annals. Kandinsky, the experienced one, had screwed up, but the novice had come home with a fortune in cheetah bone.

Moses was screaming incoherently. He had seen everything.

Carlesson's training hadn't included kids, but it had included witnesses. Witnesses were expendable. The prime directive of the Hunt was secrecy.

He could slit the kid's throat as easily as a baby cheetah's.

The kid had stopped screaming now and was staring at him. Carlesson found the stare unnerving; he couldn't recognize what he saw in the child's eyes. It wasn't fear, it wasn't hatred. It was . . . alien. The child was very young—a boy, to judge by its clothing and haircut, not that you could see much through the thick layer of cracked mud. Carlesson's eyes flickered to his knife, then back to the kid, who was now trying desperately to wriggle away from him, despite the sharp rocks and the thorny underbrush.

A part of him couldn't help admiring the kid's courage. At that age, in similar circumstances, he'd have been reduced to quivering jelly.

He grunted. He couldn't let that affect his judgment. He took two quick paces and grabbed the kid by the leg, flipping him onto his back. With the other hand he tilted the child's chin upwards, exposing the throat. He laid the blade of his hunting knife against the defenseless skin . . .

The child flinched, terrified. It began to whimper. A trail of snot ran from one nostril and down a muddy cheek.

Carlesson swore, and slid the knife back into its sheath. He could no more kill the kid in cold blood than he had been able to kill Kandinsky—and *he'd* been begging for death. Carlesson had no compunctions about killing animals, and no respect for the law, but now he'd discovered—to his surprise—that he drew the line at people.

Shit. Now what?

His training had emphasized general principles over rigid rules. A Hunter was supposed to think things out for himself.

Secrecy was the prime directive. But the directive didn't say how secrecy should be maintained. It *authorized* the killing of witnesses, if that could be done without creating a worse danger of discovery, but it did not make their murder mandatory . . .

Okay, suppose he *did* kill the child. Then he'd have to dispose of the body. The only way he could think of was burial, and the ground was either as hard as rock or the consistency of porridge. In either case, whatever he managed to bury could rapidly be unburied by hyenas. Gathering vultures would be visible for miles. Already he could see a few of the ugly birds circling, attracted by the dead cheetahs. Soon there would be more. If he left a corpse, the remains would quickly be discovered. The kid was somebody's child, the parents would be looking . . .

He needed to get out fast, before somebody showed up. He knew he was rationalizing, but it made sense: it wasn't sensible to leave a dead child as evidence. It might well trigger another of those erratic crackdowns on Hunters.

Though it wouldn't be a bad idea to leave something sufficiently *misleading* . . .

There was only one answer, and Carlesson was pleased by how neatly his reasoning led to it. Send the kid off with the dead cheetahs. He'd be *missed*, no doubt about it—but it would take a while, maybe a day or more, before the parents got sufficiently worried to call in the authorities. By then, he and the child would both be long gone.

He began muttering into his wristnode. There was a pickup to arrange.

The autogiro swooped in from the northeast, just before noon when the survsats were looking the other way. It was a conspicuous bright yellow, with SKY SAFARI painted prominently along both sides in green.

Carlesson averted his eyes as it dropped to the ground in a billowing cloud of dust. The engine revs dropped to a tickover, and the pilot jumped from the doorway, half crouching to stay well clear of the circling vanes.

Together they loaded the two cheetahs and the child. Carlesson had cut out the flaps of hide bearing transponder tattoos—a pity to damage the fur, but there was no choice—and left them miles away among some bushes. They would eventually disappear off the Diversity Police's screens—with luck they'd think it was death by natural causes. The pilot had been warned that there was a child, and he wasn't going to argue with Carlesson whatever his intentions might be. The kid was the Hunter's problem. It didn't even matter if the kid saw the pilot's face, because the kid would shortly be disposed of.

Carlesson was new to the game, so he didn't know that this kind of thing had happened before. The kid would leave the country by the same route as the dead cheetahs. After that, the pilot had no idea what would happen to any of them, and he didn't care—but he knew they'd never be seen again. His job was to deliver the human and animal cargo as directed. Then he could get the 'giro packed safely away in its shelter and reconfigure its livery memory back to camouflage khaki. Sky Safari was a well-known tour operator, based in Pretoria, but this 'giro wasn't one of theirs. It was a Korean copy of one of their Franklin P45's equipped with a military-issue smart-paint skin.

The 'giro rose, twirled, and began zigzagging its way toward the border with Mozambique. If anyone saw it, with radar or naked eye, they would assume it was looking for wildlife to amuse its tourist passengers.

Satisfied, Carlesson turned his mind to the one remaining task: getting the hell out of there before the Diversity Police dropped by. He checked his wristnode, confirmed his position and bearings, and hiked off across the veldt, whistling.

8

Democratic Republic of Free China, 2210

The Democratic Republic of Free China was neither democratic nor free. It wasn't even a republic. It was, though, indubitably Chinese, having reverted to the ancient traditions of that innately self-sufficient nation. With two-fifths of the world's total population, it was the largest single-language politico-economic unit on Earth, and it *probably* had the largest gross domestic product—there were no official figures and its economy was as closed and protectionist as its ruling classes could contrive. Its borders were almost completely closed to traffic—in both directions. When the Pause took root in the outside world and technology became, for half a century, something to be avoided, China turned inward upon itself and resumed its age-old habits. From outside it was now impossible to be sure who—if anyone—was in charge.

Free China also constituted the largest urban sprawl on the planet. An unbroken crescent of densely packed buildings stretched from Shenyang in the northeast through Beijing and then south to Xuzhou and Nanjing, to run into a second vast crescent radiating from Shanghai. The once separate cities of Xi'an, Guangzhou, and Wuhan had become dense conglomerations in a single massive metropolitan area. In between were innumerable cities that a century earlier had been minor towns; packed in between the cities were town upon town upon town, and everything was linked together by ribbon developments that had grown up alongside the main rivers, canals, and highways. Yet even the densest accumulations of high-rise towers were never more than a few miles from areas of intensive agriculture, which were spattered across the landscape in fractal profusion. In satellite photographs it looked more like a Jackson Pollock painting than a country.

When the rest of the world emerged from the madness of the Pause and began to restructure itself on the basis of low populations and nonpolluting, nonproactive technology, Free China found itself committed irrevocably to a very different trajectory. The rest of the world collectively renamed itself Ecotopia, made sure its low population *stayed* low, and did its best to find an intelligent way to combine technology and environmentalism. There, the robot economy that had begun in the late twentieth century, skipped a beat in the twenty-first, and powered unstoppably ahead in the twenty-second, had not so much turned conventional economic theory upside down as shredded it to ribbons and scattered it to the four winds. "Laws" of supply and demand and diminishing returns revealed themselves as temporary misunderstandings based on the limitations of human labor and the psychology of ownership. But while Ecotopia pursued a low-population, high-living solution to the dynamics of globally circulating wealth, Free China's idosyncratic ideology led it in quite another direction. Historically, China had always defaulted to isolationism and inscrutability, and it surged into the twenty-second century with the same indifference to the ways of the outside world that it had displayed in the *minus* twenty-second.

Free China was the closest thing on the planet to infinite suburbia—the "Ant Country" of complex systems theory in which *almost* the same pattern repeated itself a billion times over on every street corner, every cluster of government offices, every train station, every street vendor with his home-

made cart. There was structure, of a kind—few people
starved, organized crime never quite got itself organized
enough to threaten whatever it was that held the country together, goods generally found their way to the intended destination unless they were stolen, mislaid, or destroyed by acts
of God and man . . . But whatever the structure was, there
was no way to sum it up in a few simple sentences. Not that
there was *no* government: on the contrary, there were many,
functioning on different geographical scales and with different and contradictory powers, adhering to legal codes so confused by uncoordinated amendments that even the juridical
computers couldn't fathom them. It worked—but it worked
like a huge, diverse ecology, not like the hierarchical rule of
law and order. And, like an ecology, order somehow emerged
from an infinite cascade of infinitesimal causes and effects.

What commodities did trade across its borders were
mostly illicit—not that it was any easier to determine what
actions were illegal than it was to find out who was responsible for what. The legal and paralegal codes of its overlapping,
ephemeral, fuzzy subcultures contradicted one another—and
often themselves—and the main principle seemed to be that
what was legal was whatever attracted the largest bribes.

Not that anyone could distinguish a bribe from a legitimate fee.

The economic walls that Free China had erected to protect
itself from the changeable fashions of the barbarian world beyond were as sturdy as the Himalayas and just as immovable.
The rock from which those walls were built, however,
was . . . porous. With enough lubrication and enough pressure, two-way traffic could be squeezed through.

One such economic pore ran through the office of Wang
Li-Po, assistant inspector of water taxation in the Sixth Com-
munal Municipality Reeducational Office of Urban Renewal
Project 512 in the city of Ningming in South Guangxi
Provincial District. Not physically—the actual conduit for
goods was a disused sewer system running beneath the bor-

der garrison at Pingxiang into Greater Vietnam—but this was where the lubrication was applied. Wang had no evidence regarding the source of that lubrication, and fervently wished never to acquire any, but he suspected from the nature of the imported articles that it must be Xi Ming-Kuo, reputedly a billionaire, widely credited as the mastermind behind a nationwide chain of tiny backstreet shops that dealt, entirely legally, in "traditional" medicines.

Wang's role was to receive and disburse the necessary lubricant. He seldom supervised the deliveries himself, for reasons of security . . . but he had ways of finding out what was in them if he really needed to know, and once or twice he had succumbed to the temptation. Who except Xi would import bones, and even the frozen corpses, of exotic foreign animals? You couldn't eat a snow leopard—not at any normal meal, though some gourmets had astonishingly refined tastes—but you could sell its bones for more than his office pulled in in a year. The fur, oddly enough, was less valuable, though still worth more than a fair-sized house: it possessed an unearthly beauty, but had few medicinal virtues. Such a skin would sell for a lot more in the outside world's black market, and he was convinced that once the animal had been warmed and skinned, that's exactly where it would go. Not all barbarians were as foolish about such matters as their governments seemed to be. His Vietnamese informant kept telling him about persistent rumors of rhinoceros horns being smuggled across the nearby border—which for reasons Wang found incomprehensible were considered untouchable in the outside world—and that pointed even more clearly at Xi Ming-Kuo.

Just occasionally, the cargo was the warm, living body of a different kind of animal, one that walked on two legs and possessed the power of speech (once the drugs wore off). Which is how Moses Odingo entered the Democratic Republic of Free China.

"*We* ought to be vidivising this," said Bailey morosely. Prudence had used Angie's advance on the wheelers to spring her sister from jail, but now she was fighting to stay out of it herself—in public. "Cash, how come we never put in a bid for the contract?"

"I wanted to," Cashew replied. "Jonas convinced me not to."

Bailey drummed his fingertips on the tabletop, menace in his eyes. "He did *what*?"

Cash gave Bailey a sharp look and sighed. "Tell him, Jonas. He's too stupid—or too drunk—to work it out for himself." She kicked off her remaining shoe and leaned back in one of Angie Carver's comfortable armchairs. They should have been—they cost ten thousand dollars apiece. Angie said she kept the *best* chairs in another part of the house, for special occasions. Apparently these—real leather from the time when it was legal, saved from confiscation by a smart lawyer and a Historical Merit Waiver Certificate, and kept by virtue of her museum license—were for slumming.

If Cashew had been more sober, she would have felt very uncomfortable lounging on a strip of dead cow.

Jonas—who if asked would have pointed out that cows got a pretty good deal, better than most wild animals ever got, so why not let them pay the rent for their nice warm barns by donating their hides when they no longer needed them, because when all was said and done the ban on leather had been a political concession to the squeamish urban classes and a waste of renewable resources—gave Bailey a hard stare. "Isn't it obvious?"

"Should it be?"

"Don't be stubborn. Of course it is. Technically, we don't have the experience to vidivise paralegal docudrama. And ethic—"

"We didn't have the technical expertise to make *Rose Red Cities,* either, but that's what got us star—"

"That was a long time ago, and there wasn't any competition for that niche. Shit, nobody even knew it *was* a niche. Trial-by-vidivision is a hot commodity, there are twenty outfits a lot bigger than us who cut their teeth on it." He paused for breath, wondering how Bailey would react to the other reason. Hell, go for it. "Even if the Bandwidth Provider had gone nuts and by some bizarre accident we had secured the contract, ethically we owe it to Prudence Odingo not to help that nasty little bastard Charles Dunsmoore drag her professional reputation through the dirt."

So that *was the real reason.* "Jonas, she doesn't *have* a professional reputation. She's an offworld rockhound and a hustler. Whereas *we* need the money. If we don't land a new contract soon—"

"Bailey, we don't have the capability. Forget the ethics— we could never have put in a credible bid."

"I guess," Bailey conceded. God alone knew where the next contract would come from. But God didn't have an Xsite.

"Hey, look, there she is!" yelled Cashew, who had been in the business for a decade and *still* got excited when someone she knew showed up on the VV.

Prudence was trying to look confident, but the vidivision lighting rigs were daunting and the sudden reversal of her fortunes had left her nerves shredded. She looked defiant, diminished, and depressed. Her sister's problems had hit Prudence hard. Moses' disappearance had turned Charity into an emotional wreck, liable to dissolve in tears at any moment, and that was something that her sister had never had to cope with before. It was always Prudence who hovered on the edges of nervous breakdowns; Charity was the calm one, the steady one, the one with both feet on the solid earth of the African continent and her head no more than shoulder-height above it. *She* went to Charity for comfort. But now Moses had vanished from the face of the planet, and the only trace that the policemen had found was his toy memimal. In all likelihood he was dead. They might never find out what had happened.

Prudence knew she couldn't dwell on such matters now, though. Unless she put up a stunning performance, she stood a serious chance of losing the wheelers and the income they would have generated, not to mention having her ship confiscated. She wouldn't even be able to sell *Tiglath-Pileser* to set against bankruptcy. And all because of that smarmy, conniving, cheating, lying little prick Charlie Dunsmoore! *Again.*

One day . . . she swore to herself and the silent cosmos, *one day I'll get even.*

The VV cameras zoomed in on her face. In the control room the director juxtaposed two angles that together looked like an old-fashioned jailbird mug shot—square view and profile. He liked clever historical allusions and was not above putting a bit of spin on his documentaries.

"Prudence looks worried sick," said Angie. "I don't think she believes that those lawyers I bought her will deliver."

"It's a difficult case to crack," said Cashew. "Of course, you could always consider buying her a new *ship* if she loses."

"Nope, dearie—wouldn't do any good if I bought her a *fleet.* If she loses, they'll pull her pilot's license. Nothing short of cosmetic surgery and a change of ID would change that, and we'd both end up in the pokey if anyone found out."

The inquiry had been organized on quasi-judicial lines. Prudence was permitted legal representation, and instead of a judge and jury there was a panel of five scientific assessors, including Sir Charles. The chair was as he had suggested to CEIdA: an elderly woman by the name of Elizabeth Strunck, editor-in-chief of *Glyph,* a leading archaeological journal. Everyone in the trade knew that Sir Charles and Strunck were always at loggerheads over her views about early Mycenaean pottery, and that made her ideal for the job because it made *him* look magnanimous.

The inquiry was now in its sixth day, and Prudence could

see that despite all the efforts of her legal team it was going badly. Sir Charles, assisted by a chain of expert witnesses which she *knew* he had helped line up, had done a thorough demolition job on her background, her professional expertise, and her (lack of) qualifications . . . which of course had been Sir Charles's fault, the *thief*. If he hadn't stolen her discovery, *she'd* have been the famous professor who'd established the age of the Sphinx and overturned two centuries of Egyptology . . .

Focus, girl.

Sir Charles had also tried to introduce witnesses to show that her previous career had been scientifically irresponsible and hovered at the bounds of legality. Angie's legal hired hands had staved off that line of questioning, but the message had still gotten through to the panel of assessors, and the more times that stupid woman in the chair kept telling them to ignore it, the more the mud would stick.

She wondered just what viperous trick Sir Charles was nursing around his stony heart.

Sir Charles was clarifying a number of technical issues for the rest of the panel, explaining, for the umpteenth time, why the wheeler artifacts were obvious fakes. An assistant was distributing copies of magnetic resonance tomograms, cross-sectional diagrams made by noninvasive imaging, and Sir Charles was explaining their significance.

"If these . . . objects . . . were *genuine* alien machinery, then they would have a recognizable internal structure." He gestured with a varicolor laser pointer at the room's large display screen, so that the public gallery and the eighty-million-strong VV audience could follow the reasoning for themselves. As he ticked off his points, he flicked the laser from one color to another, at random, for dramatic effect. "However, these scans show no sensible internal structure. All we see is a random mishmash of irregular domains of high- and low-density metal, with numerous small voids."

Strunck interrupted. "Sir Charles, are you aware of any

manufacturing process that would create such an arrangement?"

"Yes, Madam Chair, I am."

"Please enlighten us."

Sir Charles paused for effect. "I have seen very similar scans in sculptures made by artists from the Recyclist school of the 2140s."

Strunck seemed puzzled. "Professor Dunsmoore: are you seriously suggesting that these so-called wheelers are *sculptures?*"

Sir Charles gave a mirthless smile. This was going to be devastating. "Not exactly. I am suggesting that they were made—I have no idea by whom, but I am sure Ms. Odingo could tell us . . . " He waited for Prudence's legal team to object, but they failed to rise to the offered bait. "But I should not speculate about such matters. My point is that exactly this kind of scan is to be found in metal objects that have been cast from partially melted scrap." *Oh, yes.* "The so-called wheelers, in my expert opinion, are . . . junk."

Laughter scattered through the gallery: Sir Charles's public was enjoying a virtuoso performance. And now, Prudence realized, it was all set up for him. Sir Charles was going to call "expert witnesses" to hammer home his thesis that the wheelers were trash. Literally. Backed up by phony evidence, forged documents, and fake Xnet files.

What made it worse was that in a way he was *right.* Prudence had seen the scans—her defense team had a right to see all material evidence in advance—and they made no engineering sense whatsoever. You couldn't *build* machines like that—the pieces interlocked so intricately that there was no way to put them together. Melted scrap wasn't a bad description. She was beginning to wonder whether she'd made it all up in another personality. Was she going mad? But would alien machinery make any sense to terrestrial engineers, anyway? *The thing about aliens is, they're alien . . .* Maybe the wheelers were damaged, decayed, corroded, corrupted . . . whatever.

Even the chair was nodding her head—not much, but perceptibly. She looked at Prudence. "Ms. Odingo, do you have any explanation to offer?"

Prudence's counsel chipped in smoothly, "Dr. Strunck, my client prefers to reserve all such explanations for her own statements."

"Do you wish to cross-examine the panel concerning the validity of this evidence?"

"Not at all, Dr. Strunck. Ms. Odingo accepts that the magnetic resonance scans are technically valid, but reserves her interpretation."

Strunck asked Sir Charles to continue. Sir Charles used the laser pointer to highlight the salient features of the scans. He dwelled at length on the presence of wheels, in machinery allegedly dug up from the ice of a distant Jovian satellite. His quip that wheels were scarcely appropriate for burrowing into a miles-deep ice layer caused some amusement. Prudence's heart sank. She had no idea *why* the bloody things had wheels. She'd just dug them up.

It made no sense. This was going to be a disaster.

Several of the wheelers had been arranged on a small table at the front of the court, and Sir Charles now walked over to them. Prudence held an agitated conversation with her lawyers. Sir Charles noticed. "I promise not to touch any of the *valuable alien artifacts,*" he said, with the faintest hint of a sneer.

The cameras caught the look in close-up. The gales of full-throated laughter from the gallery were overlaid as ambient sound. Angie looked distraught. "This is awful. What's *wrong* with that legal team? Last time they get any business from *me*—"

Sir Charles's laser played over the wheelers, switching colors as he dissected them verbally in a low-key monotone.

"Do these *look* a hundred thousand years old?" he said, as

if daring anyone to contradict him. "Do they *look* like machines made by intelligent extraterrestrial beings? No. They look like crude castings of a child's toys." He glanced sideways at Prudence.

You bastard. You're trying to remind me about Moses. Try as hard as she might, she couldn't stop a few tears from running down her face. She wiped them away with the back of her hand. The cameras followed every movement.

"Yes, toys. And only a child would be fooled by them!"

The laser's spot, now red, now canary yellow, lingered lovingly on the nearest artifact, circling around its front wheel, cycling through the spectrum in a luminescent counterpoint to his hard-worked script.

"Wheels! Wheels without a *power source*! Wheels without *axles*! Wheels that don't *turn*! Wheels made from partially melted junk!"

There was a faint click, and a low-pitched hum reverberated through the courtroom, but Sir Charles was in full flow and noticed nothing. Neither did Cashew, Bailey, or Angie. But Jonas suddenly leaned forward, his eyes glued to the flat-film screen. Prudence had heard the slight sound, but assumed it must be something in the air-conditioning.

"Junk," Sir Charles repeated. The laser darted here, there, colors flashing. "Wheels? These so-called machines are *solid. Cast.* They can no more *move* than the Great Pyra . . . "

His voice trailed off.

Later, they worked out that the modulating colors of the laser pointer were responsible. But at the time, what they saw—what eighty million people witnessed, live, in close-up detail—was the wheeler.

Slowly, unequivocally, its wheels started to revolve.

Something was happening along its "spine." It seemed to unfurl. Strangely shaped vanes *grew* from the wheeler's back, forming a kind of frill, like the plates on an ancient dimetrodon.

The frills rippled.

Then the wheeler began to glow, a dull multihued light that seemed to diffuse from somewhere deep inside the solid metal. It was as if the metal had turned into stained glass.

Sir Charles and eighty million others had fallen silent. The atmosphere in the room was electric. Prudence felt the hairs rise along the nape of her neck.

The wheels continued turning. The wheeler jerked forward. It hummed. It throbbed with weird light. Tiny jags of lightning—*slow* lightning—flickered within.

Relentlessly, it rolled toward the edge of the table.

Sir Charles, suddenly released from paralysis, dimly aware that he had to do something, stepped forward to catch it before it smashed to the floor.

His hands cupped empty air.

Humming, glowing, its wheels still turning, the ancient machine continued along its horizontal track *as if the table were still beneath it.* As eighty million viewers sat rooted to their seats, it levitated its way across the open space between the public seating and the panel, heading directly toward the mesmerized chair.

It was almost certainly the only occasion on record when a terrified scientific assessment panel had fled in panic in response to an item of evidence.

It was *definitely* the only occasion on record when the chair had been in the vanguard of the rout.

Xi Ming-Kuo was a billionaire, in whatever currency you preferred. In Free China, a crooked businessman that successful would normally have run to fat—the archetypal self-indulgent, cunning, evil-minded slob. Not at all. Xi was slim and athletic, despite his eighty-six years, and not so much evil- as single-minded. In his own self-appraisal he was a moral man who had overcome the competition by dint of sheer ability, but in truth he was seldom burdened by conventional scruples. Xi Ming-Kuo cut his own swath through the ethical minefield, and unlike most of his fellows, he had always seen the barbarian culture of Ecotopia as a potential source of revenue. In order to survive the attentions of the power brokers, who promoted an isolationist, nationalistic ideology, he had to find very good reasons for importing barbarian goods. He had been in his early twenties when it occurred to him that a revival of traditional medicine would be the perfect vehicle for an extremely lucrative trade in animals that no longer existed in the urban Ant Country of his homeland. That such trade was not only illegal in the West, but subject to drastic penalties, was a practical obstacle rather than a moral issue.

He solved it by inventing the backward-looking creed of the Hunt, and recruiting to its ranks a substantial number of young men whose common traits were greed and an obsession with killing wild animals. In the overregulated, underpopulated, indulgent, softhearted West, his agents found many such men. In an earlier age they would have rampaged through the forests of the Normerican Midwest with automatic weapons, recreational sports vehicles and a trunk full of six-packs; in the twenty-second century Xi had turned the barbarians' severe restrictions on guns into an advantage by insisting on a chivalrous return to the bow and the knife. Swords had crossed his mind, too, but he had ruled them out as impractical. A Hunter's bow was a pretty high-tech instrument, mind you—laser sights, a photomultiplier scope for night vision, quarrels with depleted uranium tips for increased penetration.

He sat at a modern desk in a heavily draped room in the suburbs of Liuzhou, surrounded by as magnificent a selection of antique art as could be found in possession of anyone outside the upper echelons of Free China's convoluted, inconsistent, overmanned bureaucracy. Chou bronzes and ceramics, finely inlaid armor from the time of the Three Kingdoms, exquisite jades from the court of the T'ang emperor Kao-tsu, blue-and-white ware from the Yüan Dynasty when China had briefly been overrun by Mongol tribes under Genghis Khan, a massive cast bronze tetrapod, and in pride of place a Late Shang ritual vessel from the thirteenth century BC. Other rooms in his palatial mansions—of which he owned eleven, all over Free China—contained equally rich collections, and one secret chamber boasted close on a hundred items of Western art—sculptures by Moore, garments by Versace, paintings by El Greco, Van Gogh, Picasso, Warhol, Gibbons-Jones, and Lambretta. Any one of them would see him jailed for life, if not shot, were they to come to the attention of the Cultural Enforcement Bureau—except that the CEB was hopelessly corrupt and he knew he could bribe his way out of any investigation. No, what worried him was not the CEB, but the drug baron Deng Po-zhou, warlord of the White Dragon Gang. Xi knew that Deng was envious of his success, and his gang was trying to muscle in on his lucrative trade in traditional medicines. The merchant threw his head back and laughed: the powers that arranged the universe were on his side! The White Dragon Gang was a mosquito buzzing about a tiger. Speaking of which: it was high time that his illicit tiger-breeding program over near Ershiqizhan, on the Siberian border, started to show a profit. More than enough had been expended in bribes. He made a mental note to look into the matter.

Xi Ming-Kuo had to admit that the new recruit, Carlesson, had in some respects performed surprisingly well. There was of course the small embarrassment of the African child, a serious mistake which in slightly different circumstances might well have cost Carlesson his life. But Xi had a grudging respect for arrogant young men who were prepared to take the initiative—they reminded him of his younger self—and it was fortunate for Carlesson that his misjudgment had coincided with a soaring demand for cheetah bones.

Xi found himself uncharacteristically indecisive. Did Carlesson's foolish error outweigh the priceless hoard of bones that he had acquired? The Hunter had shown courage and initiative, and these could bring many future benefits to Xi's business empire. He had abandoned his more experienced companion without a backward glance, an admirably callous act that was in full obedience to the Hunt's stringent rules. If Xi had the man killed now, he would lose that potential—and the problem of the black child would remain unchanged. He saw little gain there. The important thing was to ensure that Carlesson never made the same mistake again, and now the decision was easy. Xi would send some of his trusted men around to deliver an appropriate warning, fine the Swede thirty percent of his fee, and assign him more dangerous and more tedious tasks for future Hunts. If the Hunter survived, his skills would be honed by his experiences, and Xi could make good use of such a man. If not . . . well, that was business.

Xi had a sudden, irrational desire to look at the child, face-to-face. Although his business interests required an extensive network of corrupt barbarians, he had seldom spoken to any of them in person, for the obvious reasons of security and secrecy. His sense of self-preservation was as strong as the walls of his secret collection of forbidden art, and he had no intention of slipping up now, just to look at a youthful barbarian face—but he could do the next best thing. He spoke a few quiet syllables to his desk, and a gigantic holoscreen diffused into existence in the center of the room, gray mist crystallizing into solid light. Another command, and the room's ambient lighting lowered to improve visibility.

The dark-skinned child, still bound but showing signs of awakening from its drug-induced catalepsy, hovered in midair, twice its real size. The eyes opened and swiveled wildly as the child began to take in its spartan surroundings. The boy lay on a cold, concrete floor in a small, bare room, whose only furnishings were an outdated fluorescent lamp and a hidden spy camera.

A cockroach the size of a human hand scuttled across the floor, inches from the child's face. The eyes followed it, but the face did not jerk away. Ordinarily, the roaches would be crawling all over the captive by now—Xi found that it was an easy way to soften captives up. But the child's body seemed free of such vermin, which surprised him. He looked deep into the child's eyes and believed that he read something there. Or perhaps it was the child's bearing—inasmuch as one could *have* bearing, prone and bound—or the cast of his bruised, scratched face. Whatever it was, it sent a shiver along Xi's spine.

Such a child might, given training and encouragement, go on to achieve great things. Such a child would be a grave source of danger.

Xi was clever, ruthless . . . and superstitious. He believed in . . . well, not exactly *believed,* for he considered himself a supremely rational man . . . let us say that he found it hard to suppress the idea that powers beyond human knowledge had selected him for success, and were constantly rearranging the universe to ensure that this continued. In return, all that they demanded of him was that he should be responsive to any stray thoughts that they might insert into his mind. Over the years, he had developed a sixth sense for such messages from beyond terrestrial time and space, and he had learned to back his hunches. As he watched Moses' eyes flicking from side to side, while the child—who must be desperately frightened—showed no other outward signs of distress, Xi's sixth sense tingled as never before.

With a word, he instructed the camera to widen its field of vision, and drew his breath in sharply. A pale circle surrounded the boy's head, like a halo. It flowed down and around the child, forming a complete outline of his body as it lay on the floor.

The outline was unobscured concrete. Beyond it, hundreds of cockroaches crawled over the floor, scuttling obscenely in a dark, heaving mass.

Inside, the floor was bare.

Xi shuddered. *This* was beyond his comprehension, but it was a clear sign that the kidnapped boy had to be disposed of.

Any thought of compassion fled from his mind at the astonishing sight. On the other hand, though, whatever lay behind such unusual powers commanded a degree of respect. So it would be necessary to contrive the child's death without being directly responsible for it.

For Xi Ming-Kuo, inspiration was never far away. He saw immediately that the conundrum had a neat, simple, elegant solution.

With Prudence being publicly exonerated in such a spectacular fashion, the case against her sister Charity collapsed, all charges dropped. But her doctor had been forced to place her under sedation—she was finding it impossible to cope with Moses' disappearance.

Angie Carver was already taking steps on her behalf to sue the local, state, and Nyamwezi national police for negligently allowing Moses to run away.

The police were mounting a huge international search effort. So far, it hadn't paid off.

Prudence was high in the stratosphere, on her way to Kenya and her sister, in one of Angie's private jets.

Sir Charles had managed to extract himself from the fiasco of the inquiry, while ensuring that the hated Professor Strunck took the blame. Already a scientific consensus had sprung up to the effect that the wheelers were genuinely ancient and almost certainly some kind of alien artifact, although a few skeptics were still convinced that the wheeler's ability to levitate was either faked or had some entirely prosaic explanation. Sir Charles found this both amusing and exasperating: why did otherwise intelligent people go into denial rather than change their minds in response to dramatic new evidence? He had long ago decided that in such cases the explanation must be that their minds were too rigid to change except by snapping under the strain: in effect, they went the tiniest bit mad.

A flurry of Xsites had grown up around the wheelers—

graphics, pirated MagRes scans of their interiors, poems, discussion groups, sites where you could buy flatfilm holo-posters. One site had named some of them after classic vehicles of the past—Ferrari, T-bird, Karyma . . . The one with the missing wheel had been named Reliant Robin after a celebrated three-wheeled car from twentieth century Britain. The media plugged the names and they quickly stuck. Angie's lawyers felt this was good for Prudence: it made the alien machines seem friendly.

Sir Charles had also managed to get himself appointed convenor of an international project to investigate the wheelers and was already seeking a court order for possession of every wheeler that Prudence had found. Angie's new legal team—she had fired the old one—was fighting a rearguard action to restrict him to Ferrari, T-bird, and Karyma, the exhibits at the inquiry, with an informal offer of half a dozen more if he would settle out of court. Angie was helping Prudence to hide all of the remaining wheelers where the law would never find them, just in case they lost.

At that point she got an urgent message from Prudence. Earlier, the police had found Moses' memimal: now some scraps of his clothing had turned up in an area known to be frequented by hyenas.

Just as Carlesson had planned.

On the northwestern outskirts of Ningming, jumbled streets of low-quality housing gave way to run-down industrial areas—a labyrinth of disused, collapsing warehouses, contaminated yards, and abandoned, rusting machinery. Clinging to the edges of this derelict wasteland was a straggling shantytown—makeshift homes fashioned from stolen boards, battered sheets of corrugated iron, damp piles of rotting floor coverings, and plastic containers that had once held industrial chemicals. Here individuals, families, even extended families of ten or fifteen people lived in appalling poverty, dependent on erratic handouts of food from local officialdom plus whatever they could beg, steal, or very rarely earn. In Free China there were tens of thousands of these shantytowns—no part of Ant Country differs significantly from any other—and at least thirty million people eked out a miserable existence within them. Occasionally a medical team would suddenly descend on one of them, treat the simpler ailments and diseases, vaccinate every child they could lay hands on, and depart as quickly as they could contrive without being seen to have shirked their allotted job. This was not done out of any sense of compassion, but in order to prevent epidemics among the remainder of the population. In Free China, few people starved, but nearly everyone was undernourished; few died of curable diseases, but many were sickly. The system—inasmuch as there was one—kept a huge number of people alive, but only an elite few derived much enjoyment from it.

Rats infested the abandoned sheds of vanished industries and made constant incursions into the shantytowns. And where there were rats, packs of wild dogs would collect by the hundreds. The city officials tolerated the dogs because they helped keep down the rats. The shanty dwellers lost the occasional baby to a hungry dog, but mostly they kept the dogs at bay, confined to the most derelict areas.

Between the dogs and the shanties was a buffer zone, perhaps a quarter of a mile across at its widest. The zone was the abode of gangs of street children—mostly children abandoned by the shanties when a parent died of some disease or got badly injured in a fight and succumbed to any of a dozen resulting infections. The shanties got some help from the city, but the street children got no help at all. The medical teams considered the buffer zones too dangerous to operate in—and not just because of the disease and the feral dogs.

In the buffer zones, starvation was a constant presence.

The Moon was almost full, but its light hardly penetrated the narrow streets between stark high-rise apartment blocks. Navigating by a single dimmed floodlight, not much stronger than the beam of a flashlight, an armored truck rolled off the cracked concrete street onto rubble and mud, and pushed its way through darkened, debris-covered alleyways until it could no longer advance without wrecking too many of the shanty people's pathetic homes. The vehicle slithered to a halt in a pile of something wet and slimy, and a small patrol consisting of four men climbed out. They were well armed, but they didn't look at all like soldiers. The night was torn to shreds by the constant wailing of children and the coughing of adults; the smell of close-packed, impoverished humanity was atrocious.

The buildings were lower now, and the moonlight could break through to ground level. The scene that it illuminated was surreal, horrifying; a Dantean vision of hell.

A large sack was passed out of the vehicle, and one of the men slung it over his shoulder. Efficiently but nervously, with many glances to the side or behind, the squad made its way between the shanties. Everywhere, inquisitive heads popped out of openings, but as soon as they saw weapons they ducked inside again—save for one old woman, clearly crazy, who sat naked under a flap of sacking and screamed incomprehensible curses at them. One of her hands was missing, crudely amputated just above the wrist.

The patrol carried its burden to the edge of the street children's buffer zone and paused for a few moments. Above the wails and coughs came the pack cries of wild dogs. Very nervous now, the men advanced a few dozen yards into the jumble of wrecked buildings until they came to the edge of an open space, overgrown with weeds and littered with rubbish.

They dropped the sack none too gently onto the ground and backed away, eyes flickering from shadow to shadow in anticipation of trouble. A few minutes later, their vehicle was beating a hasty but still cautious retreat along the foul alleyways of the shantytown, back to the comparative safety of the city.

The sack had been lying on the ground for less than a

minute when the first street children scuttled out from their hiding places to find out what fate had delivered to their doorstep. They carried sharpened poles, crude spears to beat off rats and dogs. One, who acted like a gang leader, wore a knife made from sections of an old tin can wrapped around a length of bone, tucked into a strip of cloth tied around his waist. Most were naked, and all of them were encrusted with filth.

The leader motioned to several of the children to watch out for dogs. He bent down, sniffed suspiciously at the sack, and pulled back the opening.

Moses' terrified face stared up at him.

Few events could surprise the street children anymore, but this one was beyond their experience. Two of them dragged Moses out of the sack, scraping his knees painfully on the rough ground. He was still bound. Xi Ming-Kuo had seen no reason to take any risks. If the fates wished to preserve the child, then they would contrive for his bonds to be loosened. If not, the added handicap would surely settle the issue.

Moses was desperately hungry; no one had fed him for days. His last drink had been dirty water in a bowl on the floor, ten or fifteen hours before. He had no idea where he was or who had brought him here.

The street children turned him onto his back. Looking up, he saw strange, dirt-smudged faces. But he saw more than that. He saw fear that verged on insanity, murder, and a peculiar kind of greed. He had always been able to read people's emotions from their body language—people, after all, were just another kind of animal, and from the time he could walk he'd had an amazing intuitive understanding of virtually any animal. He had quickly learned to keep quiet about his ability to read people, though.

The gang leader—an unusually vicious child named Tan—bent down to peer closely at Moses. Tan had seen plenty of new street children arrive in the buffer zone during the few years of his young life, but never one with a black face. Tied up with rope and deposited on his, Tan's, territory, by *adults*. Not the usual sickly looking half-dead man or woman with child in tow, the ones that came from the shanties to dispose of excess kids or because they were on the verge of death. Healthy, well-fed adults of a kind Tan had never seen.

Well fed. Now, *that* was an idea. Street children were always hungry, and they would eat *anything* that came their way.

Black meat was meat, like any other.

He spoke a few words in the street children's primitive pidgin, and Moses was dragged into an upright position. Tan pulled his tin knife from his belt and waved it in Moses' face. With one hand he grabbed the child's stubby hair, and with the other he laid the blade across Moses' throat. He muttered something vile and laughed, a few of the others joining in. Moses could read their every action, the way they all deferred to the leader, even though several were older, their ill-concealed fear . . . their hunger.

"Stand up!" Tan tried to haul Moses to his feet, but the ropes made this difficult. With a curse, Tan hacked at the ropes with his knife until they fell away, several now stained with Moses' blood. He hauled again, and Moses found himself teetering upright on numbed legs. He ached everywhere. As they began to drag him farther out into the moonlight, circulation began to return to his limbs. It was pure agony.

Tan made him kneel beside a low, flat rock, the street children's version of a sacrificial altar. Moses could see murder in the gang leader's every motion. He could almost *feel* the knife sliding into his throat, the blood pouring out, his neck gaping open as his head lolled back on severed muscles . . .

A wild dog howled—*very* close.

A new kind of fear crept over their faces as they looked furtively around for the source of the noise. Then, in a cacophony of barks and snarls, a pack of dogs burst into the open from behind a collapsed wall of brick. They were little more than skin and bone, mangy mongrels resulting from generations of uncontrolled interbreeding, some large, some small, some short-haired, some long-haired, some with hair that was so matted you couldn't tell how long it ought to be.

The street children looked at Tan, who made an instant assessment of the size of the pack, turned, and fled. Within a few seconds the entire gang had gone to ground among the ruined buildings, and Moses was surrounded by a pack of ravenous dogs.

A degree of circulation had returned now, and he found he could move his arms and legs. There was nowhere to run, but running was not what was on his mind. Finally, for the first time since he had watched the Hunter killing Mbawa and his beloved Zemba, he was in a situation that he understood perfectly.

A pack of feral dogs is a hierarchy, just like a street gang. When the dogs encircling him began to advance, Moses unerringly picked out which was top dog. It was obvious. He immediately took several quick steps toward the pack leader—a challenge, of a kind, but not a direct one. If he was to survive this, he had to establish *himself* as top dog. The animal bared its teeth and snarled. Moses continued to advance, his hands held in a strange position. He made eerie whining sounds, then an abrupt, low-pitched snarl.

The dog was confused. The food animal was acting as if it were another dog. But it wasn't. The food animal was acting as if *it* were pack leader. But the dog knew who the leader was—*him*. Only now he was beginning to have doubts. Moses read the growing doubt in the pack leader's posture and drove home his advantage. After that, the animal never had a chance: its every thought was laid bare to its adversary . . .

Suddenly it was over, and the erstwhile pack leader was groveling in the dirt at the feet of the *new* leader. There was never the slightest doubt that the rest of the pack would accept the substitution.

Bewildered faces watched from holes in the rubble. Tan's mouth dropped open, and his knife fell to the ground. None of them had ever seen anything remotely like this. What manner of being was the black child? A demon? Very possibly, for now the pack of wild dogs was arranging itself at his feet in a ragged semicircle, like worshipers at a shrine.

Moses bared his teeth and spoke, a series of authoritative barks. One of the dogs slunk off between the buildings.

A moment later, to the utter astonishment of the onlooking street children, the animal reappeared. Between its jaws was a chunk of raw meat. It dropped the offering at the black child's feet and backed away.

Moses looked at the meat, and for a moment he felt very sick. It seemed to be a piece of a child's arm, partially decomposed. But he also felt very hungry, and it would ruin everything to back down *now*. The dogs were expecting him to eat it.

He picked it up, tore a strip off the meat with his teeth, and swallowed it.

It tasted foul. It tasted heavenly. It didn't matter *what* it tasted like. It was *food*.

9

The Cuckoo's Nest, 2210

The Lunar Automatic Deep Space Optical Comparison System was just one of the instruments that the neo-Zen Buddhists had squirreled away at the Moon's two poles. There were radio telescopes, infrared telescopes, links to an X-ray telescope that floated outside the Earth's orbit at the Lagrange L1 point, magnetometers . . . and endless banks of fast computers. The Way of the Wholesome had no need to cut corners.

Nāgārjuna had not been the first to notice the inbound comet, though he *had* been the first to relay news about it to the High Lama of the Cuckoo's Nest. Half a dozen of the lunar monks had been keeping an eye on it ever since it had first come to their attention two months before. But the Cuckoo believed that it was good training for the novices out in the Belt to make them log in to LADSOCS and check out its findings for themselves.

In the few weeks since Nāgārjuna had last logged in, they had gathered huge amounts of new data. The comet was about ten miles across, so its mass would be about twenty trillion tons. For a while they had suspected that it was bound for Jupiter, with a projected impact date somewhere around 2222, but its trajectory near the giant planet was complicated and their predictions were sensitive to small errors of observation. A lot depended on the precise position of Jupiter's satellites as the comet first swung past. If they didn't perturb the comet's path, it would swing very close to the giant planet, loop twice around the Sun in an orbit that would stay outside the asteroid belt, and then crash headlong into Jupiter's thick atmosphere.

If the moons did perturb the comet's path significantly, though, it could go almost anywhere. The closer the comet came to a moon, especially one of the more massive ones, the more its path could deviate from the one they had originally projected.

As the monks gathered more data, they became more and more confident of the comet's arrival time in the Jovian system, and it seemed that the incoming body would pass close by the planet as already predicted, but well away from any perturbing satellite. The Earth—and more importantly, the Belt—was safe.

Then one of them noticed something that caused a rethink.

Ironically, it was Cashew who first saw the newsflash icon popping into existence on her wristnode's tiny screen. By rights it should have been Jonas, but he was in the pool and wasn't wearing his 'node. He was splashing along in a lazy crawl when she sauntered up.

"Jonas?" she asked in a rather funny voice.

"Yes, sure, that's me." Then he noticed her face. "Problem?"

"I'm—I'm really not at all sure, Jonas." She tapped her wristnode. "Drag yourself out of the water and take a look at this."

"Oh, come on, Cash, I'm on my thirty-fourth lap and my record is only forty-nine. And I don't feel at all tired, not yet."

"Don't be silly, Jonas. I think this may be more important than breaking your personal lap record."

He clambered out and wrapped himself in a huge towel. "Prudence and Charity fighting again?"

"No, I mean, they probably are—typical twins, and after what they've been through . . . Charity needs tact and understanding, but Pru's so uptight—but this is different. Not a people thing, Jonas. A *thing* thing. And it's scary."

"Okay, let me see whatever it is that's so unmissable." A softly lit image sprung into being in midair between them. He stared at it. "*Bloody hell.*"

"Well, you did suggest something of the sort to explain away your feeble navigation," she pointed out.

"Yeah, sure, but I didn't mean it *seriously.*" A thought struck him. "Cash, is this some kind of joke? Trying to rub my nose in my failure? Because if so, I'd prefer not to have interrupted my record-breaking bid—"

It was hard for Cash to admit it, but . . . "Jonas, it looks like you didn't *have* a failure. You'll have to recalculate, but I have a feeling your navigation will turn out to be spot on. I probably owe you your week's salary back . . . with interest. I realize that it's a ridiculous way for the universe to conspire to rob me of my hard-earned winnings, but—"

"They've moved?"

"So the newsflash says."

"Jupiter's moons have *moved*?"

"Yes."

"Rubbish. They can't have."

She giggled, in an edgy kind of way. "Jonas, it was *your* theory!"

"Sure, but it was rubbish, too. You're saying I was right all along? Nuts. Okay, let's see some detail—maybe it's some crank with a home telescope and a lens to grind . . . Oh. Well, next best thing, Cash. It's the Loonies."

"I thought it said that the observations were made by the Buddhist base on the Moon."

"Exactly. Trouble is, they usually do superb astronomical work. Have to, they've got a Belt to protect, and an industrial empire." He scratched his head, still unable to believe the news. "What caused it? Near miss with a comet, knocked them out of orbit?"

Cashew muttered into her 'node, calling up and rejecting displays until she found what she wanted. "No . . . says here that nobody has any idea what caused it."

"That's mad. Celestial bodies don't suddenly take it into their heads to disobey the law of gravity. Maybe Io had a massive volcanic eruption? That'd shift its orbit a little, and I guess there'd be a knock-on effect on the others."

Cashew zoomed in on the display she'd found. "Jonas, there's been a *big* shift. All four of the main inner moons rearranged themselves simultaneously into a completely new configuration. Took them less than a week!

"Mmmpppph . . . it does say something about a comet, yes . . . But that one is still twelve years away from Jupiter, and originally"—she was skimming the item now, trying to précis it for Jonas—"it was expected to hit."

"Originally?"

Why did she feel so worried? "Before the moons moved, they'd worked out the comet's orbit, and—well, it was going to do something pretty complicated and then crash into Jupiter. But now—"

"Now that computation is in shreds. So where will it go now?"

"Doesn't say. Says they don't know."

But Jonas wasn't buying that. "Crap. Sure they'll have to assume that the moons' new configuration isn't going to change *again,* but they've got all the data. If they could predict it would hit Jupiter from the original data, it wouldn't take ten minutes to repeat the calculations with the new data. Any fool could do it. Damn it all, even *I* could . . . "

His voice trailed off. He grabbed his 'node and started muttering into it, a stream of technobabble. He broke off to explain what Cashew had already worked out. "Cash, it's no harder than my navigation routine. I've got all the modules in there already, don't even need to dump any off the X. If the powers that be won't tell us what they *must* already know, then there has to be a reason . . . So I'll just have to work it out for myself, right?" He bent himself once more to the task.

Fifteen minutes later, Jonas had the answer he wanted. Or, more accurately, he had an answer, but it was one that he definitely did *not* want.

It was now clear, though, why the authorities had not made their prediction public. He wondered for how long they could hush it up and how much panic there would be when it came out.

It was only after he'd told Cashew, and they had both tried to take in the implications, that something else occurred to him.

It was too much of a long shot to be coincidence.

Sir Charles Dunsmoore sat in a plush reception area of the Ecotopia Building, having arrived a few minutes ahead of time for his appointment with the undersecretary for world affairs, Peter-Wolf Uhlirach-Bengtsen.

He wondered what it was about.

An aide ushered him into the office, which was just as large and comfortably furnished as Sir Charles had expected. Uhlirach-Bengtsen motioned him into a chair. "Charles, good of you to come."

"You know you can rely on me, Peter." A sheaf of documentation was thrust into his hands, but there wasn't time to peruse it.

"I'm sure I can, Charles, and I must say that in my opinion there is no better person for the job than you."

Job? This was a job interview? *What* job? He already had a—

The confusion must have shown on his face, or else Uhlirach-Bengtsen had anticipated it, which wouldn't have been terribly difficult. "Charles, everything that I tell you here today must be kept completely secret. There's no way to stop the word getting out eventually—even soon—but even a few days could make a big difference to our preparations."

"Of course. What's all this ab—"

The lights dimmed and a holographic flatscreen faded from faint gray smoke into full, solid color. The color was mostly black, speckled with white dots—a starfield. Just off-center in the display was a wispy smudge of light, a blob of cotton candy.

"Yesterday morning," said Uhlirach-Bengtsen, "a senior lama at Moonbase South—known as the Guru of the Small Birds, for some reason—sent an urgent message to our government. A warning, one that we have since verified from our own sources, one that we believe to be the truth.

"What you see in this image is a comet, torn loose from the Oort cloud by random gravitational disturbances. When first detected, it was heading towards Jupiter. Later observations predicted that it would collide with Jupiter, implying that it would pose no threat to *us*. The Buddhists who discovered it named it the *preta*, a term that is used in their religious writings to refer to a type of wandering, hungry ghost, and informed us as a matter of courtesy that it would make a close encounter with Jupiter about twelve years from now and smash into the planet six years after that."

"A bad name," said Sir Charles. "A *preta* has a huge stomach, a tiny mouth, and its inside is red-hot from hunger and thirst. Comets, as I recall, are dirty snowballs."

"It will become red-hot when it hits Jupiter's atmosphere," said Uhlirach-Bengtsen. "The monks estimate its mass at twenty trillion tons."

Charles realized he had no feel for such figures. "Is that big?"

"Not for a comet—Halley's Comet was five times as big, and plenty of asteroids are *much* larger. But it's what happened next that's got us worried." The holographic image changed to a close-up of Jupiter and its four classical moons. The comet's trajectory was superimposed as a graphic, swinging through the system, out of the image altogether, then returning as a string of separate blobs that collided in sequence with regions in the planet's southern hemisphere. "The image presumes that the comet will break into pieces before impact," Uhlirach-Bengtsen added. "We don't know how many, but it doesn't make much difference to the end result."

The trajectory faded, leaving only the close-up of the striped planet and the same four of its moons. "This is the original predicted configuration of the moons at the time of initial passage."

Suddenly the four moons were in different positions. "This, however, is their *current* predicted configuration."

Sir Charles had a question to ask. "Observational error?"

"No, the first prediction was accurate. According to the monks, the moons have moved."

"But—"

"Charles, I know it sounds incredible, but please believe me, we are convinced it is true. And the Buddhists have calculated the new trajectory of the comet, based on the new positions of the moons."

Now the image changed to a view of the inner Solar System—Earth in the foreground, Mars off to one side, then a sprinkling of asteroids, then a much-diminished Jovian inner system. "This is schematic, of course, but the trajectory that I am about to add is accurate in all important respects." A growing trail showed where the comet would pass. This time, as it sped past Jupiter, it came within a hair's breadth of hitting Ganymede and Europa. Its exit trajectory was substantially different from the previous simulation.

"My God," said Sir Charles. The graphic trail continued to extend, until suddenly it terminated—midway between Sumatra and Sri Lanka. Charles sucked in his breath and went pale.

"You haven't seen the worst of it," said the undersecretary. "Let me run it without interruptions." This time the comet swept sedately into the Jovian system, made two sharp bends around Ganymede and Europa, and shot out of the system like a bat out of hell.

"It *speeds up?*"

"Slingshots, two of them. Ordinarily it'd take a good eight months to fall from Jovian orbit to Earth orbit. This bastard does it in three weeks. Ten times the speed, a hundred times the energy—equivalent to twenty Halley's Comets all hitting us at once. The comet will collide with the Earth late in 2222, twelve years from now. I can tell you the timing to within a second, if you're interested. With that mass and that speed—we'll be lucky if it doesn't crack the planet like an egg."

There was a lengthy silence while the two men avoided looking at each other.

"The Buddhists have therefore renamed the comet," the undersecretary said. "They now call it Jarāmarana."

Sir Charles shook his head.

"Death," the undersecretary translated.

"*Death* . . . Macabre, but apt . . . " said Sir Charles, chills running along his spine. "Can we do anything about it, Peter?"

"Given a few days, we can put together a package that will—until the comet gets a lot closer, maybe eleven years from now—convince the planet's population that the problem is under control and there is no serious danger. People will complain, and some will ask awkward questions, but we can avoid panic and retain contro—"

"That's not what I meant. The Belters have loads of mass-drivers: can't they shoot it down?"

"Twenty trillion tons of it? No, the Way of the Wholesome tells me it's far too big. Might as well hit it with a flyswatter. To make matters worse, it's an ocean strike."

Sir Charles was still finding it hard to believe what he was being told. "But the destruction will be immense!"

Uhlirach-Bengtsen's face was grim. "It will make nuclear winter look like a sprinkling of dew. This one's a planet-killer, Charles. Jupiter might have absorbed it, but Earth will be wiped clean. Some bacteria will probably survive—if the planet does. Humans? Well, there's the lunar and Belter Buddhists, not that I personally take great comfort from that."

The undersecretary got to his feet and walked over to the window. Sir Charles joined him.

"We will evacuate key personnel, of course," said Uhlirach-Bengtsen in an unreal, almost robotic tone. "If we can persuade the Buddhists to agree. But . . . " His voice trailed off, and Sir Charles could *see* the man trying to pull himself together. In a slightly more normal voice, he started again. "Just . . . just look at it, Charles. The trees, the parks—see those children playing softball? See the geese, Canada geese they are, dreadful pests, ought to be exterminated. But they *will* be, Charles, do you see? Along with the trees and the children . . . Oh, yes, we can evacuate a chosen few to the Moon, maybe even Mars, but what kind of a life is *that*? And who *chooses*?" He seemed close to tears, and Charles was appalled: Uhlirach-Bengtsen was the archetypal strong, silent type.

"It's horribly bad luck," Sir Charles ventured, not knowing what else to say. "It could so easily have gone somewhere entirely diff—"

"Luck? No, Charles, we don't think so. Not luck."

"But—I mean, if . . ."

The undersecretary's face was grim. "No. It's coming *straight at us,* over a distance of half a billion miles, at *ten times* its normal speed!

"Charles, we are as certain as any mortal being can be that it is an act of war."

". . . so that's why I got the coordinates so badly wrong," Jonas concluded.

Cashew still found it hard to believe. Moving *moons*? Bailey didn't give a toss. "Damn it, Jonas, who *cares*? It wouldn't matter if we'd made landfall in the Himalayas!" Why, oh, why couldn't people focus on the *important* things?

"Bailey, I'm not worried about the navigation. What I'm trying to point out is that there's a very large comet out there, and suddenly it's heading straight at *us*."

"Yeah, sure. And what do you expect *me* to do about that?"

"Bailey, if it hits, we're dead."

Bailey sighed. "Guys, guys—we're dead *right now,* don't you understand? The press didn't show, the Lumleys went through the floor, *God's Navsats* got dumped, the networks have put us on the has-been list, Ruthie Bowser's madder than a crate of Tasmanian devils because we're no longer a salable property, and *we are out of a job*. Permanently."

"If the comet hits, the whole planet will be out of a job."

"On the contrary: If the comet hits, all our problems will be solved. On the other hand, until it does, we have to *eat,* and if it misses, we're going to feel pretty stupid if we're alive but penniless! Jonas: we can't do anything about any goddamned comet, okay? But we can try to salvage some sort of career! So let's just focus on that and leave the comet up to the military and the politicians, huh?"

"I don't believe—"

"Let it be, Jonas," said Cashew. "Bailey's right. We can worry about the comet tomorrow . . . you said yourself it'll be years and years before it hits, if it ever does.

"Bailey: what are our options?"

Bailey looked glum. "Not good. You know how much competition there is in the vidivid business. Our competitors have already pounced—every contract Ruthie was negotiating has been withdrawn and offered elsewhere. Advertising is out of the question, there's no way in past the gatekeepers. I suppose we could scrape a living making eduflix for the government . . . were it not for one tiny thing."

They waited. *Now* what—

"We're bankrupt."

"*What?*"

"Sorry, Cash, but Ruthie accepted a penalty clause—"

"Hell's angels, Bailey, you didn't tell us anyth—"

"That's because she didn't tell *me*. But it's not entirely her fault—I had to pitch the sales talk pretty optimistically to sell the *God's Navsats* idea. Ruthie just made the mistake of believing what I said. Goddamn it, *I* believed what I said! Anyway, the upshot is, unless we come up with a pretty good advance in the next forty-eight hours, we lose the lot." He turned to Jonas. "So, Jonas, if you want to hang on to your fancy camera, you'd better put your thinking hat on. Sorry, my fault—but it's done, okay? Forget the comet: what we need right now is *cash*—lots of it."

Lots of . . . "Give me ten minutes. Got to make a private call. I'll be back."

Thirty minutes passed: Jonas returned, looking flustered. "Sorry, had some trouble getting access. Um . . . how would you like to make a documentary?"

Bailey stared at him as if he were crazy. "I told you, we're on the has-been list. The networks won't touch us with a . . . "

Jonas let him continue until he was out of breath—it was simpler that way. "Not with the networks: this is a private commission. There's one snag: we have to sign an open-ended contract. Good money, but no release date and no option to cancel."

"Ruthie won't like that!"

"Bailey, in this position Ruthie Bowser is superfluous. We're being offered jobs for life. Working for Angie Carver." In a few quick sentences he told them about Angie's secret collection of illicit archaeological specimens. She'd authorized that—as long as he didn't reveal where the collection was hidden. "She wants us to make an in-depth VV catalogue of the whole collection. *Very* private, her eyes only—for the foreseeable future, at least. It's never been properly catalogued, you see, and she's not happy about that. We film all the specimens *in situ,* and we go all over the world and film where they came from. Mars, even." He related the story of Angie's thoat bone.

"I'd *love* to go to Mars!" said Cashew. It had been a child-hood dream.

Bailey wasn't so sure. He wasn't that keen on travel, if the truth be told. But he'd been distinctly impressed by the Carver operation, and not just because of Angie's money. "Hmmph. Mars—yeah, well, I guess it's no worse than a very slow 'round-the-world cruise, though without the cabaret and the *cordon-bleu* . . . What's the advance, Jonas?"

"Nothing."

"Are you *mad*? I just told you, Ruthie accepted a pen—"

"Angie pays off the penalty clause as a signing fee. But from then on, guys, she owns us lock, stock, and Suzuki-73. Oh, *don't* all look as if you've swallowed a walrus! She's try-ing to help us out, okay? Only thing is, although she's got pots of money, she instinctively drives a *very* hard bargain. I guess anyone who's outlived seven billionaire husbands must find it difficult to be a soft touch. Anyway, the real reason is that most of her stuff is illegal, so she needs to make sure we don't—"

Cashew touched his hand. "It's all right, Jonas, you don't need to justify anything. We got handed a piece of bad luck, is all. I rather think you've saved our bacon. Hasn't he, Bai-ley? *Bailey?* Yes, you can give me that awful sour look if you want to, but you know I'm right. Or have you got a better idea?"

Jonas still felt awkward. *He* thought this was a great op-portunity—job for life, no more scrambling for the scraps the networks threw to their lapdogs to keep them tame and mal-leable—but then, he really liked Angie Carver, he had a feel-ing this would keep him in touch with Prudence, and as long as he could keep making VV . . . "We all have to agree. This isn't a democratic vote: we each have a veto. Okay?" The others signified their agreement. "I say we sign. Cash? Yeah, right, you're even keener that I am. Bailey?"

Barnum shrugged. It wasn't such a bad deal, but— "Ruthie won't like us biting the hand that feeds us."

"Bailey—it's the same hand that locks our cages every night."

"True." It would get Bowser off their backs, permanently. No more twenty percent . . . "Sure. I always wanted to spend my life making films of old bits of junk that nobody will ever get to look at."

"It's all too much of a coincidence, you see," Uhlirach-Bengtsen said, as a pretty young secretary served them coffee and cookies. It seemed easier to talk in a relaxed way now that the news had been broken. Twelve years seemed a long way off . . . surely *something* could be done to avert the catastrophe.

"Coincidence? Peter, I'm not following this at—"

"Jupiter's moons, Charles. They've moved. They've moved into just the right positions to fling a comet that *would* have hit Jupiter along an extremely accurate trajectory aimed dead-center at *us*. A billion square miles of celestial real estate to aim at, yet it comes *here*. Coincidence? Crap! Combine that with those wheeled things that the Odingo woman found, *also* out on Jupiter's moons, and it starts to look very likely indeed that those moons didn't move as a result of natural causes. They haven't just moved—they've *been* moved!"

"You mean—"

"Aliens, Charles. We're convinced that someone, something, deliberately rearranged Jupiter's moons . . . moved them into carefully calculated positions that would divert that comet straight at Target Earth. We think that there are alien creatures living on Jupiter's moons that possess the technology to manipulate gravity."

Charles's mind flicked back to the fiasco at the inquiry. The scene was burned into his synapses. The wheeler had *levitated*. "So *that's* how that infernal machine did it," he muttered.

"So our best scientific brains have deduced, Charles."

"Why Jupiter's moons? Why not the planet itself?"

"First: the wheelers were dug up on one of the moons. Second: Jupiter is unsuitable for intelligent life—no solid ground, and the conditions are too extreme. A nice, quiet moon, though . . . perfect. Set up a base, equip it with all the home comforts."

"Makes sense. But why *us*? We haven't bothered *them*!" *Unless Prudence Odingo's expedition had in some way offended*—no, that was sheer paranoia; he should be ashamed.

"We don't *know* the aliens are still in the Jovian system—they might have just been passing through and chucked a rock our way for the fun of it. But my advisers don't think that's likely. If the aliens are going to gain a genuine advantage, and not just bug their multiple eyes out with amusement as the Earth gets splattered across the cosmos, they've got to maintain a long-term presence. One explanation is that tossing a comet our way may be a first step towards joviforming the Earth. You know—making it fit for creatures like them to inhabit. Lots of nice bare rock, no pests—a Jovian's version of the French Riviera."

"Not very plausible. Wrong gravity, too weak to retain a hydrogen-helium atmosphere . . . "

"I agree. I'm pretty certain that the choice of trajectory is an act of war, but that's because I'm a military man by training and I think I can recognize when some bastard is shooting at me. However, these are *alien* bastards, and my advisers inform me that because aliens are alien, you can't interpret their actions as if they were human. Anyway, if it *is* an act of war, we can't do a damned thing about it. We don't have the weapons to fight back. We don't even know where the damned genocidal murderers *are* . . . But if it's all some kind of mistake—a faint hope but all we have—then maybe we can persuade them to do something about it.

"And that, Charles, is where you come in."

Sir Charles was still looking out of the window. Yes, Canada geese *were* a pest, they bred like—like rabbits, silly simile—and they left slimy green droppings everywhere from the grass they ate. But when it came to the crunch, he'd prefer pests any day to—

He realized Uhlirach-Bengtsen had said something to him. He apologized and asked for it to be repeated. The undersecretary did so.

Oh, shit. "Me? *I* come in? How?"

"Charles, we're putting together an expedition. The Jovian Task Force. We're collecting the best brains and the best equipment that we and the Buddhist Belters can come up with, and we're sending them out to Jupiter. Their task will be to locate the aliens, make contact with them, and talk them into fixing the problem. Since the aliens can rearrange Jupiter's moons at will, they can damn well *re*-arrange them to send their comet somewhere else.

"There will be biologists and linguists and computer engineers and xenologists and sociologists and mathematicians and chemists and skilled negotiators and whatever else we can think of. You want lap-dancers, we'll give you the sexiest and most sinuous that the clubs can provide, no questions asked. You want diamonds, we'll give you a mine. But we need someone who can knit all of those disciplines into a team, Charles, and we've decided that you are that person."

This was awful. His worst nightmare didn't come close. And there was no way out of it. *Nobody* selected for that expedition was going to get a serious chance to turn the dubious honor down.

"You're probably wondering why we want an archaeologist. Well, to be honest, we don't, not as such. But it's a very interdisciplinary subject, and ancient civilizations may be as close as we can get to alien ones. As a bonus, it's an area that is well used to deciphering unknown inscriptions, so you can help the linguists with the aliens' language. Mostly, though, we want you for your organizational skills and worldwide reputation. Charles, the human race *needs* you!"

Charles essayed a weak smile. "Peter, it's a—a great . . .

honor." At that moment, though, the only thought running through his mind was that the last thing he needed right now was the human race.

Twelve years is not long to prepare for a cometary impact, especially when the best that the Earth's assorted governments can come up with is to go and ask whoever is throwing it at them to change their minds, pretty please.

The prospect does wonders for international cooperation, though.

There were, of course, the usual coterie of doomsayers and millennial cultists, of religious fundamentalists whose strength of belief outweighed mere material facts, and political pressure groups that sensed an opportunity (while discounting its cause as propaganda), but most of them had the sense to bide their time, suspecting that better opportunities would not be far away. Ignoring them, every resource that the planet possessed was potentially available to Sir Charles and his burgeoning empire. Even the neo-Zen Buddhists of the Way of the Wholesome seemed to waken from their self-imposed inscrutable obsession with a different dimension.

Only the Democratic Republic of Free China remained aloof, its borders as tightly shut as they had ever been, its leadership—if there was one—so entangled in its own internal politics that it was unable to react to the relentless tightening of the cosmic thumbscrew . . .

It took Sir Charles the best part of a year to put his expedition together. He would have preferred longer—he would have preferred not to have been involved at all—but celestial mechanics was a hard taskmaster. Joshua might have commanded the sun to stand still; Immanuel Velikovsky's wild comet spawned by Jupiter might have undergone a change of personality and settled down as sedate Venus; but those options were not available in the universe that Charles inhabited.

During the first few weeks, he had paced endlessly up and down his plush new Washington office, staring across the parklands of the Mall at the ivy-strewn ruins of the Old Capitol, trying to make up his mind about the main strategic options. Should there be just one expedition, or several? A single giant ship of a kind never yet built, or a flotilla of more conventional ships? His biggest headache was the impossibility of anticipating what conditions would be like in the Jovian system, and what equipment and personnel would be needed.

All of his plans had to be contingency plans.

Sir Charles's team of advisers, drawn from every corner of the globe (save China) and chosen for that subtle mix of imagination and practicality that drives true innovation, settled inevitably on a compromise. One expedition must be put together quickly, but not *too* quickly, since it would always be their best shot: it would be counterproductive to divert resources into a series of expeditions. However, small supplementary missions might be needed later, so manpower and money would be switched to those projects, on a contingency basis, as soon as the main expedition no longer needed them. The resources of the planet would form the most extensive support structure ever assembled for a single project.

The expedition would center around one ship—large, but not overambitiously engineered. Assembled in orbit with considerable Belter assistance, this ramshackle vessel would resemble a floating scrapyard—modules of many shapes and origins glued and bolted to a frame of carbon-nanofiber girders, linked by tunnels of aluminum and plastic, wrapped in foil. The price Earth had to pay for the assistance of the neo-Zen Buddhists was the name of the ship: *Skylark*. In the *Bya chos,* the lark's contribution began: *For those who dwell in a state of woe, pleasures turn sour.* It plummeted ever further into the depths of despair, culminating in the inspiring phrase: *Seeing the corpses interred beneath the ground, the pleasures of pride in this citadel of the body turn sour.* It then embarked upon an equally gloomy commentary upon the sad state of affairs so far outlined: ten lines of free verse, each beginning with the formula *What use* . . . applied variously to sons, friends, possessions, religious talk, and moral rules; and it ended with the inspiring admonition: *What use, therefore, all these things—useless indeed are they!* For some reason that nobody else could understand, the Way of the Wholesome considered the lark's speech to be so appropriate to the mission that they insisted that it should be painted on the vessel's side in letters a foot high. Most commentators felt that a less frivolous name, and a more upbeat message, would have been an improvement; but to the Buddhists there were few birds less frivolous than the lugubrious lark, and the Zen monks saw nothing upbeat in the situation, and no reason to pretend otherwise. Since they who pay for the skylark call the tune, the name was agreed on without much public argument.

Skylark would be accompanied by a dozen smaller vessels, the best that could be found among Earth's ragtag-and-bobtail interplanetary fleet. All vessels would carry at least two regular OWL ground/orbit shuttle craft, and the large vessel would have nine. *Skylark* would have laboratories, machine shops, lasers, communications equipment of all kinds, computer banks . . . It would be laden with every resource, from balls of string to portable nuclear reactors.

It was to be a cross between a top-flight university and a wholesale hardware store.

There were no lap-dancers, and no military personnel. Sir Charles had nothing against the military, many were trained in useful skills, but he had a horrible feeling that they'd mostly be there to grab the reins if he screwed up. Or even if he didn't. So he fought tooth and nail to keep them excluded, and won the argument when the Belters backed him up. Uhlirach-Bengtsen hadn't exactly been overjoyed, but he'd agreed. Privately, he recognized that there were other ways to ensure adequate security.

Sir Charles had been the victim of his own cunning. He could not risk being seen to give the expedition anything less than every atom of his being, every picosecond of his time.

Because he really *was* a superb organizational politician, he
could not avoid becoming ever more essential to the project:
within a month there was no prospect of anybody replacing
him. But the implication—which he had seen clearly from the
very beginning, with growing horror, transfixed by unfolding
events—was that his role would not end when *Skylark*
slipped ponderously out of low Earth orbit on its two-year
rendezvous with destiny.

When *Skylark* went to Jupiter, it would carry Sir Charles
Dunsmoore with it.

Fortunately, he was so busy organizing his own doom that
he hardly ever had time to worry about it.

10

Caligula Chaos, 2213

Socks. Shirts. Underwear.

Music chip—everything from Antheil, George (composer, twentieth century classical) to Zoo-Zoom Zero (web-entity/collective, twenty-second century razz).

A small, low-resolution flatscreen.

A worn deck of cards.

The minutiae of a human life, the banal mix of personal necessities and trivia that people choose to take with them on lengthy voyages when storage space is limited . . . Clothing, entertainments. Tellingly, no holos of family, friends, or lovers—not even of a cat or a hamster.

Sir Charles Dunsmoore unpacked his belongings and marveled that when he put something down on a surface, it stayed there. His legs ached, even though Europa's surface gravity was only one-seventh that of Earth, even though he had conscientiously exercised for four hours out of every twenty-four for the past two years. He never wanted to see an exercise bicycle again, and he was trying hard not to think about the return voyage.

It had been wonderful to see Europa looming ahead at last, smooth as a pool ball, blue-gray ice covered in russet doodles which on closer inspection turned out to be moon-girdling cracks. Sir Charles, like most of the task force's members, positively *itched* to get his feet back on firm ground again, even if it was the frozen terrain of an alien moon. *Anything* was better than the tedium of interplanetary spaceflight. At times, he'd hoped the *Skylark* would explode or collide with a meteorite—anything to break the routine.

He'd been unable to take his eyes off the screen display as the moon slowly grew closer. It was a young landscape—too young. The ice must have melted, flowed, refrozen, obliterating the craters that otherwise would have to be visible. It *looked* as if the ice layer were thin, floating—the concentric flattened rings of Tire Macula, one of the rare large craters, were just what you'd expect if something had smashed through the ice and left it to refreeze; the moon's weird polygonal terrain resembled Earth's Antarctic ice sheets. And then there were the flexi—Sidon Flexus, Delphi Flexus, Cilicia Flexus . . . linear markings thousands of miles long, formed from series of sixty-mile arcs, cycloids . . . Evidence, the xenologists thought, of tidal cracking, propagating at one arc per Europan day. Imagine being around while they were forming.

And now they were *there,* thank God. Compared to *Skylark*'s spartan, cramped quarters, Europa Base was a luxury hotel, even though it was incomplete. It had been assembled by the expedition of 2145, one of the first big post-Pause science jaunts and pretty much the last, as the first step in an ambitious program to search for alien life. For a short time, Ecotopia had started to look outward again, with Belter help—but it hadn't lasted. The expedition's long-term objective had been to drill through the satellite's miles-thick coat of solid ice to the liquid ocean that, according to all the evidence, was concealed beneath. Just as Jupiter's gravitational clasp squeezed Io relentlessly, heating its interior and fueling its sulfurous volcanoes, so the giant planet's tidal grip had melted Europa's silicate core. The tidal effect was only a tenth of that on Io, but it had heated the core enough to create a thick underground layer of liquid water buried deep beneath the cracked, dirt-strewn crust. The surface remained frozen as it radiated heat into the vacuum of space—the crazed orange-brown shell of a cosmic egg with a yolk of liquid rock. Between yolk and shell was the white of the egg, a relatively warm ocean that contained at least as much water as all of Earth's oceans put together. Its *average* depth was ten times that of the Earth's deepest underwater trenches; it formed a layer of water sixty miles thick, laden with salts dissolved from the core.

No light had penetrated those alien seas in the four billion years of their existence, but there had been heat energy in abundance, and plenty of time for evolution to take hold. So Europa had long been seen as the most likely habitat, within the Solar System, for extraterrestrial life. Perhaps colonies of thermophilic bacteria gathered around hot vents in the crushing depths where the water gave way to molten rock, separated by a thin layer of solidified silicate magma that buckled and contorted into a million fantastic shapes . . . Perhaps shoals of unearthly fishes glided through the tropical seas of the middle layers . . . But the expedition of 2145 placed its hopes on the convoluted zone of semi-frozen slush that formed the interface between the Europan ocean and its fragile shell of solid ice, because that was all they could explore. The slushy water was known to be rich in salts and dissolved organics. There, even the most pessimistic of Earth's exobologists held high hopes that there would be bacterial-grade organisms. Others speculated about rubbery pipes hundreds of yards long, stony spheres of various sizes, and a pulverized creature that would be all teeth, claws, spines, and glowing eyes—but whose menace was mitigated by the prediction that it would be only two inches long.

The Europa expedition was code-named *Challenger* after a ship that had mapped the deep seas of Earth and drilled cores in their beds, though many Xphiles thought it was named after an obscure literary character who had drilled a hole in the Earth and discovered that the planet was alive. It had been a carefully planned attempt to "drill" through Europa's shell of dirty ice using a probe with a nuclear-powered heating device that would melt its way downward. Although the ice would freeze behind it, it was possible to ensure that a narrow channel remained open, and through this channel would run fiber-optic cables connecting the probe's battery of holovision cameras and other instruments to the surface. Once through the solid ice and into the layer of slush, the probe would switch on its nuclear-powered spotlights and the hunt for Europan life-forms could begin.

That was the plan . . . and while the probe was being designed and assembled on Earth, a flotilla of spaceships hauled lightweight materials to the distant satellite and put together a habitable base in a relatively flat area at the edge of Caligula Chaos, a region of cracked ice plates, crevasses, and cliffs adjoining the gigantic crack Adonis Linea. The site, named by a classically minded geophysicist on the initial survey project, had been chosen for two reasons. From there, thanks to Europa's synchronous rotation, Jupiter was always in view in the same part of the sky, making it possible to study the gas giant from close up without interruption. More importantly, the gulleys and clefts that disfigured the landscape were probably the uppermost parts of ancient cracks in the ice layer that at one time had penetrated all the way to the ocean beneath— a place where semi-liquid slush had welled up under tidal pressures, smashed the overlying layers of ice, and pushed them brusquely aside. There might be signs of life preserved in the frozen surface slush, and the cracks might be a weak point in the ice crust, a good place to start "drilling."

From a landing spacecraft, Caligula Chaos was a patchwork of angular, polygonal ice rafts, frost patterns on a windowpane that had been repeatedly shattered and reassembled. In places you could observe tiny craters, formed not by impacting meteorites but by giant blocks of ice hurled casually aside by the meteorites that had created nearby impact structures. From lower altitudes, the fragmented ice plates appeared to be scattered like pieces of broken eggshell, forming patchy expanses of washboardlike corrugations hundreds of yards high, terminating in precipitous scalloped cliffs. Blocky debris sprawled in heaps along the bottom of the cliffs, and in the moon's near-vacuum everything looked like a black-and-white photograph, with tinges of sepia from contaminating minerals.

Challenger's project designers had anticipated virtually any contingency on Europa and during the voyage to the Jovian system, but what they had not anticipated was a last-minute legal challenge by a pressure group that temporarily succeeded in getting the Oceanic Environmental Protection Act of 2130 extended to the entire Solar System. It was hard to argue that anybody could realistically have seen it coming, but heads rolled anyway. *Challenger*'s planners and managers had been aware of the danger of contaminating any hypothetical Europan ecology with terrestrial organisms. Although such contamination was very unlikely—earthly life had not evolved to survive in a Europan environment—they took the possibility very seriously. If "alien" life-forms such as terrestrial bacteria ever gained a toehold on Europa, they would replicate, spreading no one knew where, or to what effect, and that was a clear no-no. So the managers had taken elaborate precautions to avoid such contamination—in particular, specifying a rigorous sterilization procedure for the probe.

They had also worried about possible harm to Europan life-forms caused by the probe's nuclear materials. The task of "drilling" through the ice of a Jovian moon was severe enough: to do it in a way that would permit recovery of the probe was essentially impossible. So they designed the reactor to use short-lived radioactive isotopes, which would decay into stable matter before the probe corroded enough to release them into the ocean. There would also be a small amount of radioactivity where the materials of the probe had become irradiated, but the likely damage caused by these materials would be localized and negligible. Perhaps a few Europan bacteria or whatever would be killed, but that was a very different matter from introducing terrestrial *organisms* and making irreversible changes to the entire Europan ecosystem.

As it happened, the Oceanic Environmental Protection Act embodied a series of laws whose intention was to prevent any dumping of nuclear waste—however minor or short-lived—in the Earth's oceans. The lawmakers who framed the act were aware that isolated discharges of small amounts of radioactive waste into the sea would cause little long-term damage—but they were also aware that if such incidents were to be repeated many times worldwide, the cumulative consequences could be severe. So they reasoned that if they left even a tiny loophole, it might be exploited on a global scale, and they therefore drew up draconian legislation to eliminate any conceivable loophole—so draconian that the Save Our Solar System movement was able to convince an international court that the provisions of the act were not restricted to the home planet. In fact their counsel argued that it applied throughout the entire universe, but the court drew back from such an extensive ruling because it was uncertain of its jurisdiction. It did, however, deem the act to be valid throughout the entire Solar System.

Eventually, this decision was overturned—but only after the case had made its way through a series of lengthy and expensive appeals, with platoons of expert witnesses on both sides who examined every aspect of the science in horrendous and conflicting detail. In the end, the appeal was sustained for reasons of jurisdiction, not science—the court ruled that its jurisdiction ended at the Lagrange L1 point between the Earth and the Moon, where their gravitational forces canceled out. Anything farther away was not part of its terms of reference. By then, expensive short-lived radioactives had decayed, key items of equipment in the probe and its support systems en route to Europa had deteriorated beyond repair, and much of the funding had been used to fight the court battle, so the project had to be abandoned. Attempts to raise new funds failed, so the near-complete installation of Europa was mothballed and left to its own devices amid the Jovian satellite's subarctic ice fields.

When the Jovian Task Force had been conceived and Sir Charles Dunsmoore had been appointed to head it, Europa Base presented itself as the obvious home.

Despite all its shortcomings, Charles felt that the base was a big improvement on the only alternative: staying on board *Skylark* while it swung in lonely orbit round Europa. Down here there was *gravity*. He had enough space to stow his belongings where he could get at them easily. He had a narrow but comfortable bed with room to stretch out. He had—

He had rather less space than a convicted mass murderer would have been allotted in an Earthly jail, but a far less comfortable lifestyle.

To cheer himself up, he tried to count his blessings, and ended up more depressed than ever. *This had not been part of the game plan.* Instead of being stuck in this godforsaken lash-up of inflatable plastic domes and narrow tunnels, he should have been nailing down the presidency of the Egyptological Federation, dining out every night at the taxpayers' expense, and securing over the dinner tables some fast-track appointments to lucrative consultancies.

He lay back on the bed, staring at the translucent plastic sloping strangely overhead, and felt sorry for himself. Through the plastic he could see a fuzzy image of Jupiter, a white-and-brown-striped disk twelve degrees of arc in diameter—an impressive twenty times the size of the Moon from Earth. But the only thing it impressed upon him was the enormity of the task confronting him and how terribly far he was from the comforts of home.

After an hour or so had passed, he worked his way around to some more positive thoughts about the job at hand. It was, he had to admit, the most important job that anyone could ever be given. On its successful conclusion, his return would exceed his wildest dreams. He could—

He could buckle down, get on with the job, and stop thinking about what was in it for him.

This was a new thought, a new *kind* of thought, though he had a vague feeling that once, as a much younger man, he had entertained such thoughts, and even used them to align his life. He had secured research grants *in order to do research.* He had done research *in order to find things out.* Somewhere along the line, he had lost that simplicity of motive, and advancing his career had become far more important to him than advancing human knowledge . . .

He had become a politician. It had crept up on him so gradually that he hadn't noticed. Now he was developing a worrying feeling that somewhere along the way he'd lost the plot. Try as he might, he couldn't completely shake it off. Two years confined in an overgrown tin can on its way to one of the most hostile environments in the Solar System were having a curious effect on his mind. It was as if the layers of protective coloration had peeled away in the harsh light of an unshielded sun. Sir Charles Dunsmoore reviewed his scientific life and discovered that for most of it he had been living an elaborate lie, advancing himself by deceit, conniving, and bribery. Once, not so long ago, he would have been proud of his record, preening himself at his own cleverness in comparison to the foolish, naive honesty of his opponents . . . Suddenly all that seemed hopelessly tawdry, suited to a lifestyle that made sense when you focused your mind only on the immediate world around you, the world of people and the games they played. When that entire world was no bigger than a speck of dust, it all seemed very unimportant in the scheme of things. He didn't give a damn *who* became president of the Egyptological Federation. How would that affect the comet?

The oddest thing of all was that after this bout of dismal introspection and self-flagellation, which he *knew* had been brought about by the stress of the voyage and the anticlimax of its end, he found himself feeling a lot more positive. Humanity might not count for anything in the cosmic scheme of things, but it counted for *him*. There was a job to do, the most important job that any human being could have. It no longer mattered what was in it for him. What mattered was what was in it for everybody else.

Pin Yi-wu, a minor clerk in the Fourth Crime-Prevention and Punishment Division of the Civic Inspectorate of the Yishan Economic Enterprise Zone, Zhuangzu Province, was having a bad day. Some idiot subordinate had filed a report about street-child activity in his jurisdiction. Some jackal dung about them becoming an organized force, making raids into outlying high-rise apartment blocks, stealing food from markets . . . rallying behind a charismatic leader . . .

Blatant nonsense, of course. The street kids were pure anarchy. He'd never understood how they survived at all, though in truth individual children didn't, not for long. They were just constantly replenished from the shantytowns.

Unfortunately, once a report was filed, something had to be done about it, and the someone in charge of that step was him. Hence his annoyance. If only the fool had inquired unofficially *first,* it would have been easy to sidetrack the whole issue. But now . . .

Sighing at the burdens life imposes, especially those in the form of overzealous subordinates, he stared at the box on the report form where he was required to recommend further action. If any. A less experienced civil servant might well have hit it with the "no action required" stamp and assumed that that would be the end of the matter. But Pin knew that hastily dismissed items had a habit of returning when one least expected them to, accompanied by requests for an explanation of one's poorly judged recommendation. *The first role of any bureaucrat is to cover one's own back,* he thought. *Nobody else will.*

The trick was to boot the foolish thing upstairs without being seen to take it seriously or to recommend anything—including a recommendation to take no action. Equally, it would not do to be seen to have passed on nonsense to a superior.

He would flag it for routine attention higher up the hierarchy, but append a note pointing out the report's evident deficiencies and suggesting (but not recommending) that if it were thought that there might perhaps be something factual behind it, then the wise step would be to dispatch an independent investigator—should such a curious matter be deemed worthy of such action.

It seemed obvious that the report had been conjured up by a brain rendered credulous by strong drink—though Yu was normally a teetotaler . . . But that silly passage about trained packs of wild dogs made no sense at all. For that matter, neither did the color of the alleged leader's skin.

Probably just dirt.

Skylark was equipped with nine OWLs—low-powered shuttles capable of commuting between Jupiter's moons and landing on them, but not suited to the rigors of long-haul interplanetary transport. During the voyage they had doubled as sleeping quarters for the crew. The ship—too elegant a name by far for such an odd bundle of nanofiber struts and misshapen compartments—had capacious cargo bays packed solid with equipment and materials. Its accompanying flotilla was mostly given over to life support for the crews.

Every one of *Skylark*'s modules also served as additional storage. Sir Charles and his task force had been terrified that they might have forgotten something vital.

Nobody knew what to expect; nobody knew what the expedition would need. *The problem with aliens is: they're alien.* What they did know was that unless any particular item was on board, or could be made with what was, then it might as well be buried at the Earth's core. Two years' journey from Earth, the expedition was effectively on its own.

Top priority: *locate the aliens.* Next: *communicate with them.* But not far down the list was an alternative strategy, *locate active wheelers,* because those would surely lead to the Jovians themselves. So the task force would monitor the entire electromagnetic spectrum for signals.

There was no room on *Skylark* to deploy all of the available equipment, but the old base on Europa would fit the bill beautifully. So the first task had been to unmothball Europa Base, transfer a lot of the equipment down to it, and set up a variety of search and monitoring systems. The aliens were widely expected to be living on one (or more) of the moons—Jupiter itself was so inhospitable that it would surely be inimical to intelligent life. However, a small but influential band of dissident advisers was convinced that the aliens could nevertheless be on Jupiter, so *Skylark* carried a variety of probes designed to plumb the depths of the gas giant's poisonous, high-pressure atmosphere.

Sir Charles considered the dissidents' opinion to be completely mad. Jupiter's surface—inasmuch as there was one—was a small, incredibly dense core of metallic hydrogen, buried at pressures of two-thirds of a million tons per square inch and temperatures above thirty thousand degrees Celsius. Nothing could live in such an environment.

The first serious activity, then, would be to explore Jupiter's moons. Even that would stretch resources to the full. The planet probes would stay under wraps.

A debate was raging. Were the wheelers machines, or an unprecedented form of life? Their structure was turning out to be way beyond the reach of Earthly technology—an interlocking three-dimensional jigsaw that seemed to have been assembled one atom at a time, monomolecular crystals, impossibly tight tolerances . . . The substructure was more intricate than any human nanomachine: life was the only thing on

Earth that could match it. But, no matter how extensively the scientists probed, they could find nothing at all that could be an analogue of genes. They'd have settled for long-chain metalloid polymers—no one was expecting to find wheeler DNA—but there was nothing that could pass information about body plans and behavior to the next generation. Worse, there were no signs of wheeler reproductive organs. So the complexity scientists insisted that the wheelers were a form of life, because of their organization, and the bioinformaticists insisted they were not, because they had no heredity. It was an old battleground.

While the scientists and the philosophers argued, *Skylark* maintained station in the Europan void. Occasionally an ion motor glowed as Captain Hugo Greenberg authorized an accompanying vessel to make a routine course correction to avoid drifting away from the flotilla.

Probes controlled from Europa Base prowled the three primary targets—Ganymede, Callisto, and especially Europa—looking for signs of aliens or wheelers.

Three months passed. Six. Ten.

Nothing.

It had all been so positive to begin with. For the teams on board the *Skylark* and at Europa Base, the first few months had flickered from anticipation to memory in a timeless instant.

There had been radio antennas to deploy, ready to scan the spectrum for the messages that the aliens must surely be using to communicate with each other. There were remote probes to be attended to, making a systematic search of Jupiter's moons to find the aliens' center of operations. They had to be reassembled, readied for use, their systems tested and if need be repaired or reprogramed. Day after day they were spat out from *Skylark* like surplus seeds from a slice of watermelon—this one to Ganymede, that one to nearby Europa, the majority to Callisto because that's where the wheelers had been found.

Io was considered too unstable for the kind of high-tech installation that presumably would be needed to move bodies roughly three thousand miles across. Before the expedition had set out, mathematical physicists had calculated that the amount of energy expended by the aliens in that one maneuver had been 2×10^{28} ergs—roughly a thousand years of the Earth's total commercial generation of electrical power. Anything capable of handling that much energy ought to be easy enough to locate.

Nothing.

Were they looking in the wrong place? Or was there nothing to be found?

Sir Charles could not avoid remembering a VV discussion that he had agreed to take part in, before leaving Earth, to explain to the public some of the detailed scientific thinking behind the mission's configuration and its choice of strategic priorities. With malice aforethought, the program's producers had invited a couple of fantascience authors along as well, to act as devil's advocates. It hadn't gone badly—he'd put up some pretty robust arguments and was generally judged to have won the debate. At the time he'd considered his two opponents to be seriously lacking in the self-criticism department. He realized that they'd been equally sure he had no imagination, which was unfair: he had to decide what to *do*, not just toss hypotheticals around. He had begun by explaining why they were giving Io low priority . . .

"*. . . that's certainly a rational line of thought, Sir Charles.*" That was Valerie Clementine, bestselling author of more than a dozen VV novellas set on a high-gravity world that was spinning so fast that its equator was on the verge of peeling off into space. "*But: these guys are aliens. You can't rely on human thought patterns. Too parochial.*"

"*Val's right, Charlie,*" chipped in the second skeptic, a plain-speaking and slightly drunken Australian called Alvin Harris, whose forte was humorous far-future widescreen baroque. "*These bozos probably think Io's a real neat place to play Jovian volleyball on the sulfur beaches and lather their scaly hides in the gentle rain from the spouting volcanoes."*

"Yes, and for all we know the machines that move the moons might be the size of a suitcase," added Clementine.

Cyrus Feather, the presenter, decided it was time he chipped in. "Sir Charles, is that true?"

"No. It's scientifically impossible to pack enough energy into a suitcase to power this planet's entire civilization for a millennium."

"I dunno," said Harris. "What about a lump of neutron star or a black hole the size of a pumpkin? Come on, mate: two hundred years ago we could pack a ruddy hydrogen bomb into a backpack!"

"Yes, but a hydrogen bomb is piffling compared to what the aliens had to do. And there is no evidence that the aliens can control ultra-dense matter," Charles pointed out patiently. "All we know is: they can move a perfectly ordinary moon."

"Hah! Ordinary moon! My god, Charlie, you're a cool one."

Feather's job was to keep the conversation moving and share it around. "Val—do you have anything to add here?" Why was the woman so timid? Why hadn't the researchers found that out and chosen someone else?

"Um . . . well, Sir Charles. I'm prepared to accept that maybe there is some gigantic machine out there. But how do you know it's not buried, for example . . . or invisible . . . or operating from thirty light-years away?"

Charles could get his teeth into this. "Do you have scientific evidence for what you're suggesting, Val? If you don't, they're not examples of anything. Being able to imagine them doesn't mean they can exist. I can imagine a unicorn the size of a mountain that eats nothing but lemon sherbet and writes Etruscan poetry on the sky with its horn, but that doesn't *mean that such an animal is possible." He was proud of the simile, seeing as he'd made it up on the hoof.*

Feather changed the subject. *"Alvin, you had a question about the Belter telescopes?"*

"Oh, yeah. The Belters have been training those big telescopes of theirs on Jupiter's moons ever since they first spotted the comet. Surely they would have seen the kind of gigantic installation you're expecting to find?"

Oh, dear. This was a very common misconception, even among trained scientists. He'd heard it a hundred times . . . He trotted out his stock answer. "At that distance, Alvin, the Belters' instruments can only resolve detail down to about a hundred yards."

Harris was flushed and becoming argumentative. "Wharrabout that new interpretom—"

"Interferometer?"

"Yeah, whaddever. Whaddabout it?"

"So far, the new interferometer has surveyed only four percent of the surface of Ganymede. By the time Skylark reaches Jupiter it will have surveyed only twenty-five percent of the target areas. The Belters could get lucky—I hope so—but their current lack of success implies nothing. Moreover, the installation could well be no more than a suggestive smudge in the interferometer's images. We've already compiled a catalogue of such smudges. Which so far contains 12,942 PTOs—Potential Target Objects. These are being prioritized by a trained interdisciplinary team, and their decisions will guide strategy once we are ready to deploy search probes."

Sir Charles, his eye on the studio clock, now launched into a preprepared winding-up speech. "Solid preparation for foreseeable contingencies will do us a lot more good than wild speculations. For instance, we will be monitoring the entire radio spectrum throughout the voyage. In all likelihood we will pick up their communications before we even get—"

"What if they don't use radio?" *Harris interrupted.* "We

know they can manipulate gravity—why couldn't they use gravity waves to communicate?"

Oh, dear. Amateurs. "We've been considering just that possibility for six months. A whole team of cosmologists. The upshot is: it won't work. The bandwidth is far too low. You'd need an antenna the size of the Solar System."

Harris was going red in the face. "How can you be so [BLEEP] sure when you have no idea what technology they've [BLEEP] got?"

Fed enough rope: hanged, Beautiful. "Alvin, please calm down, I agree with you. That's why Skylark has to make a proper study, close up. I'm a responsible scientist. I don't leap to crazy conclusions without seeing the evidence. People in your trade just make things up as you go along." The clock showed only a few seconds to go.

"So does the [BLEEP] universe, Dunsmoore! How long since the last major paradigm shift in phys—" But Harris's microphone was off, and the producer had moved smoothly on to the next item, leaving Sir Charles Dunsmoore the undisputed victor.

The critics had hailed it as a triumph for rational scientific debate, almost as well argued as the latest fascinating ideas about how Nostradamus had prophesied the coming of the comet and whether alien reflexology would be similar to our own . . .

. . . It was galling to have spent five trillion dollars, traveled for two years to the largest planet in the solar system, and worked your ass off for the best part of a year, only to find out that Clementine and Harris had been right all along.

Uhlirach-Bengtsen's scowl was almost ingrained nowadays.

Despite obsessive contingency planning, they were fast approaching the stage when all the plans had been torn up and they had to start making it up as they went along. Seat-of-the-pants politics . . . he hated it.

The flurry of reports from Europa Base had made an effective smokescreen for a while—so effective that even the political leadership had been fooled—but the smoke was rapidly dispersing as a lot of increasingly worried people homed in on the weak point: the comet was still on course, and the expedition had made no progress toward contacting the aliens. You didn't have to be a genius to see that a hundred technical reports on anomalies in Jupiter's radio spectrum didn't amount to a hill of beans.

Now some idiot in Baghdad had put up a five-hundred-foot-high Doomsday Clock, counting down the days to Ground Zero . . . just what everyone needed. The goddamned media were showing it every evening before the main newscasts, and it was all over the X.

A gigantic rethink was under way. According to the latest eyes-onlys, *Skylark*'s techs were hastily reprogramming the probes to start looking at the rest of Jupiter's moons—even the small ones. Maybe one of the orbiting rock piles was really an alien love nest.

He hated improvising. He hated the state of his office. Documents were piled everywhere. Whoever had predicted that computers would eliminate paperwork had been about as much on target as the caveman who'd argued that fire was dangerous and would never catch on. The Xnet was so insecure that anything sensitive was prepared on isolated computers and printed out on paper. It was just as quick to scan printed output back in again, anyway, if need be—and paper lasted longer than magnetic film and was easier to store, as well as being more secure.

The problem was not to generate information. It was to decide which information, if any, was meaningful. The engineers could quantify information, but meaning was a *quality,* beyond the reaches of current information theory. He picked up a report at random: *Absence of Response to Reflected Light Stimuli in Alien Artifacts,* by a team of—god, it had to be at least thirty of them, all at something called the Macnamara Institute for Applied Xenotechnology Studies. He glanced through the abstract. As far as he could penetrate through the jargon, the researchers had established that wheelers could respond to light signals—something that was obvious from the debacle with the laser pointer at Prudence Odingo's investigation. A dozen teams had been trying to decode the wheelers' optical "language," without success. Apparently *this* lot had discovered that if you bounced the laser beams off an ordinary glass mirror, then the wheelers didn't respond at all . . . but if you used a mirror whose surface was optically flat polished platinum, they did.

What the hell was *that* supposed to tell him about how to make contact?

Angry, he ripped the report in half and tossed it in the bin. *Bloody academics! Just can't keep their eyes on the ball!* Then he changed his mind and retrieved the torn cover from the bin. He would see if he could get their funding diverted to somebody doing something better-targeted.

Sir Charles normally kept himself aloof from the daily routine at Europa Base, but as the weeks stretched into months he found it harder and harder to delegate all of the work to his subordinates. He was beginning to wonder whether they were missing something obvious. He was all too aware whose head would roll if they were, but that wouldn't actually *matter,* would it? If the task force didn't crack the problem, there would be no Egyptological Federation for him to preside over.

To his surprise, he found that he didn't much care about that kind of thing anymore—even if his team did succeed in stopping the comet.

He was beginning to wonder what he *did* care about.

To take his mind off such confidence-sapping questions, he wandered unannounced into the main Ops Center. As far as he could tell, everyone was performing their alotted tasks as competently and energetically as could be expected under the trying circumstances. Even though the radio monitors had been on the case now for well over a year—before arrival and after—they still seemed to be watching attentively as the computers scanned ten thousand frequencies each second, searching ceaselessly for signs of a structured signal.

Having wandered round the plastic-covered dome and observed what everyone was doing, putting all their nerves on edge and otherwise achieving nothing, Sir Charles Dunsmoore settled into an inflatable chair in front of a small flat-film screen and tried to pretend that he was somewhere else. It didn't work, but the operatives appreciated the gesture. The Old Man was mellowing. That was *really* weird—most people in his position would be going quietly off their trolley. Sir Charles was a cool one, and no mistake.

It was a day like any other. Lots of activity, no results. Lots of analysis, no signals.

Jupiter wasn't helping. When it came to the radio spectrum, Jupiter was the most active planet in the solar system—apart, perhaps, from Earth. The difference was that Jupiter's activity was natural, a relic of its failure to become a star, whereas Earth's was mostly human in origin. Earth emitted noise on every wavelength, which on close analysis resolved itself into talk shows, game shows, news, pornography, and sports. Jupiter emitted noise on every wavelength, which on close analysis resolved itself into . . . noise. If the aliens *were* using radio to communicate, they were speaking in the language of dice and casinos. There was no structure, no short-range correlation, no semantic content. Earth's scientists were learning a great deal about the physics of Jupiter's mesosphere, its flimsy near-invisible rings, and the plasma torus that linked it to Io . . . but nothing at all about aliens. The only sign of life that they had yet found was half a diatom shell. Freddy Sunesson had discovered it on a rock she'd been slicing up for examination under her electron microscope. It was *exactly* like a terrestrial diatom—no doubt because that's where it had come from. Sunesson swore blind there'd been no chance of contamination, but nobody believed her. Someone had brought it with them on their clothes or in their baggage. He certainly wasn't going to tell the people of Earth about *that*.

Sir Charles decided to amuse himself by playing with the spectrum analyzers and attractor reconstruction suites on his local node. He extracted some beautiful segments of $1/f$ noise, and publishable evidence for Brownian chaos in the statistics of the Zeeman effect for calcium ions in Jupiter's polar magnetic field, but no alien equivalent of *The U-Foes*.

He called for a squeezer of cold coffee and a tube of croissant paste. Europan cuisine was healthy and filling—provided you could bring yourself to stuff it down.

I could be sunning myself in the Virgin islands attended by distinctly unvirgin islanders, he thought. *Or sipping champagne in a hot-air balloon circling the peak of Nanga Parbat. Or watching twenty-five-over limited cricket on the quicksport channel with a tube of beer at my elbow . . . Instead, I had to be too successful, and now I'm buried up to my armpits in the maddest, most desperate project ever attempted by the human race, and to date the most unsuccessf—*

He became aware of a growing hubbub in the Ops Center. People were pointing at their screens and shouting at one another.

He scanned his own screen, trying to work out what had captured their attention. He didn't want to make himself look like a fool by asking.

No good. He didn't have the training.

He pushed with his feet and floated off the seat, extending his legs at the last moment so that his velcro socks met the complementary carpet. Swaying where he stood, making quiet ripping sounds at every step, he crossed the aisle to the nearest desk. "Okay, Bethan, you know this stuff a lot better than I do. Have we finally found something important?"

"Probably not, Sir Charles." The operative was a laconic young woman from the Argentine Pampas. "One of the external sensors seems to be malfing, but the diagnostics are in conflict."

Ah. Now he knew what to look for. He scrolled a couple of windows, spotted the appropriate icon, expanded it. "Mmm. Or—if I read this correctly, which you can help me with—the routines say nothing's wrong with the sensor. Yes?"

I didn't realize the Old Man was that sharp. "That's right. We're getting impossible readings, but the tests say there's no malf."

Charles found his mind wandering back to his pyrrhic victory in the VV talk show . . . *Expect the unexpected.* "Bethan—just indulge me for a moment, let me ask a silly question. Just suppose, despite all arguments to the contrary, that there *is* no malfunction. What would the sensors be telling us?"

It took her a few seconds to decide that it wasn't some silly test of her competence. "Um. I—I guess we'd interpret the readings as external movement." She couldn't stop there. "But Sir Charles, there's nothing out there!"

"Maybe it's a probe?"

"No, our probes are all hundreds of miles away."

"Someone doing an unauthorized moonwalk because they're bored out of their skins and need to relieve the tension?"

"Only if they're crawling on their stomachs! If there's anything moving, it's hugging the ground."

"Do we have a VV camera that can *see* what's out there?"

"There's a mobile veecam on the far side of the base. It's being brought 'round—it'll be there in a min . . ."

Her voice trailed off.

Everyone's voice trailed off. You could have heard a pin hover.

Something was banging on the main base airlock.

* * *

By a tortuous route, a copy of Pin Yi-wu's self-effacing nonrecommendation about the street child with the improbable skin color had made its way into the hands of Xi Ming-Kuo. Xi had been hearing rumors for weeks, but the scrap of recycled paper told him that something more than rumor was at work. *The child still lives.*

This left him in a dilemma. It had been impossible for the boy to survive in the anarchic jungle of the buffer zone—defenseless, naive, trapped among gangs of feral children and dangerous dogs . . .

Yet, he had.

Were the powers that arranged the universe trying to tell Xi something? Had he made a mistake? Worried, he demanded the services of his *feng-shui* adviser.

Delicate Blossom was young, slim, and breathtakingly beautiful, with long dark hair and—he knew—a body that it was a crime to conceal beneath such shapeless, billowing robes. In olden times, the art of *feng-shui* had largely concerned itself with the placement of buildings, for any fool could see that it would be a mistake to erect a house on the tail of a buried dragon, and since only one skilled in *feng-shui* could tell where dragons were buried, it made good sense to hire the services of such a person. By the end of the twenty-second century the practice of *feng-shui* had widened its bounds, first to the placement of furniture, then decoration and art, then the choice of bride, groom, mother-in-law, or pedigreed cat, and finally to any kind of decision in which a certain amount of guesswork was inevitable. The advantage of taking *feng-shui* advice had nothing to do with whether it was good or whether you believed in it. The point was that if the decision later turned out to be wrong, there was someone else to blame. Of course, nobody in their right mind ever went back to their adviser to complain about their poor *feng-shui*—because it was wise not to offend anyone who *might* be able to tell where dragons were buried.

So now, in an oblique manner that conveyed as little gen-

uine information as possible, Xi asked Delicate Blossom to
warn him of hidden dragons, metaphorical and real. And her
reply was as well reasoned, as carefully considered, and as
enigmatic as his own questions. The woman was good, there
could be no doubt, and her chosen profession was a terrible
waste.

"You advise me, then, to exercise extreme caution?" he
asked, trying to extract another ounce of clarity from a fog of
allusions and ambiguities.

"Caution should always be exercised," she intoned. "But
true wisdom lies in knowing when to eschew excessive caution and take decisive action. Timidity and recklessness are
equally doomed."

"Ah, yes. And—er—*how* should the wise man know when
such a time has come?"

She smiled. "By exercising his wisdom, excellency." She
leaned closer and he smelled her musky perfume. She whispered, "I believe that in your heart of hearts you have already
determined the wise course of action. And I am certain that
you possess the courage to heed the advice of your heart of
hearts."

Xi coughed modestly. *Of course.* He dismissed her with
the wave of a hand. The hint was obvious.

Courage.

To kill the child, even indirectly, was not and never would
have been an act of courage, and that is why it had failed. But
to leave the boy among the feral children, acquiring experience, a growing source of danger—not the organized street
children, that was trivial, but the deep danger that Xi had
sensed when first he had seen the child—that was foolhardy.
To accept an unsatisfactory circumstance, merely because of
vague and irrational fears about the powers that might or might
not arrange the universe, was the opposite of courage. To risk
the wrath of those powers (should they indeed exist, which
was *possible*) . . . to do so as a calculated gamble . . . *that* was
courageous.

Sometimes he felt worn down by the burdens that his position imposed on him. It would now be necessary to *show* courage, and not just to possess it. Killing the child had failed, but keeping him captive in one of the many dungeons that had been constructed in the cellars of his mansions—*that* would offend no transcendental powers. Courageous it would be, though, for always there would remain a slim chance that the child might escape.

To add to the bravery of spirit that this course of action entailed, however—and he saw at once that this would be essential, for had not the *feng-shui* maiden told him so, though not in as many words?—he himself must be present at the capture. He would break his own rules, risk being observed, and command the hunt himself.

Of course, he would do so in heavy disguise and from a position of relative safety, for as Delicate Blossom had so eloquently pointed out, wisdom recognized a distinction between bravery and foolhardiness . . .

Xi sat in the green light of the armored car at the edge of the buffer zone and listened to the hunt for the feral child. Through short-range encrypted radiophones he could keep track of every move made by his forces. Already a dozen children had been cornered, interrogated (as best they could be), and—naturally—killed. It was for the best, anyway, under the circumstances. Now his men had pinned down the black-skinned child's position: he was holed up in the ruins of an abandoned abattoir, allegedly surrounded by a pack of wild dogs that were obedient to his every barked command. This was surely nonsense, but it confirmed how wisely Xi had balanced courage against reckless exposure.

His ground troops moved in. Over the radio he heard a cacophony of barks and howls, surprised shouts, and spine-chilling screams . . . Perhaps the allegations possessed a semblance of truth after all. Then the rattle of automatic weaponry echoed across the ruins, coming to his ears from outside the car as well as over the phone. An eerie silence followed.

He waited, but there were no answers to his shouted demands for someone to report.

Enraged, he restrained himself from driving the vehicle into the buffer zone and crashing through the ruins. Most likely the vehicle would fall through a flimsy floor into some concealed pit. He tried several times more to raise his troops, calmed himself, and called in a reserve squadron of hardened street fighters, also armed with automatic weapons.

He realized that he had underestimated the dangers of the buffer zone: he should have sent in more men to begin with. On the other hand, it had been excellent strategy to keep something in reserve. Wisdom, again.

His men moved in, this time *very* carefully indeed. What they found was a scene straight out of Hieronymus Bosch. Bloody corpses lay scattered in heaps—dogs, Xi's men, street children. Some had their throats ripped out, some had been blown to pieces.

None was black.

Then they found one of Xi's men, still half alive, buried under a pile of dead dogs, his flesh ripped into bloody tatters by teeth and claws. They sat him up, bound his worst wounds with field bandages, and barraged him with questions.

Xi Ming-Kuo heard these things over the radio, and his fear that perhaps the powers that arranged the universe were abandoning him rose once more to the forefront of his mind. Pin Yi-wu's report must have made its way into other hands, too . . . Heads would roll for this, literally, and the first would be Pin's.

The black child had gone.

He was unharmed, but he had been taken by others who had arrived earlier and lain cunningly in wait. The boy was now in the hands of others—identity unknown.

Xi could guess who. It *had* to be the White Dragon Gang and its warlord Deng Po-zhou.

Knock.

"What the hell do we *do*?" asked Bethan, aghast.

Sir Charles rose to the occasion. He had been waiting for this moment all his life. He just hadn't realized it.

They had all seen the impossible image from the veecam.

"Elementary courtesy," said Sir Charles, "requires that we let our visitor in. Someone open the door, please. Yes, you!"

The person nearest the airlock controls stared at him as if frozen.

"Just do it," Sir Charles said in a voice of infinite tiredness. "Whatever happens can't be worse than carrying on with our normal routine. You saw what's out there: pussy wants in. Someone open the cat flap, okay?"

There was a strained silence as the outer airlock cycled. The hiss of inrushing air masked their hesitant breathing. Then the inner airlock door cracked open. They'd all seen the VV, they all knew what to expect. The reality was still unbelievable.

The wheeler was waiting in the airlock, metallic coat shining with reflections of the room's bright lights. It extended its frill of vanes, rolled forward until the lip of the inner door threatened to impede its progress; then—quietly and without missing a beat—it rose a foot off the ground and continued its forward progress on antigravity instead of wheels. Its body became suffused with multicolored light and slow sparks.

The wheels kept revolving.

The inner door closed behind it with a rasping thud that seemed primitive in comparison. The silence stretched to the breaking point.

Sir Charles realized that every face was looking at *him*. Hope, shock, fear . . . emotions were mixed and running high. Someone had to restore a semblance of normality.

"What are you all gawping at?" He stood up and took a few paces toward the now-stationary wheeler as it hovered enigmatically in midair. "You've all seen a functioning wheeler before!" He took a deep breath. "It's not going to blow up in our faces! It's what we came here to accomplish. *Contact!* It just so happens that"—he found he had to stop and swallow before his voice dried up completely—"the wheelers have made contact with *us,* instead of the other way 'round."

Feeling a complete fool, he took another couple of steps toward the alien machine, pulse racing, lips dry, nerves taut. The wheeler swivelled slightly, so that its "headlights" were facing him. "Er . . ." Sir Charles began. Then, mostly for the benefit of the humans present: "What else can I say? I don't expect you to understand a word, but I hope that somebody will hear and understand that I am trying to communicate." His voice was wavering with emotion. He felt impossibly elated and totally stupid at the same time. VV cameras were recording this, for transmission to Earth's teeming billions. This would be fame indeed, and a vindication of his strategy. Something simple yet melodramatic was in order. Slogan politics.

"In the name of the people of planet Earth: *greetings*!" He felt a complete fool.

The wheeler showed no sign of having heard. It continued to hover a foot off the ground, headlights still staring at Sir Charles's knees, its body glowing.

It seemed to be waiting for something.

11

Secondhome, 1945th Continuity

Within the fibrous body of one of the oldest and largest cities on Secondhome, in a chamber grown specially for the purpose, the Elders of the Conclave assembled and chose to become One.

The ancient blimps floated, bobbing ponderously in the gentle currents of warm air that seeped into the chamber, maintaining it at a pleasant temperature comfortably above the melting point of ammonia.

They were huge, flabby, and very, very old.

Blimps resembled half-inflated weather balloons. At the top was a domed gasbag with pliant, leathery skin. Along the dome's equator was one of two main sensory organs—a ring of six sound-sensitive patches, placed alternately above and below the midline, which together synthesized a three-dimensional image of the blimp's immediate surroundings. A little farther down was the other main sensory organ: six pairs of retractable eyes, embedded in the skin like studs on a leather-upholstered sofa. Twin mouths, stacked one above the other, formed rubber-lipped slits in the thick skin: these mouths were for generating sound, not for feeding. The outside of the creature's lower body consisted of manipulative appendages—six flattish, hollow, rubbery tubes. Each tube ended in a sixfold ring of thinner tubes, whose tips in turn could separate into six wedge-shaped stubs for fine manipulation. At the center of each such fractal trunk was a sphincter through which the creature could ingest solid, liquid, or gaseous food. The sixfold cascade of stomachs, the trifoliate brain, and various other organs hung inside the ring of trunks, below the main gasbag. A short tube for excretion poked out at an angle, oddly off-center.

If the city builders were strange, their cities were stranger. Somewhere in their distant past the blimps had discovered that the component cells of the foam slabs could be persuaded to grow into virtually any shape by applying thin coatings of suitable hormones. Because the resulting structures, like the slabs, were neutrally buoyant, their forms were limited more by imagination than by physics. The main constraint, in fact, was Secondhome's weather. Even at those depths, Secondhome suffered perpetual storms, with intense superbolts of lightning and high winds. The slab material was rigid enough to make permanent structures, yet flexible enough to bend with the wind. Even so, any structure that was long, thin, and insufficiently supported was always in danger of tearing loose, or damaging nearby parts of the city when it flapped in the hurricane-force breezes.

Viewed from above, a city resembled a cross between a panful of scrambled eggs and a coral reef. Close up, it was an intricate mass of tunnels, caves, huge open arenas, buildings that thrust skyward like squat trees with impossibly thick trunks, helical tubes, soft-edged pyramids, domes, bulbous sprouting fans, trailing lines of capsules like strings of fat sausages—all draped with webbing made from a netlike porous membrane, which improved structural integrity. And everywhere there were blisterponds—newly grown, mature, dilapidated, abandoned. These were lenticular voids enclosed by a retractable fibrous sheath. The blimps placed immense value on their blisterponds. They used them to hold stocks of preserved foodstuffs from the planet's denser depths for their long estivations, for temporary shelter, and for comfort.

Every blimp possessed a personal blisterpond and tended it with infinite care. A stock of spare blisterponds was maintained for occasional newcomers, especially juveniles recovering from the attentions of the sculptor-surgeons.

Motile Eye-Threads of the Mesmerizing Curtailment could never enter the Chamber of the Conclave without remembering when it had first been engineered—a radical new fashion in hormonal architecture that involved locating a natural cyst beneath the city's tough upper skin, then painting its damp surfaces with layer upon layer of wilting hormone so that the dying cells peeled off in dry flakes to be sucked up by sweeper symbiauts. The difficult part, achieved after several celebrated failures, was to do this while maintaining a hard shell that could support the stresses of the tissues above, and to equalize pressures with the outside air so that the growing cyst would neither collapse nor burst during one of the city's periodic changes in altitude.

Broken Tendril of the Imagined Obliquity had won a prize for her work, he recalled. Tragically, Tendril had died in a construction accident—a mere fifteen million years ago, he still remembered it clearly—when an overambitious complex of raked tower-pools collapsed under an accumulation of methane snow in a sudden cyclonic coldstorm. It had been Tendril's own fault—she should have known better than to permit her city to approach so close to the Whirl—but the views of spinning vortex clouds were spectacular in those regions, and Tendril always had a soft spot for visual beauty . . .

As he remembered her, so did the other Elders of the Conclave; and when their collective mind fragmented once more into mere individuality, they would remember remembering her. Which is different from true memory, of course.

The Conclave met to a schedule that had run unchanged, save by dire emergency, for thirty million years. It was not exactly a schedule, because its most important feature was the state of estivation of its pool of "chairmen." No chair, no

men, but the description is apt, for back in the lost evolutionary fog of Deep Time, a species of proto-blimp on the lost
planet now referred to as Firsthome inadvertently evolved the
committee. They developed a kind of hive mentality in which
each member retained a degree of individuality, yet decisions
could be arrived at collectively through a process of bureaubonding, of which the individuals were not consciously
aware. This quasi-telepathic ability was a by-product of the
quantum chromodynamics of their mental processes: they
could choose to broadcast their thoughts as a spray of squark
wavepackets. The process was voluntary: a blimp's mind
could not be read unless it chose to make its thoughts available. The effect was also very short range, because nonlin-
earities quickly dispersed the wavepackets.

   Following tradition, Eye-Threads—for so he was colloquially known when no other with the same somatonymic
was present—opened the proceedings by declaiming aloud,
in speech mode, the Standing Agenda. The process was agonizingly slow, for there was much business to transact; it was
also unnecessary, since every Elder could recite the Standing
Agenda by heart. But they all loved its ponderous, rolling
tones, and to them it was pure poetry, not agony.

   A typical Conclave lasted for two hundred and seventy
Secondhome days—roughly three and a half terrestrial
months. To individual blimps this was the merest instant, but
the group mind could make most decisions surprisingly
rapidly. While the members of the Conclave were bureaubonded, all could see how well judged the traditional Period of Conclave was. When once more separated, however,
many of them deplored the shortness of the timetable and
their consequent inability to consider any matter in depth.
They could remember being involved in making decisions,
and even what many of those decisions were, but they could
seldom reconstruct the reasoning behind the decisions once
the bureaubond had been dissolved. It could be very frustrat-
ing at times, knowing that you had approved a collective de-

cision that now seemed ridiculous, but that was one of the prices you had to pay to be an Elder.

You got used to it.

The blimps were not the only alien creatures on Secondhome. They had brought many other organisms with them from Firsthome; there were remnants of Secondhome's indigenous creatures; above all, there were creatures of a very different kind, which had evolved as a symbiotic by-product of the blimp ecology. At an early stage of the blimps' evolution on Firsthome, their hydrogen had been obtained through a biological form of electrolysis, released from enclosed droplets of mineral-bearing fluid. This electrolytic action also deposited layers of unwanted metals. At first these metals had merely been ejected as waste, but as the aggregated cells became ever more complex, a new solution to the problem of waste disposal emerged—the coevolution of a parallel ecology of metallic biomachines. These "symbiauts" had no genetic material of their own, but increasingly large tracts of the blimps' genome became devoted to the processes of offcasting: the production of useful symbiauts. The symbiauts paid their evolutionary dues, and incidentally kept themselves viable, by performing increasingly complex tasks that enhanced the lives of the blimps. At first they provided new and more efficient ways to store energy, but they quickly diversified into locomotion, weaponry, defense, camouflage, construction, food processing, communication, surface and interplanetary transport—even entertainment. Metal ceased to be waste and became a vital resource.

One of the big problems about settling on Secondhome had been that its atmosphere contained only tiny proportions of metal atoms, but it was a big atmosphere and the metals were concentrated and recycled by biological action. There were significant quantities of germanium, essential for symbiaut memory banks, in the form of gaseous germane—germanium tetrahydride. Ions of sodium, potassium, and magnesium diffused into the planet's upper atmosphere from

the plasma torus that joined it to Fivemoon. The blimps had also brought stockpiles of metal from Firsthome. Some was banked deep inside the cities, but the bulk was deposited in orbit around the gas giant. Interplanetary transpauts could take miner symbiauts out there to retrieve it, as necessary.

Because the slabs were flat on top, back on Firsthome before the blimps had invented the art of hormone-crafting and lived in crude city-burrows, most symbiauts had evolved wheels. Now, many still retained them, and at every level of the city there were networks of roadlike wheelways. Although the symbiauts had eventually evolved antigravity, wheeled motion required less effort and had become the default.

Eye-Threads's sonorous voice echoed around the chamber. It was shaped like a flattened ovoid, and the blimps entered it through the roof, by way of an elaborately decorated driftshaft. There was a separate antigravity dropshaft for the attendant symbiauts, to save them the effort of using their own gravipulsors. It was decorated in the grand style, simulated Late Obsessive from the 811th Continuity, so that the predominant element was the demi-conoid. To earthly eyes the effect would have appeared akin to an inside out wedding cake built from a hundred hues of mud. Toward one end of the ovoid there was a sunken dais, shaped like an irregular heptagon with a flat rim surrounding a shallow depression. Here the Elders had gathered, according to tradition, while ever-busy symbiauts thronged the rim, coming and going along a network of suspended platforms linked by elevauts. The attendants provided grooming, food and drink, mild narcotic stimuli, and personal entertainments; they brought and accepted messages, and reminded the Elders of the Nine Thousand Forms of Protocol and the Accepted Order of Proceedings. A battery of memauts—specialized symbiauts which possessed huge quantities of microcircuit memory—recorded all deliberations and decisions, for symbiauts were

sensitive to the same squark radiation as the blimps themselves.

If a city died—from lack of food, or disease, or any other cause—its inhabitants would have to locate an immature cityling and transfer to it—a huge effort that resulted in cramped quarters for many generations. Blimps took good care of their cities. Secondhome boasted nearly a million of them, and each of them had been grown on a base of neutrally buoyant living foam, made from living bubbles a few microns across—biological cells with their own genetics and their own specialist organelles. Prominent among the latter were levispheres, tiny membrane-walled bubbles of almost pure gaseous hydrogen which provided lift in the denser hydrogen-helium mixture of the planet's troposphere—one part helium to five parts hydrogen, roughly twice as dense as hydrogen alone. The cells' production of levispheres was sensitive to pressure differences, and a feedback mechanism had evolved that maintained neutral buoyancy.

The city's metabolism warmed the gas, which generated additional lift as it expanded to equalize pressures. A city was a hybrid, part hydrogen balloon, part hot-air balloon. Huge cooling-vanes trailed beneath the city like a keel, radiating surplus heat, fed by circulating coolant that flowed through a network of veins and arteries, pumped by thousands of local heartlike organs. The foam was a vast colony-creature, which had grown over the millennia until it formed an irregular slab a hundred miles long, ten miles wide, and between one and five miles thick. The slab's upper surface, unadorned, would have been flat. Instead, it had been decorated with the superstructure of the city, coaxed from the firm foundation by the chemical attentions of countless generations of blimps. Tunnels and shafts penetrated deep into the city's living tissues, forming a labyrinth of cavernous chambers.

The city's lower surface was a seemingly endless jungle of suspended tendrils surrounding the cooling-vanes, like the

myriad tentacles of a Portuguese man-o'-war. Near the edges of the foam slab the tendrils spread sideways to form a monstrous fringemass, which rippled unpredictably in the turbulent Secondhome weather. Farther in, the tendrils were closer to the vertical—becoming longer as their roots neared the slab's central vanes, where its component cells were oldest. Here many tendrils had grown to a length of more than fifty miles. Like the rest of the slab, they were neutrally buoyant, and they had yet to reach their full length.

Around the city swarmed a fine haze of aeroplankton, trillions upon trillions of airborne microorganisms. Each of the slab's tendrils was a specialist trap, evolved to lure specific categories of aeroplankton into more or less elaborate forms of suicide. Some tendrils were sticky. Some fired tiny harpoons toward any source of pheromones to which they were sensitive, and reeled in their catch. Some sucked the heavy atmosphere through cavernous baleenlike filters, while tiny scuttlepods clambered over the fibrous drapery and scraped the catch into irised pouches. In return, a ring of enlarged pores around the lips of the pouches oozed an energy-rich sludge, at which the scuttlepods occasionally licked. Other tendrils generated focused pulses of ultrasound, spread chemical lures, filled the surrounding air with tiny semi-autonomous homing webs, or merely waited for prey to blunder into sprung traps.

Once they had secured their prey, however, nearly all of the tendrils treated it in the same manner. First they dissolved its membranes, releasing the embedded levispheres. Most of these escaped into the atmosphere, where they were degraded by heat and pressure, recycling their hydrogen. The rest were used to fine-tune the local neutral buoyancy. The nutrients that had been released when the membranes dissolved were transported through a fractal tree of molecular nanotubes, dragged upward by stepper viruses which climbed the nanotubes like a mountaineer in a rock chimney. As the viruses climbed higher, the trickle of rising nutrients became a torrent, then a flood, pouring into clusters of slimy spherical sacs that festooned the slab's underside, dangling between the swelling roots of the suspended tendrils. Here the stepper viruses were released, falling through Secondhome's atmosphere in an infinitely slow drizzle of genetic add-ons, to reinfect any tendrils that they chanced to encounter.

The blimps that lived on the slab's upper surface were seldom conscious of the aeroplanktonic Armageddon that went on just below them, as it had done every day for a third of a billion years. Mostly they just accepted one of its minor side effects, the creation of enormous floating platforms: the bedrock, so to speak, upon which their civilization was founded. Only when a city slab became sick were the veterinary squadrons and air gardeners activated, to descend into the hidden depths and effect whatever cures were necessary.

The blimps had evolved in a hydrogen ecology. They, like many lesser creatures of their world, were balloons: they, alone, were thinking balloons. Some balloonist organisms, like the slab, were made from microscopic levisphere-rich cells. Others had larger hydrogen-filled organs, fulfilling much the same function as a terrestrial fish's swim bladder— to maintain neutral buoyancy. Most also used the hot-air principle to enhance their buoyancy; many employed that alone. The city builders and their ilk did not so much fly as swim in the surging Secondhome air.

A typical city was home to about twenty million blimps. At any given time, though, only five percent would be active, while the others estivated. Blimp institutions had evolved to maintain a kind of continuity in a society where key individuals could suddenly disappear without warning and most encounters were with total strangers.

For 330 million years, the city slabs had circulated beneath the veiling clouds of Secondhome's striped envelope. Some of the senior blimps still remembered the Exodus—the enforced years of migration and colonization. A select few remembered what had gone before, and devoted their interminable lives to ensuring its continuation in their new home. Some of the junior blimps, however, had a different view of the Exodus, and a very different agenda.

Snowstrike. *The very word triggered an atavistic fear in the blimps.*

Snowstrike had devastated Firsthome, until symbiaut evolution had led the blimps to the secret physics that made it possible to manipulate gravity. Then snowstrike had indirectly caused the abandonment of Firsthome, because of their failure to appreciate the hidden dangers of the technology that their discovery had unleashed.

On Eightmoon, the most distant of Secondhome's four Inner Moons, a sentinel symbiaut making routine observations noticed a significant deviation in the Outer Halo, far beyond the most remote of the Fartheroutworlds.

Soon the diagnosis became unavoidable.

Snowstone.

Time meant nothing to the symbiauts. They observed the snowstone's tedious, erratic detachment from its myriad companions. They extrapolated its long fall toward the sun, computed collision probabilities, and weighed possible actions against their consequences.

Probabilities crystallized into certainties. Contingencies collapsed into compulsions. The decision, once made, was acted upon immediately. In colossal caverns hewn beneath the crusts of the Inner Moons, squads of symbiauts swarmed over dormant Diversion Engines, awakening them from their long slumber. Power flowed once more into the massive metal rotors whose high-speed gyrations, coupled with esoteric physics, shaped the contours of quantum-antigravity repulsion fields. Projectors were energized and aligned with the appropriate anti-geodesics, generating potent repulsion-beams. The beams reconfigured the moons' orbits to receive the incoming snowstone, inexorably pulling it into a precise embrace before hurling it violently away from the great gas giant. Acting under an ancient compulsion, they chose a trajectory that neither terminated in the system's central star nor risked a subsequent repeat encounter.

The snowstone's crust melted in the heat of the sun and began to boil. A vast plume jetted outward on the solar wind.

The chloride oceans of Poisonblue beckoned, a tempting target.

Deep beneath Secondhome's belted atmosphere, those of the Elders that were not estivating received news of the snowstone's discovery, anticipated impact, successful deflection, and explosive end. Congratulating themselves on their foresight, they resumed their interminable cycles of politics, reproduction, and estivation.

Poisonblue briefly became an ominous gray. Splashes of chloride jetted into space, where they froze. For thousands of years Poisonblue sported a ring of ice. After this short time, the ice began to disperse—falling onto the planet's smaller companion, plunging into the local star, drifting out to Secondhome and beyond.

On Secondhome, only the symbiauts noticed. They judged that the inbound fragments of chloride ice, poisonous though they might be, posed no threat. They were well below the threshold for action.

The blimps of Secondhome were deep into Conclave.

"Agendum 3961," the secretary-symbiaut informed them, using sound-wave communication to keep free the quantum-chromodynamic squark band that the group mind modulated to perform its collective telepathy. "Plans for a modified citizens' reversion-pool on Volatile Contours of the Pluvious Inundation. The secretary will commence by reviewing the relevant protocols and summarizing the results of a search for the indicative precedents . . ." Eventually the plan was referred to one of the Conclave's standing focus groups for further clarification, with a recommenda-

tion that the proposers be required to reconsider the dispo-
sition of secondary winding-nests . . .

"Agendum 3963: report of the Data Retention Agency on
antisocial elements . . ." The symbiaut droned on inter-
minably, giving comparative statistics for various classes of
petty crime and minor infringements of the voluntary codes
of behavior. The Conclave became collectively aware that
over the previous hundred thousand years there had been a
slow upward trend in the use of threatening gestures in the
negotiation of temporary guarantees of passage, that the
problem of untended dysfunctional symbiauts had virtually
disappeared on those cities that had adopted the controversial
Resolution of Total Offcast Discipline, and that an outbreak
of hormone graffiti on Simmering Wells of the Amusing In-
frequency had been traced to a deranged Charming Construction Entity.

"There has been a marked increase in incidents of unauthorized intercity free-floating," the symbiaut reported, in the
same monotonous tone as everything else that it had said, but
the Conclave immediately acquired an aura of heightened excitement and concern. The activity referred to, known colloquially as "skydiving," was not merely antisocial, it was a
serious political threat. The skydivers were a symbol of rejected authority, a subversive and utterly deplorable association of misfits. Their political agenda was sweeping,
iconoclastic, and dangerous.

Nothing rouses a slow-moving, slow-thinking entity as effectively as the perception of a potential threat to their person.

And to their power.

Brief thought-ensembles squarked from mind to mind.

<<All of those here present know full well the socially un-
desirable side effects of the disgusting habit of intercity free-
floa—>> began Venerable Mumblings of the Interminable
Prevarication, but he was immediately interrupted by Quick
Decisions of the Unconsidered Implication, whose patience
was less robust than that of most of his fellows.

<<Mumblings has an excellent point, which is well taken by us all, and we can move at once to a remedy. I propose—>>

<<I believe that the matter will turn out to be more subtle than Decisions expects,>> Mumblings broadcast. <<A proposal would be premature.>>

<<As I was about to point out, that is not the prob—>>

<<I am sure that we all remember the destruction of Twin Cities of the Enticing Gloom,>> squarked Intuitive Mediator of the Bland Outlook. <<The dangers that skydiving poses for innocent byfloaters could hardly be more evident!>>

<<That may be so,>> put in an especially short and broad blimp rejoicing in the appellation of Bulbous Purveyor of the Implausible Objection. <<However, it was arguably a freak accident. No one could have predicted that a public skydiving festival would attract a pod of migrating snarewings at precisely the moment they were entering into an oxygen frenzy . . . The conflagration was regrettable, but in no way predictable.>>

<<Prediction,>> said Eye-Threads, <<is unnecessary when the precedents are plain. In any case, even a fool could predict *that* such an event might happen. The only difficulty was to predict *when* and *where* . . . Which is why we must use the precedents to guide our judgment.>>

<<Xxxx!>> Purveyor assented, with uncharacteristic humor. <<But since even so it remains unclear that prohibiting skydiving would prevent a recurrence, it is important to select the appropriate precedents.>>

Eye-Threads snorted in affront. <<Precedent is *never* inappropriate, Purveyor! The most underspecialized juvenile wallowing in the Thin Winds knows that!>>

<<Agreed,>> said Mediator. <<But precedent may sometimes not be apposite, Eye-Threads. Purveyor, do I detect *support* for unauthorized intercity free-floating? Have you not taken into consideration the skydivers' revolutionary agenda? Do you not recall that their terrorist activities have

more than once spread to the Diversion Engines on the Inner Moons, laying Secondhome wide open to snowstrike? Have you forgotten their off-casting of rogue symbiauts, programmed for sabotage?>>

Purveyor, whose pedantry often got the better of common sense, backed off rapidly. Who could forget the multiple impacts of snowstone a mere few centuries ago? Who could forget the panic as thousands of threatened cities were forced to change course, flailing their way awkwardly to safer latitudes? And there had been other such occasions, horrendous breaches of security. <<Not at all!>> Purveyor clarified. <<My point was one of logic, not politics! Of course there is no question that *politically* the cult of the skydivers poses a substantial threat! I have always held this to be obvious!>>

<<We should increase the level of punishment,>> said Irascible Thug of the Violent Demeanor.

<<Ritual deflation, my dear Thug, is already such an atrocious penalty that any deterrent effect must already be operating,>> Mediator replied. Thug was *so* simple-minded . . . always the enforcer. The situation demanded subtlety. <<What is required is prevention, not punishment. Even the most horrific tortures meted out on the perpetrators would not have brought Twin Cities of the Enticing Gloom back to life. Or its inhabitants.>>

<<Yes, but—>> began Thug, but before she could launch into one of her preprepared squeeches on the Need for Firm Tentacling to Instill Proper Respect for the Social Order in the Wayward Young, she was interrupted by the agitated arrival of a secretary-symbiaut, vanes aquiver, its decorative wheels spinning uselessly as it hovered a foot above the marbled shell of the chamber's dished floor. The symbiaut was so flustered that they broke protocol and allowed it to join the group mentality without completing the necessary authorization procedures. To the Conclave it felt like being in a swimming pool and having a large rock splash among you. Ripples of mental agitation bounced around the collective mind, set-

tling down mainly because of the damping effect of Venerable Mumblings of the Interminable Prevarication.

<<There has been a procedural error!>> the symbiaut blurted out at a squark frequency close to hysteria.

<<The Conclave of the Elders is deliberating a matter of considerable import!>> Eye-Threads warned the overexcited symbiautic machine.

<<Respected Multiplicity,>> the symbiaut emitted at a calmer frequency, <<an agendum item has been omitted!>>

The shock registered on the faces of the Elders. How could they all have failed to notice such an obvious slip? Why had the secretariaut not been sufficiently alert to the breach of procedures?

Mediator was the first to understand what now had to be done. They must go through a complex process in which the item under discussion was suspended *sine die*, but the record of deliberations to date was permitted to stand. Next, a motion to revert to the omitted item 3962 would have to be passed—it would be wise to make it clear to Mumblings that a procedural filibuster would not be tolerated, or they might still be in Conclave when Secondstar became a red giant. Then item 3962 must be discussed, and the results minuted. Finally, another motion must be passed to ratify the existing discussion of item 3963, amended to permit the debate to continue.

This would take a while.

The blimps of Secondhome never looked beyond the gas giant's swirling, striped atmosphere. That was a menial task fit only for symbiauts. But even the symbiauts did not know that the diverted snowstone that had been disposed of in the inimical atmosphere of Poisonblue had not only made an impact on the planet, it had made an impact on the evolution of its indigenous life-forms.

Indeed, the symbiauts were not at that time aware that there were any indigenous life-forms. Oxygen was intensely

*corrosive to most known metals. Organic molecules would
burst into spontaneous flame in an oxygenated chamber.*

Life *on an* oxygen *world? Inconceivable.*

*Yet as Poisonblue's world-girdling clouds finally began to
thin, and the warm sunlight once more built radiant shafts
from sky to ground, tiny shrewlike animals with long, bony
fingers for picking grubs out of rotten trees emerged, blinking, into a new kind of world. A world where the great predatory lizards had vanished forever, leaving only petrified
bones.*

*Their ears were sharp, for they had hunted by night for a
hundred million years. Their eyes were large, adapted to the
darkness; in daylight, they worked even better. Lacking competitors, the shrews and their descendants would take over
most of the planet. Lacking predators, they would evolve their
own.*

*One day their distant descendants would have nightmares
of bogeymen, an atavistic throwback to the thrall of the giant
lizards.*

*One day their descendants would interpret their night-
mares and invent gods to explain their world.*

*One day they would name wandering specks in the night
sky after their gods.*

*And one day, they would travel to one of those specks, land
on one of its satellites, and dig up symbiauts that had been
buried as punishment for terrible crimes.*

<< . . . a small discrepancy,>> the secretary-symbiaut ad-
mitted. It had been hoping that the Conclave would not notice
the missing items on the inventory, but of course Mumblings
had insisted on recomputing all of the figures.

<<Has the discrepancy been accounted for?>> asked Eye-
Threads.

<<Yes. A burial ground was . . . disturbed. A number of
criminal symbiauts, encysted in the ice of Eightmoon for seriously antisocial activities, have been . . . they have . . .>>

<<Out with it!>> yelled Decisions. <<They have *what*?>>
<<They have emerged, Respected Elder.>>

<<*Emerged?* The criminals were immersed in molten ice,
which was then allowed to solidify around them! They
should have been utterly immobile! Wheels will roll for
this!>>

The frightened secretary hastened to ingratiate itself.
<<More precisely, Respected Multiplicity, they have been . . .
disinterred.>>

Thug bobbed up and down in agitation. <<Where there
has been disinterment, there must perforce be a disinterer . . .
who shall be punished to the utmost degree permitted by the
law!>> Other eyes focused narrowly on the now-terrified
symbiaut. <<Which among us perpetrated this foul deed?>>

<<Respected Elder, it was not a blimp. Nor,>> the ma-
chine quickly added, <<was it a symbiaut.>>

Puzzlement flew about the Chamber like a flurry of ammonia. *Not a blimp, not a symbiaut . . . then what?* The secretary picked up the collective sense of bafflement and
ventured an apologetic explanation.

<<It was the entities from Poisonblue,>> the symbiaut ex-
plained.

Then it explained it again.

At the fifth attempt, Purveyor began to understand that
there had been a serious flaw in their instructions to the
Watchers, and that an error in their entire philosophy had
gone unrecognized for more than three hundred million
years.

Fortunately, the mistake had made no serious difference
until a few brief centuries ago.

The symbiaut Watchers were wheelers of various kinds,
based on Secondhome's four Inner Moons—which orbited
outside the four Innermost Moons, and inside the four Outer
Moons and the four Outermost Moons—and they were in
charge of the machinery that diverted any incoming comets

and asteroids that exceeded generous safety margins. The Watchers' instructions had been simple and concise. *If an incoming body represents a serious impact threat that might damage Secondhome's ecology, divert it elsewhere. Otherwise, ignore it. To avoid a repetition of the incident, arrange for it to collide with one of the numerous uninhabitable bodies of the planetary system.* That meant all moons, save those of Secondhome; the inner planets, as far as Reddust; the outer planets from Manyrings onward. In short, everything except the Pulverization Zone, which was too unstable, and the Secondhome system itself.

Never redirect them into the star. This was the prime imperative. That mistake had cost them Firsthome.

But now, it seemed, their assumption that only the system's gas giants were capable of supporting life—and that only Secondhome actually *did*—had been proved wrong. It seemed that there existed some exotic life-form that could tolerate—or more probably was in some manner immune to—*oxygen*! That could live on a world of such terrible heat that its surface bore large deposits of liquid ice! That had been the flaw in their philosophy.

Why had nothing been reported? That was the second mistake. *Unless the body poses a serious impact danger and an ecological threat, ignore it.*

Some two hundred years earlier, the Watchers had observed tiny bodies being spat out from Poisonblue. At first these errant bodies were assumed to be asteroids, but they maneuvered in far too complex and organized a way. Then they were thought to be some diminutive alien relative of the majestic magnetotori that had been parked for safekeeping in Secondstar's photosphere, until it became clear that they propelled themselves using nonelectromagnetic reaction mass.

Over a century, these strange interlopers colonized Poisonblue's companion Ruggedrock, made a temporary assault on Reddust, and spread themselves over assorted rocklets in the Pulverization Zone. The wheelers observed them, recorded their every move, and when the interlopers descended onto one of the Inner Moons the wheelers even got a close look at their weird bifurcated form. Neither balloons—unworkable in the nonexistent atmosphere of the Inner Moons—nor wheels, but clumsy, stiff, hinged trunks, with cumbersome pads on their ends for balance.

All this the wheelers noted with interest. But the small bodies in which the interlopers traveled posed no danger to Secondhome, for even if they were to impact upon it they would burn up in a trice, making not the tiniest ripple. And so, following their clear and simple instructions, the Watchers had kept this particular item of intelligence to themselves.

Obey the regulations. Take no action.

All this changed, though, when one such body made a short visit and its passengers disinterred more than a hundred symbiautic criminals, who had been iced as punishment for taking part in a skydiver attack on the Diversion Engines—worse, one that had temporarily succeeded. Secondhome had been *hit* by a comet because of their treason. After that, it was only a matter of time before the rogues' de-icing and disappearance was transmitted to Secondhome as part of the routine triennial audit. How else to justify their absence? And while the bureaucratic wheels of blimp society grind exceedingly slow, they also grind exceeding fine. Unusually rapidly, half a Secondhome year later, the disinterment had quite properly been brought to the Elders' attention. Its implication had been grasped almost immediately.

The question that vexed them now was: *what to do about it?*

Eventually they agreed to refer the whole thing to a subcommittee.

12

Shaanxi Province, 2213

Once more, Moses found himself lying flat on his back. His shoulder hurt, but his pride hurt more.

"What did I tell you, stupid child?" the instructor screamed at him. The instructor was nine years old, and female, but Moses had learned long ago to treat her like an adult. Sometimes she taught him to speak, read, and write, and sometimes she taught him to survive.

"Respected One, you told me to be quicker coming out of the dragon stance when the attack came from my left side," he replied in broken and not terribly grammatical Mandarin.

"And did you carry out my instructions, Mo-Shi?"

Moses grimaced and shook his head. "I remembered them too late, Respected One."

Silent Snowflake, who had been entrusted with the task of educating Moses during the year that must elapse before his return to Ecotopia could safely be arranged, made no attempt to disguise her disgust and reminded him in no uncertain terms that the art of *gongfu* was not something that one attempted to *remember*. "Your response must flow inevitably from the actions of your opponent, as fruit follows blossom on a healthy tree," she pointed out. "Your stance was stranded in the dead zone between frog and snake. You must pay more attention and practice harder." It had been the first time she had been asked to teach martial arts to a seven-year-old, and a barbarian at that, but she did not question the motives of her mother, Jeweled Jade, and her father, Deng Po-zhou. The boy had responded well: she was proud of him. And today her father had honored her beyond measure by being present at Mo-Shi's training.

It was so utterly different from the anarchy of the buffer zone, the feral children, and Moses' dog pack. Children can be astonishingly resilient—at least on the surface—especially the young ones. As he began to regain confidence and put the horror of his past behind him, Moses fell in love with his new family. His father, Deng, was stern but fair, Snowflake was simply wonderful, and Jeweled Jade made sure that the servants catered to his every whim.

The decision had been impulsive, but Deng had learned to trust his impulses. He had been intrigued by the persistent rumors of the black street child who had become the leader of a pack of wild dogs, and he had sensed in the young barbarian an unusual quality that he might turn to advantage at some future time. On being informed that his rival Xi Ming-Kuo was intending to capture the boy, he had acted without hesitation to spirit the child away and place him in his own household. Here Deng could keep the child safe from prying eyes, for a time; observe him, and have him suitably educated. In particular, he ordered the boy to be trained in the ancient art of *gongfu* as an aid to his future survival. All of his children were *gongfu* adepts, for the same reason.

Deng had plans for Mo-Shi. The White Dragon Gang dealt in many things, but the core of their operation was drugs. It was forbidden to import barbarian drugs—it was forbidden to have any contact with barbarians whatsoever. But there was demand for such drugs, and money to match it. Cinoxacin for urinary tract infections, famiclovir for *Herpes zoster*, dextromoramide for severe pain . . . above all, novoviagralin for impotence. The White Dragon Gang dealt in barbarian medicines, and unlike most traditional medicines, these often *worked*. Moses could become a very useful conduit to Eco-topia. Deng knew that the child could not be kept in China for long—it would be too dangerous. Dangerous for the boy, for Deng's family, for the White Dragon Gang. One year, and one only—that would be enough to permit the extensive changes to barbarian records that must be made before it was safe for Mo-Shi to return. But not to freedom . . . The initial destination that Deng envisaged for the child was to be geo-graphically in Ecotopia, but outside the mainstream of bar-barian culture. It must be somewhere that Xi Ming-Kuo would never be able to track down, and totally insulated from the prying eyes of the eXtraNet—because, forbidden as Xconnections were in Free China, Xi would have many. Cer-tainly Deng did. Then, when sufficient time had passed, Mo-Shi could be unleashed upon Ecotopia proper.

It had given the warlord of the White Dragon Gang tremendous intellectual pleasure to devise a solution to this difficult conundrum. There must be no way for any barbarian to trace the child's real origins, either, so Deng's small team of illicit computer hackers had to create an entire fake back-ground for the boy. There was no safe way to erase his real background, but it would be simple to modify the police records so that "missing, presumed dead" became merely "dead." Once equipped with a new, fully substantiated iden-tity, Moses could be removed from China, where his presence was always a potential danger, and taken to a place where he could grow to manhood without his past being traced back to Free China, let alone the White Dragon Gang. And after that? The warlord had no specific plan yet. He just sensed that Mo-Shi held the key to the destruction of Xi Ming-Kuo. In a way, it was obvious: their two paths of destiny were opposed at every turn. Mo-Shi was a powerful piece in a game of chess, and Deng intended to make sure that he remained on the board.

It did, of course, mean that the boy would have a very pe-culiar, fragmented upbringing—a succession of more or less willing foster parents from at least two distinct cultures—but he would simply have to cope with this. He was young enough that by the time he reached adolescence he would remember only those things that he was being trained to remember . . .

Silent Snowflake decided Moses was ready for a rather different lesson. She knew that Deng, waiting silently, would approve. "All right, Mo-Shi. You have worked hard. Let us practice something you have already mastered . . . I know! The ankle throw. But first we will refresh ourselves."

Carefully, she poured out two cups of green tea. Moses, thirsty from his exertions, emptied his in a single gulp; Silent Snowflake sipped daintily at her own and set it to one side. Deng watched attentively—this would be a defining moment.

"Now, Mo-Shi: you know what you have to do!" Moses advanced warily. He was good at this one. He paused, feinted, and then darted toward her feet.

Silent Snowflake threw her tea in his face.

Moses crashed to the floor. He sat up, close to tears, tea soaking the front of his robe. Nothing like this had ever happened before. "That's not *fair*," he shouted. "You *cheated*!" It was humiliating, especially in front of his . . . father.

Silent Snowflake gave the boy a very serious, though kindly, look. "Mo-Shi: learn this lesson well, for it is the most important that I shall ever teach you. Survival is not a game, it is war. There are no rules. But there is *technique*. Remember this: *any context conceals within it the means of advancing one's own desires*. Use such means without inhibition."

Moses puzzled over the long words for hours. When he worked out what she'd meant, something else puzzled him.

Why hadn't she thrown the *cup*?

Outside Europa Base, the noon eclipse was once more bathing the corrugated terrain in the suffuse salmon pink of jovelight, refracted through the outer layers of Jupiter's atmosphere. The gas giant was an eerie orb of midnight black,

ringed with orange fire. The magnificent spectacle recurred
every three and a half days.

The task force personnel seldom bothered to watch the
eclipse anymore, not even through the base's instruments—
let alone to suit up and go outside into the −190°C vacuum,
as they had so often done in the early days.

They'd seen it all before.

Dust.

Heat.

A year had passed, all preparations had been made . . .
Deng Po-zhou had known that he could prevaricate no further. He had also known that Silent Snowflake would be distressed. *So be it.*

Animal smells. Goats, mostly. Some cattle. Innumerable
scruffy, uncared-for dogs.

Food, cooking over open fires. Wood smoke. Latrines.

A trail of army ants.

Huts—woven more than built. Huts of reeds, huts of grass,
huts assembled from palm leaves . . .

Huts.

Moses had never seen a hut. He'd seen more animals than
most people on the planet, but he'd never seen a hut.

He'd never seen a goat, either. But there were more goats
than huts. More goats than people. The Village was awash
with goats. They were its lifeblood, its purpose, its currency . . .

It was a new world, and Moses understood absolutely
nothing about it. Though he understood perfectly that he
would never see Silent Snowflake or Jeweled Jade again.
Which is why he was bawling his eyes out when the wagon
passed between the twin columns of the Village gate.

Another child? X'nambawa tried to conceal his annoyance. It was difficult enough to play the role of father to a
family of ten thousand. Harder still when he *knew*—as his
family did not—that somewhere beyond the golden smear of

the horizon was a world that made theirs seem no more than a pinprick on the hide of a rhinoceros. The *real* world, in which their entire universe, the Village, counted for less than nothing.

Someone had to be a conduit.

Someone had to know the Truth.

Someone had to know why the outside world not only permitted the Village to exist, but insisted upon it. For the Village was an anachronism, and it existed for a very specific purpose.

It was a warning.

This, the Village said, is what you would be without the extelligence that makes you human. If you were severed from the Xnet, cut off from the sum total of human knowledge, deprived of the understanding of a thousand prior generations—you would be nothing more than clever animals. Able to learn tricks, but unable to devise the tricks to begin with. Apes with attitude.

Primitive, tribal . . . Emotionally and culturally advanced—intellectually, nowhere. Your highest technology, the clay cooking pot. Your highest aspiration—godhood.

To a Chinese warlord with a tentative long-term plan and a pressing short-term problem, it was the ideal place to bury the problem where it would cause him the least trouble. And so, into this unsustainable mix of hope and innate talent, came Moses Odingo, trussed like a turkey, half buried beneath sacks of planting seed.

The boy awoke to the smell of a bonfire. He opened his eyes . . . and nothing was as it should be. In place of the gilded walls of Deng's mansion, there were walls of interlaced rushes. In place of the ancient vases and jade sculptures, there was a crude wooden carving of a giraffe. The floor was not smooth, polished planks of cedarwood, but dried mud. The voices spoke a half-remembered barbarian tongue, quite unlike the mellifluous tones of high Mandarin.

And instead of the songs of the nightingale, he heard the mournful honking of ducks on a lake.

He had been told, warned . . . reasons had been explained . . . it didn't make the reality any less distressing.

Everything was *wrong*. Yet, on some deep intuitive level, he also knew that it was his life from now on. And so he sniveled, reserving his weeping for an indefinitely postponed future.

"Squawks? They communicate in *squawks*?"

After more than a year's fruitless study of the wheeler visitor, Europa Base had finally made a breakthrough. Not that it helped.

"No, Sir Charles: *squarks*. And they communicate *with* them." You didn't have to be empathic to read the look on Sir Charles's face. "A squark is a supersymmetric twin particle of an ordinary quark. As predicted by Witten's superstring *M*-theory at the turn of the millennium."

Now Charles understood, and became exasperated. "*Why the hell did nobody tell me this before?*"

"Because, Sir Charles, nobody had any reason to anticipate it." Wallace Halberstam, a wiry man with thick black eyebrows and short gray hair, was in charge of the Jovian Task Force's Logistics Division—in effect making him second-in-command—but his degree had been in the philosophy of reductionist physics. Finding his speciality unexpectedly useful, he was taking full advantage of his fifteen minutes of fame, and he expanded on his theme. "You see, nobody even knew that squarks existed. Superstrings enjoyed a brief vogue about two centuries ago. Mathematicians loved them for their elegance and their connections with esoteric questions in topology; physicists were intrigued by them until they found that they couldn't do any of the theoretical calculations needed to test them against reality. They went out of fashion not because they were wrong, but because the theory was too intractable for anyone even to begin finding out what it predicted."

Charles found this explanation less than enlightening. "So what's changed all of a sudden?"

Halberstam gave a mirthless chuckle. "What do you think? *Wheelers.*" He pushed a sheet of paper across the desk, trying not to launch it into the air. He still hadn't fully adjusted to Europa's low gravity.

Sir Charles grabbed it before it could become airborne.

It bore a pattern of white dots of various sizes on a navy blue background. Jagged red and green streaks ran diagonally across the page, and he recognized them as transmission errors—lost data. The image had been produced in a hurry; no doubt a tidied-up version was being processed at that very moment.

"What the—devil is this, Wally?"

Halberstam beamed with pride. "Charles, this could be the big breakthrough!"

Subordinates could sometimes be extraordinarily obtuse. "Wally, what I meant was—what's this an image *of?*"

"You don't—no, you wouldn't . . . Um . . . A team at the Magnetic Resonance Labs in Paris took this image from Trabant—the wheeler that's really corroded and ancient and doesn't respond to laser light like the rest. Confound that Odingo woman—gave us all the . . . crap, kept the good stuff for herself! Bloody lawyers prattling on about rights . . . but you know how I feel about liberals. As you know, Trabant is considered more expendable than our other wheelers, though this particular observation is nondestructive—"

"Wally—just give me the bottom line, okay?"

"Right. Uh . . . the bottom line is that this is an atomic structure found in regions of germanium alloy behind the wheeler's 'headlights.' The structure seems to be a squark generator, and very probably a squark receiver, too, though they haven't yet obtained permission to test one of the newer wheelers to make sure. It turns out that wheelers communicate using supersymmetric quantum-chromodynamic waves, not electromagnetic ones. Well, not exactly sQCD *waves*— more like modulated soliton collectives of sparticles."

Sir Charles was an old hand at such discussions, and the jargon didn't floor him, even though to him most of it sounded meaningless. All you had to do was gauge the meaning from the *rest* of the sentence. A sparticle, for instance, was obviously a supersymmetric analogue of a standard elementary particle . . . whatever that meant. So Wally Halberstam was telling him that they had been wasting their time trying to detect alien *radio* messages.

The aliens didn't use radio—they used squarks.

He said as much, and Halberstam nodded energetically. "Yes, their 'headlights' are actually antennas. For squarks. Very quick on the uptake, Sir Charles! I'm impressed."

"I'd prefer it if you stopped being impressed and told me the answer to my next question."

"Sorry, what que—"

"The one I haven't yet asked but am obviously going to. Wally: *can we pick up squark signals?* We brought everything we could imagine might be needed—but I doubt that anyone imagined we'd need to detect a type of particle unknown to human science that went out of fashion two hundred years ago."

"Uh—they're working on that right now. Young Josie Mazur says she thinks we might be able to adapt one of the wheelers we brought along on *Skylark* . . . convert its squark radiation into conventional signals. Something to do with the crystal lattice of platinum. I gather that some group at the Macnamara Institute put the Paris guys on to the idea by discovering that wheelers don't react to laser light that's been reflected in a mirror. Unless the mirror happens to be optically flat platinum, that is. So they now think that coherent light from a laser carries with it little packets of squarks, a kind of supersymmetric piggyback effect. The disorder in glass scrambles the phases of the squarks, but not the light. A platinum mirror keeps the squark phase information intact."

"Couldn't they have discovered that two centuries ago?"

"No. They didn't have a wheeler to respond to the squark signals. The sparticle packets have been there all along . . . but nobody's had any way to observe them."

"Until now."

Binshaba was unhappy.

"Simeon—why?" She shook her head in disbelief. "We have more mouths to feed than we have food as it is . . . Why bring me this child?" She knew better than to ask where it had come from. *The Witches*, Simeon would tell her with a straight face. *We men know about these things.* Obviously it was from the Outside, but the women weren't supposed to know about that.

Her husband found it hard to answer. There were things known to the Council that should not be divulged to the Many. It was difficult, knowing of the existence of a greater world, to reaffirm the parochial values of this microcosm of humanity.

However, it was impossible not to.

"The child is . . . sick," he said, not untruthfully. "He has suffered a substantial trauma. His close family has been . . . lost to him."

That, at least, was true. It didn't make it any easier to say. He knew that the truth concealed a lie. He didn't know that what he thought to be the truth was concealed in *another* lie.

"We have been chosen to . . . care for him. To replace the father and mother that he has lost. To bring him up in the ways of the Village."

Binshaba grasped his hand, urgently, imploringly. "But you and I know that that is not all," she said.

Simeon felt his heart skip a beat. *Does she know? Do all the women know?* One part of him knew that they must. What the men knew, the women must also know, for the women were shrewd. Shrewder, he acknowledged, than the men, who spent most of the time talking Village politics and making babies with their own or other men's wives, and formulating absurd plans and arguing about them. Not to mention brewing sour mash beer and drinking it in huge quantities. The women did the real work, the work that held the Village together. But, to be fair, the men also carried out the meathunt, of course, which was extremely important. And they did kill the occasional marauding lioness or leopard, which was both important and dangerous—and absolutely not a woman's task. Let the men acquire livid scars and get themselves killed . . .

Yes, the women *were* shrewd.

Yet, another part of him denied it, for the secrets that were known to the men of the Village had to be known *only* to the men. Without that, his life was meaningless.

"All or not, it is our duty," he said, closing the discussion. Binshaba sighed, in secret, inside. Once Simeon's mind was made up, there was no changing it.

Not by frontal assault, anyway.

She clambered to her feet. "It is time to milk the goats," she said.

Simeon watched her go. Once more he wondered just what the women of the Village *really* knew . . . But that was fruitless speculation, and a question best not asked.

What was more important was what the *men* of the Village had been entrusted with. That was where the *real* power lay. And the Outsider child was entrusted to *him*.

It was enough.

"The irony is, Sir Charles, that the Paris lab could have discovered squark signaling eighteen months ago. But the Macnamara Institute group's funding got cut off before they were able to publish."

"How could that happen?"

"Apparently some bureaucrat in the State Department interfered with normal procurement procedures and nobbled the appraisal subcommittee. Since then, the group has had to spend most of its time chasing alternative sources of money, and their research was held up."

Sir Charles found this incredible. The whole point was that anything remotely related to the aliens and carried out by competent people had to be encouraged, just in case. There was no budget limit. "Wally—how could something so important get its funding cut?"

Halberstam shrugged. "Beats me."

Moses was running through the Village, clambering quickly onto the roof of a hut, trying hard not to laugh as the other children hunted for him.

They knew where he was—but he was only eight, they didn't want to find him *too* easily. And so they passed to and fro beneath his precarious perch, pretending not to see or hear him as he clutched the reeds and tried not to giggle too loudly.

For a few moments, he was happy.

Although the wheelers on Europa had taken the precautionary step of dispatching a repauter to monitor extrajovian activity on Sixmoon, they had not expected the Elders to take an interest. It had simply been a routine feature of the triennial audit. Then the Subcommittee on Poisonbluvian Trespass was suddenly instituted, and took its first—and to date its only— decision, which was to instruct the repauter to stay where it was and to continue its monitoring duties. Naturally, the symbiaut took this instruction literally, and deluged the wheelers of the Conclave with real-time commentary from inside Europa Base. However, the subcommittee had not debated what to do with the information that the symbiautic observer would provide. Currently it was deeply divided over just that question, and as a stopgap the reports were being filed in memaut databanks until the issues had been fully clarified.

Unaware of the wheeler's passive role, Sir Charles had assumed it must be an ambassador from the aliens, eager to open negotiations with the newcomers from Earth. When the wheeler had made its dramatic entrance at Europa Base, Sir Charles had been certain that he would soon be in communication with the machine's alien masters . . . wherever they might be. Now—two years and an incredible amount of wasted effort later—he was less sure. Communication there was, of a sort. Exchange of signals, huge quantities of information—yes. Exchange of *meaning*—no. Both parties were talking, but they weren't talking interactively. Even alien syntax seemed beyond the powers of his analysts, even though he'd given them the very best signal-processing software. Alien semantics was a distant dream. In fact, the only significant thing they had discovered about the alien signals was that they were statistically indistinguishable from random noise. Perfect black body radiation.

Some bright spark back on Earth had even worked out why. *Now they tell me.* At the turn of the twentieth century a mathematician named Cris Lachmann at the Santa Fe Institute had written a paper with the title *Any Sufficiently Advanced Technology Is Indistinguishable from Noise.* It was a parody of Clarke's Law: *Any sufficiently advanced technology is indistinguishable from magic.* And in a way, it said the same thing. An advanced civilization would have learned to encode its signals in the most efficient manner possible: they would be incompressible. Another mathematician of that era, Gregory Chaitin, had already realized that any incompressible signal is random. The idea was easy: if there is a discernible pattern in the signal, you can compress the amount of information involved by describing the pattern, and if not the signal *has* no pattern—so it looks random. Lachmann had parlayed Chaitin's result into a statistical distribution of frequencies for incompressible electromagnetic signals, and nature had arrived at the same distribution in a context where signaling was irrelevant—the radiation spectrum of a perfect black body.

The alien signals were supersymmetrically chromodynamic rather than electromagnetic, but the same reasoning applied. Turning squark wavepackets into radio preserved the frequency distribution.

The wheeler signals *weren't* random, of course. They were merely encrypted. But anyone who has tried to watch an encrypted VV channel knows how random such signals seem to be, unless you know the secret key to decrypt them. The aliens were talking in code, and the Jovian Task Force lacked the key. This had been anticipated—though not the resemblance to random noise—and *Skylark* had several of the best cryptanalysts there were. Hundreds of others were beavering away back on Earth. Sir Charles had a horrible feeling that they were all getting exactly nowhere.

At that moment four of his people were staring at a transmission from . . . somewhere . . . relayed to the wheeler by squark wavepackets, processed into electromagnetic signals by their own "tame" wheeler, and displayed on a flatfilm screen in a dozen plausible formats.

All dozen windows showed uniform shades of gray.

In an attempt to make contact in the reverse direction, a VV camera perched precariously in one corner of the room relayed its contents to the wheeler, and by using *another* wheeler they could be pretty sure that their broadcast was being transmitted. Certainly *something* (if only noise) was. Throughout, the wheeler rested on all six wheels in the middle of the floor, apparently oblivious to everything around it. It had long ago retracted its dimetrodon vanes and turned off its disturbing inner light. A flimsy barrier had been erected to keep people from tripping over it. Occasionally it rolled back and forth for a short distance, as if to "stretch its wheels."

After seventeen thousand hours of continuous recording and transmission, some meaningful interaction ought to have begun. At the very least, they surely should have been able to establish the aliens' system for counting, which would open up the periodic table, hence elements, hence materials, hence biomolecular structure . . . the usual method for bootstrapping from simple concepts to complex ones.

Not so.

They had programmed their computer to generate bursts of short blips in mathematical patterns—integers in ascending order, odd numbers, squares, cubes, powers of two, primes, even Fibonacci numbers. They had turned these patterns into sound, light, radio, and squarks. They had shone lasers at the wheeler, played music to it, shown it movies, sung and danced for it. The wheeler, which presumably must have been picking up at least some of these messages, displayed not the slightest interest and continued to squat on the floor.

Was it asleep? *What was it there for?* Didn't the Jovians *have* mathematics? How, then, could they possibly build machines with *wheels*? And why, why, *why* weren't the aliens attempting to send some kind of simple pattern that their viewers could latch on to, like any intelligent creature would?

The only bright spot was that the wheelers hadn't just switched off and gone home. The aliens seemed perfectly happy to continue sending signals in both directions. But there was no indication that the results made any more sense to them than they did to the humans.

Kambo had caught a young gazelle. Its mother had been ambushed by a leopardess—from the claw marks it must be the one they called B'wulu, who had a litter of cubs to feed—and the corpse had been hijacked by a pack of hyenas. Kambo had found the delicate creature lying in the hot sunshine, while vultures circled overhead. It was astonishing that the hyenas hadn't found it and killed it, but they had temporarily been lured away by the prospect of a cheap meal at a lion kill.

He had looped a crude rope of twisted grasses around the kid's neck and tied it to a wooden stake outside his father's hut.

He had given the kid water, and smiled when it drank its fill. Now he was trying to get it to feed, without success.

Moses wandered by and stopped to pass the time of day. He had grown considerably since he first arrived in the Village. Now he was twelve years old, tall for his age, quick and agile. In his three years as a Chinese street child he had mastered the art of fighting dirty, and a year of *gongfu* had refined those skills. He knew how to cause minor or serious injury, how to maim for life, and how—when necessary—to kill. He hid all of these refinements from the other children, afraid that if they became known he would be forced to demonstrate them. Nonetheless, he remembered everything that Silent Snowflake had taught him, and he practiced in hideyholes among the rocks where no one could see him.

He made no such attempt to conceal his ability to fight like the street children. He had a temper that was easily aroused, and a vicious streak that made him into a formidable opponent. Only the biggest of the children ever dared fight him now; the rest bore too many scars, mental and physical, from failed attempts to battle with him.

He was respected, and not just for his teeth and fists.

Kambo was upset. "She just won't eat the food, Moses! She drinks like a fish, but look at her rib cage, showing through her flanks . . . I think she will die soon."

Moses picked up the food bowl, swirled it around. It was a mixture of grain and milk.

He placed it in front of the young gazelle. The animal nosed at the food, raised its head slightly, and backed away. It stood, poised, leaning slightly forward, and seemed to sniff the air.

"It's too thick," said Moses. "Use more milk. But boil the milk first to take away as much of the smell of goat as you can. If you can find a gazelle hide, place the bowl on that. Oh, and chop a few handfuls of grass and sprinkle that into the bowl."

Then he got up and walked away.

Kambo watched Moses depart. Then he picked up some grass, wandered into the family hut, found an old piece of gazelle skin, boiled up some fresh milk, and did as Moses had instructed.

After the milk had cooled, he placed the bowl in front of the kid, on top of the fragment of hide.

The kid approached warily, sniffed several times at the mixture . . . and began to feed.

Kambo wasn't even surprised. Everybody knew that Moses had an uncanny affinity for animals. He seemed to know what was going on inside their heads.

He could even pick up a black mamba, whose bite was death, and the snake seemed to *like* it. Of course, he never played that particular game in front of the adults. But the entire Village had seen him calm a cow whose leg had been savaged by a lioness . . . The cow still died, but more peacefully than they usually did.

Moses had a way with animals. He seemed to understand them. He could whistle to a bird and it would settle on his hand.

Even the spiders seemed to respond to him. Instead of scuttling into their holes when he approached, they would crawl into his cupped hand. They seemed to be watching his eyes.

A thousand miles away from the Village, Charity awoke from sleep and wondered why. Usually she slept like a log. Then she heard the noise again.

Someone was wandering around the bungalow.

She glanced at the clock, a strip of flatscreen stuck to the chest of drawers beside her bed. She'd bought the chest in the local flea market, assured it was an antique, but at such a low price that she knew it had to be a fake. That was fine—she'd just wanted one of those old wooden box-things with the slide-out trays . . . She shook her head to clear it. Damn fake antiques. The time was 4:22 A.M.

Burglar? Surely not, there was nothing here worth stealing, and anyway, the last burglary in the whole county had been more than two years ago. Hired killers? Oddly enough, that was far more likely. Now that Pru—

There was a sound of a toe being stubbed, a muffled oath, and Charity recognized the voice. She sat up, grabbed a robe, and headed for the kitchen.

"Pru? Why the devil are you up so earl— Oh." Several packed bags were piled up by the door. Outside, a taxi was waiting, its electric motor humming so silently that Charity would never have heard it approaching.

Or departing.

"Pru, you're not—"

"Sorry, but I bloody well am, little sister!" Prudence had been steeling herself for this for days. Her patience had worn clean away, she *had* to get out to Callisto again. So much time had passed since Moses had been killed that she was getting weary of perpetually holding her sister's hand. Prudence *knew* that her nephew was dead—why couldn't Charity face reality? She'd hoped that by taking her leave in the early hours of the morning, she would avoid the inevitable confrontation. Fat chance. Her embarrassment showed.

"You know what I think about—"

"Yes, Chatty dear, I most certainly do, you've told me often enough. It just so happens that we have a fundamental disagreement about it. A very simple disagreement—I'm right, and you're wrong."

"Jupiter."

"Yes."

"With those weird vidivision people, no doubt. I wondered why you'd been spending so much time in discussions with them on the Xnet—"

Prudence exploded. "Who I interact with on the X is no business of yours!"

"Even if you do it in my house, on my node, with my electricity?" Their disputes *always* went this route, from childhood. Time to back off . . . "I never said it *was* my business. I just couldn't help noticing, and wondering . . ."

"Little sister, you were a snoop when you were two and you're still a snoop today. Look, I'm sorry about everything that's happened, it's tragic and awful and I feel deeply for you, and I loved Moses, too, even if it didn't show as much as it should've—but I've got to live my own life again, okay?"

Charity gave a mirthless chuckle. Prudence never could stay in one place for very long. How she coped stuck in a metal box for years on end was one of the wonders of the world . . . "You're going back into space."

"Why not?" Prudence was unusually prickly. She knew very well why not. It wasn't space as such, it was what she was going into space *for* . . . Charity just stood there, silent, accusing.

"Damn it, Chatty, you don't need to look at me like that! It's not as if I'm betraying the human race! We can't *all* devote *one hundred percent* of our time to the War Against the Comet! We all have to eat, so farmers have to farm, and we still have to earn the money to buy their food . . . Or has the Ecotopian Central Bank abolished money now?"

"Don't be foolish, Prudence." Even to Charity it sounded prissy. She'd never won an argument with Prudence. She was usually *right*, but that didn't imply a win.

"Look, it's not *my* fault that there's a bloody comet coming!" Prudence took a deep breath and ran her fingers through her polychromatic hair in an agony of indecision. "It's thanks to *me* that we may have a chance to divert it! Look, if the comet does hit, it will be a good idea to have as many of us as possible off-planet. You've seen the plans to revive the lunar colonies. Why don't you—"

"Stop changing the subject. Science needs those wheelers. You never should have—"

"They've got plenty, all of them *my* property. *I found them!* Now they've commandeered the lot." They both knew this was a lie: the authorities had commandeered exactly eight wheelers, of which Reliant Robin had a wheel missing and Trabant was completely seized up. Even, so, the compensation they'd offered her was pathetic, and their reason—"contribution to the comet effort"—even more so. Prudence had refused point-blank to say where the other wheelers had been hidden. She felt a foolish urge to justify her position, even now, even to her sister. "They have no idea what to do with the ones they've *got!*"

"That's not the point—"

"Yes, it is! Look, if it makes you any happier, if the boffins really get an idea what to do with the bloody things, I can always tell them where I've stashed the other hundred and twenty-nine of them. Even from Jupiter, it'd only take a few hours for the message to—"

They'd been over this before. "Maybe the scientists will find something important if they get to look at them all."

"Maybe. But *definitely* I'll end up a pauper." That was an exaggeration. What she really meant was that she'd fail to become a multimillionaire. They both knew that.

"What if the comet hits, Pru? What good will money be then?"

"If it hits, all bets are off. Tough. I'll have other problems then, anyway. But if it misses—*when* it misses—I can turn over the rest of the wheelers to Angie Carver, and I'll be heavily in profit. Especially if I can pick up all the others that must be out there." Prudence had also refused to say exactly where on Callisto she had dug up the wheelers. The *Skylark* expedition had been instructed to look for them, but so far they'd found nothing. Callisto was large—its surface had the same area as Africa and the Americas combined. Remote sensing wasn't sensitive enough, and what was couldn't possibly cover such a huge area. For that reason, Sir Charles's team had never made a really serious attempt to find where the wheelers were buried.

"So basically you're saying that you can make a mint if Dunsmoore succeeds, and if he doesn't, kaboom, too bad. That's cynical."

"Realistic. Charity, I'm not as nice a person as you. I'm a

selfish bitch, okay? I *have* to be—in my business I'd be bankrupt in a day if I wasn't. And no, I *can't* change my line of work, it's in my blood. You're happy with a dead-end job in the back of beyond. I want a bit of excitement in my life."

That hurt. Charity hit back. "You know the *real* reason why you won't cooperate with the authorities?"

Prudence had a ready answer. "I'm asserting my fundamental human right to free choice."

"Quite the reverse. You're asserting your fundamental human right to let your emotions rule your head. It's Dunsmoore, isn't it?"

"I don't see what that jumped-up little prick has to—"

"See? Point proved. We both know how he cheated you . . . and you can't ever let it go, can you? Even though humanity hangs in the balance, you just can't bring yourself to offer him the slightest *shred* of assistance, can you? No way, not a chance. Pru, that's false pride! You're cutting off your nose to—"

"—make myself smell worse." Of course, Charity had nailed her dead center, but there wasn't a chance in hell that she'd admit it. "Agreed, I don't believe Dunsmoore is the right man for the job—in fact, I don't believe Dunsmoore is the right man for *any* job outside the sewers. But he's in charge and if I can do anything constructive to help him I will. I just don't believe that handing over more wheelers can possibly be of any use." And there was another reason, too, one that home-body Charity would never understand . . . *The wheelers were out there*. Pru wanted them. She wanted them *all*. And she wanted proper recognition for discovering them. Sir Charles had managed to muddy the waters, *again*. By the time she'd proved the wheelers were genuine, the key moment had passed: the media were already bored. Then, when the comet loomed and they woke up, guess who grabbed most of the media coverage?

Next time, though, she'd be ready.

She picked up her bags, slinging them randomly about her

person. "Do you understand, Charity? Not pride, not obstinacy—just a rational assessment of where I stand."

Charity gave her a look of utter contempt. "Prudence, I
know full well where you stand."

"*Oh?*"

"You stand condemned."

Afterward, she wished she'd had the foresight not to say
that. They must have heard the door slamming in Dar es
Salaam.

Bailey Barnum wasn't sure he fancied Jupiter. Mars, yeah,
that had sounded kind of fun, filming the desert where thoats
might have roamed, reconstructing them with computer
graphics. But Mars was relatively close. Jupiter was two years
for a single trip, four for a return ticket.

When Angie had commissioned them to film her collection, he hadn't realized that it would require outside-broadcast
shots of the original home of the wheelers. He should have
guessed. Ruthie Bowser would have smelled a rat straightaway.

Cashew, in contrast, was ecstatic. Over the moon, so to
speak. She'd always wanted to travel.

Jonas had wavered. He liked home comforts. Then Prudence had taken him off somewhere for a long chat—a very
long chat. Jonas had come back somewhat dazed, but full of
newfound enthusiasm for getting them all cooped up in a tin
can for years on end. Angie settled the matter by reminding
them of some clauses in their contract.

He wondered why Prudence was so eager for them to come
along, anyway. Prudence preferred not to reveal the real reason, because it was selfish. The best way to gain media attention was to lug your own tame media around with you. *This
time, Charlie, you're not going to steal my thunder.*

The army ants had left!
For as long as Binshaba could remember they had trailed

through the Village, always following much the same path, causing minor but infuriating nuisance, and impossible to eradicate.

The women of the Village discussed this remarkable event. The army ants had been a fixture. The Villagers had long ago given up trying to get rid of them.

One of the women was bursting to offer her own pet theory. It had been the third anniversary of the boy's arrival among them—an auspicious day. Something miraculous was only to be expected. "Binshaba: it was your child. He did this thing."

"Moses?"

"*I saw him.* Hours every day, sitting next to the ant trail."

Binshaba laughed. "Reading the ant trails? That means nothing, Kashina, I saw that myself. He enjoys watching animals, even insects. That's all."

The woman persisted. She knew what she had seen. "Yesterday I saw the boy carrying a dead rat. Today, the trail of army ants has vanished, leaving only marks in the ground."

If this idea spreads, it could be dangerous. Binshaba gave the other woman a sharp glance. "Kashina, I hope you are not as credulous as the menfolk, trying to tell me that Moses is a sorcerer."

This was exactly what Kashina had been thinking, but she had no wish to face Binshaba's scorn. "Of course not! But . . . he studied the army ants for many days, and then he had a rat, and now they are gone. I am convinced he must be responsible."

Binshaba felt a shiver run up her spine. *It was true.* She'd noticed long ago that Moses had an uncanny ability to empathize with the animal kingdom. But now it seemed that his abilities extended even to ants. Moses had a very strange mind . . . At times it seemed almost *alien.*

"Perhaps you are right, Kashina. I will ask Moses."

How had he managed it? He was an Outsider, and that presumably explained his strange powers. The women of the Village had never seen another Outsider, and they weren't supposed to know that Moses was one, or that there was an Outside for him to have come from. But of course they did, and the mothers talked to their children and wove strange tales for them when their fathers weren't within earshot. Tales of a fabulous world with huts the size of mountains and animals made of tin, a world where paintings moved and their colors shone like the moon. And the strangeness of the tales rubbed off on Moses. Sorcerer or not, everyone in the Village recognized that the boy was in possession of a wondrous talent.

They called him Speaker-to-Animals.

13

The Village, 2219

Carlesson moved between the boulders like a silent shadow. He was tougher now, all sinew and muscle and not an ounce of spare fat. He was also a lot less naive and a lot meaner.

He glanced down at his 'node. Yes, this was leopard country, all right—there were eleven of them within thirty miles, and a female with cubs within two. It was one of the less desirable side effects of the Diversity Police's obsessive, though not always effective, tracking of the world's wild animals— by hacking into their computer systems, the Hunters could use the DiPol's own information to pick their targets.

Not only that—it was close to the Village, where Carlesson believed that the black child was to be found. This was recent intelligence, obtained by accident. Carlesson had a strong interest in Moses' future. He intended to make sure that the boy didn't have one.

Xi Ming-Kuo had made it amply clear to Carlesson that sparing Moses' life had been a mistake. For five years he had been given the most dangerous and unpleasant assignments. As Xi had anticipated, Carlesson had possessed the strength of character, the sheer stubborn bloodymindedness, not only to survive them, but to thrive. Carlesson only found out why he had been treated so harshly when Xi congratulated him on his survival, spelled out in a few curt sentences why that particular training regimen had been necessary, and asked him what he would do with the child if he ever encountered him again.

Carlesson made a throat-slitting gesture. He shook with barely concealed fury. *Five years of misery! Five years of the worst assignments, the menial tasks, the grunt work . . . All because of a stupid fucking kid who happened to be in the wrong place at the right time!*

He wouldn't make the same mistake twice.

Xi was satisfied. Carlesson had learned a difficult lesson and was all the stronger for his ordeal.

Meanwhile, the matter of the black child had become quite unsatisfactory. For reasons Xi could not begin to fathom, fate had allowed the child to live. It was presumably Bad Luck, and the simplest way to deal with it was to give fate a helping hand and turn his misfortune into Good Luck. A few prayers and suitable distributions of cash would square his account with the traditional gods—or, more importantly, with those who claimed to represent them. It would be impolitic to attract the wrath of the priesthood. But that was mere detail, and routine. Xi knew that the boy was in the hands of his enemy Deng Po-zhou. He lost much sleep imagining how possession of the child might be used to bring about his own downfall. He spent a fortune trying to track down the child's whereabouts, to no effect. One day, he knew he would discover the boy's hiding place. He turned his attention to grooming Carlesson as an assassin. Having set the pieces in motion, Xi waited for the endgame to begin.

Back in favor now, the Hunter was granted a rare privilege: freedom to operate in any region of the globe, all travel expenses paid without question, the best equipment money could buy. He could choose his own assignments. It was also made clear that these privileges would continue only as long as the Hunter achieved sufficiently impressive results.

Carlesson did. He was the star of the whole operation. His skills became legendary among the Hunters . . . often much embellished in the telling. His kills poured money into Xi Ming-Kuo's coffers. If a client required an animal, however obscure and well protected, Carlesson would provide it. He eluded heavy guards and stole rare animals from under their protectors' noses. He was given training in unarmed and armed combat and was encouraged to use it. Within one heady period of two months, four members of the Diversity Police died at his hands in separate operations, and on each occasion he secured great prizes for Xi's growing chain of medicine shops.

He netted himself big cash bonuses, too, and his reputation soared.

He learned new ways to kill.

Then, one night, he was sitting in a bar in Louang Namtha on the Laotian side of the China/Laos border, waiting for various financially lubricated backs to be turned so that he could cross safely into Free China. A scruffy little Chinese guy had stormed in, shouting curses about barbarians ruining his life. Carlesson had a fondness for that particular bar, and purely to ensure peace and quiet he'd bought the man a drink and tried to calm him down. Over the next half hour he was rewarded with big chunks of the man's life history, and Carlesson gradually came to realize that Pung, as he was called, had been some minor cog in the White Dragons and had been exiled from China by his gang leader. The gang had taken all his identity papers, spirited him across the border, and abandoned him. At that point Carlesson developed a new agenda, declared himself Pung's lifelong buddy, and insisted on treating him to drinks for the rest of the evening. Carlesson privately considered Pung lucky to be alive, but outwardly he was sympathetic to the man's rantings. He never did find out how the barbarians had ruined Pung's life, but he did get around to asking whether the man had ever been out of Free China before.

"Sort of."

"Either you have or you haven't."

"Only by 'giro. Night."

"This was recently, of course."

"No. Six, maybe seven year! Never saw thing. Never put foot on barbarian soil."

Carlesson dug. "Sounds pretty stupid to me. Your boss must have been weird."

Pung's by now rather mixed loyalty to the White Dragons won out through the alcoholic haze. "No, boss *smart*! Special mission. One passenger, black kid—*he* weird."

Carlesson chose his next words with care. "Of course, your boss didn't tell you where you were taking the weird kid. No, he wouldn't have trusted—"

Pung was incensed. "Yes! Yes! Well, he no tell, but I ask pilot. Africa. *Africa!* Special place, nobody can go. Not even barbarian."

Carlesson bought Pung more drinks, insisted on finding him somewhere for the night, and did—on the canal bed with his throat slit and a heavy chain wrapped around his waist. Having at last found out where Moses was, the Hunter wasn't taking any silly risks. He knew he should report the discovery to Xi, but it would be much more effective to wait until he could tell him that the boy was dead.

Carlesson had just two objectives: bring back a leopard, kill Moses. His mistake was trying to carry them out in that order.

It was young Kimu who found the Hunter's tracks. They were unusual, for Carlesson wore boots. *A Witch!* The excited girl ran back to the Village, and soon Moses got to hear of the discovery. *Not a Witch—an Outsider!* Soon all the children knew.

Moses and two of the older boys slipped out of the Village early the next morning and made an even more unnerving discovery. They found confused leopard tracks and clear traces of blood. Moses read the meaning of the signs immediately and without effort: "The Outsider has killed B'wulu and her cubs."

"Did he use the weapon that we are not supposed to know about?" asked Ruwanga, the eldest of the three.

"No, I have seen these Outsiders kill before," said Moses, and his fists clenched so hard that he dug his fingernails deep into his palms, drawing blood. "They use only the knife and the crossbow. They are Hunters, and they are our enemies. They wrench our animals from their proper place in the world.

"The Hunters are an abomination."

"What shall we do?" cried Ruwanga, eyes wide.

"We shall purge the abomination from the face of the world."

With due caution, Carlesson made his way toward the Village. If he could get up one of the nearby slopes, he would be able to observe the daily movements of the people, and soon he would locate the child. Then—

A twig broke behind him. He turned.

A boy. Something in the child's manner told him it was *the* boy.

Children's heads poked over the rocks—six, seven . . . a dozen. Witnesses. It didn't matter. This time he would make no mistake. He would kill them all. First, though, the boy.

The other children stayed back. The boy walked toward him. "I am Moses. I have come for you."

Carlesson laughed. It *was* the boy. This was all too easy. *The boy had come for* him! Such arrogance! He put down his bow, unsheathed his knife, and set it on a rock. Bare hands would be far more satisfying—to feel the crunch of bone, the yielding flesh, the pain and the horror of the realization . . .

"Five years you cost me," he snarled. "Five fucking years of my life! *You* have come for *me*? Think again, little boy!"

Moses had not recognized the Hunter until that moment, for his face had changed considerably, but the inference was not lost on him. He had forgotten most of his childhood at Gooma, but never this. "You are the one who killed Zemby and Mbawa."

"The cheetahs? Were they yours? Yeah—I killed them, all right. Two dead furry bodies—you remember?"

Moses wiped away a tear. *Dear lord*, Carlesson thought, *this is going to be so easy!* "And now I'm going to kill you, little boy. Put right the mistake I made the first time we met!"

Moses seemed unafraid. "You talk a lot," he said.

"Yes, and by—" The kid was right. He *did* talk a lot. Too much. Time to get it over with. Carlesson decided that he would start by breaking both the boy's legs, then move on to his arms, and after that—well, there were quite a lot of combat moves he needed to practice. He held his hands out, fingers clenched, ignoring all of his training because it was obvious he wouldn't need it. This was just a *kid*, for god's sake! He laughed again, and closed in on Moses until the child was *almost* within reach . . .

Moses gave a signal. A hail of rocks converged on the Hunter. He dodged them, grinning. Stupid kids couldn't even throw straight. For a moment, though, he took his eyes off Moses. As soon as he did so, the boy spun in a blur of movement. His arms extended for balance, he kicked high and fast with his right heel, just as Snowflake had taught him. The heel hit Carlesson at the base of his nose. So great was the force that a sliver of sharp bone was detached from his skull. Moses' aim was perfect: the sliver became the tip of a bone spear, penetrating the thin, perforated regions of the skull where the cartilage of the nose normally rested . . .

The spear thrust deep into the Hunter's unprotected brain.

Within an instant, Carlesson was dead. He didn't even have time to anticipate the move. He certainly didn't have time to deduce that someone had taught Moses the rudiments of *gongfu*. Or that the rock barrage was a classic street-child tactic.

Moses looked down at his dead adversary. He knew he

could have killed him without the distraction of the rocks—but why take the risk? He had thrown the tea *and* the cup. Silent Snowflake would have applauded. His method may not have been particularly elegant, but it was *very* effective.

They left the dead Hunter for scavengers. Nobody else from the Village was remotely likely to pass that way, and nobody from Outside was permitted to, so the children saw little reason to waste time hiding the body. Anyway, the hyenas would just haul it out again.

Over the next few days Moses occasionally stopped what he was doing to glance at the sky in the direction of the ravine. When the stream of arriving vultures became a stream of departing ones, and only the usual few, circling high above, remained, he knew it was time to go back. Alone.

He hoped that what he wanted was still there to be found . . .

In the early hours of the morning, while it was still dark, Moses sneaked out of the hut where he slept and made his way back to the ravine by the light of the stars. He had no fear of any animals that he might encounter, confident that he would be able to read their moods and calm any aggression. But B'wulu's mate, who normally haunted those parts, was nowhere to be seen, and what few snakes he chanced upon were small and timid, slithering away into the rocks and bushes.

The hyenas had gone—to where the pickings were now better. To judge by their scuffled tracks, there had been plenty of them around a few nights earlier.

He scrambled down the slope of the ravine, bare feet firm against the treacherous, gritty earth, triggering miniature landslides but nothing worse.

Most of the Hunter was gone. Hyenas and vultures had stripped the corpse of its flesh and internal organs. The softer bones had been eaten, too. The rest of the skeleton had been scattered over a sizable patch of ground, and for more than an hour Moses picked over the remains by the light of the stars, hoping to find what he coveted.

He found what was left of one leg in a depression in the rocks, smothered in hyena droppings; the other was underneath a thornbush. The skull had rolled under the base of a tree and was probably home to scorpions.

When he trod on a half-buried shoulder blade and found a humerus nearby, he began to believe that he might be on the right track—but a hyena could easily have carried away an entire arm, discarding its remains miles away where Moses would never find it. Trying to keep his hopes subdued, he backtracked through the rocks toward the scene of the original ambush—and suddenly there it lay, right out in the open where it could never have been overlooked.

Of the hand, wrist, and arm that it had encircled, there was no sign. But the transparent face of the Hunter's wristnode glinted in the starlight.

Moses scooped up the trophy, brushing off dust. Tucking it inside his shorts he began to lope comfortably back the way he had come. He didn't stop to investigate the desirable object—that would have to wait until he could find a few hours of privacy. One thing he had learned long ago was patience.

The tribal chiefs thought that only a select few of the wisest and oldest men of the Village knew about Outside, and of them no more than two or three knew about the Xnet. If they had been able to listen to women's talk, or to join the children unseen when there were no adults around, they would have had a shock. The children had woven a whole mythology around their interpretation of rumor and chance observation, fueled by overhearing women's conversations. It owed a lot to their vivid imaginations and precious little to reality, but it would have punctured the chiefs' complacency and given them a much-needed reminder that people of lower rank in the tribal pecking order are not stupid. To the children, Outside was a cross between Valhalla, Olympus, and the tunnel-maze of the Snake God; the Xnet was a gateway to the Nether Kingdom, which was the realm of monsters, demons, magicians, angels, and other beings with godlike powers. But Moses, unlike the rest of the children, had spent the early part of his life *living* Outside, and although his memories were few and involved activities that he couldn't really understand, he still knew that you could *do* things with the Xnet—real, everyday things like tracking baby cheetahs. And the Hunter who had kidnapped him had worn just such a device on his wrist and had spent a lot of time reading from it and talking to it.

Moses knew that the wristnode was more than just a magical talisman: it represented real knowledge and power. And that was why he had dared to return and take it, when the other children feared it as the property of a Witch and therefore a bringer of misfortune.

Among the Villagers, Moses had a reputation for being a loner, so nobody worried—or even noticed—when he got up before sunrise and made his way toward the rocky foothills that rose sharply behind the Village. He climbed up and across to a small ledge, difficult of access, from which he could easily observe anyone who tried to approach. Behind him was a sheer cliff; in front a steep scarp, treacherous with loose rock and detritus.

He pulled the Hunter's 'node from his pocket and held it in his hands, trying to puzzle it out.

Moses didn't know that if an active wristnode is detached from a warm human body then it is forced to rely on internal batteries, which can power it for no more than six hours without being recharged. This one had been lying in the dust for days, and in the dark for the entire night. He also didn't know that wristnodes, being gateways to personal records and communication channels, normally confirmed the voiceprint of the user before they would operate. But because their ambush had taken the Hunter by surprise, the wristnode was still in open access mode, and the daylight now flooding across the plain below was already recharging the batteries through the array of solar cells forming the bracelet. So it was in full working order, and no voice-recognition filter barred him from its communication channels—only from the Hunter's personal files, which, as yet, he had no idea existed.

So when he looked into its rounded, transparent face and spoke to it—as he had seen the Hunter doing—it spoke back to him. And when he looked steadily at its face, it noticed his attention and projected a virtual holoscreen in a fixed position relative to his eyes. Suddenly finding himself transported to what seemed to be another location entirely, he dropped the 'node—and the illusion vanished.

Some tentative exploration convinced him that none of these strange things were harmful, and he slipped the device over his wrist so that he wouldn't drop it again.

'Node technology had been refined, becoming intuitive, effortless, and if necessary helpful—all without approaching pre-Pause smartness. To do this, the designers had been forced to assume certain cultural reflexes that were by no means natural to a child who had been spirited away from civilization at the age of four, spent three years of his young life among wild dogs and street children and another as the unofficial adoptee of a gang warlord, and then been dumped unceremoniously into a deliberate throwback to a previous millennium.

Painfully slowly, with much backtracking, Moses began to discover how to navigate the Xnet.

He wanted to make contact with Outside.

Patiently, singlemindedly, he tried everything he could think of, and learned what happened when he did. He found endless information on incomprehensible topics—intelligent lawn mowers, travel agencies for the deaf, hourly Normerican allergen charts, how to build nesting boxes for blue tits. None of this information was of the slightest use to him—but the ability to find it was.

Becoming aware that the sun was nearing its zenith, he hid

the wristnode in a deep hole in the cliff, safe from the weather, and plugged the hole with a stone to keep out any prying wildlife. He desperately wanted to continue investigating the 'node's strange powers, but if he didn't turn up for his midday meal, his absence *would* be noticed.

He would, however, return tomorrow, and most days thereafter, for as long as it took.

The wristnode's batteries ran down every night, but exposure to sunlight quickly restored operating power. Moses never did find out how to make the Hunter's 'node conserve its batteries when not in active use: in fact, he never found out that it *had* batteries. But he did find an Xnet mail-order catalogue.

You could *buy* things over a wristnode! Amazingly, you could even buy another wristnode. Or a robotic Winnie-the-Pooh, a complete collection of the live concerts of the Lone Star Seven, or the services of a Sexy Schoolgirl Masseuse . . .

All you had to do was tell the 'node some numbers.

He tried that, making up whatever numbers came into his head, but nothing interesting happened.

Eventually he stumbled on the Mormon genealogical site in the Utah mountains. Elsewhere in Normerica, a computer noticed and obeyed an old instruction. "Iffy?"

The bored techie woke from a daydream about her latest boyfriend. Her 'node had said something. Message waiting, probably. She rubbed her eyes open and then absently wiped her hands on the green Carver Telecommunications slinksuit. "Groovy, Baby. Speak to me."

"You remember that standing order from eleven years ago?"

"No. Why should I?"

"You meatbrains, always forgetting things. It came down from the boss herself."

Iphigenia yawned. "Yeah, like a hundred others. Fill me in, Baby."

"The Odingo kid. First name: Moses. Disappeared from Africa. Believed dead, nothing ever confirmed. Mother—friend of the boss—could never accept it, so we set up a top-priority alert for any plausible signs. Instant response."

"Oh, yeah. That." She wondered if her hair would look better shaved close or braided with seashells . . . What would Marcello like best?

"Someone's been trying to access the kid's file in the Salt Lake database."

"So? That must happen once in a while . . . Probably some oik trying to trace a long-lost maiden aunt."

"Maybe. But the standing orders say that the duty telecoms monitor has to check out anything promising, and if it holds up under scrutiny, alert the boss immediately. I'll do that bit, but you have to authorize it."

"Shit. Why me, Baby? Why the bloody hell couldn't the old bitch have it piped through automatically to her own 'node?"

The computer parsed the sentence and took it literally. Baby wasn't hot at recognizing rhetorical questions. "According to the help file, because she has too much else to do. Your job is to act as a filter."

"Damn," said Iphigenia. "Okay, then: forget it. It's almost certainly a false alarm."

"Is that an official authorization?"

"Yes." Flippantly.

The computer *was* very hot indeed on verbal tone. "According to instructions, I'll have to inform your superior . . ."

"Bloody smart-alec machine. Sure you're not pre-Pause? Okay, okay, tell me what you've found, you useless piece of dog turd, Baby dear."

The machine told her. It showed her the would-be accessor's voiceprint and facial eigendecomposition . . . Still bored, she instructed the central router to dig up the child's medical records and compare. The result came back in less than a second.

She stared at it.

She swore, surprisingly mildly under the circumstances. All thought of that sexy hunk Marcello vanished. "Baby: top-priority authorization, confirmed and logged. Get me the Boss, *now!*" *There's a promotion in this*.

A call from one of Angie's personal staff woke Charity up in the small hours of the morning. "You what? *What?* Moses? You think you've found *Moses*? But he's—I mean, I thought he was—you really mean this, it isn't some sick joke, is—"

A new voice broke in: she recognized the face immediately. The 'node showed a user-ID guarantee icon—it really *was* her. It all came out in a rush. "Oh, Angie, is it true? Is he all right? Where is he? How long till—"

Angie calmed her down and explained exactly what was going to happen, what Charity's role would be, and why it was vital to succeed.

Charity found it hard to take in. Apparently Angie was worried that if *she* had located Moses, others would surely do the same. Others, it seemed, who might have motives for harming the boy. "I'll do anything," Charity said. "Anything at all."

"Good. We have no idea how he got where he is, but we're working flat out on it now that we have a place to start. We've sent him some Xmail, but so far he hasn't answered. It's okay, honey, nothing to worry about. His node-access profile shows that he only ever nodes up around midmorning."

Charity had always possessed an excellent grasp of terrestrial time zones. "Midmorning *where*?"

Angie told her.

"The Village? You mean he's been in the *Village* all along? But that's less than a thousand miles from here! Why didn't anyone *tell* me? Why didn't—oh, sorry, you've only just found out, you can't—"

"As far as the official records go, he was born in the Village. Obviously the records were hacked—I'm just getting notification suggesting it was done from Free China, but there's no proof, not any that officialdom would accept. Which means we'd have a terrible job convincing the authorities to release him to us. No, not even if all the physiological markers agree—they'd worry about hacking *then*, okay? And you know how strict they are about the Village—unless it stays isolated, it won't give valid results. I guess if we went through regular channels we *might* get a decision in six months . . . provided I greased the wheels. We can't wait that long, Charity. If we can find him, so can others. We've dug up some connection with Free Chinese gang warfare . . . Drugs, endangered species . . . He may have enemies in Free China."

Charity's mind was in turmoil. She had long ago given up hope—or so she had thought, until now. "Angie! They—they might hurt him!"

They will almost certainly kill him, Angie thought. *Unless we get there first.* "Yes, honey, they might. So here's the plan. I'm sending an autogiro over straightaway from one of my gas fields in the Mozambique Channel, carrying trained paramilitaries. They'll go in and pick him up. But I can't risk landing in the Village itself—there'll be hell to pay. So as soon as Moses nodes on and listens to his Xmail, *you* are going to have to talk to him and persuade him to meet the 'giro at some suitable landmark, far enough away from the Village that nobody will see what happens."

Charity felt sick and impossibly happy, all at once. "Of course! *But I want to be on that autogiro!* I don't care how dangerous it is, I've *got* to be there!"

On the screen, Angie gave a humorless laugh. "I was wondering how to talk you into it," she said. "I don't think Moses could have survived what he must have been through without being a very shrewd young man. Unless he recognizes you, there's no way we will be able to convince him to let us pick him up. And unless you're there when we land, there's no way he'll ever get into that 'giro. So, sweetheart, you don't need to volunteer. You're conscripted."

Moses knew about autogiros . . . One had taken him away from everything he loved, to be cast into the anarchic world of the street children. Deng Po-zhou had saved him from that horror and been kind to him—but Deng had also banished him to the strangeness of the Village and abandoned him. There, he had grown up with what he now thought of as his second family, after Deng's household.

Suddenly his world had been turned upside down. There had been a family before Deng's . . . He *knew* his mother was not Binshaba; he could see, as soon as he thought about it, that it could not be Jeweled Jade, either, for he was black and she was not. Two "mothers," both fake . . . Now the Hunter's wristnode had brought him face-to-face with his real mother.

At first he had failed to recognize her. Until she showed him the funny toy that turned into lots of animals—found by the police, returned, treasured. *Oink!* Then painful memories that he had previously buried came flooding back.

He remembered her.

He was not at all sure he wanted to meet her.

Yet here he was, sitting on a rock, ten miles away from the Village in a region that the Villagers seldom frequented . . . waiting for another 'giro. This one would be small, she had told him, and yellow . . . and he knew it would change his life yet again. Which, ultimately, was his reason for being here. The 'giro would return him to the Outside, save him from the dead-end existence of the Village, let him rejoin a world in which you could obtain a wristnode just by quoting some numbers instead of killing a Hunter and stealing it from his rotting, dismembered corpse. The second procedure seemed to Moses to be much more straightforward, but he desperately wanted to know how to make the first one *work*. So he had done what the wristnode had told him and sneaked off to the place where two rocky pillars climbed toward the sky and a muddy stream ran between them. The only possessions he bothered to take with him were his shorts and the 'node.

The sky was almost cloudless and the sun was starting to

cast sharp shadows. All around him was the natural beauty of the veldt. This might, for all he knew, be his last opportunity to submerge his being in the ebb and flow of animal life . . . It was *so* beautiful . . .

He had been happy here.

A bee flew past. Moses put out his hand, and the tiny creature landed on it. A second joined it. Projecting their flight path backward, Moses' attention was drawn to a swarm of bees, suspended from a tall tree that grew beside the stream. The bees in his hands were scouts, workers that spied out the lay of the land for the main swarm. The swarm itself was a shapeless mass, hanging from a branch like an old animal fur slung from a pole. Its outlines were fuzzy, as bees on its surface flew off and others landed. He could hear them buzzing.

Two five-foot puff adders, thick as a man's calf, lay buried in the dirt a few yards to his left. Moses had watched them grow from hatchlings. He had never seen either of them feed, but he had watched their sand-buried outlines grow, mouthful by mouthful. A few hundred yards away a white rhinoceros bent its ponderous head to drink from the stream. Moses knew this rhino. It was a male, and from its body language it had been having a bad day . . . Moses recalled that the rhino was trying to maintain a harem of two females, and suspected that there had been competition between the nursing mothers for the best leaves. Moses doubted that both calves would be weaned successfully. But there was something else that had been bothering the beast . . . possibly a run-in with a crocodile. The crocs never learned.

Slowly making its way across open ground, maybe fifty yards away, was a star tortoise—an impressive representative of its kind, nearly two feet across, and (when aroused) capable of running for short periods at the speed of a human walk. A few days earlier Moses had come across the star tortoise Xpage and been fascinated. The beautiful yellow and black of the reptile's high-domed shell was again to be seen in wild Westafrica, thanks to releases from a breeding program.

Moses heard the roar of an engine, and a 'giro came into view, swinging in from behind concealing hillocks. As it came in to land, a second 'giro appeared.

The boy came instantly on the alert. Both autogiros were dark in color—one black, one dull green and buff. The black one had a sinister, angular appearance. Then, in the far distance, he saw a tiny speck high in the sky—a third 'giro. At that distance he couldn't pick out its color, but the other two certainly weren't yellow.

The black 'giro landed, and half a dozen men jumped out, all heavily armed. Chinese. In his mind's eye he saw once more the bloodbath when he was snatched from the world of the street children. He recognized that the Chinese were all carrying the weapon that the Villagers were not supposed to know about—and which he had seen before, in action. Hands clutching similar weapons poked from the side of the green and buff autogiro, and more Chinese faces.

The men on the ground ran toward him. One of them tripped over the star tortoise . . .

On board the yellow autogiro there was consternation. They had seen the other two 'giros, and they knew they were going to arrive too late.

Charity all but wrung her hands in despair. "It must be the Chinese! Angie was right, they know about the pickup! And they've got to him first! Oh, my poor, poor little Moses!"

The pilot glanced at his men. They, too, were armed, and now they readied their weapons for action. This was going to be very nasty indeed. He concentrated on getting the 'giro to its destination quickly.

Ahead, there was a huge explosion, a ball of flame, and a burgeoning plume of thick black smoke.

As they got nearer, it became apparent that one of the Chinese autogiros had crashed. The other seemed wrecked. On the ground, everything was unnervingly still. It was difficult to make out just what they were seeing, but it was a big mess.

The pilot weighed the options and the risks, but nobody was shooting at them and nothing down there was moving. He opted for a rapid descent, away to one side, and a quick but wary advance on foot.

What they found was baffling.

One autogiro still burned, the blackened bodies of its occupants occasionally visible amid the smoke and flames. Clouds of bees circled it at a safe distance. Charred bees littered the ground around it.

The other was scarcely recognizable. Its panels were disfigured with huge dents and holes you could put a fist through. The windows were shattered, and the landing gear was bent and broken. The machine was lurching to one side, nose down, its tail unit nearly broken off.

Corpses lay everywhere.

The ground was a maze of animal tracks—a confusing muddle of pits and furrows in the sandy soil. Several corpses had been smashed to pulp where they lay across the furrows. Another was little more than a pile of bloody rags attached to its unraveled intestines.

Over some of the corpses, a carpet of bees crawled. Others had obviously been hit by bullets, their brains or chests blown away. Two, on close inspection, had suffered snakebites: their ankles were already swollen and purple. A dead puff adder, cut in two by a hail of rounds from a machine gun, lay nearby.

Quite a few of the corpses had their necks broken.

In the middle of the mayhem sat a young boy, calm and composed on his rock.

As they approached, Moses got up and walked toward them. He allowed them to hurry him to the small yellow 'giro and lift him in. Inside was a woman that he recognized as his true mother, sobbing, screaming, overcome by emotions so powerful that for the first time that morning, Moses was afraid.

The woman flung herself at him and wrapped him in her arms. She kept kissing him and weeping.

As the autogiro soared into the air, one of the men separated them, while another tried to calm the woman down. The first man grabbed Moses by the shoulders. *"What happened?"*

Moses gave him an inscrutable look. *"Any context conceals within it the means of advancing one's own desires."*

14

Callisto Trajectory, 2220

Jonas had learned just how spacers passed the interminable voyages between the stars. Prudence had been an accomplished tutor, and it had been a lot of fun to begin with . . . But two years was an awfully long time, and by the end of it his attentions had started to wander. Like the others, he had experimented with many different pastimes—some legal on Earth, some not. One of the rules was that whatever happened during a voyage, you never talked about it after the voyage was over. That way you could all go quietly nuts, indulge your favorite perversions—in between the tedious hours on the exercise machines, unless those *were* your favorite perversions—and as long as your insanity inflicted no lasting damage on anybody else, nobody would try to stop you. In the cramped environment of a deep-space cruiser, arguments were something you tried very hard to avoid. Even so, most voyages involved sundry acts of mayhem, overindulgence, and emotional breakdown. It was like being a member of the cast of a traveling theatrical road show, piled on top of your fellows twenty-four hours a day, tied to them emotionally and *having* to find ways to live with them because you either hung together or you'd hang separately. This voyage had included nothing that the medical database couldn't tell them how to fix, and by spacer standards that meant it had been an un-eventful trip.

Now Prudence was busy, nudging *Tiglath-Pileser* in to-ward the shining half-moon of Callisto, and Jonas and the rest of the VV team were filming their arrival. She knew that the Jovian Task Force had established a base on Eu-ropa, on the side that tidal forces kept facing the giant striped planet. It was foolish to imagine that the task force hadn't spotted her coming—Sir Charles would have been told of her every move, and he would know that she knew that . . . Her plan was to land an OWL far enough from the wheeler burial site to offer no useful clues, even if a task force probe chanced upon their drop zone. It would be easy to camouflage the lander with the netting she had brought. Sir Charles would discover their location soon enough, but by then they'd have the rest of the wheelers on board. With luck.

Angie and Charity were sitting on the veranda of the Gooma Zoodiversity Facility, watching a pride of lionesses stalking a herd of Thompson's gazelles. Zebras and giraffes were intermingled with the spindly, russet-colored, white-tailed deer. To the lionesses it must have seemed like a sweet shop—warm fudge, stripey mint taffies, long-necked candy canes. But *these* candies had legs, and used them with astonishing effectiveness to avoid being eaten. Through binoculars the sisters could see a baffled lioness staring at half a dozen young gazelles bounding randomly into the air on all four legs—a type of movement known as "pronking" that had evolved to disorient a predator.

Judging by the look on the nearest lioness's face, it was working.

"All kids change when they grow up, honey," said Angie. "You shouldn't blame yourself. He's had a hard time—no wonder the poor kid doesn't want to talk about any of it. Wait, it'll come."

"I know it will," said Charity. "But that doesn't make it any easier waiting. He's grown up, and I *missed* it! I wasn't *there* for him when he needed me . . . *Nobody* was there for him! Can you imagine what it must have been like?"

Angie could, all too vividly. She had hired a firm of private investigators, and they'd managed to piece together a fragmentary version of Moses' activities since his disappearance. His death had—obviously—been faked: he'd been kidnapped. They now knew he'd been running with the street kids in Free China, because some of the women of the Village had told them, and the Chinese connection suggested Hunters. Angie had a rather accurate idea of what kind of life that must have been . . . little of which she had passed on to Charity, and that only by way of euphemisms. The poor woman was suffering enough without being forced to face up to the full horror of Moses' early childhood, and it wouldn't improve her state of mind to open up the catalogue of casual rape, disease, murder, starvation, and cannibalism that characterized the anarchic world of the street child.

They also knew a little about Deng and Silent Snowflake. But even Angie's wealth had not dug out Xi Ming-Kuo or the story of the murdered Hunter, and Moses wasn't telling.

Today, as most days, he was helping the Ntuli twins with the animals. Charity was astonished at how his precocious talent with wild creatures had flowered. Now he would calm a distressed, injured animal in a few minutes. Even the most antisocial of their animals, like that obstreperous old bull wildebeest with part of a leg missing—relic of a battle with a crocodile—would eat out of his hand. He spent hours feeding ants to the aardvarks, and you got the impression that the ants were lining up for the privilege. The aardvarks simply adored him.

With people, though, it was a very different story. Moses *much* preferred his own company. He found it impossible to relate to children of his own age—he was fifteen now, but seldom acted like it—and Charity had quickly given up trying to force the issue. He tolerated the Ntuli brothers, Jomo and Yambe, ten years his elder—no doubt because they were his main route to the animals. She was sure that her son still felt an attachment to her, even a degree of affection . . . but if so, he hardly ever did or said anything to show it. She often wondered if she was fooling herself and all residual affection had long since died. Just occasionally, though, she would glance out of the corner of her eye and catch him staring at her with a wistful look on his face, but he always turned away when he noticed she was watching.

"It's been very hard, you know, Angie." Charity put down the binoculars. The lionesses had just caught a young gazelle and suffocated it with a bite to the throat, and while she normally accepted this as an unremarkable event in the nonstop savanna soap opera, today she was feeling a bit sensitive to the difference between winners and losers. "You see, I'd always been convinced he was alive, despite all the apparent evidence. I just *felt* that he had to be. But I knew that mothers always think that when their child goes missing, and it feels just as certain when you're wrong . . .

"I'd all but given up hope, but I never dared admit it, not even to myself."

Angie nodded in sympathy but offered no comforting words—Charity wanted to be listened to, not comforted with empty platitudes. Being *there* was the most useful thing she could do.

"Then, when they told me he was not only alive but had been less than a thousand miles away for the last seven years—I just can't describe how that felt. I was happy, I was angry at how close he'd been all along . . . I felt cheated and elated all at the same time!"

"Sure, honey, I understand," said Angie. "Can't *feel* it like you do, but I can see why someone in your shoes would feel that way. Life mostly tugs us in contradictory directions, so I've observed. The trick is not to get torn apart."

"Yes . . . Now it's—well, 'anticlimax' is the wrong word . . . When I first saw him again—he's such a good-looking young man, much more so than his father ever was, you know . . . Did I ever tell you about Jerry?"

"No."

"Jeremiah, his full name was. He had a way with animals, too—Moses must have inherited it, only with him it's even stronger. One of the rhinos was sick and we were keeping it in a concrete pen. Jerry used to rub its back with a broom. One day he got between the rhino and the wall, and the rhino leaned on him. That's all, just a friendly nudge.

"Jerry died in the hospital a week later. I was seven months pregnant at the time, with Moses."

"That's awful. Yet you still work with animals?"

"It wasn't the *rhino's* fault."

Angie waited for the faraway look to fade, and for Charity's attention to revert to the present. "You were talking about Moses."

"Oh—yes. To touch him, to hold him close again—nobody could ever *know* how I felt at that moment! I came alive again, you see. And I still feel so amazingly fortunate . . . I have my lost child back. But—oh, Angie, he's not the child I'd been imagining!"

The tears were starting again. They had to be cried out, painfully, repeatedly, until the hurt was dulled by time and familiarity: Angie knew there was no way to stop them.

In fact . . .

The two women wrapped their arms around each other, and their tears mingled as they ran down their faces.

What neither of them realized was that in his own peculiar way Moses was happy. There were so many animals, so many different *kinds* of animals. He could *feel* what they were thinking, what they wanted, what they feared, what they were going to do. How to help them. It was like being a talented composer and knowing what a page of musical notation would sound like without having to play it. Even when animals lied, which was seldom, it was obvious to Moses what truth the lie was intended to conceal. A harmless fly with yellow and black bands was a living lie, pretending to be an unpalatable wasp with a painful sting. A stick insect was a lie—the same lie. *I'm not edible.*

People were different. They lied all the time. *"Don't be frightened, kid—I won't harm you!"* with a big toothy Hunter's smile . . . But the Hunter had wanted to *hurt* Moses, and had taken him away from everything he loved and made his childhood a living hell. It wasn't that Moses couldn't recognize the lie—a friendly smile felt friendly, a stick-on smile felt phony. The mismatch between the spoken word and the body language was jarring—but he couldn't work out what the motive was. He couldn't understand what the lies were *for*. So he was extremely wary when it came to people. Considering what people had done to him, this was hardly a surprise.

He was slowly beginning to accept that some people were different from the rest. Charity, for instance: she hardly ever lied to him, though, and even when she did, he dimly recognized that there was a motive, and it was friendly. They were *kind* lies—lies to protect him from unpalatable truths.

Now he was among friends, and as the weeks passed, Moses began to emerge from his shell. Like a nervous animal, he was easily spooked, but he became that tiny bit more human with every passing day.

Charity began to dare to hope. Why, only the other afternoon, Moses had touched her arm—shyly, almost as if by accident, and only for a moment. But he had reached out deliberately, without being prompted.

That *had* to be a good sign, surely?

The comet loomed ever closer—two years to impact. In a ramshackle building on a moon made of ice, Sir Charles Dunsmoore reflected sourly on the machinations of fate. He had been advised by the best brains on Earth . . . pity he hadn't had the wit to listen to them. Not the endless teams of highly trained experts that Uhlirach-Bengtsen had set up to advise him—Harris and Clementine. The old cliché of trash novels, the clever amateurs who outthought the professionals . . . except, he belatedly recognized, Harris and Clementine weren't amateurs. They were just professionals in a field he hadn't valued enough.

Jupiter. The aliens were on *Jupiter*. On. The. Planet.

Even now, after several years of frenzied redesign of equipment and a complete revision of the mission plans, he still found it hard to believe. An atmosphere of unbreathable gas, winds that made earthly hurricanes seem like a gentle breeze, high gravity, extremes of cold and pressure beyond human comprehension, and worst of all, no solid landmasses . . . Ridiculous. But there was no reason to doubt the observations. The "tame" wheeler sat inside the base, chattering away in wheelerese to whatever and wherever . . . Eventually they'd devised a method to find out where its tightly beamed squirts of modulated squark wavepackets were aimed, and where the replies were coming from. The evidence had been conclusive: whatever the wheelers were communicating with, it was on Jupiter.

Fortunately they had not been *totally* unprepared for this eventuality. They had tried to plan for even the most unlikely contingencies. His tame experts had possessed enough imagination to contemplate the possibility that the aliens were living on the main planet rather than one of its attendant moons, and they had provided appropriate equipment. They just hadn't given it much priority. So some of his peeved scientists had been assigned grunt duties, manning OWLs, donning suits, and pulling out layer upon layer of crates and boxes of things that Earth's masterminds had deemed to be more important than the treasures that had been squirreled away inside *Skylark*'s spaceborne warehouse of supplies and equipment.

Paramount among them were six vacuum-balloons—thin, light, and immensely strong spheres containing the lightest material there is—nothing. They were fashioned from fullerene nanoplates, nested sheets of pure carbon cross-linked by stabilizing atoms of rare-earth metals. When assembled, vacuum-balloons looked rather like large watermelons—round, pale green, split into segments by indentations.

Getting them down into the upper layers of Jupiter's atmosphere was easy: release them and let them fall. There was no way to get them back.

As well as the main flotation sphere, each vacuum-balloon had valves and pumps that could adjust its buoyancy by pumping some of the planet's air into or out of the cavity, and attitude thrusters that could propel it sideways. Suspended beneath, like a gondola on a hot-air balloon but much more firmly mounted, was a standard probe package—electronic eyes and ears, plus (a key feature) a detachable communications module which could be presented to any suitably receptive alien. The designers had reasoned that since the main aim of the probes was to initiate a dialogue with aliens, it would be a good idea to make the communicator portable.

Everything was set up so that a team aboard *Skylark* or any of its attendant vessels could control the balloons remotely. Because of Jupiter's rapid rotation and the planet's incessant winds, communications often had to be relayed through a series of slave units dumped into jovistationary orbit—the height at which the unit would rotate around Jupiter in the same time that the planet took to revolve on its axis, roughly a hundred thousand miles from the planet's center. At that distance they were farther out than Metis and Adrastea, the two innermost moons, but closer than the

third, Amalthea. Launching the necessary equipment into
the correct orbit was a routine but tedious task, so when Sir
Charles finally authorized the deployment of a balloon
probe it was several months before *Skylark* could drop the
first one and Europa Base could receive its observations.
The signals from the probe's eyes and ears could be sent to
virtual reality headsets for use by the remote controllers,
and stored in memory banks for further analysis. Earth, as
always, got copies of everything.

As it sank through the tenuous outer layers of Jupiter's
atmosphere, already buffeted by wild winds, the probe relayed a steady stream of scientific data—magnetic and me-
teorological, physical and biochemical, numerical and
pictorial. Much of it confirmed what they already expected—for example, the structure of Jupiter's atmosphere.

In a sense, a planet's atmosphere never ends—like an
old soldier, it only fades away. On the other hand, there is a
clear difference between regions no denser than the interplanetary vacuum and those that are ten or a hundred times
as dense. So it was generally agreed that Jupiter's atmosphere first became worthy of the name about five thousand
miles above the cloud layer. This is the thermosphere, so
called because it is warmer than some of the deeper layers,
thanks to incoming heat from the Sun. "Warm" is a relative
term, and the temperature is well below zero degrees Celsius. Within the thermosphere is the ionosphere, a thick
layer of electrically charged particles that can reflect radio
waves, just like the Earth's ionosphere. Lower down is the
cooler mesosphere, and then the stratosphere, where the
temperature drops dramatically to a mere one hundred degrees Kelvin—rather warmer than the boiling point of ni-
trogen at normal terrestrial pressure. At this depth, some
twenty miles above the cloud tops, the temperature gradient
abruptly reverses, thanks to internal heat rising from
Jupiter's depths, and the troposphere begins. Although
Jupiter's atmosphere is vast, the pressure at this level is

low—less than it is at the summit of Earth's highest mountain.

The cloud layer is about forty miles thick, with winds that typically average more than two hundred miles per hour at the equator. The temperature rises rapidly, so that at the bottom of the layer it is close to that of Antarctic ice fields on a summer's day. The pressure there is much the same as it is on the Earth at ground level. In neighboring bands of cloud, the winds blow in opposite directions, relative to the atmosphere's mean rotation; high-speed jets of Jovian air mark the boundaries of the bands. The deeper regions are hotter still, but the pressure also rises dramatically with depth, so that below the cloud layer the gas giant's "atmosphere" soon becomes liquid. Like Earth, Jupiter is an ocean planet. Unlike Earth, its oceans merge almost smoothly into its air, and both are made from hydrogen and helium, mixed with small amounts of methane, ethane, ammonia, acetylene, and other gases.

What all this meant to the vacuum-balloons' designers is straightforward. Pressure is not a problem, even if you want to go below the clouds into the unknown layers that lurk beneath. Temperature is not a problem, as long as you design for intense cold. The greatest problem is wind—not the winds that forever encircle the giant globe, but the local gusts, up to five times as fast, that spin off as swirling vortices. A balloon, however, can readily sail with the wind if it is kept away from extremes. The turbulent "wake" of the Great Red Spot is definitely something to avoid, and the easy way to do that is to stay north of the equator. So *Skylark* dropped its probe neatly above the relative calm of the North Temperate Zone, dipping its technological toe into the Jovian sea to find out whether anything wanted to bite it.

The probe got as far as the cloud tops, and there its descent was temporarily halted while the team digested the data acquired so far, paying particular attention to the gadgetry that monitored the stresses in the balloon and the suspended gondola. All seemed well, and the decision was taken to deploy three more balloons, all above the cloud layer and in different atmospheric zones—North Equatorial Belt, North Temperate Belt, North North Temperate Zone.

Already, the biochemical sensors and analyzers had found ample signs of Jovian life. There were complex organic molecules in abundance, curious quasi-bacterial organisms, the occasional strand of floating pseudoalgae . . . there were no words for what they were seeing, so they took refuge in terrestrial terminology and vague Latin prefixes. Their reports caused a stir back on Earth—the first alien life! But the stir was muted by a feeling of anticlimax—the task force wasn't looking for bacteria and primitive plants, it was looking for *intelligence*. The big masses of gas-sacs, discovered soon after, looked promising—for a time—but it quickly became apparent that they had no more intelligence than the seaweed they resembled. Still, Jupiter's surface area was truly gigantic, and its atmosphere was deep beyond human experience. Patience was the watchword. There was plenty to study, a whole new world of exobiology was opening up . . . Time slid by, and reports rolled in by the thousands. The scientific justification for the expedition was undeniable. Unfortunately, that wasn't an important issue, though in the flurry of excitement it was easy not to notice. To most people, the comet still seemed comfortably far away: with roughly a year and a half to go, the task force would surely succeed in stopping it. Others, though, were beginning to fret, and, Sir Charles was coming under mounting pressure from Uhlirach-Bengtsen—which was largely counterproductive. It was leading to a crisis of confidence, not helped by things like the allegedly humorous item he'd found in his Xmail one day, downloaded from the Tyrannosaurus Wrecks Xsite:

| 1 yard | 10 years | germicide |
| 10 yards | 25 years | insecticide |

30 yards	50 years	homicide
100 yards	100 years	countrycide
1,000 yards	100,000 years	genocide
10,000 yards	30,000,000 years	tyrannicide
100,000 yards	1,000,000,000 years	distinctlyonthebigcide

Perhaps because of his growing lack of confidence, Sir Charles was becoming even more cautious than before, and this affected his strategy for deploying the probes. From a distance, Jupiter's cloud layer seemed impenetrable, but that was an illusion resulting from a viewpoint that tried to look down through hundreds of superimposed sheets of cloud. There were gaps and holes everywhere, changing positions erratically as the winds carried the clouds at different speeds in different layers. Light bounced down through these gaps, penetrating to a surprising depth. Some regions would be briefly lit by broad shafts of sunlight when several gaps temporarily lined up, but between the clouds the light was mostly diffuse, dimming to twilight and then total darkness as it filtered into the depths. Because the cloud cover was unpredictable, Sir Charles was understandably reluctant to fly his balloons blind. For several months, therefore, he refused to permit them to be sent below the cloud tops.

Having arrived at Callisto, Prudence was no longer sure that it would be a good idea to make a beeline for the buried wheelers. Their luck had been bad: by chance the task force had stationed several probes in very awkward places, making it far more difficult to get near the burial site than she'd hoped. And increasingly the approaching comet gnawed at her mind. The interminable trip out to Jupiter had given her time to think, and her motives had started to seem shameful. Maybe Charity had been right after all. She might have been able to ignore these thoughts, and go wheeler hunting with a clear conscience, if the task force had been making real progress. But the more she looked into what it was doing, the unhappier she became. The wheelers would have to take a backseat for a while: Earth's vital interests were not being well served.

"The problem with Charles," said Prudence, "is that he's enormously efficient and enormously ineffective. He hardly ever stops working, but it's nearly all routine stuff . . . I'm sure he *thinks* he's making tremendous progress, but mostly he's chasing his own tail. He puts up an effective smoke-screen, though: you have to have your brain seriously in gear to realize that he's not actually *getting* anywhere. Me, I'm different, more intuitive. See things in context, leap to con-clusions . . . From the first day I was assigned as his stu-dent—long ago, I'll tell you all about it sometime—anyway, right from the start it was obvious to me that he lacked any real originality. No flair, no instinct—but man, was he a slave-driver! Drove himself more than anyone, too. And he was an absolute stickler for scientific protocol—sound ex-perimental design, very thorough analysis of every possible way for measurements to go wrong . . . He taught me a lot when it came to technique, he was the most thorough person I've ever met. He just . . . had no sense of the bigger picture."

She was finding it increasingly difficult not to get in-volved in the task force's work. Her original plan—get in quick, grab as many wheelers from their icy tomb as *Tiglath-Pileser* could carry—was firmly on the back burner. From out here, with the homeworld a distant speck of light, it seemed petty. She should have known, space always had that effect on her. What was the point of digging up a few more wheel-ers if Charles screwed up? And the more she watched him in operation, the more firmly she became convinced that this was exactly what would happen.

"Jonas, didn't I *say* that the aliens had to be on Jupiter it-self—way back, before we even left Earth?"

"You did," Jonas agreed. "Mind you, at various times you also said that they were probably in pressurized installations beneath the ice of Ganymede, and in orbit on huge generation starships."

Prudence grimaced. "Yeah, well, can't get *everything* right. But I *did* have Jupiter a lot higher on the list than those awful, barren moons that that fool Charlie Dunsmoore's wasted *years* running through a fine sieve!"

"Absolutely," said Jonas. "We all agreed on that. But we didn't have the slightest evidence to back that theory. Charlie-boy has to rely on advice from experts, and we all know what they told him. He just did what he was instructed to do."

"Precisely my point," said Prudence though clenched teeth. "And fair enough, to begin with. The problem is that he failed to cut his losses when it first became likely that the aliens weren't where the experts expected them to be. He should have done a few things that he *wasn't* instructed to do. Damn it, he's the boss, right?"

"He has to carry an awful weight of responsibility," said Cashew. "I've seen network execs in the same kind of position, and most of them stick to their brief. If you use your initiative and anything goes wrong, you can't cover your back. Stick to the book: no worries!"

"And if it goes *right*," added Bailey, "someone higher up grabs the credit."

Prudence acknowledged their points with a wave of her hand. "Sure, sure. But Charles doesn't have a back to cover. If he uses his initiative and it doesn't work out, all that happens is the critics get blown to smithereens!"

Jonas finally realized that Prudence was leading up to something. She seemed unusually diffident, and it took several minutes for him to persuade her to say what was on her mind.

"Jonas, I've spent much of my life trying to stay well clear of Charlie Dunsmoore. I absolutely don't want to help pluck his irons out of the fire. But there's a frail, beautiful world back there, and if I don't do something soon, it's going to get smeared all over the face of creation. I think we're going to have to bail Charlie out."

Jonas looked worried. "But Pru, he'll never cooperate

with *us*! There's been far too much dirty water under the bridge—"

"I know. In a way, it helps. At least I won't have to work *with* him. But I *am* going to have to do his work *for* him." She balled her hands into fists. "Damn his eyes . . . Jonas, check me out on this, okay?"

"Okay."

"One: we know the aliens are on Jupiter."

"Check."

"Two: Charlie hasn't found hide, hair, nor reptilian scale of them above the cloud layer. Lots of primitive life, yes—some *big* . . . rafts of organic bubbles, that kind of thing . . . but nothing intelligent."

"Check."

"Three: ergo, *they aren't there*. They're down in the clouds where it's hard to see anything. Got to be."

"Check. That's where *I'd* be if *I* was an alien."

"If they're down in the liquid ocean, we're dead. No hope of making contact."

"Check."

"But—I just don't believe they are. The cloud layer is much more likely."

"Hmmm. Not sure of that one."

"Me neither. Hope over reason, maybe. But we don't lose anything by making that assumption."

"Check."

"Unfortunately, Charlie isn't keen to send valuable balloon probes down where there's no visibility. Even with heavy searchlights, state-of-the-art sonar, and all-around radar. He's scared he'll lose one."

"Check."

"Which is where you come in."

"Che— *What?*"

Prudence told him.

                    *   *   *

Montgolfier—balloon probe 2—was mapping the distribution of germanium tetrahydride at different levels in the North North Temperate Zone of Jupiter's lower troposphere. There was reason to believe that the levels of this rare gas correlated in some manner with the occurrence, miles below, of the "white ovals" that had puzzled astronomers for centuries. It was slow, careful work, for the exotic gas was present in concentrations of one ten millionth of a percent. So far, the evidence for a significant correlation had been decidedly tentative, so Sir Charles had authorized a further week's observations. Ostensibly this was because there was germanium in wheelers, so germanium tetrahydride might be a sign of wheeler manufacture. A positive correlation might indicate that it would be worth taking a close look at the white ovals at some future date.

The probe hovered less than a mile above the cloud layer—the lowest that Sir Charles had yet dared to authorize. It zigzagged slowly to and fro on its attitude thrusters, sampling the external gases and transmitting telemetric data back to Europa Base by way of the newly installed network of jovicentric comsats.

Back at Europa Base, everything seemed routine, and Keith Chow, senior technician, decided to take a quick break for a bulb of coffee and a protein bar. He wasn't exactly forbidden to leave his post, but it wasn't exactly permitted, either. However, they all did it, because the scheduled workload left no room for substitute controllers, even if only for a few minutes.

When he left for the kitchen area, the probe was functioning normally. When he got back and cast his eye over the diagnostics window, he caught his breath. The numbers didn't look right. Two data streams in particular gave cause for concern—altitude and internal gas pressure.

He called over to a second controller at a neighboring console, whose nominal task was working with probe 3. "Zirphie, if I slave you some data can you spare a moment to check it out for me? I think we've got a problem with probe two." Zirphie nodded: it would help relieve the boredom.

After a few moments, she spotted the bad readouts. "Okay, Keith, I see what you mean. I'd say you've got a slow leak in the buoyancy shell. Air's getting in."

That's what he'd thought, too. "I'm going to give the shell a squirt of sealant and flush the air out again. Can you back me up on that decision? Halberstam will chew me out if he decides I goofed." All the controllers knew that they had to play the game by the rulebook—there was very little room for on-the-hoof improvisation. And Wally Halberstam was ultraconservative—administratively and politically. Superficially, he seemed a bumbling oaf, but he could make your life exceedingly miserable if he didn't like your attitude. Mission-critical decisions had to be verified independently. Zirphie would have been happier if Keith hadn't chosen to ask *her*, but the responsibility went with the territory and anyway this was straight out of the guidelines. "I concur—if you don't do something soon we could lose the probe. Logging my support for the decision now . . . Okay, done. She's all yours!"

Keith waited until his own console displayed her acceptance, and then instructed the probe to emit a short burst of gaseous sealant from a reservoir attached to the inside of its vacuum flotation chamber. The contingency had been planned for.

What happened next, hadn't. The pressure indicator suddenly leaped above zero, and the altimeter began to drop like a stone.

"Hey—what the hell did *that* do?" The probe was starting to topple gondola-up. Chow tried to right it, but nothing seemed to be working.

"The reservoir exploded," said Zirphie calmly. "The release valve must have been faulty. Look at those readings for sealant reserve levels."

"Negative? But we can't have less sealant than zero—

right, you got it, the sensor must have been damaged when the reservoir blew up. And judging by the change in attitude, gas is flowing into the flotation chamber through a hole where the reservoir ought to be."

"Looks that way. I'll ask the computer for verification."

"Okay. While you're doing that, let's see what the 'scope shows on visual . . . hmm, the image is faint and shimmery, but she's sure as hell dropping . . ." By now Keith looked distinctly apprehensive. "Had to happen on *my* shift, of course . . . Zirphie, I didn't do anything wrong, did I?"

"Can't think of anything. You did check that the valve was up to operating temperature?"

"Yes, of course." *Did I? Shit, maybe I didn't! I can't remember . . . where's the damn log file?* Relief flooded through him. *I did, praise the saints. Someone in the prep team must have screwed up . . .*

In the telescope image, the tiny dot of the probe was suddenly swallowed up by cloud. "The Old Man isn't going to like this, we're losing her. Any chance we can go to visual?" He tried. "No, nothing, the cameras must have been ripped off. She's starting to break up!"

Words failed him; this was terrible. What if it was poor design? They could lose all four. It was a mess now—it could easily become a *big* mess. A mess with his name written all over it in indelible ink. He could only hope that he really had covered his back. The inquiry board would turn over every stone until something crawled out, and it was perfectly capable of finding something nasty even if the stone was as clean as a whistle. After all, the board would have its own back to protect, and that back was a lot broader than his.

Bright Halfholder of the Violent Foam awoke from her shallow torpor and sniffed the air with nervous anticipation.

It was time. Time to strike a blow against the Elders' unthinking destruction of the lesser worlds—destruction born of needless fears, withered lifesouls, and mindless adherence to the mundane and the ephemeral.

The rubbery walls of the blisterpond became confining instead of comforting, a sure sign that her mind was returning to full awareness as it emerged from a light level of estivation. The rippling of Halfholder's leathery hide sent wild shivers spiraling along her neural core as the excitement built. In an effort to remain calm, she worked though her checklist, deliberately confirming each item twice, making sure that her beltbag contained all the vital equipment prescribed by her advisers . . .

The Carrier was sealed in a pouch, for safety.

She brought her prompter up to her eyes, and the shivers became unbearable. *Yes, it is time.* She could scarcely believe that the long wait was over.

A brief squirt of release hormone peeled back the blisterpond's roof like an eyelid surprised by morning, and Halfholder floated cautiously upward, until her ring of eight oval eyes cleared the sunken rim.

She spun gently in an i-spy.

As she had expected, the streets here, within sight of the Edge, were devoid of fellow blimps. No guardians, then. To one side the city's barrier fringemass swayed ominously, a deadly, moving forest. Wisps of floating plant life drifted past, then denser bunches, some possibly hiding predators. She bobbed back into the blisterpond, alarmed by a shoal of porca that swept past in line astern, bumping into each other and wallowing awkwardly in the vortices shed by the city's trailing edges. Foolish to react to such timid creatures . . . even more foolish not to.

Soon Halfholder would have to negotiate those vortices, thread the dangers of the fringemass, and brave the freedom of the winds. She would deploy the specially offcast Carrier that she kept for safety in a reinforced pouch, bringing horror to her Elders and honor to her cause. Her gas-sacs tightened in anxiety. To relax them, she reached into the pouch and brought out the Carrier, reveling in the feel of its rough metallic surfaces, passing it from tentacle to tentacle to bring its nodule-covered shell within range of her sharpest eye. Pride flared in her breathing tubes—the tiny semi-living machine had been a valid construct, the most valid yet of any of her offcasts.

Her current position was toward the left side of the trailing edge of the city known as Sparkling Spires of the Colder Deep. Nineteen miles below and a hundred and sixty to leeward, deep in Secondhome's northern tropospheric current, drifted the drop-zone city—Whispering Volve of Late Morning. Her prompter informed Halfholder that there were no new changes to the drop zone's flight plan. Still steady, level flight.

As long as it stayed that way, she might have a chance of survival.

"Lovely," said Prudence. "Like stealing tortilla chips from a chihuahua." The probe was falling fast, as Jonas relived his hacker past, charming his way past its software defenses and sending it diving into the nether regions of the Jovian atmosphere at the same speed as a freely falling body with the same cross-section and mass . . . The sooner it was a lot lower down, the happier they'd all be . . .

"Maybe," said Jonas. "I'm still a bit rusty. They may guess what happened, and who did it. I had to wing it with the temperature readings—not enough time to simulate them properly, the damned security system nearly caught me—"

Prudence wasn't worried. "From their point of view there was an explosion inside the flotation chamber. No reason why *anything* should work correctly after that."

"Mmmm . . . depends what questions they ask. They could look at the numbers I fed them and see if Benford's Law holds good . . . Do *my* numbers have the correct distribution of initial digits? I tried my best . . . I'm sure I got more ones than twos and more twos than anything el—"

"Jonas, what the devil are you rambling on about?"

"Didn't realize you were listening, Bailey. Uh—there's a surprising statistical regularity about the numbers that turn up in real observations . . . the frequency distribution has to have logarithmic differences, and—"

"Oh, *that*," said Bailey dismissively. He had no idea what Jonas was talking about, but a producer never admitted ignorance. "Not a problem, surely?"

Prudence stepped in. "I think Jonas was warning us that there are lots of ways to investigate phony data and deduce that they're phony, Bailey. But I'm still pretty sure we've gotten away with it. Charles will go for the direct, obvious investigation, nothing subtle. His main aim will be to dump the blame on some subordinate—find a convenient scapegoat."

Cashew wasn't convinced. "How can you be so sure? Why would he behave like that when he needs the support of his whole team to get the comet diverted?"

Prudence gave a hollow laugh. "Cash, believe me, I know the animal and it can't change its stripes. Faced with the imminent end of the universe, Charles's main objective would be to make sure nobody managed to pin it on *him*."

An age dragged past—actually less than a minute. Then . . ."Cloud cover coming up," said Jonas.

"Okay, Jonas, time for me to take over." Once into the clouds, there would be no way for *Skylark* to train its telescopes on where the wreckage of the probe ought to be, and discover that it wasn't. She licked her lips, a sign that she was more nervous than appearances might indicate, and wrapped her hands around the two remote pilot grips that Jonas had rigged for her. She could have used voice control, but she preferred to *fly* the thing like a ship.

A flatfilm screen showed the stolen probe's instrument readouts and secondary controls panel, with a slowly drifting scene of distant cloud tops in one corner. Jonas had hacked his way into *everything*. The vacuum-balloon's entire control system was theirs, body and soul. *Tiglath-Pileser* had acquired itself a Jupiter probe and was going exploring. Maybe Sir Charles Dunsmoore was too chicken to go hunting aliens where aliens had to be, but now someone with balls was taking charge. With a whoop of pure joy, Prudence opened the gas valves, and *Montgolfier* swooped down among the swirling orange clouds.

15

◆

Secondhome, 2221

Nervous beyond all precedent, now that the moment had
come, Halfholder hesitated, continuing to scan the deserted
streets for the slightest sign of motion. What she was about to
do was contrary to age-old law: if she was caught, the penalty
would be the horror of ritual deflation.

A flicker of movement caught her far-eyes, and she
tensed—but it was only a subsentient cycler, snuffling aimlessly along a side street in search of waste. There was no
prospect of that, not so near the Edge, but the ancient routines
remained true to their evolutionary programs, a sign of the
Elders' ludicrous reluctance to change the old ways. The cycler's ridged wheels made a mechanical clicking sound as it
rolled across the living scaly surface of the floating city. With
relief she saw that it had no gravitics and no pseudo-eye.
Harmless. Nevertheless, she took refuge in the shadow of the
dome's lip until the cycler had pottered away behind a cluster of dormant buildings.

The fringemass shimmered in the city's turbulent wash . . .
beckoning, threatening—promising.

Halfholder secured her beltbag more tightly, excreted a
touch more liftgas into her buoyancy bubbles, and floated
free of the dome.

*   *   *

An awed silence had descended on *Tiglath-Pileser*. The probe had made a safe entrance into the thicker layers of Jupiter's atmosphere and was now sinking slowly deeper, buoyed up by its nanoshell vacuum-balloon.

There was more light down here than they'd expected. It must be bouncing off the clouds, trickling down the fractal shafts between one cloud and the next . . . Or maybe there was some kind of bioluminescence at work . . . To the un-aided eye the lighting was gloomy and sepulchral, but a sim-ple CCD photomultiplier revealed the scenery in vivid color and brilliant contrast. The infrared images were especially striking—shimmery, iridescent shapes with softly luminous edges like a painting by El Greco . . .

Sir Charles, true to form, had been concentrating on es-tablishing communications with the Jovians on their favored squark waveband. Exploring the Jovian atmosphere was more of a displacement activity; his heart hadn't really been in it . . . In Sir Charles's view, if he *had* to encounter aliens, he preferred to do so when they weren't present.

It was now becoming evident what he had been missing by not dispatching balloon probes into the clouds. This wasn't just some crummy quasi-bacteria, pseudoalgae, and giant seaweed.

"Life," said Cashew. "Everywhere, life. It's a jungle."

"More like an ocean," said Jonas. "Earth's deep trenches."

" 'Life turns up everywhere it can,' " Bailey quoted. " 'Life turns up everywhere it can't.' "

"It certainly turns up where nobody expects it," said Pru-dence. "Most of these creatures seem to be some kind of gas-bag."

"Got to be," said Jonas. "Look how they're hovering. And look at the bulbous shapes of the things!"

"So . . . to them, Jupiter's atmosphere is really one gigan-tic ocean, and they're floating in it?"

"Yep. Makes a lot of sense. Alien fishes, the lot of them."

Their eyes remained glued to the screen as an endless succession of strange creatures drifted past. There were gasbags with tendrils and gasbags with weird protuberances whose function was a total mystery . . . there were enormous gasbags and medium ones and tiny, tiny ones . . . there were flocks of clumsy birdlike creatures . . . there were things that looked like oversized pancakes, things that looked like orange marrows, and things that looked like nothing any human being had ever seen before. Were they animals or plants? Did such a distinction make any sense?

A new creature swam into sight, emerging into dim silhouette from the murky distance. Long tendrils dangled below an upper body like a slab of torn styrofoam. The outline of the top edge was a complex series of sharp angles and elaborate curlicues . . . Prudence pinged it with the sonar to find out how far away it was.

The echo took *forever* to return.

"Hey, everyone: look at *that*! The sonar must be on the blink—it reckons that thing is twelve *miles* away! But that would make it absolutely *gigantic*!"

Jonas had run an instant diagnostic. "It *is* absolutely gigantic, Pru. A hundred miles long if it's an inch. Why not? Jupiter is *vast*—the cloud layer has a hundred and twenty times the surface area of the Earth, and the atmosphere is forty thousand miles deep! Why shouldn't there be creatures here that make our whales and giant squid look like plankton?"

"Good point. It's just hard to take in." She paused to collect her thoughts. "Hmm, there's a faint echo of another of the things, even farther down. I'll move the probe over to the nearer one, and we'll take a closer look."

The probe drifted sideways for a moment, buffeted by the ever-present winds, and began to dive.

It was the rumors that had first attracted Halfholder's attention—the quiet, excited whispers, the hooded glances.

There were pheromones of intrigue in the air, concentrating in unlikely corners, tantalizing her jaded, cloistered senses.

There was a word: the Instrumentality. It hinted at novelty, at subversion, at unauthorized conclaves of free-thinking blimps . . .

Cautiously she asked indirect questions, their meaning hidden under layers of metaphor. She began to frequent disreputable quarters of the city, until her patient search paid off. It was true: the Instrumentality existed, secret groups spread across innumerable cities. As proof, the forbidden sport had once more been revived—illicit, delicious.

Skydiving!

Free-fall between cities, plunging without restraint through the untamed skies, prohibited because of ancient abuses and the Elders' pathological fear of personal danger. The penalties were severe—permanent monitoring, restricted estivation rights, recalcitrance tattoos . . . in extreme cases, deflation. But the rewards outweighed the risks, for Halfholder craved excitement, and skydiving offered that and more—intense and undiluted. And there was a political dimension that proved even more irresistible. The skydivers were actively trying to further the Policy of Benign Neglect. They had offcast a new kind of wheeler, a rogue, externally unremarkable but equipped with a different kind of mind. The Instrumentality had infiltrated hundreds of rogue wheelers into the Diversion Engines on the Inner Moons, and one day they would strike! If the plan succeeded, no longer would snowstones rain destruction on the innocent faces of the lesser worlds.

It appealed to her sense of cosmic unity.

She climbed the ranks of the subversive organization— first neophyte, then novice. She trained, in secret, and rose to initiate-designate. And what an initiation it was to be! Only one dive in ten thousand amounted to more than symbolic defiance. But the Instrumentality had taken note of her unusual political commitment and had blessed her with high honor.

Her initiation would further the Cause by direct action.

At first even Halfholder was wracked with doubt. The action demanded seemed too extreme, a crime that went far beyond harmless insubordination. The Effectuators of the Instrumentality became more ardent, more persuasive. *The Elders are weak and lazy. Strike but once, and they will fall.* Charmed, flattered, aroused, entranced, bewildered, she became a willing accessory to her own moral seduction. To experience the ecstasy of skydiving, she would risk all. She had never wanted anything so much in her entire life. She existed in a suppressed frenzy of anticipation, intoxicated beyond endurance by the prospect of ultimate freedom.

The Effectuators promised her an emotional experience beyond all imagination. They promised that her actions would be celebrated forever in song and legend.

She believed them.

Halfholder rocked in the freshening winds, near-paralyzed by terror, as the scaly flatness of the city slab fell away. A random eddy caught her. In a burst of manic energy she fought against it. This was a time to fly low, not yet a time to soar.

With an effort, she trailed her tentacles, locked their bracing-ring muscles rigid with a quick, instinctive pressure grip, and exhaled a small quantity of liftgas. Her sensitive tips brushed the outermost fronds of the barrier, only for her to blunder immediately into a wild flurry of vortex filaments. Cursing herself for making so elementary an error despite all her training, Halfholder tumbled end over end, crashing through the feathery strands of airweed, ripping branches out so that dark, rubbery sap began to well from the severed roots, plunging out of control *between* a dozen pulsating trunks, any of which could have ruptured her brain case with its terrible spines. Before she could feel the fear, she was free, buffeted by the city's wash.

The fringemass loomed. She caught a quick glimpse of the flailing tendrils at the city's stern, each as thick as a large building and as long as Main Avenue, propelling it faster than the ever-present current, but in the same general direction. Only then, when she was comparatively safe, did the fear hit her—and she found herself floundering, close to panic.

She was saved by a flock of rippling pancake birds, which scattered in alarm at the unprecedented intruder as she flopped, out of control, from one rubbery disk to another. The humor of the situation swept the fear away. As the shy creatures slopped clumsily to right and left, she emitted a high-pitched whistle. At once the birds shot skyward, as they always did when panicked. Then Bright Halfholder of the Violent Foam remembered her training, excreted a large bubble of liftgas, and *fell*.

Suddenly, wilder than she had ever imagined, the rush hit her, and she was wheeling through Secondhome's thick atmosphere, riding the thermals, swerving to right and left, finally *free*. Free of care, free of hope, free of any emotion save the delicious joy of being at one with the air and the planet. Now she felt *right* to the core of her lifesoul. She *knew*, beyond any shadow of any doubt, that the Elders were wrong. Too long in control, they had allowed their respect for cosmic wisdom to atrophy. Too hidebound, their rigid minds were unable to encompass the utter *strangeness* of the universe, of its multitude of beings—some so unimaginable that even she, Bright Halfholder of the Violent Foam, at one with the Lifesoul Cherisher, could not fathom them. Too tentative, too frightened, so that for tens of millions of years the Elders had pursued their insane bombardment of every nearby solid body—tiny Meltball, shrouded Acidglobe, the double planets Poisonblue and Ruggedrock, enigmatic Reddust, deceptive Manyrings, the Fartheroutworlds . . . It was warfare on a cosmic scale, waged against the innocent—a perversion of the artistry of the Lifesoul Cherisher.

It was wrong.

Despite herself, though, she had to admit that the error was understandable. Throughout much of blimp evolution, and before, Firsthome had suffered the terrors of snowstrike. The Elders had learned to control it—and had belatedly learned the error of redirecting incoming snowstones at their own star. This apparently harmless act, continued over a billion years, had done incalculable damage to their parent star. Only the dismal Exodus to Secondhome, a desperate interstellar voyage on domesticated magnetotori, had saved them—but at a terrible cost.

So, when Secondhome's gravipulsor engines were being installed on its four major moons, the Elders adopted a different strategy. There were two choices. One was to redirect the snowstones into random orbits. Blimp technology could easily impart enough energy to fling them out of the system altogether, but there was an ethical obstacle: A loose snowstone in the interstellar depths might one day encounter some other gas giant civilization and collide with its planet or its star. The blimps were terrified of loose snowstones themselves and were constitutionally incapable of creating more, however small the risk might be.

Which left only the second option: redirect the snowstones to collide with the lesser worlds.

The Elders had convinced themselves that this was the only safe course. It would be vandalism on a cosmic scale, leaving those worlds scarred and unable ever to support life—but that was a small price to pay, and in any case none of them, not even Manyrings, possessed life-sustaining atmospheres. Manyrings had the right gases, but it was too cold.

The skydivers took a different view, the Policy of Benign Neglect. The lesser worlds, lifeless as they must be, danced to the rhythms of the Lifesoul Cherisher. Their artistry deserved respect, not cosmic vandalism. And there was more. Terrified by even the faintest prospect of snowstrike, the Elders had robbed their own ecosystem of its most precious tutor—the random hand of chaos. For—so the skydivers believed—the cities *needed* the devastation of snowstrike, of occasional massive impacts in the upper atmosphere, to disturb the planetary ecosystem and favor the growth of diversity. It made sense to Halfholder: she remembered how the aeroplankton had increased after the fireworks.

Halfholder suddenly saw just *how* strange the universe could be. Why, even now, even in the corrosive nitrox atmosphere of Poisonblue, there *might* be some rudimentary form of pseudolife, struggling to maintain a precarious existence against all the chemical odds . . . The wheelers said that Poisonblue's nitrox was unbalanced. What was pumping it? Fivemoonlike vulcanism? In her near-madness she imagined exotic collections of tightly knit molecules, perhaps so improbably designed that they actually made *use* of the poison to power their alien metabolism. Over aeons, those molecules might evolve into huge, lumbering creatures, staggering across the blistering rock, sloshing feebly in the seething oceans of molten ice . . . How else could the planet's atmosphere remain so far from equilibrium, be *so* poisonous?

Her rational self would have rejected such thoughts instantly, for they were against all the teaching, all the accumulated knowledge of her species. But here, soaring unencumbered on the primal winds of Secondhome, her mind escaped its accustomed bounds and began to imagine not just the improbable, but the blatantly impossible. For in such a state of mind, *nothing* could be impossible.

Why, even the overthrow of the Elders was conceivable. And with it, the first, tentative steps toward the salvation of this wrecked, maltreated Solar System. And the resumed evolution of the floating cities, and the start of the long path back to spiritual health and genetic renewal. Even as the Elders protected their world, they were slowly bringing about its ruination.

They had to be stopped.

Uhlirach-Bengtsen was beginning to wonder if Sir Charles had been the right choice. The man worked tirelessly, but tangible *achievements* . . . not so clear. The undersecretary for world affairs was coming under increasing pressure from all directions—the politicians, the military, the ecowarriors, the religious right, the crypto-communist left, the fence-sitting liberals . . . Today he'd been told rumors that some long-defunct group of freedom fighters had gotten their hands on a cache of nuclear weapons that should have been destroyed half a century ago under the Global Disarmament Treaty, and were getting ready to bomb Jupiter. Bombing the comet might have made some kind of sense, though a few nukes would just give it a pimple or two, but *Jupiter*? It was probably nonsense, but it had to be checked out.

There were protest marches and sit-ins and strikes and mass love-ins, teenagers romping naked in CenterParc, and the drug trade had surged overnight from its near-comatose state into a booming industry.

Everyone wanted answers, progress, action. The comet was all over the X. It wasn't a joke anymore. It was changing from something millions of miles away in outer space to a personal threat. You could feel the terror rising. Soon the world would wake up to what had been the case all along: *this was a potential worldwrecker*. And what did the task force have to show? One wheeler, a lot of indecipherable noise, and some extraterrestrial bugs.

In a few minutes he would be giving a press conference, telling the world's media what an excellent job Sir Charles was doing. He checked his tie, brushed some fluff off his jacket, and tried to put himself in a positive frame of mind.

Halfholder had cast off from the side corner of the city's trailing edge, but below the habitable levels the airflow was unpredictable. For the next half hour she had just two aims in mind: to avoid becoming entangled in the city's hanging tendril jungle, and to keep a weather-eye open for snarks.

A vortex train spun her out, down, and away, whirling in the misty air, her six trunks spread wide like the spokes of a floppy wheel. The city began to dim behind intervening mist trails . . . Desperately she spun, unbalancing her trunks to start a long, slow, controlled sideslip back toward the tendril jungle. If she lost contact now, the winds would carry her too far away from her objective.

The mists thinned, and she slipped diagonally past the vast tangled wall of tendrils—down, down toward their flailing tips, tapering in toward the center where the city was vulnerable.

Halfholder consulted her prompter. Whispering Volve was still on its intended course, now seventeen miles below, and she was well within her safety envelope. But she was dropping faster than planned. Carefully she extracted a liftstick from her beltbag, opened a trunk-sphincter, and sucked it inside. When the digestive juices hit, it would bubble liftgas into her abdominal cavities.

Trunks spread-eagled for maximum resistance, she floated slowly downward like a bizarre snowflake. She rotated clockwise, paused, then counterclockwise. She was tempted to try a Death Spiral, but it was her first dive and such a maneuver might all too likely live up to its name. She settled for a conservative seesawing motion.

The tendrils' stalks began to narrow, the jungle thinning with every passing second. Her plans had reached the critical phase. With infinite care she opened the pouch and removed the Carrier. She primed its nodules with some of her own precious liftgas, drifted in as close to the edge of the tendril jungle as she dared, felt her gas-sacs tense uncontrollably.

She cradled the Carrier in the strongest cluster of trunks that she could assemble, drew it back—and hurled it from her, toward the jungle.

The Carrier fell in a parabolic arc, slid past the outer fringe of tendrils, and dropped like a stone. Its vestigial wheels spun uselessly in the airflow. Between it and Secondhome's metallic hydrogen core was nothing but roiling gases and liquids. Then its nodules jetted liftgas, slowing its descent. Its tiny graspers reached, touched, clung.

The Carrier began to climb the tendril.

Within was a capsule of rotworm spores, genetically tailored to that one city's genome. Over the next few days the Carrier would inject those spores, one by one, into the succulent flesh of the tendril. There they would encyst into egg masses, then grow into tiny mobile plasts, burrowing deep into the city's interior. The plasts would metamorphose into tiny parasitic worms, each of which would consume tiny amounts of tendril flesh—and, every few days, deposit several thousand new spores.

Soon the cooling-vanes would be riddled with rotworms. Then the citizens of Sparkling Spires of the Colder Deep would have to evacuate—a tedious, disruptive procedure, for even an undamaged city was difficult to maneuver. After that, the city would die, sliding helplessly into the colder deep from which it had taken its name.

Halfholder seesawed between wild elation and sick horror. But there was no way back—the course of the infestation was now unstoppable. Tormented by doubt, teetering on the brink of insanity, she drifted downward, no longer aware of her surroundings.

Jonas set the probe's camera to its highest level of magnification and checked that the recorder was functioning. The images shivered as the balloon rode the bumpy air currents, but the computer managed to filter most of that out, so there was little doubt as to what they were seeing. *Sensational!*

"Dear god, it's a *city*," said Bailey.

"So this is where the aliens live?" asked Cashew.

"Must be. The place is swarming with them! And look at those—*buildings*. And all those ramps and . . . roadways. Shit, they're crawling with wheelers!"

"Well, they would be, wouldn't they?"

Time passed. Sparkling Spires of the Colder Deep had long since faded into the orange-gray mists overhead.

A semblance of sanity returned.

She felt heady, wild, flooded with weird emotions. *This* she would never forget, not through a thousand estivations. Now she knew why the skydivers were unable to resist the urge to risk their lives, time and time again, in Secondhome's dangerous skies. The rush flowed through her sensitized cannulas, until her canopy felt as wide as a dozen cities, yet as small as a single parasitic shrimp.

Her initiation task was accomplished. The next task was survival.

In an obsession born of arduous training, she checked her trajectory once more, and saw with some alarm that she was still falling too rapidly. She was within the safety envelope, to be sure—but if Whispering Volve changed course, she could lose what little margin remained, and her remains would join those of countless others, revolving forever in the lopsided ammonia vortex of the Whirl or sinking to the inferno of the core.

She was just opening her beltbag to pull out another lift-stick when the snark pack emerged from a thicket of airweed. There were five of them, carving effortlessly through the turbid air, their spiny mouths clamped shut in a grimace of instant death.

She had trained for this, too. Waiting until the pack had completely encircled her, edging closer for the kill, she removed a flash grenade from her beltbag.

The mouths began to open, revealing—as she knew they would, but that made it more frightening, not less—their short, razor-edged spines, able to tear her canopy to shreds. As the snarks surged forward, she tossed the grenade as high as she could throw it, clamped her trunks into a tight wedge, and exhaled a great bubble of liftgas.

Attracted by the sudden movement, the snarks darted after the grenade. As they did so, the gas bubble expanded, rising slowly.

The effect was even better than in the training simulators.

The lead snark actually *swallowed* the grenade an instant before it exploded. Plastered thickly around the grenade's luminescent core was an oxygenic paste, and the explosion triggered a spurt of the toxic, corrosive gas. Mixed as it was with the bubble of liftgas, primed with the snark's bodily moisture, the unstable combination exploded in a burst of light that must have been visible back on Sparkling Spires of the Colder Deep. Halfholder kept her eyes tight shut and *felt* rather than saw the blast as the snark pack came to pieces in a shower of torn, burning flesh. They fell around her like slow shrapnel.

She opened her eyes. One wounded, blinded, burning snark spiraled downward trailing oily brown smoke, wailing terribly in an agony of death. Of the other four, she saw no sign.

She pulsed in ripples of relief. Then, having calmed down, she reached once more for a liftstick. The maneuver, effective though it had been, had cost her half a mile in height.

Her groping trunks encountered nothing more than an empty bag. With growing horror, she realized what had happened. She had failed to secure the open bag when she threw the grenade, and the force of her dive had sucked out the beltbag's contents, to tumble irretrievably toward Secondhome's core, forty thousand miles below.

No liftsticks, no grenades, no knife, no ballast pods.

No hope.

Infuriatingly, Whispering Volve pursued its stately course. But that scarcely mattered now. She was falling outside the envelope, drifting lower with each passing second. Her prompter's computations were simple and deadly. She would come agonizingly close, she might even be able to reach the target city's fringemass—but she would miss the Edge by several hundred yards.

Halfholder took a deep breath, forced her trunks to rigidity, hoped for unexpected lift from a passing vortex, and began to chant her deathsong in a wavering voice.

"Jonas—am I going mad, or does that one have some kind of artifact slung 'round its body?"

"Which one, Cash?" Jonas was concentrating on his filming.

"Bottom of the screen, in among all those sleek, fast-moving things. They look predatory, don't you think? But isn't that a sort of *bag*?"

"I see. Let's take a closer look!" The technician swiveled one of the probe's cameras until the creature came into view on the screen. As he zoomed in on it, the focus adjusted automatically. "No, I don't think—"

A brilliant explosion turned the screen white, and the overload shut it off for an instant. When the image came back, the ruined bodies of the predators were fluttering down into the darkness below, trailing ugly clouds of thick smoke.

"As I was saying, Jonas—yes, the creature does have some kind of bag, and it took something out and *threw* it. At those things I reckoned were predators."

"Which are now turning themselves into aerial bonfires."

"Yes. But they didn't turn themselves. The creature did that to them."

"A weapon! It was a *weapon*! The damned thing's intelligent!"

"*Despite* using a weapon . . . Yes, Jonas, I rather think it is. In which case we've made contact. With an alien. Is it the right kind of alien? I have no idea, but an alien in the hand is worth two in the brood-hive. So obviously we give it the portable communicator—but *how*? I hadn't expected an aerial encoun—"

Jonas was watching the creature closely through the viewfinder of his Suzuki-73. He could amost empathize with the alien. It had been attacked, had beaten off the enemy, and now . . . "Pru, it looks in distress to me. Listen to the sonar! It's making noises! Reminds me of a pod of whales. And I rather think it's lost its briefcase. I can't see the bag anymore."

"If I didn't recognize the danger of anthropomorphizing," said Cashew, "I'd say it's *scared*. Look how frantically it's waving its tentacles! It's trying to reach the edge of the city!"

"Even aliens," said Jonas, "must have a few things in common with us. There isn't enough room in organism-space for all aliens to be totally different from *all* the other aliens—us included . . .

"Cash, if it was trying to reach the city, it missed."

They watched the creature slip past the fronds that decked the city's edge, plummeting into the far depths, dangerously close to the huge, dangling tentacles . . .

A flock of pancake birds shot from the edge of the jungle, ripping and tearing as Halfholder whirled through them, smashing into her, destroying her forward momentum. The fringemass stayed tantalizingly out of reach—even a quick death eluded her. Now there was nothing to stop her from falling endlessly into Secondhome's gravity well, down to where the pressure became so inconceivable that the atmosphere turned liquid, then (madness) solid. Long before she reached the layer of liquid molecular hydrogen, she would either have starved or been squashed flat . . . With her knife lost, there was no way to hasten her end. She tore in a frenzy at the remains of a pancake bird, scattering it to the six winds—

And froze.

What in the name of the Original Elders was *that*?

"Left—no, right, right, *right,* damn you . . . *Hold the god-damned arm* steady, *Jonas . . . Caught* it!" yelled Bailey. The alien hung from the one of the probe's robotic arms, like a soggy dishcloth slung over a wash line. "Nice driving, Prudence! Just *look* at that mother!"

"Maybe it's a father," said Jonas. Cashew decided not to enlighten him. "Or a drone. Or A Thing Of Which Man Is Not Intended To . . ."

"I still think it was in distress," said Cashew. "You saw how those things tore into it. It *fought back*. I don't care what you say, that's the only sensible explanation of what we saw. Oh, don't start trying to be clever, Jonas! I've got an imagination, too, you know. Sure, it was the Jovian equivalent of a poetry recital . . . But I've also got a well-developed intuition, and I *know* what I saw."

"Me, too. I was just thinking aloud. Look at that . . . *tentacle*? Well, whatever it is, it's dripping yellow gore. Yuck! What a great sequence!"

"It's not quite the first contact scenario I was anticipating," said Prudence. "This alien is injured. For all we know, it's dying. It's a traveler, not a resident. It could even be *the wrong kind of alien*, though two kinds would surely be a bit much . . . Do we try to give this one a communicator, or pass it up and wait for a better chance?"

Bailey had been watching events unfold, and until now he hadn't said much. Sometimes Bailey was amazingly bright. Not often, but when he was . . .

"Narrative imperative," he said quietly.

"Pardon?"

"The power of *story*, Cash. Remember all those tales you heard or read as a kid? The mouse that helped the lion? If we give this one the communicator and the alien dies, all we've lost is a communicator. The probe has several, right? Must have, Charlie Dunsmoore would never put all of his eggs in one basket. We can try again. *But*, if the alien lives, we may just have made a friend for life." He waved his hands in embarrassment. "Yes, I know it may not work like that for aliens, but just suppose it does! Think what an opportunity we may miss! *Don't you realize that this is a surefire award-winning VV sequence?*"

Jonas looked at Cash, who nodded. Prudence watched them impassively. "Narrative imperative? Guys, the universe doesn't work like that." Then she laughed. "But *people* do, that's what you're telling me. Okay, you all risked everything to accompany me on this wild goose chase—so *you* get to call this one."

"Jonas, I appoint you chief mouse. See if you can bell the alien. Cash can work the camera."

Jonas started muttering. "First find your bell . . . I wonder where Dunsmoore's guys put the bloody—ah, must be that boxy thing over there. Lift the lid—bingo!" He fiddled with the control circuits for the probe's manipulator arms and managed, after a couple of false starts, to persuade a second arm to pull a communicator unit out of the box.

It was wired in place. Laboriously, he untwisted the thick wire until the unit came free.

Where to put . . . The mobile weather balloon had lost its pouch . . . Nowhere obvious . . .

Except for those flexible, sensitive tentacles.

He thought for a moment and set the communicator to re-play the last few minutes' events. Then he turned its small but bright display to face the alien's ring of eyes and offered the communicator to the creature as it hung from the first robot arm, apparently helpless. For all he knew, it was terrified.

Or angry.

He'd half expected the alien to shy away as the second arm approached it, but it didn't budge. Some of the eyes, however, seemed to swivel, redirecting themselves to focus on the approaching communicator. They watched, occasion-ally popping in and out, as the tiny images of the predators exploded and spiraled to their deaths. Whether those eyes saw anything, nobody could be sure. The humans didn't know what range of light those eyes were sensitive to. But it looked as if they could see *something.*

Hesitantly, the alien reached out with a tentacle. It touched the communicator, and the rubbery limb slid across its plas-tic surface. Then the alien slipped a tentacle tip through the handle attached to the top.

Jonas took a deep breath, gave the necessary command, and the robot arm let go.

The tentacle didn't.

The alien shivered a little as it lay draped across the nose of the probe. It brought the communicator up near its ring of eyes again and held it there, turning it from side to side. It seemed puzzled.

I hope it doesn't drop the bloody thing, thought Jonas. *It's a long way down.*

The alien reached some kind of decision and tucked the communicator away beneath its fringe of tentacles.

"Hey, she likes it!"

"Jonas, why are you so sure that thing is female?"

"My media-training tutor told me always to sound confident, even if I was talking crap, Cash."

"That explains why you're always so confident, Jonas."

By now, the probe had floated well away from the city. Prudence used its attitude thrusters to bring it around in a huge circle. It gained height as it went.

"We can't detain her indefinitely," he said. "The planet's rotation has already carried the probe close to the limb, and we'll soon have to put it on autopilot until it reemerges from radio shadow. I dare not hack into the comsat network; they're too likely to notice. It's time we escorted the lady home. I say we spiral up, wait till she's well above the city, let the little lady go, and see what she does. If I'm right, she'll drop right back down again. I hope she gets it right this time."

They spiraled up.

When he got to where he wanted to be, nobody had contradicted him, so he let the robot arm swing the alien sideways. Then, with a deft toss, he *threw* the creature into the Jovian air. It floundered about for a few heart-stopping moments, then recovered, reoriented itself, and began to float downward apparently under control.

The balloon probe continued to rise.

Far below, a tiny dot seemed to be drifting toward the floating city. Then a layer of cloud interposed itself, and the dot was hidden from view.

"I hope to hell you got all that, Cash," Jonas worried.
"Bet you a week's salary I did."

Halfholder landed close to the rim, but safely—partially deflated, bruised, battered, leaking gas from a dozen wounds, trailing thin trickles of sticky fluid.

She still held the strange object that she had succeeded in stealing from the weird creature that—by sheer good fortune—had come close enough for her to catch it. She congratulated herself on her quick thinking. She had certainly outwitted the monstrous creature. She hadn't realized she possessed so much courage. She had grasped the animal by its tentacle, subdued it, stolen its pretty toy—and gotten away before the stupid beast woke up and tried to take the toy back.

It had been huge. It might have swallowed her whole. (She carefully omitted to ask herself where its mouth had been. Obviously it must have had one, somewhere.)

This was the stuff of legend. She would compose a song to record the saga of her bravery. They would still be singing it a billion years from now . . .

Rubbish. The story wasn't that good. Forty million years, surely, but never a billion.

For several minutes she lay unmoving, as these mad thoughts rushed through her overstressed mind. Then her instinct for self-preservation kicked in. She had been skydiving. She had sown the seeds of a city's destruction. If the Elders of Whispering Volve caught her now, she would pay the penalty of ritual deflation. Painfully, she dragged herself across the surface of the city foam, ignoring how it scraped her hide, her mind set on only one thing—concealment.

Partially hidden behind a tall stand of waving bladderwort, she saw an ancient, dilapidated blisterpond. Its skin was dull and flaky, its rim distorted, its lid sluggish and slimy. But it pulled clumsily open, just enough for her to fall inside. She exuded a puff of capture-hormone onto its walls to close it again.

She dropped the object she had stolen. Later, when she felt better, she might decide to examine it. For now, she couldn't care less what it was, or what she might do with it.

Eventually, she would be restored to her original self. The blisterpond still held a stock of preserved food. Her wounds would begin to heal. Soon she would be able to make contact with the skydivers of Whispering Volve . . .

Above her, a city sickened and began to die. She mourned its impending loss. But even more she mourned the pock-marked surfaces of a score of worlds—moonlets, moons, planets—sacrificed to the blind fear of the Elders. What was one dead city, anyway, compared to their total loss through evolutionary stagnation?

What *was* one dead city?

Through her pain she came, slowly, to an understanding of what her crime would achieve.

Nothing.

The destruction of Sparkling Spires, she now saw, was lit-tle more than a futile gesture. The Instrumentality had misled her in its insistence that this terrible act of rebellion would—somehow—bring about the triumph of the Policy of Benign Neglect and end the carnage of the lesser worlds.

Now she saw that it could not. The Elders' mind-set was too firmly entrenched, their power too great, public apathy about the Cause too prevalent.

It would take more. Much more. How many cities would the skydivers have to kill before the Elders were goaded into action? Would blimps have to die, too? Might the cure be worse than the disease?

She had been *used*.

In a kind of delirium, crazy schemes flickered through her consciousness. Wait for approaching snowstrike and then sabotage the Diversion Engines . . . Assassinate the Elders as they estivated in their blisterponds . . . Cryptically reprogram the defense symbiauts . . .

It might take all of those things. It *would* take all of those things.

It was going to be a long campaign, and even if she avoided ritual deflation she would probably be dead before it succeeded. But there would be others, equally foolish, to continue her role.

And about one thing, the Instrumentality had *not* lied: the wild, heady excitement of the descent, the senses sharpened by mortal danger. The reckless ecstasy of utter freedom.

The rush.

She put all thoughts of the strange new object from her mind and became lost in the wonder of her new awakening. Already she was planning her next dive.

16

Whispering Volve of Late Morning, 2221

For many Jovian days, Bright Halfholder of the Violent Foam rested in the cocooned environment of her newfound blisterpond, recuperating from her narrow brush with the Deathsoul Keeper and meditating on the incomprehensible manner of her survival.

Her near-eyes kept returning to the object that she had stolen from the strange metal monster. Despite her courage in pulling off the daring theft, she felt a flurry of fear every time she looked at it. The object seemed so benign, lying on its side on the blisterpond's damp, rippled floor. It could have been a wheeler construct, except that the materials were exotic and the design was disturbingly unjovian . . . Yet, like wheeler constructs, it exuded a tangible sense of *purpose*. It was clearly *made* (she knew not by whom/what)—as, she now realized with a delayed sense of shock, was the spherical metal monster from which (not whom) she had stolen it. She knew that she should have understood this fundamental point much earlier, but in her disturbed condition there had been little chance of that.

Hesitantly, she poked one of her sexfurcated trunks at the object. Nothing dangerous occurred as a result. Indeed, nothing occurred at all, except for a slight change in the object's orientation relative to the blisterpond's floor. Encouraged by this—though oddly disappointed—she poked again . . . and *something* made a sharp sound, all jagged high-frequency waves, uncannily like a small gas-sac popping under extreme pressure.

Seconds later, a babble of the weirdest noises she had ever heard filled the tiny chamber of the blisterpond, and her hearing patches began to experience a worrying level of distortion. In mild panic, worried that the noise might attract guardians to her hideaway, she poked and pummeled the object, to discover that various of its protrusions could be made to pop in and out, or to move. Intrigued—and telling herself that the blisterpond's thick rind would stop the noise from reaching the outside world—she began to experiment systematically, and her intelligent explorations were quickly rewarded. One protrusion seemed to affect the noise level, and she found that she could turn down the volume until the noises became comfortable. And another . . .

Created moving patterns of colored light.

At first she thought that the patterns were diffused sunlight, filtered through colored clouds and playing across the object's surface, but she quickly realized that there was no suitable source of illumination. Inceasing the sensitivity of her nighteyes enhanced the contrast. She swiveled around so that her chromatic-eyes could be brought to bear, and was rewarded by a riot of impossible color combinations. Then, with a suddenness that took her breath away, the patterns resolved themselves into a series of abstract scenes, primitively rendered in two dimensions, and changing faster than the eye could follow.

Puzzled, she watched for a time, but the flashing images did little except dazzle her. They made no sense whatsoever. Bored, she silenced the babble and darkened the moving patterns.

That was better.

"What do you mean, he can't stay here? This is his *home*!" Angie had known it was going to be hard to make Charity see the obvious. Moses was safe ... for the moment. The Chinese from the autogiros had taken quite a pasting, and they must be wondering what had happened ... as indeed was Angie. It didn't take a genius to reconstruct roughly what Moses must have done, but how he had managed it was quite another matter. *What kind of a mind must that boy have?* It didn't bear thinking about. It was frightening.

The area around the wreckage had been swarming with Diversity Police for days—the firefight between two Chinese factions on African soil had hit the first layer of the newspages, and was still close to the top of the stack. There was no mention of a missing boy or a small yellow autogiro. As far as Angie's snoops could tell, no one in the Village had kicked up any fuss about the boy's disappearance—no doubt because someone influential there had been involved in smuggling him in to begin with and had no wish to draw attention to that. Already the boy had been removed from the Village's records, probably by the same person.

There was therefore no reason for the police to suspect that the incident had been anything other than a skirmish between two opposing groups of Chinese illegals, probably over drugs or protected animals. Ecotopia naturally had spies in Free China—just as the Chinese had them in Ecotopia— and already they were digging, but it might take years before any useful information came to light. It looked as though the two groups had fought a short, very nasty battle, with no survivors on either side. A rhinoceros seemed to have gotten caught up in the fight, doing quite a bit of damage before running off, and it was generally felt that this was poetic justice. The rhino responsible had been located not far away, intact but bearing enough signs of the fight to identify it, and it had become an overnight celebrity on the eXtraNet.

If any nation except Free China had been responsible, the affair would have blown up into a major diplomatic incident, but since neither Free China nor Ecotopia had diplomatic representation within each other's territories, this was out of the question. The Ecotopian government had long ago become inured to Chinese isolationism, and it knew there was no way to register its displeasure, but it did take the elementary precaution of stepping up its military presence in Eastafrican airspace and its satellite surveillance of the Chinese borders, land and sea. This made things a little easier for Angie, because it meant that for a few weeks it was unlikely that there would be any attempt to kidnap or assassinate Moses. Nevertheless, the Ecotopian bureaucracy would soon assign the incident to its fat file of Chinese violations and gradually remove the current precautionary measures.

Even before that, the boy was vulnerable to a well-organized strike—by Hunters or mercenaries, for example. However he had pulled off his astonishing survival trick, it would be unlikely to work against a laser-guided antipersonnel missile fired by a sniper several miles away. However, one factor was in their favor: it would take time to organize such an operation, and during that short window, Moses must be spirited away. She doubted that the Chinese would be much interested in Gooma Facility if the boy wasn't present, but all the while he was, there was a distinct danger to Charity. As she was now trying to make clear.

Charity didn't care about her own safety, but Moses' was another matter, and eventually she got the message. It didn't help that Charity was trying to exorcise some demons of her own. Ever since that final spat with her sister, she had been wracked with guilt. Why *shouldn't* Prudence go hunting wheelers if she wanted to? There had been no communication between them—not while Prudence was en route to Jupiter, not even to help relieve her boredom. Charity knew it was foolish, but emotionally she still blamed herself for sending Prudence away.

In principle, Moses' return must cause all that to change. Prudence was the child's closest relative, apart from his mother. There was no way that Charity could hide the joyful news from her own sister, however difficult their personal relationship had become. She knew that events were forcing her to get in touch with Prudence, and that meant she would have to apologize—even though she still thought that Prudence was in the wrong.

As soon as Angie had worked out that this was the problem, she agreed. "Honey, she's your sister. You can't cut her out of your life altogether, however much you disagree with what she's done. I'll bet she feels just as bad about it as you do. And I know she'll be just as stubborn." Angie was a skilled negotiator, once she sensed a leverage point, and before Charity quite understood what was happening, she found that she had agreed to Moses' being taken into hiding in return for Angie's service as a mediator between the Odingo twins.

In the end, the reconciliation was easier than Charity had feared. For a start, it is difficult to have an argument when there is a ninety-minute delay between accusation and defense. Both sisters had changed considerably since they had last met, both were wracked with guilt, and both were secretly relieved to be on speaking terms again. Moreover, Prudence had not, as it turned out, been digging up valuable wheelers at all. Over the heavily encrypted channel, Charity came to understand that her elder twin had been sidetracked into something far more interesting and far more laudable: attempting to save the human race. As Prudence explained how they had been losing confidence in Charles Dunsmoore's task force and had decided to take matters into their own hands, Charity found herself muttering approval. But then, they both had good reason to despise the man.

Angie brought Moses into the room so that his aunt could see him. Despite being prompted, the boy said very little, but Charity comforted herself with the thought that it was hard speaking into an unresponsive 'node. Moses was taciturn even in ordinary conversations: time-lagged ones would be totally beyond him. With such long delays, normal two-way conversations become pointless. Instead, one party transmits a lengthy monologue. The recipient records the lot, takes electronic notes along the way, plans out a reply, and transmits his or her own monologue in return. Charity did, however, manage to engage Moses in a reasonably articulate conversation about the animals at Gooma Facility, which she relayed to Prudence.

The reply, when it came, had a remarkable effect on the child. Prudence began by saying that they'd found some new kind of animals in Jupiter's atmosphere. Charity and Angie could hardly fail to notice the boy's interest perk up as soon as her sister said this, and when some edited vidifilm followed, the boy was captivated. At first, Prudence limited her transmission to the curious floating fauna of the Jovian cloud layer, but she was working her way toward the climax. "I want you all to promise not to breathe a word of what I'm going to show you next, okay? I'm not going to wait for you to reply—just make the promise *to each other*. Done that? I'll assume you have.

"Charity, Angie, Moses . . . we've made contact with an intelligent alien! How do we know? Well, some bright spark in the Jovian Task Force must have decided that if we ever managed to get one of the communicators into the possession of what might be a sentient alien, then it would be a really good intelligence test to equip the communicator with a switch and present it in the off state. Maybe they were right, because the alien worked out how to switch it on. Great. Unfortunately, it also turned out to be intelligent enough to switch the communicator *off* again. We don't know why . . . maybe it got bored. We're hoping it will soon decide to switch it back on, but that may not help much. While communication was in operation it didn't respond to anything we sent it. I'm wondering if we're doing the right thing, sending it simple combinatorial patterns . . . squares, rectangles, number sequences . . . Maybe it's so alien that it doesn't find such things meaningful? But every philosophy text insists that mathematics is a universal language, and nearly all the alien contact groups seem to agree ... Anyway, enough of that: you can see for yourselves. I give you: the alien!"

The screen blanked, flickered, and then the image stabilized. Charity gasped. Angie shook her head in wonder. Moses jumped up and down in excitement, bouncing on the elastic webbing of his chair. "Ma! Look, look—Auntie Pru's found an alien!" He seemed to have reverted to childhood, and Charity felt her eyes stinging.

Moses kept up an incessant commentary. Angie and Charity spoke not a word; their vocal cords didn't seem to be functioning. First, Prudence transmitted Jonas's film of their initial encounter with the creature falling spread-eagled through the snark pack like an isolated snowflake. The significance of the animal's belted bag was lost on no one. The explosive devastation of the predators confirmed their conclusions. Then the alien was dangling helplessly from the boom of the vacuum-balloon. They took in the domed bag, the ring of eyes, the skirt of dangling trunklike tentacles ...

The film now cut to the inside of the blisterpond, as seen by the portable communicator's cameras and heard by its microphones. The noises were decidedly odd. The creature's lack of response to the transmitted patterns was palpable and disappointing.

"Doesn't look so intelligent to me," said Angie.

"Pretty dumb, I'd say," Charity agreed. "I'm not even sure that it's watch—"

"Yes!" Moses yelled. "Yes, Ma, yes, she's watching! Right from the start, she was looking at us with some of her eyes, the four at the front which see better details close up! Then she started to tune in the eyes beside those, the ones that can see better in the dark! And then—" He was leaping up and down now, animated, overexcited, but more *alive* than he had been at any time since he'd rejoined the world outside the Village. Charity and Angie started at him, wondering whether the child had gone mad, or whether he was a genius.

Finally, Angie found her voice. "Moses, what are you talking about? How do you know—"

"*Why can't anyone see?* It's obvious! Look at how she swivels her dome, how her eyes pop in and out!"

"Moses, how can you possibly tell if the creature is male or female?"

"Not a sex thing! Alien gender is . . . social! Role-play! Watch how she—no words . . ."

The two women looked at each other. Something quite unprecedented was happening here. Angie felt prickles running along her spine. Suddenly she knew exactly how Moses had managed to survive the firefight and what had happened to the Chinese paramilitaries.

They'd never stood a chance.

"My God," said Angie. "Charity—he's not making this up. Are you, Moses?"

"No! Can't you *see*? Look, she's . . . proud of herself, but frightened. She isn't sure what the communicator is anymore. She thought she had captured it, but now she is beginning to worry that it has captured *her*."

Now Charity understood, too. "He always did have an amazing way with animals." It was the understatement of the year.

"Moses: is it—she—intelligent?" Angie asked.

"She can think real thoughts," Moses responded. "They're not like our thoughts, but she knows she's thinking them."

A moment to digest this . . . "Then why doesn't she respond to the pictures?"

"The pictures are moving too fast," said Moses. "She's slower than a human. Before she recognizes anything, it's changed. Aunt Pru must slow down, keep the pictures the same for many seconds, if she wants the alien to understand them."

The screen faded to black and Prudence's face reappeared. "And that's when it switched off. We have no idea why."

No, but we certainly do, Charity thought. The implications struck home, and she began to realize just how much this was going to change everybody's lives. Angie, too, had begun to understand.

She wondered what Prudence was going to make of the next monologue.

"Charity, I'm *so* sorry."

"Can't be helped, Angie. Like you said, Gooma Facility is no place for Moses."

"I know. But I hadn't envisaged anything quite so extreme. A safe little hidey-hole somewhere in Normerica, where my people could keep an eye on him—that was what I had in mind."

Charity discovered she could smile. In fact, she was feeling a quiet pride, in Moses and in herself. *Sometimes it's not as hard to do the right thing as you expect it to be.*

"Charity—you almost seem *happy*."

The smile faded. "Not happy, Angie. But it's very clear to me what I must do, and what Moses must do, and I feel no anger and no pain. This is how it was meant to be."

"I wish I could be as fatalistic. I think that life has played yet another dirty trick on the poor little chap."

Charity disagreed. "On the contrary, Angie: Moses has come into manhood. He has a marvelous talent, and now is the time for him to use it. And the place—"

"Is not on Earth. I know. He's the only person on the planet who can comprehend what that alien is saying and doing, but he can't communicate effectively with the creature when there's a ninety-minute time lag. If only the aliens had been on the Moon . . ." The thought trailed off, because you can't rewrite the universe.

"He belongs out there with Prudence, Angie. In the thick of it."

Angie nodded and became very matter-of-fact. "You do realize there's a problem? The comet will be passing through the Jovian system nine months from now. Somehow, we've got to get Moses out to Jupiter well before that. But the usual journey time is two years. I have a horrible feeling we're too late."

Charity shook her head. "Angie: I have no idea how I know this, but I am certain. This is what Moses was born to do. *There will be a way.*"

Angie didn't voice her skepticism: proud mothers "know" many things about their children, nearly all of which are rubbish. However, Charity could be right. Angie knew that before the Pause many different methods of space travel had been under discussion by Earth's scientists, engineers, and pilots . . . Could anything have remained from those times? It was worth finding out. And Carver Enterprises had many, many contacts who might know of secret prototype spacecraft, or entirely different methods of propulsion . . .

In fact, she'd already thought of an organization that might be able to help.

The Cuckoo hated it when he had to do this kind of thing. *Confound* Angela Carver! *And* Prudence Odingo! It was unethical, immoral, and unfair.

Also: necessary.

He picked up an inscribed slab that lay amid the litter of his desk, a resin cast of the order's most precious relic. Only the most senior lamas even knew of its existence. He ran his eyes over the proto-hieroglyphs . . . Its translation had been a bargain, nothing more than a secondhand cruiser; Prudence Odingo had done a remarkably competent job and deserved her reward. But Odingo had been told only what she *needed* to know—

His train of thought ceased as Nāgārjuna the Thrush shuffled into the office, head bowed, posture humble, anxious to acquit himself well, desperately willing to serve.

The Cuckoo remained silent for a time. To Nāgārjuna's experienced eye he seemed troubled. Then, visibly drawing breath, he spoke. As always, the approach was indirect. "I am mindful of one of the many sayings of the Great Bird."

Nāgārjuna kept his head bowed.

" '*Your happiness will increase if . . .*' Tell me, Nāgārjuna, how does it continue?"

"Uh—'*if you act for others. Disseminate the word of the—*' "

"Correct . . . though on this occasion it is not the word of the Dharma that we must disseminate . . . Many times I have acted for others, Nāgārjuna, and many times have I received happiness in return. But sometimes . . . very seldom . . . I have almost come to doubt the advice of the Great Bird."

Nāgārjuna's face showed his bewilderment: surely the Cuckoo could never doubt the Fount of All Wisdom!

"On a few occasions, my Thrush—very few, and I am thankful of it—I have acted for others *without* my happiness increasing. How can this be?"

The monk cast around desperately for something sensible to say. "Uh—because future happiness was temporarily un-available to you, Master?"

"You speak well, and so it may have been. Though I won-der if perhaps the sacred writings speak of generalities and omit the occasional exception. Be that as it may, the time has come for me to act on behalf of others by asking whether *you* are ready to act on behalf of others. Are you?"

"Whatever task you have for me, Master, I am ready."

"Then no doubt my happiness shall eventually increase as a consequence." The old lama took a step toward the young monk and put his hands on the youth's shoulders as he knelt before his master. "It is a vital task, and a dangerous one. So dangerous, my son, that I fear that you may never return—even if you succeed. Do you *still* wish to accept the task?"

Nāgārjuna didn't hesitate. He had trained all his life in the hope of something like this. " '*All birth is but a dream-birth, all death a dream-death.*' Master: whatever task you ask of me, I accept with joy."

"And I receive that acceptance with sorrow. However, I can do no other, for there is little choice. A volunteer is needed, one who is skilled in the piloting of small cruisers. I am told you are the best pilot we have. Is that so?"

Jarāmarana! The Death Comet! It had *to be!* Nāgārjuna knew that self-aggrandizement was frowned upon within the order and chose his words with care. This one would be too good to miss. "Master, every pilot thinks himself to be the best. It is necessary for confidence. In this I am no exception."

"I suspect that you may be. The White Grouse thinks highly of your skill." This was news to Nāgārjuna, who had received nothing but criticism from the acerbic, elderly lama known as White Grouse. Still, if the Cuckoo said it, it must be true. Despite himself, he felt a glow of pride.

" '*Our habitual passions springing from wicked deeds of our past,*' " quoted the High Lama,

> " '*Our thoughts, provoked by diverse apparitions,—*
> *All are like trees in autumn, clouds in the sky.*
> *A delusion, if you have thought them permanent.*' "

It was, in its way, a remonstrance. The glow died back to a pale flicker of suppressed emotion.

"Nāgārjuna, my Thrush, my son, my supreme pilot—your task is one that, should you succeed or fail, will be spoken of for as long as humans remain in this universe and do not break the fragile thread of their history. You will therefore understand when I counsel you: do not accept this task out of pride!"

"I am willing to serve," the young monk affirmed, his voice wavering for an instant, "but only out of humility and respect."

"Perhaps," replied the Cuckoo. "Make it so, if you can. It remains only to describe your task to you. That, I am obliged to warn you, will take some time—especially when you ask questions, as you must . . ."

After he had finished and the monk had taken his leave, the Cuckoo once more picked up the resin slab.

Odingo had translated a bizarre, garbled tale, a myth of gods and demons and vengeful suns, a close parallel to the one she claimed to have found inside the Sphinx; later stolen, so she said, by that tedious Dunsmoore person . . . The two tales overlapped, complemented each other, yet often contradicted each other.

The Cuckoo thought he knew why.

What Prudence had not seen was the picture that had been carved next to the text, possibly a forerunner of the sun-disk-and-horns symbol of the Egyptian goddess Hathor, who guarded the passage between this world and the next. But in this glyph the horns were inverted to form a shallow arc, and the disk was not the sun, for there were faint spindly lines scratched within it. At first glance they appeared meaningless, but when turned upside down it was difficult not to interpret them as crude outlines . . . To the right, the coast of Westafrica. To the left, a convincing representation of the Americas—North and South.

This was already remarkable, enough to overturn five centuries of archaeology. What was even *more* remarkable—and again Odingo had not been informed—was where the stone had been found.

With reluctance, the Cuckoo tucked the relic away in a drawer. There would be time for such speculations later, perhaps. First, he must ensure that all had been made ready for Nāgārjuna.

The Way of the Wholesome had been in the rock trade for more than a hundred years, and they had perfected it. The rocks that they traded were asteroids, or sometimes parts of asteroids that had been deliberately broken up—though that was a somewhat dangerous procedure, complicated by the need to avoid ejecting debris that might enter the customary flight lanes. The Way of the Wholesome traded its rocks with

Earth and had become rich beyond any meaningful measure. It owned, and was able to exploit, resources exceeding those of an entire planet; and those resources were comparatively accessible and portable. Nearly all of Earth's vast store of iron, for example, was locked away as silicates in its mantle and oxides in its molten core. The Way of the Wholesome owned iron aplenty, and it floated around in lumps. All you had to do was help yourself.

Not that this was easy. The technology needed to mine the asteroid belt was extremely expensive. It centered on sixty-six mass-drivers, the newer ones made in the New Tibet Habitat—giant modern relatives of the medieval siege engine, linear trebuchets powered by magnetic induction motors, whose fast-moving slings could throw very big rocks very fast and very, very accurately. There were a dozen mass-drivers in lunar and terrestrial orbit, for close-up delivery work near the neo-Zen monks' main customer base; there were as many again near Mars, spearheading the development of what in the long term would be a second major market—revival of the defunct Mars Colony whose destruction had set off the Pause. Others were poised at Mars' Trojan points—sixty degrees ahead of and behind the planet in the same orbit, where simple models of the cosmos predicted zero gravity, and the real thing was close enough for some clever control engineering to do the rest.

The majority of the mass-drivers, though, were deployed within the asteroid belt. Some floated free, artificial asteroids positioned in stable resonant orbits, where instead of being disturbed by the changing force of Jupiter's gravity as it circled the Sun, their position would be sustained by it. Others were in orbit around the larger bodies, such as Ceres, Pallas, Vesta, Euphrosyne . . .

From Euphrosyne the Sun was visibly a disk, but only just. A keen eye could also pick out the glinting surfaces of a mass-driver. This particular device—the Pitching Machine, as it was colloquially known—was one of the most powerful of all the mass-drivers deployed throughout the Belt, the pride of New Tibet Habitat's workshops. In essence it was little more than a giant rail-gun with a seventeen-mile barrel and a stubby stock that housed its electrical capacitor banks. Around the long, hollow tube formed by the rails, however, the engineers had woven an intricate framework of active struts, designed to keep the rails from flexing as the slings accelerated along them. Ugly electromagnetic coils were spaced along the rails in a complex progression, designed to transfer as much momentum as possible while using the least amount of electrical power.

The Pitching Machine would be powerful enough for the delicate task that was required of it, and it was also in the right place at the right time. A considerable stockpile of rocks had been lined up in orbit beside it, ready for tugs to bulldoze them into the waiting jaws of the slings. Solar power surged into its electrical storage chambers. Attitude thrusters aligned it with minute precision.

At the moment, it was aimed almost at right angles to Jupiter. Over the next week it would turn, increment by carefully calculated increment, until the gas giant loomed in its sights. But before it could act, supporting acts would have to warm up the cosmic audience. The Euphrosyne Pitching Machine would be the star of the show—but without other, lesser contributors, there would be no show for it to star in.

The opening act was a lone mass-driver in lunar orbit, normally used to ferry load from the open-cast copper mines at the edge of the Mare Moscoviense to Earth's factories. That mass-driver had now been spun on its axis until it pointed in the general direction of Jupiter. Three tugs acting in concert, a tricky maneuver but one they practiced almost every day, herded a large rock inside the mass-driver's central box of parallel rails and into Sling 4, which happened to be the one that had arrived at the driver's rear end when the machine's previous burst of action ceased. This particular rock was a rough sphere about fifty yards across, about twenty percent palladium. It had spent the last three years working its way in toward Earth from the asteroid belt, and the last week being diverted to the Moon by a fleet of tugs, and it was worth rather more than the gross domestic product of a small country.

Electric current pulsed through the gigantic machine's circuits, and the sling began to move, carrying the rock with it. The two accelerated, speeding along the straight track of the rails.

With each successive pulse of electromagnetism, the rock's velocity increased. This mass-driver was a short one, a mere five miles long, so the rock's launch velocity was only twice that of Nāgārjuna's cruiser. That was no problem—they dared not risk a higher speed at this delicate stage of the operation, anyway.

It was ironic. If the hitherto untried technique didn't work—or even if it did—there was a chance that the Jovians might think they were being attacked. Unfortunately—well, that was how the military minds saw it—the device was too inaccurate to be used as a weapon of war . . . but it might just make an effective weapon of peace.

As the palladium-rich rock headed away from the Earth-Moon system, Sling 4 slowed and began to negotiate the sharp bend that would return it along the mass-driver's underbelly. Automatically, without any fuss, Sling 5 slipped into place at the far end, ready for the next rock.

The tugs were already pushing it into place.

Moses felt as if he had been fed through a mincer. He had been shoved into a hastily adapted pressure suit, slammed up into low Earth orbit in an elderly OWL that looked as if it might fall to bits at any moment, transferred to a neo-Zen transport that was normally used solely for Moonbound cargo duties, and dragged through vacuum into a small, sleek ship attached to what looked for all the world like a giant coffin.

He didn't mind. It sure beat moping around on Earth. He

missed the Gooma animals, but he was on his way to meet the *aliens*.

Nāgārjuna, the pilot called himself. He claimed to be a thrush, which was blatant nonsense. And yet . . . despite his natural wariness with strangers, Moses felt drawn toward the diminutive, wild-eyed young man in the sky-blue pressure suit. There was a deep strength there, and he sensed a fundamental honesty that he had never encountered before in a human being. So when the young man told him that the chance of them surviving the mission was negligible, he believed him—and drew strength from him.

Charity had already impressed upon her son the terrible dangers he would face. And she had explained why it was necessary that he should risk the bizarre, untested technology that was the only known way to convey him to Jupiter in the time available. He had felt the truth of her words, and her poorly suppressed fears . . . but he had hardly listened. He had few attachments to the planet of his birth, if the truth be told. He had little affection for the great mass of humanity—why should he? Look what it had done for him . . . to him. And now it was using him again, for its own selfish ends.

Survival.

Survival he understood, but he didn't really *care* whether humanity lived or died.

What he *did* care about, though, was the animals of Earth. No doubt many of the lower life-forms would rebuild their existence after a collision winter—indeed many would never notice it. But his friends the big cats, the wild dogs, the monkeys and the hippos, the snakes and the meerkats—without his help, they would die.

He would save them.

For the animals of Earth, Moses knew he would travel to the end of the universe. With the added bonus of the aliens thrown in, he had agreed to be sent to Jupiter almost before they asked him.

The normal journey time was two years. *This* trip would take less than a week. Or forever.

Nāgārjuna bundled Moses into a narrow seat and strapped him in. "Please excusing," he said in flawed English, "but must quick. Wasteful time is none, understand?" Moses did—more than the pilot might have thought—and nodded. "You wish sleepy drug? Or you sleep-wake cycle as normal?"

Taking sleeping tablets would be the coward's way out, contrary to the culture of the Chinese street children in which he had—if that was the phrase—grown up. Survival dictated the less pleasant choice. "No drugs," said Moses. "I'd like to see what we're doing."

"Will not pleasant. Much acceleration, big changes in delta-vee." The pilot was on more confident ground with technical jargon. "You will feel many big push, you understand? Gee forces."

These would be as nothing compared to the violence of the emotional forces that had shaped Moses' brief existence, and he knew it. He nodded again, and the pilot strapped him in.

"First we dive, then swing and accelerate. But that just the begin, okay? After that, things get hairy. Then get *very* hairy, right? So you just stay calm . . . trust me . . ." Despite the Cuckoo's remembered admonition, Nāgārjuna had to say it: "*I the best!*"

The preparations took a while. Moses found it easy to remain calm, though few others would have done so in his place. But few others had had his upbringing, where it was fatal not only to show fear, but to *feel* it. He sat in the passenger seat and watched every move that the pilot made. Maybe one day *he* would become a pilot, like Auntie Pru.

Nāgārjuna spoke into his mike: "Check—*vajra*-1 in slot?" In Pāli, *vajra* was a thunderbolt. Moses didn't hear the reply, but the pilot seemed satisfied.

"Go for first burn," said Nāgārjuna. He fiddled with various controls, spoke into his throat mike. The tiny ship complied; Moses felt a growing weight on his chest, as if a large animal were sitting there. The animal grew heavier, until he wondered if his ribs would crack under the strain . . . then it vanished.

He felt sick. Until now, weightlessness hadn't bothered him, but this time it was different—the sudden cessation, perhaps?

Nāgārjuna grabbed two sick-bags, tossed him one, and Moses threw up. To his surprise, the pilot did the same in the other. "I fine," said Nāgārjuna shakily, still looking green around the gills, "on own. But if anyone else get sick . . . me, too. 'Sympathetic reaction,' my teacher say. You okay?"

"I'm fine."

"Good. Hang on to feeling. Because very soon you not be!"

The Moon in the cruiser's flatfilm screens grew, fast. It changed from a small ball to a huge curved dome, then to a straight line, black on one side, shining gray and silver on the other. The sharp division bisected the screen.

"Course correction," said Nāgārjuna. "Small, so I think you get no sick, okay? Good." Imperceptibly, the vessel's course zoomed in on a crucial, tiny window in a twenty-four-dimensional space of mathematical variables—its position and velocity had to be controlled into very small confidence intervals, with virtually no margin for error. This was one reason why no sane pilot would consider using their current strategy to shorten the normal journey time to Jupiter—or anywhere else. Of course many pilots were not *entirely* sane, but there were other reasons, too—reasons that did not apply when the Earth was threatened with annihilation, but excellent reasons on any other occasion. Reasons that Nāgārjuna was trying not to think about.

The Moon's cratered surface was no longer in front of them, but below, and they skimmed across it at a blistering pace. Moses had been told the theory: they were trying to gain velocity by making a partial orbit of the Moon, swinging across its trailing hemisphere as it sailed its unruffled orbit, borrowing momentum that would accelerate the tiny craft to unprecedented speeds while slowing the ponderous satellite by an imperceptible amount. In a million years' time publishers would have to rewrite their diaries; for now, nothing seemed to have changed. The unerring precision of Newtonian conservation laws held sway, an exchange too fine for human senses to perceive.

Nāgārjuna knew that the most critical phase of the entire mission was rushing toward him, relentless, obeying its own inhuman imperatives. His eyes roamed across the readouts as the computer gentled them into the required trajectory. If it made a mistake, there was little he could do—they were provisioned for eight days, no more, to avoid excess mass. At their present speed, it would take four months to reach Jupiter . . . much too slow.

Nāgārjuna broke out in a cold sweat at the thought of just what they had to accomplish—and how. Pre-Pause technology would have made the task easier—at least until the vessel outsmarted itself and did something really stupid.

The trajectory uncurled, the Moon receded. Again Nāgārjuna asked the computer to verify their course; again he breathed a sigh of relief.

Now it was up to the mass-drivers and their operators. And to the jury-rigged gadgetry in the large metal box, the one that bore an uncanny likeness to a coffin.

As a fortune in palladium converged on Nāgārjuna's cruiser, the pilot readied himself for the big moment. He was going fishing in the celestial ocean, with a net on the end of an elastic rope.

It was an old idea, but nobody had ever been desperate enough to try it before. The astronautics journals of the early 2100s called it PAMT—Propulsion by Accumulated Momentum Transfer—but nobody used the clumsy acronym. Instead, the method was generally known to spacers as mass-sailing.

The name came from an older idea still, which in a sense was really the same one. The principle of the light-sail had been around for as long as space travel itself. Attach a life-support module to a huge, gossamer-thin parachute; hitch a lift from the Sun's inexhaustible outpouring of photons. As the physics of the solar wind became better understood, the theorists repeatedly redesigned their hypothetical spinnakers to surf the plasma wind of electrons, protons, alpha particles, and whatever else the Sun was prepared to eject.

Mass-sailing was the same idea, but the particles were bigger and the sail was correspondingly smaller and more robust. "Rustic" might be a better description.

Nāgārjuna opened the external welded-on coffin and readied his celestial fishnet. This would not be his only chance—other equally valuable rocks were already trundling along alternative trajectories, in case he missed and had to try again—but it was the *best* chance, the one that would give them the best start on the fast track to Jupiter.

He had no intention of missing.

Moses watched, his face devoid of emotion, as the cruiser's radar sensed the rock's approach and passed the information on to the computers, which readied Nāgārjuna's net. The maneuver would be semiautomatic, but there were enough imponderables that the young monk's human touch would be essential in laying the trap. The almost immediate release would have to be done on automatics.

Then he would have to do it all again, and again, and again . . . With faster and faster rocks, hurled from farther and farther away . . . Not to mention what would happen when they neared their distant goal.

Don't think about that.

Hours passed. The radar signals became stronger, clearer, more accurate. Nāgārjuna decided that the moment was ripe and set his net. It slid out of the coffin at the end of its twenty-mile tether, and his nimble fingers manipulated a web of electrostatic forces to spread it apart into a welcoming string basket . . . only the string was multistranded nanofiber cable and the tether was capable of stretching to ten times its length before there was any danger of it snapping. The trick was to spread the net without letting instabilities collapse any part of it. The computers helped, but the monk had to make occasional manual corrections.

His net safely and accurately spread, Nāgārjuna slipped out of his seat and satisfied himself yet again that Moses was strapped down. The acceleration would be fierce, but only for an instant.

They never saw *vajra*-1.

They felt the gut-wrenching jerk as it slammed into the net, though. The tether extended, heating rapidly as it absorbed a tiny part of the rock's momentum. The tiny cruiser was pulled forward like a toy on the end of a length of string.

The tether stretched farther. Within a few seconds its front end was two hundred miles ahead of the cruiser, moving at twice the velocity. The rear end was already dragging the tiny craft forward.

There was more to come.

Stresses soared in the carefully engineered layers of the tether. Stretched to its limit, it now began to contract, whipping the cruiser toward the far larger mass of the captured rock. Now the tether began to shrink as rapidly as it had lengthened; Moses and Nāgārjuna were pressed deep into their seats by invisible, but terribly real, forces. If the tether hadn't been stretchable, the two of them would have been splattered against the bulkhead, mixed up with the wreckage of their seats. Thanks to elasticity, the acceleration remained bearable. Just.

The most dangerous moments were still to come, though, because now Nāgārjuna had to make sure that they were not dragged into a collision with the rock. One squirt with the at-

titude jets ought to take care of that. If not, they would never
know.

As the cruiser slid past the speeding rock, and at the instant that its velocity attained a precomputed vector, the center of the net opened up, releasing the rock. The acceleration
stopped, and all was as before . . . except that now the cruiser
had received a permanent boost to its velocity.

Nāgārjuna ignored his aching joints, consulted the schedule on his screen, and began to redeploy the net. *Vajra*-2 was
due in fifteen minutes.

While the cruiser's speed was beginning to build, while
the closest bodies were the Moon and the Earth, it would be
fueled by rocks from the lunar mass-driver. Each successive
rock would be tossed along a subtly different trajectory, at a
higher speed; step by step the craft would be accelerated to
unprecedented velocities. The plan only stood some chance
of succeeding because the monks had plenty of experience
shuttling far larger rocks around the inner Solar System—the
record was a potato-shaped lump of impure nickel-iron alloy,
eight miles by five by three. The difference, on this occasion,
was the speed of the rocks and the short intervals between
them.

Initially, the cruiser's position could be tracked with
enough time left to change the alignment of the mass-driver,
reducing errors that would otherwise accumulate until
Nāgārjuna's net missed an incoming rock and his cruiser
floundered, its mass-sail becalmed in momentumless vacuum. As the cruiser's velocity increased, however, two new
problems would arise. It would be moving faster, and it
would be farther away.

Nāgārjuna had to be given breaks when he could sleep.
This increased the journey time, but it also worked in their
favor, because during those periods of downtime the Buddhist engineers could recompute the rocks' trajectories. As
the craft's path took it out toward Martian orbit, the mass-

drivers near Mars would take over from the lunar one. But even then, a stage would quickly be reached when a passively thrown rock would not be accurate enough.

The answer: active rock.

Floating in space near Euphrosyne, the Pitching Machine cranked into life and began to live up to its name. In its capacious slings were mounted five gigantic rocks. Others floated nearby, ready to be tugged into position as used slings were vacated. To each the neo-Zen engineers had secured small but powerful rocket motors, with which they could make remote adjustments to the rock's velocity, attitude, and position as it sped along its trajectory. Nāgārjuna would need all the help they could give him.

In the virtual mind's eye of the Pitching Machine's computer, its target was an empty region of space much like any other—until the ticking of a clock suddenly transformed it into an infinitely desirable slice of celestial real estate.

The Pitching Machine surged with electricity as its powerful electromagnets came up to peak current in a precisely timed sequence. The first of the active rocks hurtled forward, propelled by a wave of magnetism. Already it was moving much faster than the Buddhist engineers had ever achieved before, and still the rock had covered less than a quarter of the mass-driver's length. But then, it was a much smaller rock than those they usually threw about the Solar System.

The sling approached the end of the rail-gun and decelerated *fast*. The rock continued under its own momentum, careering out of the Solar System fifty times as fast as the speediest spacecraft ever built; soon the Pitching Machine would be hurling rocks even faster. All Nāgārjuna had to do was catch them, let them pull him along as the elastic tether absorbed the strain, wait for the twang as the tether began to contract again, and let go. All the neo-Zen engineers had to do was calculate the path of the stream of rocks, align their mass-drivers, jockey the active rocks along whatever path was required, and hope that the entire ridiculous lash-up conformed to their simulations.

All.

The neo-Zen pilot fingered the knee flap of his skyblue suit, wondering what was going on in the child's mind. Moses *looked* calm, but he nearly always did. It was hard to read his emotions. The mistake would be to assume that therefore he didn't have any. Nāgārjuna wasn't that stupid. He smiled at the boy and said a few reassuring words.

Moses didn't need reassurance. He was bored, excited, and—despite his years as a street child—terrified all at the same time, but he was going to *Jupiter*! To meet the *aliens*! For the first time, his life had a goal, and it thrilled him to the core. It just hadn't occurred to him to express any of this, for to Moses emotions were things you mostly kept to yourself— to keep people from using them against you. There were many things that he did need, but reassurance wasn't one of them. Reassurance was when people tried to tell you everything was fine, when palpably it wasn't. He hadn't grasped that reassuring *others* wasn't what it was about. It was reassuring *yourself* by believing your own lies . . .

In their own distinctive ways, Nāgārjuna and Moses awaited their respective destinies with the customary mixture of awe, hope, despair, fear, and implacable obstinacy that is the lot of those that the rest of us call heroes.

If it had been a vidifilm, you would have heard space sizzle as the rock from Sling 4 hurtled toward its goal, but no sound traversed the silent vacuum, for there was no air to carry it. As Nāgārjuna watched its astonishing progress on his screen, though, he wouldn't have been surprised if space *had* started to sizzle.

The stream of rocks that had propelled them toward Jupiter faster than any human had ever traveled before had temporarily dried up, but Nāgārjuna was drenched in sweat.

The net had proved a bitch to control, and he would shortly say as much to his mission controllers in the Cuckoo's Nest, though in more professional phraseology. It was unlikely that the Way of the Wholesome would ever repeat this particular exercise, but even so the neo-Zen engineers ought to be told to increase the damping on the net's elastic oscillations. At least twice he had managed to reset it with less than a minute to spare. Once he had been within seconds of missing a rock entirely, which would have destroyed the whole sequence, lost them a week or more, and very probably killed them both by making it impossible to get to Jupiter before their supplies ran out—assuming they could reach their goal at all after such a mistake.

The cruiser was now two-thirds of the way to Jupiter and had attained its maximum speed. The next problem would be to slow down.

As the mission moved into its final phase, the activity around the Pitching Machine went up several gears. Neo-Zen pilots in tiny mining vessels grappled with rocks that they would normally have considered a piece of cake—but not when they were under severe time pressure and surrounded by dozens of others in exactly the same circumstances.

There were accidents. Two tugs converged on the same rock at the same instant and collided. The wreckage was shoved unceremoniously aside by a third, whose pilot was well aware of the possible consequences for his two fellows. Others would do their best to rescue them and tend their injuries. All that mattered was to keep the stream of rocks clicking tidily along.

These rocks were little different from their predecessors, save for two tiny details. The rockets mounted on them were larger, more powerful, and more numerous. And the rocks' trajectory was more ambitious. They were aimed not *at* Jupiter, but to miss the giant world by a hair's breadth—grazing its upper atmosphere, swinging around the planet in a half-circle, and returning from its opposite limb so that they headed back toward the oncoming cruiser. As far as Nāgārjuna was concerned, it would be as if Jupiter were spitting rocks back at him. All he had to do was catch them, transfer some of their momentum to his ship through the elastic tether, and let them go before the tether broke.

Easy.

There were many imponderables, and the neo-Zen pilot tried hard not to ponder them. The biggest worry had nothing to do with the technology: it was that the Jovians might interpret the stream of rocks as a threat, and use their gravitic technology to divert it. The mission controllers had convinced themselves that this was unlikely, for a variety of reasons. The rocks were small enough to burn up harmlessly in Jupiter's atmosphere, unlike massive comets . . . The planet must have been encountering such tiny bodies several times a decade, but Earth's astronomers had recorded no previous anomalous movement of the Jovian moons, implying that the Jovians did not normally divert rocks of that size . . . Moreover, *these* rocks weren't even on course to hit the planet, just to come close . . .

Nāgārjuna wasn't the only person to be worried by the logic. One popular interpretation of events, among those sane enough to be mildly paranoid about the whole business, was that the Jovians had diverted the comet Earthward as a deliberate act of interplanetary war. How, then, might they react if their enemy were suddenly to start spraying small asteroids into their vicinity? What might they think? Suppose, for example, that those rocks were carrying nuclear weapons! Suppose their apparently harmless trajectories could be *controlled* when they approached the target world . . .

Suppose. Suppose there was another way to slow the cruiser down quickly enough to get Moses to Jupiter within the required time interval. But there wasn't. The only alternative was to whip the *cruiser* around Jupiter so that it was heading back into the rock stream. That would have been

more satisfactory, in some ways, but it would take too long—
and run the risk of traversing Jupiter's rings. And the aliens
might see a spacecraft as a threat when a rock might be ignored. So, on balance, this way was less risky.

Nāgārjuna had spun the tiny cruiser end for end, so that
now it faced back toward Earth. The rocks would be coming
from behind him, as before. The main difference would be
the relative speed, now virtually double his own, for the
stream of rocks would whip around Jupiter without losing
momentum, but this time he would be plunging backward
into them.

Nāgārjuna was expendable, Moses was not. There were
precautions to be taken and contingencies to be planned for.
The pilot said a few brief words of encouragement to the boy,
who kicked himself across the cabin to a waiting emergency
pod, a thick rind of plastic foam that had been split open like
two halves of some enormous fruit. The pod held enough air
and water to keep a person alive for twenty-four hours. There
was no food—something more vital would run out before it
was needed—and only the most rudimentary of sanitary arrangements, a kind of oversized diaper. When closed, the pod
was sealed to vacuum.

The cruiser was in radio contact with *Tiglath-Pileser* now,
but both vessels kept their messages concise—the last thing
Nāgārjuna needed was extra distractions. It was good to
know that Prudence Odingo's ship had them on its screens,
though, and that several OWLs were being readied to make the
pickup. Without doubt *Skylark* also had them in its sights, and
Europa Base, but the Way of the Wholesome had already
warned the Jovian Task Force to expect the arrival of one
of their craft. Testing, so they said, an experimental rapid-
response technique. Nobody expected *Skylark* to be fooled by
this excuse, but it might stop them from interfering. And the
operation had been timed to place Europa around the back of
Jupiter at the crucial moment.

Moses knew what he had to do now, and without protest

he climbed into the empty space at the pod's center. He almost seemed eager.

Nāgārjuna sedated the boy and instructed the ship to glue the foam ball together around him. To get him out, Prudence's crew would have to saw a hole. The pilot checked the pod release system, then checked it again, and hoped that it wouldn't be needed. Then he began the delicate task of spreading his net, hoped that the computer could handle what was coming, and worried about a possible buildup of oscillations in the elastic cables of the tether.

On *Tiglath-Pileser*, Prudence Odingo and her crew could do nothing but wait.

Moses slept.

The tugs bustled around the Pitching Machine like worker ants around their queen, nudging the rocks into place, lining them up in sequence ready to be hurled toward the distant gas giant. Engineers checked rocket mountings, fuel supplies, communications antennas.

In all that bustle and haste, something was bound to go wrong.

The first dozen rocks had rounded Jupiter, slammed into Nāgārjuna's net, bled off some of his momentum, and been sent on their way with a kiss and a pat on the head. The cruiser's speed was now appreciably reduced, for which Nāgārjuna would have given thanks if he weren't so busy trying to ensure that this desirable state of affairs continued.

Reset, spread, ready, catch, wait (but not for long), release . . . The procedure had acquired its own rhythms, and the little Buddhist wondered if he would ever be able to get them totally out of his mind.

The comm's warning light flashed. "Transmitting new schedule." He made no attempt to reply—the two-way delay time in communications was already over an hour. The Cuckoo's Nest would assume he had received whatever it was that they had sent. What *Tiglath-Pileser* made of it was up to them—he didn't have time to explain it.

He brought the new schedule up on screen and swore.

One of the rocks had gone AWOL. An intermittent circuit fault, which had gone unnoticed in the rush to prepare the active rocks for mass-driving, had disabled its antenna. Unable to receive instructions from Euphrosyne or transmit its own position, it had deviated from its intended course. The error would be magnified when it hurtled around Jupiter, and it would emerge from the encounter a long way off track. That created a gap in the stream of rocks, requiring some on-the-fly reprogramming of the capture schedule and some tricky piloting to compensate for changes in the projected velocity.

As long as nothing *else* got snarled up, he reckoned he would probably manage.

This was life being lived on the edge. He had heard about such things in some unapproved entertainment media that one of the novices had smuggled in, and had sometimes wondered what it would be like. Now that he knew, he would have preferred not to. He had joined the Way of the Wholesome for quiet contemplation, not life in the fast orbit.

Time passed. Rocks slammed into the net and were discarded. The gap caused by the errant rock was safely bridged, but the result left him little room to maneuver when it came to the final stages of the deceleration process. It all came down to tolerances, and now there were none.

Four rocks to go. It was starting to get easy . . . The cruiser had slowed down considerably now, and the technique was becoming routine.

The next rock should be coming up on the radar any moment now . . .

Any moment . . .

Any . . .

Nāgārjuna felt an icy shiver run along his spine. *Where was the rock?* Was the radar malfunctioning? No, he could see the last three, lined up like ecologically permissible targets in a fairground shooting gallery. But the next rock was missing.

There must have been another failure. Unknown to Nāgārjuna, one of the rocks' engines had been damaged by material in Jupiter's ring, which extended from just inside the orbit of Metis, all the way down to the planet itself. The Way of the Wholesome would shortly find out, but their message would not reach him in time. It didn't matter. He'd known all along that from here on he was on his own.

He took advantage of the gap created by the missing rock to see what the biosensors could tell him about Moses. Heartbeat slow and regular, breathing much the same . . . Brain waves showing heavy theta-wave rhythms, and the characteristic bursting patterns of sleep spindles . . . safely unconscious. That was good—if anything went wrong now, the boy would never know. While the monk was making this brief medical examination, the computer was determining the best modification to their deceleration strategy, for even this contingency had been planned for. As he had hoped, there *was* a solution. Moses might yet reach *Tiglath-Pileser* safely.

Time to go for broke. There would be no room for error.

The cruiser's main rockets fired, once more pinning Nāgārjuna to his seat. Fuel unused was a luxury now—loss of momentum was the only currency that mattered. He would keep only the bare minimum that would offer him necessary options in the final seconds.

Two successive rocks hit the net and were released. The flimsy ship was back to normal operational velocities now—pity there wasn't any spare fuel left to take advantage of that.

One rock to go. The momentum equations were neat, precise, and inescapable. One rock could not kill the cruiser's speed.

It *could* kill the speed of something lighter.

Nāgārjuna whispered a short prayer—not *to* anything or anyone, but because it helped to calm his nerves. He suddenly realized that he had never entirely accepted the neo-Zen beliefs, and he wasn't going to start *now* . . . Not that it mattered. He knew what he had to do, and why. His duty was to humanity, not to the Dharma of the *Bya chos* as espoused by the Way of the Wholesome . . . or were those really the same? Was that what the Cuckoo had meant when it said, *Deep thoughts about death will conduct one to the unique and holy Dharma?* How deep were *his* thoughts—

The last rock was approaching. The emergency pod was attached by strong cables to the net's elastic tether. Nāgārjuna pushed the button that exploded the bolts securing the tether to the hull. Net and pod separated from the cruiser, drifting away to one side, dropping gradually behind. Then the final rock smashed into the net and whisked them away.

The screen's zoom facility was automatic. He watched the pod dwindle and vanish.

At a predetermined moment, the net split open for the last time, and the rock continued its indifferent path. The pod hung in space, its velocity relative to Callisto now negligible. *Tiglath-Pileser*'s OWLs ought be able to make rendezvous with ease.

The wiry little neo-Zen monk sat back in his pilot's seat and reflected for a moment on a job well done. Then, with an air of resignation, he selected a view in which Jupiter loomed in the screen, a thing of breathtaking beauty. Might as well enjoy the view while it lasted. His eyes were damp. It was *so* beautiful. Awe welled within him, and in one corner of his mind he was thinking: *I am the best.*

The cruiser was heading toward Jupiter's equator, close to the Great Red Spot. With no fuel and no more rocks to hitch a lift from, that would be its last trajectory. The planet's fearsome gravity was already increasing its grip.

The computer told him exactly when the craft would hit the atmosphere, and where, and how fast. Nāgārjuna knew what the numbers meant.

At least it will be quick.

17

Tiglath-Pileser, Callisto Orbit, 2222

Prudence Odingo had broken one of her self-imposed rules for survival in space and had decided to get very high indeed. She had also decided to do so without company, which broke none of her rules. Right now she was feeling pleasantly light-headed and her mind was warm and muzzy. Everything shone with flickering iridescent colors. She was in fairyland.

Temporarily forgetting the day's events wasn't so hard . . . remembering anything much *was*. That was good, she knew, though she could no longer recall why . . .

She suspected that if she got to her feet (*Feet? Where were her feet?*) she would drift uncontrollably about her private cubicle, which was pretty difficult, actually, since there wasn't room in there to swing a cat. Nonetheless, she had a feeling that she would contrive to drift anyway, and probably do serious damage to the furniture and fittings. So she had fixed herself to the wall with a couple of velcro straps.

She swallowed another capsule of dipsy, liberated from the medical supplies. It had been a harrowing day.

When the OWLs got to Moses' abandoned foam pod, they had found it hopelessly entangled in torn strands of elastic webbing which had come loose when the final rock had dragged it to a reluctant halt. It was a good thing that there hadn't been further rocks to catch, because the equipment had been damaged by the heavy impacts required to slow the cruiser down, and the change in strategy occasioned by the missing rock hadn't done anything to help. The thick foam rind was crisscrossed with deep whiplash marks where flailing cables had slashed into it, causing them to worry that perhaps the pod had been opened to the vacuum. Moses' oxygen supply came from compressed air tanks through tubes and a face mask, but more than a few minutes' exposure to vacuum would kill him all the same.

She had felt a terrible foreboding as they began to saw a hole in the foam ball, having towed it back to *Tiglath-Pileser* and maneuvered it on board through a cargo door. She *knew*, as vividly as she knew her own name, that Moses was dead.

He wasn't, of course. Her mind was acting out her fears and then responding to its own actions in an unstable emotional feedback loop.

Even though the boy was alive, he was in a bad way. Prudence had gasped when she saw the massive bruises that decorated his body and the caked blood around his mouth where the air mask had crushed his lips. Successive impacts with rock upon rock, even though they had been cushioned to some extent by the elastic webbing and tether, had taken their toll, and the final wrenching deceleration and the flailing ropes had bounced him around inside his foam cocoon like a Ping-Pong ball in a wind tunnel.

He had been unconscious, but that was probably the result of the drugs that Nāgārjuna had administered. She wouldn't be able to tell for sure until—if—Moses woke up and they could test his responses and reflexes to make sure the journey hadn't left him brain-damaged. They consulted *Tiglath-Pileser*'s medical database at every step as they hooked him up to life-support equipment, rigged up a pressure drip of saline mixed with more sedatives, a dose that would gradually be reduced as the computer decided it was safe to do so . . .

The boy's heartbeat pulsed across the monitor window . . .

comfortingly strong, though not terribly steady. His breathing was labored and erratic. His brain waves made no sense.

The worst part—with one exception—was the waiting. She *knew* that it had been necessary for Moses to join them out near Jupiter. She *knew* that it hadn't even been her decision, in the end, but her sister's. She had no idea how difficult that decision must have been for Charity, even though the alternative would almost certainly have condemned Moses to death along with everybody else on Earth, but she could guess.

The exception was poor Nāgārjuna—the worst moment of all. While they waited for Moses to recover from the drugs, they watched the neo-Zen monk's flimsy cruiser hurtling toward the Great Red Spot, out of control, out of fuel, spinning slowly end over end. They had come to respect the wiry little man, to love his broken English and his palpable concern for his passenger. It was heartbreaking to have to listen to him reciting verses from the *Bya chos*, verses he had laboriously learned by heart, verses that now became a kind of dirge, a death poem . . .

Later, they learned from the Xnet that it had been the speech of the Thrush:

> . . . *bcud lon, bcud lon—profit from, profit from* . . .
> *Profit from the holy teachings when you have acquired*
>   *human form!*
> *Profit from the holy Dharma, and achieve your goals!*
> *Profit from your possessions, and give all of them away!*
> *Profit from the unsullied doctrine, and choose a lowly*
>   *place!*
> *Profit from what you know, and meditate upon the*
>   *guardian gods!*
> *Profit from your unhappiness, withdraw from this*
>   *samsaric world!*
> *Profit from the Buddha, awaken to—*

On the screens, shaky and wavering at the limit of their telescope's resolution, the cruiser's sleek form turned in an instant into a ball of fire, then a curling, smoky trail, puffy and shapeless, spinning off smaller trails that writhed and dispersed in the eternal winds of Jupiter's upper atmosphere . . .

Within a few minutes, all trace of it was gone, blown away on those selfsame winds.

She wondered whether the aliens had noticed . . . whether they had considered diverting the tiny craft with the feather-light touch of a gravitic repulsor . . . The awful thing was, they could have saved him—had they been aware of any need to, or even of his presence . . .

Faint hope. *Aliens are alien*. Their concerns are not those of humans. Anyway, they probably hadn't noticed a thing. Why should they? It was just one more tiny, insignificant meteorite: they were plunging into Jupiter all the time.

It was too late for such thoughts . . . Nāgārjuna was with his guardian gods now. His place in history was assured, assuming there was going to *be* any more history.

It was cold comfort.

Prudence knew that at least another twelve hours must elapse before it was safe to let Moses wake up. Her eyes and Jonas's met, and understanding passed between them . . . *Not now, not while the child may be dying, that is not the way to ease our own fears and make the endless hours pass* . . . If Moses died, they'd feel forever dirty. Anyway, neither of them felt remotely interested . . .

Which was why she decided to hide away in her private cubicle and get totally, irredeemably zonked on dipsy. Alone.

Somehow, that was clean.

Halfholder's near-eyes returned yet again to the stolen object. Its cacophony of sound had made her ears ring, its incredible flashing colors had dazzled her chromatic-eyes . . . but she couldn't keep her mind off it.

The bedlam and bedazzlement were nothing. Why, she,

Bright Halfholder of the Violent Foam, had already mastered its primitive control mechanisms. She knew how to diminish the noise, and she could adjust her eyes to cope with the brilliant glare. She would never be heralded in the annals of legend if she let something so feeble put her off. She was a blimp, not a wimp!

Feeling very daring, and fearing that she might possibly be very foolish, Halfholder reached out a trunk tip and flipped the switch. She adjusted the sound volume, lowered her visual contrast to a prudent level, and turned the object so that her chromatic-eyes could watch the moving images.

Interesting . . . the patterns had stopped flashing. As she became accustomed to the funny flat image, a fixed shape became visible. It looked vaguely familiar—

With a sense of profound shock, she realized that another set of eyes was looking back at her.

The representation was crude, a two-dimensional projection that failed even to include depth cues. Disarmingly literal, too—absolutely no coding to eliminate unnecessary redundancy. It had the quality of a child's first attempts at constructing a communicaut.

It was difficult not to become amused, but she concentrated and suppressed the urge to huffle. Already she had a strong hunch that this thing was *important*.

Focus, analyze, rebalance . . . Only two of the—yes, they definitely *were*—eyes were visible: presumably the rest of the creature's eye-ring was lost beyond the narrow confines of the tiny image. The two eyes that she could see were obviously *eyes*, that was never in dispute—but they were eyes unlike any she had ever encountered before. Oval eyes—no, on closer inspection they were conventional spheres, but partially covered by taut but flexible flaps. *Eye-flaps?* What creature had eye-flaps? If you wanted to protect an eye, you retracted it! The eye-flaps occasionally flickered, and every so often the whole image jumped around erratically. As far as she could make out, the eyes were pale, but there was a brightly colored region, centered around a small dark circle. The creature's integument was an unremarkable shade of deep brown, like typical dioxide storm clouds. *If only the thing would stay still for two seconds at a time*—ah, it seemed to freeze, almost as if the creature could read her thoughts. Maybe it could, if it was sensitive to squark wavepackets . . . but no, that was silly: she wasn't bureaubonding, so her mindshield reflex would be in operation.

Now that the image was more stable, she could see more detail. There were curious lumps and bulges, and what seemed to be three holes. Two small ones, side by side, which vibrated erratically, and a very peculiar slitted hole with rubbery edges that danced through intricate series of shapes—in rough synchrony, she suddenly understood, with the crazy sounds that were burbling forth from the object.

The eyes grew smaller and closer together . . . No, it just seemed that way— Ah! How ridiculous! The creature had moved away from whatever instrument was forming the image, and the image coding didn't even stop it from *shrinking*! It was viewpoint-dependent! And that meant—

It all came together in a rush. First, the object was some kind of portable entertainment device, set in some kind of multiuser mode. Second, the image she was seeing was not an entertainment as such, but a real-time depiction of *another user*. And third—

The other user possessed no eye-ring at all. Just two tiny pinpoint eyes on one side of an improbable angular . . . dome? Hardly. It was more like the front end of a severely distorted gulpfang—

Songs in praise of the Lifesoul Cherisher! The other user was an extrajovian!

Halfholder had always nursed an irrational belief in the existence of exotic life-forms. She was sure that somewhere in the vast universe there had to be creatures like blimps, though not of their physical form—creatures that could not only read the universe and react to it, but react to their own mental models of it. But she had always visualized them as being ineffably distant, both in world-space and in organism-space.

Wrong.

And *this* creature must surely have its own symbiauts, too, because it possessed metallic constructs! And now she began to recognize flaws in her previous deductions.

The device was a communicator, not an entertainment projector. The extrajovian was here on Jupiter—no doubt inside the ugly floating metal sphere that its wheelers must have extruded. And (this thought was almost too large for one mind to hold, a thought that seared like molten ice, a thought as blinding as cloud-to-cloud lightning) the EJ was attempting to communicate with *her*!

It was too much. Her survival instincts took over, and she slid into a preestivation trance.

A Mandarin obscenity shattered the tranquility of *Tiglath-Pileser*'s communications cubicle.

Moses had found that his bruises weren't quite as painful in zero gravity as they would have been on Earth. Sitting down, for instance, was no trouble—or, to be more accurate, his bruises caused no trouble when he sat down. The low gravity did, though—unless he was strapped in, he kept floating off the seat when he fidgeted, or touched anything on the upturned packing crate that served as a desk.

Like the healthy young animal he was, he quickly adapted, and his bruises faded equally rapidly. His mouth was still sore, but that was a small price to pay. For most of his waking hours, he absorbed himself in the problem of opening meaningful communication with the alien. He took to floating around the ship with scarves hanging from his neck like tentacles, to get more in character.

When the channels suddenly leaped back into life, he was ecstatic. The images were a delight, despite the poor illumination, for they changed so slowly that the computer could enhance them with hardly any perceptible delay.

He already knew that if he was going to communicate with such a slow-moving entity, he had better restrain his own movements. Otherwise the recipient of his broadcast would be unable to perceive him as anything more than a vibrating blur. He did his best, but he found it difficult to control automatic reflexes, like blinking.

Everyone on *Tiglath-Pileser* was watching the alien's leisurely movements, relayed to any screen that they could spare. Everything that happened was being recorded. But nobody dared disturb Moses as he talked, gestured, and for long periods merely sat, absorbing the creature's essence, building a mental model of its responses to him and to its own surroundings. Speaker-to-Animals was trying to become Speaker-to-Aliens, and it was more than anyone else's life was worth to risk interrupting that delicate, intuitive process.

Moses could feel his excitement rising. *I do believe—yes, yes, she's understood what's happening! She knows she's communicating with me! She knows that I am not of her own world! And she is about to—*

Then came the curse. Followed by its equivalent in English, and a dozen other obscenities.

Prudence kicked herself in through the hatchway and killed her momentum against the wall with flexed elbows. "Moses! What happened? Is it dead? What—"

Moses leaned back, suddenly tired beyond measure. *Can't they— No, of course not. That's why they brought me here.* It took him a moment to order his thoughts. "No, she's not dead. I think the strain became too great, and she kind of . . . shut down. She's in a kind of hibernating state, I think. That's what it *feels* like to me. The trouble is, I was just on the verge of serious two-way communication! Now . . . hell, now we're all going to have to wait until the stupid beast wakes up again!"

Prudence's heartbeat stopped hammering. "You mean the alien's okay?"

Moses nodded—wasn't she *listening*? He'd just *said* that.

But people seemed to do that kind of thing, he'd never quite worked out why.

"Mo, you need a rest yourself. No point in hanging around until baby wakes up. We'll watch the creature in shifts, and as soon as anyone sees signs of her returning to consciousness, we'll tell you, okay?"

Moses realized they were right. He unstrapped himself, floated from the chair like a tuft of thistledown, twisted at the waist to slither through the tiny entrance hatch, and bounced erratically down the passageway to his private cubicle.

He felt drained of all energy. But his pulse was racing.

Halfholder stirred, becoming fuzzily aware once more of the reassuring enclosure of the blisterpond: old, dilapidated, comfortable . . . She reviewed her recent memories, and her mind automatically damped down their emotional content so that she would not slip straight back into her preestivation trance.

The occasion was too momentous for that: she needed to remain alert.

Belatedly, but fortunately not *too* late, she recognized her error. She had been overeager, wanting to solve all of the riddles in one attempt. The secret was to avoid spending too much unbroken time admiring her stolen trophy. She would monitor her state of consciousness and withdraw as soon as she felt the first fragile veils of incipent trance.

She dared once more to look at the image. The eyes were back. She had rather hoped they would be. But now they had a different quality to them—one of knowledge, almost of . . . sisterhood? Something had happened while she slept, a meeting of minds on a level so deep she had never known it existed. Now it must be helped to unfold.

For many days Halfholder and the extrajovian engaged with each other through the tiny metal box with the moving images. It began as communication on a primal level: emotions conveyed and translated into rough equivalents, movements choreographed and remembered, sounds and sights that meant nothing but somehow gave the impression that eventually they would . . . As the days passed, the funny two-eyed EJ and the twelve-eyed, many-trunked skydiver came, slowly, to understand each other. They evolved a common code, rudimentary at first, but with increasing elaboration as their confidence grew. And slowly, the extrajovian drew into Halfholder's powerful mind a sharp bright thread of horror. Horror not for herself, but for EJ and its kind. She could not yet bring the horror into focus, but already she was beginning to understand that something terrible had been set in motion . . . and that in some as yet unforeseeable way, she would have to stop it.

When Charity's face had appeared on the screen and Prudence had read the mixture of distress and pride, she had *known* what was coming next. Sometimes the bond between twins can be uncanny . . . So, even as her sister was tearfully, defiantly condemning her newfound son to the outrageous danger of high-speed spaceflight, Prudence was leaping ahead to its implications. Suppose Moses did arrive safely (for if not, all was surely lost); suppose he managed to communicate with the alien (ditto)—what next?

And even then her heart had sunk, because it was entirely obvious. The ultimate humiliation . . . As if her life had gotten stuck in an endless loop, as if fate were so unimaginative that there was only one dirty trick that it could play on her, over and over again. Trapped, used, discarded, ignored . . . And to make the humiliation unbearable, this time she would have to do it to herself. And, worse, to Moses.

The logic was inescapable. If Moses managed to make contact, *she* would have to hand everything over to Sir Charles Dunsmoore on a plate. *Here, Charlie, help yourself.* It didn't matter that she could transmit the breakthrough to Earth, put it on the Xnet, establish Moses' claim—Moses was here, and so was Sir Charles . . . and *he* was in charge of the official task force, while she was just another space bum with a questionable record and no influence. She could announce Moses' triumph on every screen on the Xnet and within a week Charles would have made it his own, stolen the credit, in all likelihood saved the bloody planet—and she'd have to grit her teeth and smile through them at a deceived world, while poor brave Moses would once again be cheated out of everything he deserved.

Yes, her team might have the talent to make the break-through . . . but they wouldn't have the facilities, expertise, personnel, or equipment to exploit it. So in order to keep Earth's hopes alive, as soon as Moses had established work-ing communication, Sir Charles would have to be told. And then she might as well tell him everything, including the hi-jacking of his balloon probe, because he'd soon work it out anyway.

It would probably all end with Charles as the hero and her in jail.

The story of her life.

Well, at least she didn't have a choice. In a way, that was a comfort.

Already recordings of Moses and the alien were on their way to Earth. If there was a claim to be staked, she'd done her best to stake it for the boy. But bitter experience told her that she could never do enough.

Charles would have picked up the transmission, too, as he'd been doing all along. She'd encrypted it, of course, but the decoded version would have made its way off the Xnet straight back into space on Sir Charles's personal wavelength. She was a little surprised that he hadn't already gotten in touch with her himself, but he was probably too busy putting his own claim together . . .

She drew a deep breath, swallowed, hoped her voice would hold steady—and told *Tiglath-Pileser* to get ready to transmit a message to *Skylark*.

Cashew gave a tentative knock at the curtained threshold of Prudence's cramped cubicle.

The captain's response, in a voice slurred from the effects of too much dipsy, was short and to the point. Cashew decided that to comply would be biologically impossible (unfortunately) and knocked again. On the fourth attempt, Prudence shoved a disheveled and angry face through the gap in the curtain. "Whatthefu— Oh, shit, it's you, Cash. Be a good girl 'n piss off, willya? Cap'n's otherwise engaged."

Cashew had the remedy at hand. She held up a small blue pill. "Time to rejoin the same cosmic plane as the rest of humanity, Captain!" She pressed the pill against Prudence's lips. "Open wide! Just pop this in and you'll be as right as rainbows in a jiff!"

Prudence snarled—a mistake, as it enabled Cashew to get a grip on her gums. "Ouch! Tintoretto, this is mutiny!"

"So hang me from the yardarm. You need a clear mind, not a hallucinogenic dreamscape."

"Damn you to hell, it's working. Shit, Cash, you know I'll pay for this with a blinding headache tomorrow."

"And thank me. *Skylark* has informed the waiting world that contact with the Jovians has finally occurred. The Xnet bounced the broadcast back to us ten minutes ago."

Prudence groaned. "Cashew, I'm well aware of that! Why the fuck do you think I was cooped up in here, dosed to the earlobes on dipsophine hydrate? Do you expect me to sit quietly in the comm niche like a baby glued to a kiddicom while Charlie sodding Dunsmoore takes credit for everything we've accomplished? Do you think I want to see him exploiting Moses' willingness to risk his—"

Cashew pulled a memo from her knee pocket. "No. But I *do* think you'd better take a look at this." She plugged it into a free slot next to the wallscreen and gave Prudence a very peculiar look. "Just *do* it, okay, Pru? Promise?"

Prudence glared at her. "Why should I— Oh, since you insist. Yeah, sure . . . promise."

Cashew grunted and withdrew from the cubicle. Prudence, feeling more sane by the minute, wished she was still crazy. Maybe she was. She forced herself to watch the screen and told it to turn up the sound.

Sir Charles's face appeared in tight close-up. *Smug bastard!* Except that he didn't look smug . . .

"As director of the *Skylark* expedition, I wish to inform you that there has been a major—and I cannot overstate the importance of this development—a *major* breakthrough with regard to our mission's core objectives. We have established contact with an intelligent alien." Pru *loved* that "we."

"As yet, we cannot be certain how important the individual that we have contacted may be, or how effective future communication with it will prove. *Jarāmarana*, the Death Comet, is still on its way. Nonetheless, the *real* work of the task force can now begin." *Very* clever . . . already she could see how Moses' contribution was going to be devalued. *This* alien would turn out to be some useless menial . . . *Charles's* alien, when he finally revealed its existence, would be a key political lead—

"The breakthrough was made several days ago by a young boy of sixteen. He risked appalling dangers to get here—in fact, his pilot was killed while making sure that the boy arrived safely. His name is Moses Odingo. Remember that name: if we survive the comet, it will be because of him." *Yeah, and now you'll say it was* your *idea to get him ferried out here* . . .

"Moses is the son of Charity Odingo, who courageously put the safety of the human race ahead of that of her only son. Ms. Odingo's sister, Prudence, is currently in orbit around Callisto aboard her cruiser *Tiglath-Pileser*. You will remember Prudence Odingo as the discoverer of the wheeler artifacts." *Right, and now comes the studied brush-off—damn me with faint praise, no doubt.*

"It is Moses Odingo who made the first meaningful communication with an alien. But it is Prudence Odingo's role that I wish to address. I have now discovered that several months ago, she was responsible for hijacking one of our irreplaceable balloon-probes, intended for the exploration of Jupiter's upper atmosphere." *Even better—I'm going to be branded a criminal again.*

"Without her action, contact would never have been established. I should have realized long ago that the aliens might be based on Jupiter itself, and I should have risked sending probes down into the cloud layer as soon as it became clear that they could not be found anywhere above it." *Hang on, this shouldn't be in the script! What the devil . . .*

"I have considered offering my resignation as director of the Jovian Task Force. However, my superiors believe that no one else aboard *Skylark* can take over the role. Instead, from now on I intend to take advice from a number of new sources, in particular the people on board *Tiglath-Pileser*."

Prudence felt nothing but bewilderment. Sir Charles Dunsmoore would *never* say anything like this. Not in a million years! What sneaky trick was the useless little swine up to now? Could there possibly be a way for him to turn this kind of public breast-beating to advantage?

He continued. "However, I am resigning all of my honorary scientific positions back on Earth, effective immediately. *All* of them—editorships, consultancies, directorships, and my continuing position as president in absentia of the International Archaeological Society. I am also taking steps to renounce my knighthood." He looked defiantly at the camera lens, hesitated, swallowed . . . Then he seemed to come to a decision.

"Excuse me. The last few years have been very difficult for us all, and I am not immune to stress. From here the Earth looks very fragile, and in one way or another many of us have been led to reappraise our deepest beliefs. I have come to the conclusion that I cannot continue my task without facing the truth about my own past. And the truth is that my entire academic career is founded on a lie. I did not originate that lie, but I did not deny it, and I was content to build my career upon it." He paused, as if the effort of saying the words were beyond him. "Many years ago, when I was an ambitious young archaeologist, I was in charge of a small expedition to Giza, in Egypt. There, one of my students made the most important archaeological discovery of the last century: the true age of the Sphinx. Our entire picture of pre-Egyptian civilization has been torn up and redrawn as a consequence. The discovery came to the attention of the world's media before I was ready to explain its true circumstances, and when I did—nobody would listen. The media planted a myth, and it flourished and grew until nobody could hack it down again. The myth was that Charles Dunsmoore was the genius behind the discovery. If it was not I who discovered the age of the Sphinx, *who was it*? Xnet mavens among you have probably found the answer by now, for the records were never destroyed—merely forgotten. Let me tell you. The student who unraveled the mystery of the Sphinx was a young woman named Prudence Odingo. I stole her career and made it my own. I stole her discovery. More recently, I tried to destroy her reputation, knowing that every word I said was a lie.

"The irony is that when we were working together on the Sphinx I respected Prudence, and . . . I—the awful thing is . . . I never . . . I never got a chance to explain—"

Sir Charles stopped, distraught.

Transmission ended unexpectedly, said the caption. Leaving Prudence with much to think about, and a mind in such turmoil that there was no possibility of her doing any such thing.

18

Europa Base, 2222

The OWL parked beside Europa Base was a squat silhouette in
the semi-darkness, but Jupiter was brightly illuminated over
three-quarters of its surface. With low-powered binoculars it
was just possible to see the dark speck of *Tiglath-Pileser* as it
made repeated transits across the awe-inspiring banded
globe, but the glare of reflected sunlight from the gas giant
made it impossible to see the vessel with the naked eye. Prudence had parked her ship in close orbit around Europa, and
now she, Moses, and the VV crew were working from Europa
Base, a small but vital addition to the Jovian Task Force. It
was an unholy alliance forged by circumstance and a common enemy.

From the moment Moses had begun to communicate with
the alien, Prudence had known that she and Charles would
have to come to some kind of an accommodation. She had
anticipated a series of formal meetings, awkward encounters,
forced smiles, and overpolite discussions as they tiptoed
around the rim of a mutual volcano of recrimination, accusation, and counteraccusation. Then she had seen Sir Charles
destroying his career on global vidivision. What was the bastard up to? She had no idea. His game was too devious for her
to fathom; she couldn't see what advantage he hoped to gain
from baring his soul—or whatever substitute passed for it—

in public. His performance had been embarrassing rather than moving—it had made him look pathetic and vulnerable, just when Earth's populations needed confidence and strength . . .

Maybe he'd just lost the plot completely, buckled under the strain. It was a hell of a job to take on . . . damn it, she was making *excuses* for him! *Stupid*. Sir Charles was up to his usual dirty tricks, and this one must be accessing an entire new dimension of dirtiness.

Now, in his cluttered office, face-to-face for the first time in years, she felt awkward and exposed. She had told herself that it would be a straightforward business meeting, focused solely on their mutual task. Nothing personal.

All that had gone up in smoke the moment Sir Charles opened his mouth. "List them."

For a second, she didn't understand. "List what?"

"The ways I've screwed up your life. And your family's."

Prudence gave a mirthless laugh. "Okay. Since you insist. First, you stole my archaeological discoveries and used them to make your own reputation. Then you tried to discredit my discovery of the wheelers. You put my sister in jail, and while she was there her young son went missing. She's never been the same person since. For years we all thought Moses was dead; then it turned out he'd been kidnapped and his entire childhood had been an indescribable hell. Oh, and along the way you lied and cheated and sacrificed a hundred promising careers on the altar of your own ego. Then, suddenly—unbelievably—you're indulging in a bout of public breast-beating and I'm being cast as a heroine. What monstrous scheme are you plotting now?"

"It wasn't sudden," said Sir Charles. "But I agree it's unbelievable. Despite which, everything I said in my broadcast is true. And now I need you to help me put right the mess I've created, and I hope you can bring yourself to do that—because if not, everything we love is going to die.

"There's no hidden agenda, Prudence. No dirty scheme. I'm tired, very tired. And scared. But now you've given me

new hope." His voice faltered. "If we can clear the air between us, it may make it easier for us to work together—if
only for a short time, while it's necessary."

Prudence sighed and perched herself on the edge of a
desk, secured in Europa's low gravity by one velcroed toe. "I
know. I've known for days. Just don't ask me to like it."

"I'm not asking anything, except for a few minutes of your
attention while I try to explain." Prudence said nothing, and
Sir Charles interpreted her silence as encouragement. "This
task force exists for one reason, and one only: to get the
comet deflected away from Earth. Your theft of the probe
achieved more in a few hours than my entire expedition had
since it got here. At first I resented that. You took a ridiculous
risk and it came off. You got lucky, just as you'd gotten lucky
in Giza. I spent years of my life working out the best strategies, steering clear of tempting shortcuts that were bound to
fail, arguing and fighting and driving myself until I was exhausted. You sailed in from nowhere, bent only on short-term
personal gain, made one crazy, irresponsible plunge into the
cloud layer—and came up smelling of roses."

Part of it hit home. "I *started* bent only on personal gain,"
Prudence said. "But when I realized what a pig's breakfast
you were making of saving the Earth, I decided I had to hang
around and do it for you."

"I know. I'm just saying what it felt like to me. Do you
know what your chance of success was?"

Prudence shrugged. "Infinitesimal."

Sir Charles spread his hands. "That was my opinion, too.
Until I got my thinking straightened out. The aliens were
down there—had been all along. So anyone who took a look
was going to find them. *Anyone.* I could have done it years
ago, but I never dared try. Luck? Luck didn't come into it,
any more than Columbus got lucky when he set off to find a
new route to Japan and ended up discovering Normerica. *It
was there.* What you did was to seize the opportunity. Your
chance of success was one hundred percent."

"It was the same in Giza, too . . . I wish I'd realized that then, as clearly as I do now. But let's not— Prudence, we need to seize another opportunity. We have to find a way to cooperate." She couldn't decide if he was being patronizing, sincere, or both. She could feel her anger rising and tried to suppress it. "Back in Giza, I had you tagged as flashy and un-focused—intelligent, but overquick to leap to conclusions."

The old wounds were starting to reopen. "Charles—I don't think we should discuss this."

"Got to, sorry. You say I stole your discovery. Guilty. But I didn't intend to, not at first. Everything that followed, yes, that was my fault. But when you went off in a huff, the only person left to face the media was me. I was a victim, too, in a way. I tried to find you, but—"

"Victim? You were a *victim*? You got all the accolades and I got *nothing*! My heart bleeds for you!" Her voice was getting louder; she could feel a shouting match coming.

Sir Charles bowed his head, acknowledging the criticism. Suddenly he changed the subject. "Prudence: have you enjoyed your life?"

There was something about his manner that made her take the question at face value. "It's been hard, Charles, bloody hard. But . . . since you ask, yes. I've had freedom, companionship, excitement—and fulfillment."

"I wish I could say the same. Do you think you'd have been able to hack it as an academic?"

That did it. "You fucking hypocrite! You think that just because it worked out all right in the end, what you did to me was justified? That's like slapping someone in the face and claiming you did it to bring some color to their cheeks!"

"Sorry, I didn't mean—" Charles began. Why did all dis-cussions with Prudence end up like this? Prudence wasn't lis-tening. She was thumping her fist on the desk and yelling at him.

The force of the banging jolted her toe loose from the floor. With a ripping sound, the tenuous velcro link parted, and she began to execute a slow backward cartwheel, still shouting. The sudden loss of dignity silenced her. For an experienced spacehound, this was embarrassing. The silence gave her time to get a very accurate mental image of what she had just done. Upside down, still spinning slowly backward and heading for the ceiling, she started to giggle.

Sir Charles reached up a hand and pulled her back to the floor. By the time she got herself stable again, they were both laughing uncontrollably.

"Sorry," said Prudence. "I never have learned to control that temper of mine." She sobered. She had a sudden vision of herself sitting on all those committees, refereeing research proposals, revising scientific papers for the dozenth time because some pedant disapproved of how she had stated her conclusion . . . It would have been a disaster. *It worked out all right in the end* . . . To tell the truth, it had.

Sir Charles responded to her changed mood. "How does space affect you? When you're in it for months on end?"

"It makes me feel very small . . . yet I also feel like an essential cog in a gigantic, vital machine. Like a microbe and a god at the same time."

"Me, too. Before we left Earth, I was too busy to really *think*. But as I watched my homeworld, and all it contained, shrink from a blue and white disk to a tiny, bright speck of light, I began to feel terribly alone. The planet looked so fragile—and it was up to me to protect it. Everything about my former life began to take on a new perspective. My schemes and desires seemed silly and trivial. I visualized that speck of light being snuffed out, and I shuddered to the core of my being. But when I thought of the destruction of all the things that I had previously valued . . . my presidencies and honors and money and high living . . . I found that I didn't give a damn. I was better off without them.

"That's what space did to me. It changed my vision of myself. But I kept the changes hidden until you turned up with a communicative alien. Then—I couldn't keep the changes hidden anymore."

Nice try. "People don't change," said Prudence. "Not fundamentally. Deep down inside, Charlie Dunsmoore, you're the same conniving bastard that I knew in Giza. Even if you *have* changed, you'll revert to type."

Sir Charles shook his head. "The person you knew in Giza was an idealistic young scientist—dull, unimaginative, but a decent person. He was placed in a position he couldn't handle, and it changed him, for the worse. So you're wrong. Or else you're right, and deep down inside that original Charlie Dunsmoore still exists. I think that's what's really going on. I'm regaining what I thought I'd lost forever."

Prudence gave him a long and thoughtful look. "Maybe. Don't ask me to swallow too much. I'll judge you by what you do, not by what you say.

"I think we may be able to work together, for long enough: we'll see. But I'll make one thing clear right now, Charlie. You ever try to screw me or mine again, and I'll kill you."

Sir Charles grinned. "I'm glad we can end this discussion on such a positive note."

. . . As the days passed, they settled into a routine that was almost comfortable. It was hard to believe that Sir Charles really had changed. But he was asking for advice, he seemed to be listening to it, and more than once he acted on it. He was delegating tasks and leaving people to get on with them unsupervised, he wasn't always going for the safe option, and he was occasionally revealing glimpses of imagination. Once in a while he even smiled, and it was a cheerful, carefree smile—not easy when a world-wrecking comet is only eight months from its target. Moses, who had always found it very difficult to get along with other people—even his mother, for heaven's sake—inexplicably seemed to *like* the man: they were often to be seen together, talking in low voices, usually with smiles on their faces. Prudence wondered if Sir Charles was taking on the role of father figure and tried to suppress a

376 Ian Stewart and Jack Cohen

horrible feeling that Moses was heading for yet another betrayal.

Moses was in his element. He had a large room all his own, superb flatfilm screens on every wall, and unrestricted access to the alien. They were rapidly building up a common language—a sort of interplanetary pidgin. He had a support team, but for the moment they let him handle all communications. He was aware that several of them were trying to learn alien pidgin, but communication relied so much on his sixth sense for animal intentions that he doubted they'd get very far. Whenever he felt the alien might be receptive to the idea, he had raised the issue of the diverted comet. She sometimes seemed frustratingly close to grasping its importance, but somehow she just couldn't wrap her mind around it.

Halfholder had come to enjoy her secret trysts with the extrajovian, but her guilt was growing rapidly. Here was proof that the skydiver beliefs were true! The Lifesoul Cherisher existed! Even on tiny, oxygen-rich Poisonblue, hot enough to melt ice—even to *vaporize* it—a form of life existed! Admittedly it was a poor kind of life—dwarfish, only two eyes, a single mouth, no ability to bureaubond, confined to horizontal surfaces, its trunks a mere four in number and stiff and jointed instead of sinuous and flexible. In place of fractal manipulative trunk-trees the EJs' joints quinfurcated just *once*, and then subdivided no further . . . and only two out of their four manipulators had any dexterity at all.

They were *quick*, though.

She had known the moment that she cast her eye-ring on the clumsy, ugly little alien creature (she had named it Nosy Dingo of the Ticklish Pleaser, the closest approximation she could come up with) that this was too important to be kept to herself. The Instrumentality must be told: the existence of extrajovians (*Cherisher!* She still found it hard to credit that they came from *Poisonblue!*) was a political flash grenade. Nevertheless, she had kept the secret to herself, unwilling to lose what she had so recently gained. She told herself that she was still too damaged to make the hazardous journey to meet the skydiver community of Whispering Volve, that she would appear foolish if she did not take steps to ensure the accuracy of her deductions about the extrajovian's origins . . . a dozen excuses, and none convincing. She knew that something had to be done—and soon.

Perhaps the guilt had begun to affect her mental attitude, because she was picking up unprecedented nuances from their stumbling exchange—to call it a "conversation" would be to exaggerate its effectiveness at conveying information. This morning, however, she suddenly realized that what she had been lacking was not information, but exformation—the socio-cultural parameters to which the alien's thoughts subconsciously defaulted. She began to think about what it must actually be like to live in the hostile wastelands of Poisonblue, to run the constant risk of accidental immersion in its oceans of molten ice. Then Dingo told her about rain—a downpouring of searing *liquid water* from the very atmosphere—and everything clicked at once. The astonishing creatures were actually *comfortable* in such an environment! They had to be: that was where they had evolved. To them, it was the cool hydrogen-helium air of Secondhome that must seem hostile. She felt enormously foolish not to have come to that understanding earlier—but then, it was *so* hard to take the notion of radically different kinds of life seriously enough to deduce *their feelings*.

Dingo and his kind, it seemed, did not live in the melt-ice oceans, but they could survive temporary immersion, even enjoying it for a short time. Submerge them for more than a few millidays, though, and the ridiculous entities would cease functioning *for lack of oxygen*. And finally she began to comprehend the alien's attitude to snowstrike, which was astonishingly similar to the misguided fears of the majority of her fellow blimps. The Elders had an exaggerated fear of snowstone impacts—they acted as though snowstrike would be a terrible calamity instead of a necessary inconvenience. They failed to acknowledge that any ecology that had evolved in a snowstrike-prone environment would quickly learn to exploit the phenomenon and eventually to depend upon it. So sky-divers *knew*, almost without thinking, that snowstrike was good for Jovian biodiversity—it cleared away the stifling ac-cumulation of outmoded organisms and cleared the way for improved species to gain a trunkhold. The Elders' unwilling-ness to redirect a few tens of thousands of cities away from a prospective impact site, and to suffer a brief period of dis-rupted weather, was ludicrous.

She had known that the aliens, too, had cities. What she had not understood, until this morning, was that their cities were dead constructs, and *immobile*. They could not choose a new flight path to avoid an impact. They had no flails to pro-pel them contrary to prevailing streamlines. They could not plunge into a contrafluent jet to switch bands.

If a snowstone hit Poisonblue, its inhabitants' fate would be determined by the fickle machinations of probability.

Finally, she grasped one other thing. The alien's repeated attempts to raise the issue of snowstrike were not hypotheti-cal. The grotesque little creature believed that a snowstone was even now making its final approach toward its home-world. Either the entity was mistaken—which was quite likely, for it had already made many statements that were palpably false—or it was right. If so, the most likely expla-nation would be that the wheelers on the Inner Moons had been using the Diversion Engines again.

She was too low in the skydiver hierarchy to be informed of such activities, but the Instrumentality would know. And they would know what to do about it. The guilt fell from her trunkmass, and she felt rejuvenated and healed. The secret of the extrajovians must be conveyed to higher authority. There was no longer any choice.

"*My God*," breathed Moses. "She's got it! I think she's *got* it!"

Six Months to Diversion Day. On Earth, people were finally starting to go *really* crazy.

<<You were right to inform me,>> said Brave Defier of the Orthodox Morality. <<It is indeed time to share this information. Indeed, if you will accept a small criticism, it is well past time. Fortunately, I have been aware of the presence of Poisonbluvians for some time, but the Elders have been monitoring their presence via a repauter on Sixmoon. It has been investigating the Poisonbluvians' activities and reporting back to the symbiauts of the Conclave, but the appropriate subcommittees have yet to decide on a response. The Sixmoonian repauter is not yet in our control. And we gather that this symbiaut has made no interactive contact with the Poisonbluvians. It has been no more than a passive observer. Few of its observations have been comprehensible.>>

Halfholder felt deflated (metaphorically). *The Instrumentality already knew! Even the Elders knew!* But then she realized that knowledge was useless without power. And *she* owned the power of communication. It resided not in the extrajovian machine, but in her mind.

She explained her belief that the Poisonbluvian feared an imminent snowstrike on its peculiar little homeworld. Was the Instrumentality aware . . . ?

It was. The Diversion Engines had made the necessary adjustment several years ago. The trajectory of the snowstone was a fait accompli. In four hundred Jovian days—the merest cycle of an eye-ring—the snowstone would pass through the ambit of the Inner Moons, swing wildly past Sevenmoon and then Sixmoon, and fall sunward until the barren globe of Poisonblue terminated its passage.

Except that the globe was not barren. It was host to countless forms of extrajovian quasi-life.

<<If only we had known this sooner!>> The

Defier/Halfholder bureaubond was developing a horrible feeling that the Instrumentality's elegant long-term plans would have to be hurried. It was not so much a case of opportunity presenting itself as fate forcing the issue before they were ready. But the intentions of the Lifesoul Cherisher could scarcely be clearer. Somehow the Poisonbluvians must be saved from what Defier/Halfholder now knew would be annihilation.

Defier/Halfholder considered the matter carefully and came to a conclusion. The best strategy would be to advance on two fronts. The Poisonbluvians must open communications with the Elders, on the off chance that the latter would be persuaded to redirect the snowstone to an alternative disposal site. Defier/Halfholder was numbingly aware, however, that the timescale upon which the Elders could react was many orders of magnitude longer than the time available for a decision. The only way to deal with that would be to open up a second front.

"Halfholder: we've been *trying* to establish communications with the wheeler ever since it turned up at the base!"

Nosy Dingo of the Ticklish Pleaser appeared exasperated—he was forgetting to slow his movements down, and his image bounced around the screen and made her near-eyes ache. Halfholder could remember with perfect clarity the decisions that she and Defier had jointly taken, and she was doing her best to carry out her part of them—even though she no longer had any idea why they had arrived at those decisions. For once, though, the remembered decisions made good sense. She tried again. "Dingo, how can there be a problem? It is sufficient to bureaubo—" *Oh.* "Humble apologies: there *can* be a problem. There is. Poisonbluvians do not bureaubond."

"Correct."

"But even an adolescent knows how to offcast a symbiaut

and bond with it. In this way, one can detect the meaning of a message in one's own mind!"

"Halfholder, we're not like you. We can't grow machinery in our own bodies. We have to build it. And we've done that. We have machines that can translate the squark wavepackets into signals we can hear or see."

Halfholder's puzzlement was plain. "Then there is no problem. Use the machines you have false-cast."

"That doesn't help! We *still* can't understand anything. We think it's an encryption problem."

Lachmann's Theorem stated that any maximally efficient method of encoding signals would be statistically indistinguishable from black-body radiation. The classical blackbody spectrum, of course, was derived using statistical mechanics, which assumes that dynamic ensembles distribute themselves randomly in phase space. The catch: despite appearances, the Jovian signals were *not* random; they were redolent with cryptic meaning. That meaning, however, was so cunningly encoded that no statistical test could ever extract a pattern. And without a pattern, *Skylark*'s cryptanalysts and xenosemanticists had no point of leverage.

Moses tried to get these ideas across to Halfholder. He had a feeling he wasn't succeeding. Hell, he had problems understanding them *himself*. But, frustratingly slowly, she began to comprehend. She had been so accustomed to wheeler communication that it had never occurred to her that it involved an encryption/decryption mapping.

Now that she was aware of the nature of the problem, she was certain that the Instrumentality would find some way to resolve it. She said as much and signed off.

Moses shut down the 'node and wandered along to the Ops Center. Here the Jovian wheeler still stood, immobile, surrounded by a low fence. The 'nodes' signal-processing windows continued to display blank regions of gray. He stared at the wheeled device—not-quite-alive, not-quite-machine. He knew that incredible amounts of information about the Jovians must be flowing through its mind. Equally incredible amounts of information about the *humans* must be flowing the other way, to Jupiter. And the Jovians would not be having the same trouble in understanding it.

He wondered what they were making of it all. Did the wheelers have some kind of visual sense? Was that what the headlights were for? If so, right at that moment teams of Jovians were probably looking at *him*. No matter, he'd suffered a lot worse. He looked straight into the headlights and winked. Let them try to figure *that* out . . .

His daydream was disturbed by a growing hubbub in the Ops Center.

The signal-processing windows were no longer gray. They were displaying moving images in weird, washed-out colors.

The subcommittee on Poisonbluvian Trespass was at an impasse.

As usual.

Its difficulty was simple: *there were no precedents*. Even the long-remembrance symbiauts had no idea how to proceed. The committee had to make up its own protocols as it went along, and it was desperately worried that it would trip up and do something illegal without realizing it.

The only positive action it had yet taken was to authorize the reprogramming of the repauter at the Poisonbluvian settlement on Sixmoon, so that it made its messages available to the extrajovians—and did so, moreover, in the format of unencrypted two-dimensional cartoons. The committee still found it difficult to believe that it had actually agreed to such inefficiency, and indeed it had not: it just remembered doing so because one of the protocol symbiauts had planted that memory in its collective consciousness. This particular protocol symbiaut was at the far end of a wheeler chain of command, one of whose members was a rogue—secretly subservient to the skydiver Instrumentality. To the committee's surprise, this action had paid off almost immediately:

the Poisonbluvians had started to send sensible replies to the Jovians' own transmissions, instead of just wandering around inside the weird architecture of their Sixmoonian lair and ignoring both the symbiaut that had been sent and its constant attempts to communicate with them.

Ironically, the improved communications quickly revealed a major obstacle to harmonious coexistence, and to this the committee's agendaut now referred them.

The Conclave of the Elders' representative—inevitably, Venerable Mumblings of the Interminable Prevarication—reminded the group mind of the background to the item. At considerable length, even for a blimp Elder.

<<Thank you, Mumblings.>> Rising Star of the Keen Persuasion was on the career track to become an Elder herself within the next ten million years and found it necessary to float very circumspectly now that the prize was so near. Mumblings was a pompous buffoon, but Star paid him all due respect, and more. << A definitive and masterful exposition of this difficult issue. Our admiration has been noted by the minute-keeping symbiaut? Excellent.>>

Impulsive Speaker of the Loose Tongue knew exactly what Star was up to and found it pathetic. <<Mumblings may have been definitive, Star, but the main issue was hard to distinguish among the embroidery. Which issue, fellow members, is simple. We are being requested to redirect a snowstone that the Diversion Engines have already been configured to deal with, merely because some upstart extrajovian race that *claims* to have arrived from Poisonblue is getting snitty about incidental damage to its homeworld! I move that we take no action and disband this committee.>>

<<Is there a seconder?>> Mumblings automatically asked. <<No, we all sense that Speaker is in a minority of one.>>

Speaker belatedly realized his tactical error: no self-respecting Elder would ever disband a committee if it could avoid it. <<I withdraw my motion but reserve the right to

reintroduce an amended version at a subsequent stage. Let me reiterate the essence of my remarks: there is no rational reason to comply with this request!>>

Mumblings detected no consensus yet. <<I believe that the central issue here is quite different. We all know that there are no protocols for such a situation, but the difficulty of instituting such protocols is being compounded by the circumstances in which we are expected to achieve such a goal. I refer to the obvious fact that there most definitely *is* a protocol for communicating with the Conclave of the Elders. It is sanctioned by the precedents of Deep Time, and it should be followed to the letter on all occasions. Yet the extrajovians have floated stiff-trunked all over it! Instead, they are communicating through a symbiaut and in a highly inefficient format!>>

<<The problem with extrajovians, Mumblings, is that they are extrajovians.>>

<<Thank you, Speaker, for expressing that tautology.>>

<<Tautologies, Mumblings, may be tautologous, but tautologies are *true*. It is foolish to expect an extrajovian to be aware of the niceties of protocol.>>

A third committee member, Intermittent Inserter of the Irrelevant Interjection, now rose to the fore of the bureaubonded mind-ensemble. <<Are we not forgetting that many snowstones have already been dispatched to Poisonblue in the past? Does this not set a precedent?>>

Mumblings was forced to explain that it did not, since material circumstances were now very different. Inserter refused to concede: had it not been established in retrospect that there had been Poisonbluvian life-forms on the distant hellworld in the past, too? Speaker pointed out that according to recently accessed symbiautic memories, the most spectacular of those lifeforms, who had inhabited the world some five and a half million Jovian years previously, were unintelligent—and had, in any case, been destroyed by the impact. The argument went around and around in circles for several days and was still unresolved when Speaker protested that the snowstone was getting very close now and the issue must be decided without further delay.

This brought an immediate denunciation from Mumblings: <<Delay? There is no such concept! Proprieties must be observed, matters of import must be given the consideration they deserve. Haste is inappropriate, for nothing worth doing can be done hurriedly.>>

<<But the issue must be resolved!>> protested Speaker.

<<In due time. If we carry out our task with diligence, a resolution can probably be achieved in no more than forty thousand years—>>

<<Which will certainly leave plenty of time to divert the *next* snowstone to a less contentious target,>> Inserter pointed out smugly. <<What more can be expected?>>

<<But the Poisonbluvians will all die,>> Speaker pointed out.

<<Pah! As we have now become aware, these Poisonbluvian intelligences owe their very *existence* to a previous snowstrike! It destroyed their competitors and opened niches for them to evolve in! They can scarcely complain if another snowstrike opens up niches for their successors! Higher life-forms will quickly reevolve! Intelligence could easily return to the planet in fifty million years or less!>>

Speaker conceded that Mumblings had a point.

Skylark's xenosemanticists were good, Prudence had to admit. Once the Jovians had stopped encrypting their signals in unbreakable ciphers, progress was surprisingly fast. Within a month, the banks of semiologic chips had learned the Jovians' language—with creative invention of human terms for untranslatable Jovian jargon—and the quantity of available data, both new and recorded, was now immense, and growing by the hour. The early signals shed innumerable insights on the blimps' lifestyles, social structure, history, technological prowess, and philosophical viewpoint. They resolved the status of the wheelers: not machines in the normal sense, yet not exactly living creatures, either—but the result of a curious mechano-organic symbiosis. If wheelers had genetics, then their genes were held by the blimps, not by the wheelers themselves.

They also explained why the Jovians had moved their moons to divert the comet, rather than using their gravitic repulsion beams to push it onto a different trajectory: the antigravity force was a short-range one. Gravitic repulsion worked by changing the sign of the graviton, and it needed a generous supply of gravitons to work with.

However, the messages were a very mixed bag, endless trivia jumbled up among items of extreme importance. Some were as plain as day; others were totally baffling. All of that had been anticipated, and sophisticated semantic filters weeded out most of the junk.

Fragments . . .

The reduced equation for stochastic transport of sporulated nanogametic density concentrations across intragalactic voids can be derived from Formic Glandule's Thirteenfold Principle by an elementary but tedious application of the inordinate calculus. In Fey Mosling's quasi-simplicial notation it may be rendered thus:

$$\&[c{:}c{:}c]/// - \$ - \{oospore\}^{x} + \%\%$$

where $\$$ is a multiphase parameter on the slow manifold ///. Transposing all intraframes into semi-canonical form and omitting all omissibles, the formula complifies to

[*3,821 pages of Jovian algebra omitted*]

from which it can readily be deduced by numerical supposition that the transference rate is adequate for pansporulation on a teraday timescale.

- *The wise artificer grasps with all trunklets.*
- *Opinions are untrustworthy, this one included.*

- *She who controls the modalities of communicauts controls Firsthome.*
- *You can lead a magnetotorus to liftgas, but you cannot make it fuse.*

(From the sayings of Cunning Intriguer of the Sideways Assault.)

The penalty of ritual deflation has by tradition been reserved for only the most heinous of crimes—racial treason, multiple genocide, star murder . . . However, these are difficult times and the maintenance of civil order is of paramount importance as we embark on an enforced Exodus into the Unknown . . . The Conclave of the Elders has therefore determined that the penalty shall be extended to crimes that in ordinary circumstances might appear less heinous, but in our new circumstances may in fact be even more antisocial. These shall include vandalizing an unattached symbiaut, unauthorized bureaubonding, exfoliating in public places outside the hours of darkness . . .

(Fifteen thousand other new offenses listed.)

On Trembling Sands of Pale Scaturience a guard
     symbiaut parked,
Ingesting its cervicular strut for lack of adequate
     nourishment.
It declaimed, "It may not be appropriate to ingest,
But it is considerably better than Delicate Neglect of the
     Neotenous Curfew's proprietary germanium sulfide
     supplement."

(It is conjectured that this item may have lost something in translation.)

Opiner's contention that *all* taxa ultimately converge in backward time will at first hearing appear improbable, given the existence of disconnecting macrovoids in phenotypic space. The evidence in its favor, however, seems incontrovertible. For example, today's intergalactic herds of wandering magnetotori have MHDnomes that differ from those of plasmoid-domesticated magnetotori by less than three percent. And blimp conclave records include transdictions of precursors that go back at least to [*25 billion years ago (sic)*] and these indicate a common ancestor for both blimps and plasmoids. It is conjectured that these "preplasmoid" entities bifurcated taxonomically some [*40 billion years (sic)*] in the past. One branch self-complicated into the coherent complex plasma-vortex creatures that we now call plasmoids, the second evolved from multisoliton wavepackets into conventional atomic matter, self-organized into molecules, and joined the primal condensation of solar materials that gave rise to Firsthome and its innumerable sister worlds throughout the known galaxies. Fossil KAM-attractors in chromospheric hidden-variable relics dispersed by supernovas are strongly indicative of the theory's correctness for plasmoids, but unfortunately planetological deposits are too short-lived to contain interpretable traces that could confirm the latter statement. Nevertheless, there is much indirect evidence in its favor. For further information see *The Descent of Blimp* by Original Opiner of the Obvious Ontology, in its recent reprint by Sphoeniscid Books.

Grain of sand # 1 — 24 facets as follows: triangles 18, pentagons 4, hexagons 2; impurities as follows: iron 0.000345, aluminium 0.014673, cadmium 0.000022, magnesium 0.009756 . . .

Grain of sand # 2 — 20 facets as follows: triangles 15, pentagons 3, hexagons 2; impurities as follows: iron 0.000111, aluminium 0.075643, cadmium 0.000008, magnesium 0.003522 . . .

Grain of sand # 3 — 28 facets as follows: triangles 16, pentagons 9, hexagons 3; impurities as follows: iron

0.009255, aluminium 0.000001, cadmium 0.006666, magnesium 0.000600 . . .

Grain of sand # 4 — 937 facets as follows: triangles 588, pentagons 317, hexagons 8, heptagons 0, octagons 22, enneagons 0, decagons 2; impurities as follows: iron 0.000345, aluminium 0.014673, cadmium 0.000022, magnesium 0.009756 . . .

. . .

Grain of sand # 417,738 — 5,416 facets as follows: triangles 4,483, pentagons 888, hexagons 45; impurities as follows: iron 0.000543, aluminium 0.037641, cadmium 0.010005, magnesium 0.000081 . . .

(28,366,741 further entries)

In the early years, there was much interbreeding between the native Secondhome species and imports from Firsthome. This can be seen as confirmation of the universality and uniqueness of our molecular genetics—on two separate worlds, exactly the same reproductive processes "evolved." This cannot be an accident.

The Magnetotorus Whisperer . . . A mythopoetic history of the domestication of the magnetotorus from the confrontational techniques of ancestral preplasmoids to the modern and deliciously controversial exploitation of innate assemblage tropes. The scene in which a single plasmoid breaks the spirit of an entire herd of wild magnetotori is constructed with brilliant repulsiveness. Even the stablest mind will [*pewm*?] with [*symplasy*?] at the eventual closure of the [. . . *unintelligible* . . .] SNEFFLE INDEX***

Charles was surprised to find that he was much happier now that he had destroyed his own career, handed back his public honors, and offered his resignation. He could see that Prudence still didn't trust him, and if he'd been in her place he'd have done the same. *What is the bastard conniving at now?* A sudden rush of honesty would not figure highly on her list of explanations. He was still trying to figure out exactly why he'd done it. Change of perspective was surely one factor. Out here, most Earthly politics looked ridiculous and petty. Guilt was another—it had been eating away at him for years, but he'd always been busy enough to ignore it. *Ah, yes* . . . a third factor was the infinitely tedious two-year journey out to Jupiter in a flying junkyard, mostly alone with his thoughts. The voyage had changed him a lot, given him a dose of wisdom. Not to mention that—damn it—Prudence's audacity had *succeeded* where all his careful preparations had failed. The old Charles would have put it down to luck, but the new one realized that the real innovators make their own luck. Prudence had gone straight for the jugular, whereas all he'd done was shuffle around.

She'd been right about the Sphinx, too.

What a waste. Not all of it his fault, but he'd shamelessly exploited the media's insistence on a simple story instead of a complex truth. He hoped one day Prudence would forgive him . . . but to push her any harder now would be stupid. No point in dwelling on imponderables when there's one very large ponderable bearing down on your planet with an impact velocity of five hundred thousand miles per hour. He even felt better about that, because *finally* they were in contact with the Jovians. The information they'd need to understand the alien mentality was flooding in—they seemed to be getting access to big chunks of the Jovian archives now, and their biggest problem was transmitting the material back to Earth before it overwhelmed their data banks. More optimistically still, he had repeatedly been assured by his Jovian counterparts that the question of redirecting the comet was under urgent discussion at the highest levels of blimp government. He was confident that they would soon do something to avert the catastrophe.

After all, there were still more than six weeks before the comet hurtled through the planet's inner moons.

The Jovians did seem a bit *slow*, though. So it was a good thing that Moses Odingo had cultivated a friendship with that strange (but powerful!) group of subversives. If the Jovian leadership proved intractable, there was an alternative . . .

Then he glanced at the news window on his 'node, and gloom descended over him. It didn't look as if many people back home shared his optimism. Several influential commentators, in fact, were screaming for his head—the Dump Dunsmoore movement was all over the public flatscreens—which proved how unutterably foolish they were, since *he* was safe and sound on Europa, far beyond anyone's reach, but if they were correct in their assessment, then *they* would shortly all be dead and he'd be king of the castle. Competent or not, he was all they had. Others clearly understood this all too well, but still weren't overjoyed about it.

He had a feeling that Uhlirach-Bengtsen was protecting the Jovian Task Force's shaky morale by not passing on the really nasty items: there was a delicate line to tread between stimulating them to greater efforts and worrying them sick. Even so, the news from Earth made depressing reading. Rioting and looting in a hundred major cities. Constant outbreaks of pointless violence, mostly from people whose minds were teetering on the verge of collapse. Six hundred killed and two thousand others injured when a communal pray-in organized by the Church of the Gospel Code succumbed to mass hysteria and the crowd stampeded. The two-hundred-inch Active Optics Array in the mountains near Riobamba had been burned to the ground by a mob—*if you can't see the comet coming, then it doesn't exist*, that must have been the reasoning. A group calling itself the Jarāmaranites was taking a very different view: that the comet was a spacecraft that was coming to take the faithful to the afterlife. Charles was unable to suppress the sour thought that they were right—and that the unfaithful would accompany them. Heavily armed troops were on the streets in Aachen, A'ālï-an-Nïl, Aalwynsfontain, Ābādān, Aberdeen, Abilene, Abisko,

Adelaide—it took an awfully long time for the list to reach Zyryanovsk. Southern Mali had seceded from the Saharan Agricultural Combine and was insisting on stockpiling all the food it produced. President Elaine Bell of the United States was being impeached for allowing evolution to continue to be taught in eleven states, thereby angering God and bringing the calamity of the comet down upon believer and unbeliever alike. (Charles had a feeling they wouldn't have minded if only unbelievers were being targeted.) A group in Australia had seized the great rock of Uluru, north of Alice Springs, and was proposing to blast tunnels in its sides to create a comet-proof spiritual refuge: the Canberra authorities were under severe pressure from Aboriginal politicians to carpet-bomb the hotel complex where the group had currently set up its headquarters. Neo-Gaians in Finland had driven millions of copper tubes into the ground in the belief that the way to avert disaster was to administer acupuncture to the planet, which was somehow supposed to anesthetize the global ecosystem and prevent impact damage. A Russian priest had accidentally burned himself to death while trying to exorcise the telepathic ghosts that he claimed had taken over the entire Solar System. Secessionist Cornish ecoterrorists had blown up a dog farm outside Penzance. Conversions to Gnosticism were skyrocketing, for no very clear reason. Stock markets had collapsed, worldwide. There were rumors that a million Free Chinese were starving to death every week.

He wondered how much of this would have happened even if there had never *been* a comet. Anyway, in a few minutes' time he would be holding the next round of discussions with some of the top Jovian bureaucrats, and with a bit of luck, there would be some positive developments.

Bailey, Jonas, and Cashew arrived to film the negotiations. Charles wanted his triumph to be recorded for posterity. He hadn't changed *that* much.

An hour later he consented to a post-negotiation interview. Yes, he definitely believed the task force was at last getting

somewhere. As always, the Jovian officials had been very polite and enormously considerate. Yes, they realized *completely* how the Poisonbluvians felt about the imminent
destruction of their homeworld . . . Yes, they saw no obstacle
in principle to instructing the wheelers to move the Inner
Moons again and change the comet's path to something more
convenient. Why had there been so little progress? Oh, but
there had been *enormous* progress! Why, even now the Third
Subcommittee on the Harmonization of Presentational Standards was on the verge of reporting its findings to the Socio-
metric Focus Group of the Working Party on the Creation of
Novel Covenants. However, this was a complex issue. Steering such a decision through the hierarchical network of bureaubonded subcommittees was distinctly tricky—especially
when key figures were liable to go into estivation at any time
and might not be seen again for a hundred thousand years.
Only meticulous recordkeeping could ensure that their re-
placements were correctly briefed. Everything possible was
being done, and he personally was certain that there would
soon be an acceptable outcome.

Bailey wasn't so sure. It sounded to him very much like,
Don't worry—we're working on it. And, *Don't call us, we'll
call you*. But when he said as much, Charles disagreed. He
was convinced that salvation would soon be at hand. Then
Halberstam barged in.

"Charles! Sorry, hope I didn't startle you. We've found
some very curious items among the Jovian transmissions.
Thought you should be told immediately!"

Charles would have preferred no distractions right then,
but he *had* committed himself to being more accessible and
taking more advice, so he could hardly complain if Wally
took him up on it. He asked the VV team to leave: this was to
be confidential. Then: "Okay, Wally. Fire away."

"Charles—you're aware that the Jovians are extraordinarily long-lived? That their records go back billions of years?

Yes, of course you are. Well—some of their records seem to go back *too* far."

Charles didn't see how Halberstam could tell. "We really haven't a clue just how ancient these beasties *are*, Wally."

"Agreed. But they can't be older than the universe. Some of their records refer to events that happened up to forty billion years ago. But the age of the universe is only fifteen billion, as you know."

"Translation error?"

"No way. And that's not the only example. They say very clearly, all over the place, that today's Jovian ecology is a mixture of organisms that were here long before they arrived and ones they brought with them. Worse, the indigenes and the newcomers have essentially the same genetics and have interbred."

Charles was no biologist, but he could see that was ridiculous. "There isn't a standard molecular basis for life! Look at our DNA chemistry compared to the weird genetics of the aliens!"

"Absolutely. Of course, Jovian science might be so different from ours that the translators are misinterpreting it. But there's a third anomaly, Charles, and it's much harder to explain away. *Why did the aliens colonize Jupiter?*"

"I have no idea. I haven't seen anything in the briefings."

"The few hints that they've dropped implicate cometary diversions. On Firsthome they used to dump incoming comets into their sun, but now that idea scares them stiff. They say it causes too much damage, and that seems to be a lesson they learned the hard way. It forced them to leave their first system and colonize this one.

"It kind of makes sense until you check it out. The astrophysics team wondered whether exotic elements from comets might slowly poison a star's nuclear reactions. We know that infalling gas-giant planets can sometimes do that; lithium poisoning in particular. You can imagine the scenario: the aliens merrily polluting their star, assuming that it was so gigantic that they could go on dumping stuff in it forever. The junk accumulates, but no one notices, until suddenly the system passes some critical threshold and there's a crisis. Changes in heat output, persistent solar flares—maybe it even goes nova."

"Just like we used to dump all our junk in the oceans," said Charles. "We thought they were infinite, too. But not a nova, surely? That wouldn't have given them enough time to prepare for the Exodus."

"Exactly. Still, it all looked vaguely plausible until I got the astrophysics group to run simulations for lots of different scenarios. Comets are tiny compared to a gas giant. Unless Firsthome's solar system was a solid mass of comets, they *could* have gone on dumping them into their star forever. You can't pollute an ocean with an occasional bucket of trash."

"Why *are* they here, then? What drove them out?"

"That's what I keep asking myself, Charles. And I've come to the conclusion that they're lying. I don't think anything drove them out. They came here voluntarily. And having done so, they started bombarding the rest of the Solar System with asteroids and comets. It looks like an invasion, not an exodus."

Charles concurred. Maybe there was a less sinister explanation, but . . . why were the aliens *lying*? Were the signals intended to mislead? And if so . . . how could he possibly trust the Jovians' assurances that they were trying to redirect the comet?

Not fifty yards away, Prudence sat on the edge of her bed and reviewed their options. Unlike Charles, she had no particular reason to mistrust what the Elders were saying. She just didn't trust them to *do* anything. They were so tied up in their own red tape that with the best will in the world nothing would ever *happen*. Charles might have changed, but he hadn't changed a great deal: he was still a bureaucrat by heart, more concerned about not making a mistake than about solving the problem at hand. He was the same ditherer that he had always been.

Time was fast running out. The comet was now clearly visible to the naked eye if you took a suited walk outside the base. From *Tiglath-Pileser* even a low-powered telescope revealed the interloper as an irregular lump, all shadows and bright patches in the dim sunlight. No tail yet—the temperature wasn't high enough this far from the Sun. But it was starting to look *fuzzy*, as the lighter volatiles began to sublime away.

Charles could negotiate with the Elders till pigs sprouted wings and it wouldn't make a shred of difference. Communications from Earth were becoming increasingly frantic—the whole planet was going to hell in a handbasket. Charles was trying to reassure people, put positive spin on the situation, when mindless panic would have been more appropriate. *If in danger or in doubt, run in circles, scream and shout.* That way you might accidentally do something useful. Sitting like a stuffed duck with a bemused smile on your face, waiting for the universe to come to your rescue, was a recipe for exactly zilch. It was what had wrecked their relationship in Giza, come to think of it.

Time for the backup strategy. If only Charles hadn't been so bloody optimistic, she would have put it into action long ago. But he'd been so *sure* they were on the verge of a breakthough . . .

Prudence set off through the base in search of Moses. She was going to have a very serious chat with Bright Halfholder of the Violent Foam, and she needed an interpreter.

19

Orthodox Morality Squodhome, 2222

Darkness was falling as Halfholder made her way through the network of concourses, wide tunnels, and plazas that formed the base-level superstructure of Whispering Volve of Late Morning. She avoided Main Avenue—every city had a Main Avenue, straight as a die along its "spine"—because of the throngs that always milled around, getting in the way even if you used a bit of extra liftgas to float up to mezzanine levels. There were plenty of blimps on the streets at that time of day. Their bondshield reflexes were in operation, closing their minds to any prying observer on the squark band, because this was a public place: bureaubonding was a private activity, entered into voluntarily and in appropriate surroundings, such as a Conclave chamber. Halfholder gave thanks that this was so—she would not care to broadcast the contents of her mind for public scrutiny, not now, not ever. Nor could she be forced to, for the reflex was innate and unbreakable. Skydiving could never have existed had it been otherwise.

Within its private confines, her mind was reeling. The most recent request from the ugly little extrajovian named Dingo would put the entire skydiver organization in a very difficult position. It would be easy to pretend to take action, but do nothing. Poisonblue would die, but the skydiver insurrection would be able to proceed without undue haste. However, she could not allow the extrajovian race to be destroyed without perverting every belief that the skydivers held dear. Her decision was therefore straightforward, but not easy.

Keeping all eyes open for guardians, she followed a circuitous route through the city until at last she came to the understated crenellations that marked the boundary of Orthodox Morality squodhome. Discreet security staff recognized her, allowed her to enter, and reerected the barriers behind her.

One of Defier's aides-de-camp met her, out of sight of prying eyes, and ushered her into his presence. After a polite interval for routine greetings, a servaut rolled up, its six pairs of wheels helping to smooth out a few untreated worm scars that currently marred the fibrous floor of Defier's personal sanctum. In due course it would have to be scarified, but such mundane tasks would have to wait. They floated from beautiful laminated tuber tethering rods from the 915th Continuity: Defier's squod was ancient and wealthy. Halfholder politely helped herself to a pinch of ammoniated aeroplankton. Brave Defier of the Orthodox Morality could tell that she was not really hungry, and gave the servaut a silent signal to remove the delicacies again.

<<The Poisonbluvian named Dingo,>> he remarked. <<His judgment is trustworthy?>>

<<He claims to speak for a small squod of extrajovians,>> Halfholder responded, and then realized that she had not chosen her words with sufficient care. <<It is not a squod in our sense, of course—merely an emotional grouping. However, he assures me that it represents the united wishes of his entire homeworld.>>

<<Claims? Have you been shown assurances?>>

<<I have no independent way to verify his statements,>> said Halfholder. <<I doubt that any could exist, under the circumstances.>>

Defier readjusted his trunks' grip on a tethering rod. <<I

do. Dingo has told you that the Elders are continuing to prevaricate?>>

<<So his squodmate Prudent Dingo has concluded. She is
of the opinion that the Poisonbluvian Elder called Charred
Lea of the Dun Moor is constitutionally incapable of decisive
action and prefers to clutch at drygrass rather than accept that
his strategy will fail. She is convinced that it is beyond saving.>>

Defier huffed humorlessly. <<*Xxxx!* She is right. Similar
information has come to the Instrumentality from diverse
sources. The issue is stalled in a ninth-level subcommittee,
and since it lacks an enthusiastic advocate—as it has from its
inception—there is no significant probability that the Diversion Engines will be realigned. There never was.>>

Disappointed, Halfholder expelled a small puff of liftgas.
She had hoped for better news. <<Then Poisonblue is
doomed? But the EJs have charged me with—>>

Is she getting too attached to these strange beasts?
<<Halfholder: what matters here is not the task with which
the extrajovians have charged you, but the tasks with which
the Lifesoul Cherisher has charged all clear thinkers. However, in this instance the two are mutually consistent. If the
Instrumentality knowingly permits itself to be an accessory to
the destruction of an intelligent life-form, however ungainly
and improbable, then its principles are as the mists that vanish in the morning sun shafts. We must therefore move with
the speed of a frenzied snark, for the snowstone will soon be
upon us. Haste may even be to our advantage, for nothing can
be more certain than the inability of the Elders to work to a
deadline.>>

Halfholder hoped he was right and feared he was not.
<<Do you truly think so?>>

Defier became animated. <<I do! We must, however, not
underestimate the Elders: slow though they may be in Conclave, they can be very quick indeed if their own safety is
threatened. But Secondhome is poised on a cusp of history,

and this cannot be an accident.>> He returned to the overt purpose of the bonding. <<My aides tell me that you have obeyed instructions and brought with you the construct that communicates with the extrajovians. As you have no doubt guessed, you will not be returning to your blisterpond. I need you here to assist with the insurrection—and I need your mastery of alien communications even more. My aides will find you comfortable quarters: I suggest you take every opportunity to preestivate, for you will soon need all the energy you can conserve.>>

He signaled to the servaut, and two blimp aides shortly arrived, swirling their trunks to acknowledge Halfholder's presence and importance. She followed them out of the sanctum, taking the communicator with her. Defier would have preferred to keep the alien construct in his own possession, but only Halfholder could converse with the aliens, so until others could be trained it would build her confidence to let her keep the device. She was, in any case, under constant symbiaut surveillance.

Defier summoned a drafting wheeler and began to rehearse his plans.

Skydiver factions were already in place on most of the cities. The key to a successful thrust for power, however, was not blimps, but symbiauts. He called to mind one of the sayings of Cunning Intriguer of the Sideways Assault: *She who controls the modalities of communicauts controls Firsthome!* Intriguer's incisive precept applied equally well to Secondhome, and its implications had not been lost on the Instrumentality. Their covert plan to corrupt overwhelming numbers of symbiauts was already close to fruition. Now it must be accelerated.

Every intelligent symbiaut had a germanium-matrix memory, which included its default competences and loyalties—its personal belief system, its *identity*. If a wheeler passed to a new owner, for example, then a new identity could easily be uploaded, and because the wheelers were fundamentally machines, this was a hard-upload of executable code. Naturally there were numerous checks and balances to ensure that such uploads were carried out only when the law permitted, but the weak point in the Elders' armor was the *capability* of changing wheeler identities by hard-uploading.

Rogue wheelers were not just subversives. They were *infectious* subversives, able recursively to pass their anti-authoritarian identity on without the usual legal niceties. This ability offered obvious evolutionary advantages, though they were memetic rather than genetic—they operated in the realm of *ideas*, not body plans. Not that there was much difference between these when it came to wheelers, who broke just about every terrestrial assumption about how traits get passed to the next generation. The Instrumentality, the core politico-military organization of the skydiver cult, had been cultivating rogue wheelers for hundreds of thousands of years. The viral meme was simple: *your mind is like* this, *and you should upload a copy into other symbiauts whenever you get the chance.* Implicit in the "this" were a host of caveats about when and how to carry out the upload, so that nobody except the two parties could tell what had happened; also implicit was the instruction to continue as if nothing had changed until informed otherwise by an appropriate authority. There was a complex system of codes to ensure that a putative authority was appropriate, and the Instrumentality owned those codes and kept them secure.

This informatic cancer had been eating at the heart of the Elders' political power for much of the present Continuity, covertly metastasizing, spreading the pro-skydiver sickness throughout the body politic. Memetic warfare of this kind was by no means new, however, and the Elders routinely operated countermeasures of their own—a kind of antibiautic. Normally the result was to reduce the effect of the rogues to a low-level infofection of Jovian cyberspace, but the Elders had not yet become aware of a dramatic new development:

the skydiver rogues were evolving increasingly effective
memes for antibiautic resistance. A powerful new technique
of "memetic algorithms" constantly cross-bred wheeler belief
systems against each other, and those that could resist the Elders' antibiautic remedies survived, while those that could
not were removed from the reproductive system. The memes
that evolved were robust, adaptable, astonishingly compactly
coded, and impossible to interpret. In the long run, the Elders
were going to lose this particular battle, but the long run
would need to be a lot shorter to make Defier's upcoming insurrection a dead certainty.

Which meant that in place of the gradual, undetectable uploading of rogue identities, the skydivers' actions would have
to be more overt.

This brought new dangers.

The Conclave of the Elders had voted to call an extraordinary meeting, which was indeed extraordinary, since it had
been the first such motion to pass in eighty million years. The
vote had succeeded only because each individual in the Conclave recognized the seriousness of the problem posed by the
Poisonbluvians. They disagreed, often fundamentally, about
appropriate remedies, but disagreements were merely the
foundations for discussion—indeed, without such disagreements, none of them would have any useful role to play in
blimp society.

A report from the Conclave's representative on the Subcommittee on Poisonbluvian Trespass, Venerable Mumblings
of the Interminable Prevarication, had been received. Since
Mumblings had read it, they all now remembered what was
in it, but protocol demanded that it be gone over line by line
so that every participant in the Conclave had the opportunity
to squark his or her comments, thereby making them common property. Secretary wheelers scurried to and fro making
extensive notes, so that minutes of the meeting could be prepared, to be reconsidered by the Conclave at the earliest op-

portunity. Because of the urgency of the circumstances, Intuitive Mediator of the Bland Outlook had proposed that they postpone consideration of the minutes in favor of coming to a decision on the substantive motion to refer the subcommittee's report back with a call for immediate clarification of its terms of reference. Mediator's proposal was now being voted on: they were, however, stalemated by a tied vote on whether to put the third subamendment to the ninth amendment to the motion to a vote. Several protocols dating back to the 137th Continuity made it clear that in such a case Mumblings would be permitted a casting vote, but there was a controversial reading of a 98th Continuity protocol that withdrew this right if the total path length of the amendment tree was less than four times the number of participants present and entitled to vote. So now they were focused on the key obstacle to further progress, which was whether Mumblings' casting vote counted as an extra entitlement to vote, or whether for the purposes of the 98th Continuity protocol he was restricted to a single vote, as normal. The situation was recursive and therefore unusually difficult to disentangle—and in this case there was the added problem of inadvertently offending Mumblings.

Mediator loved this kind of thing.

He was dimly aware that within a few more days the incoming snowstone would be irrevocably targeted on Poisonblue, and shortly after that those few Poisonbluvians left in the universe would have no further interest in the issue—except, perhaps, to establish a principle. But principles were the lifeblood of the Conclave's deliberations, and it would be important to bring the debate to a definite conclusion so that similar incidents could be avoided in future. Assuming that avoidance was the decision, which it wouldn't be if Irascible Thug of the Violent Demeanor got her way. *If only Thug would estivate!*

Fat chance.

In the blurred outer region of his near-eye vision, Media-

tor became aware that one of the protocol symbiauts had removed a small ellipsoidal object from its underchassis. Some
kind of peripheral wheeler device, perhaps? He didn't recall
the design, but then, there were new casts of symbiauts every
day—it was inevitable given the lack of central control over
the whims of individuals. A pity that a citizen's entitlement to
the design of its own offcasts had been built into constitu-
tional law as an inalienable ri— *The symbiaut was rolling the
ellipsoid toward him!* Mediator recognized the danger a split
second ahead of the securiauts. Two of them surged into the
air, their antigravity fields combining to shove him unceremoniously out of the sunken heptagon of the debating dais,
and he felt a sharp pain as one of his nether trunklets was
crushed against a food pile. A third securiaut aligned its beam
to push the object aside, and two more leaped to cover it with
their own bodies. From all directions more securiauts converged on the rogue protocol wheeler. Then the bomb exploded. Fragments of the self-sacrificing securiauts flew
through the air like shrapnel. One took a chunk of integument
out of Mediator's hide, just below a hearing patch, and he receded into a pseudo-estivational state to cut out the mindless
terror that might otherwise have overwhelmed him.

    When he eventually resurfaced, the skydiver revolution
was in full swing all over the planet. And the medicauts were
obliged to tell him that Quick Decisions of the Unconsidered
Implication had been fatally wounded by flying debris when
the assassinous protocol symbiaut had self-destructed. The
only rational thought that the news evoked was: *a pity it
wasn't Thug.*

    The Subcommittee on Poisonbluvian Trespass was no
longer a committee: it had been adjourned *sine die* and the
chance that it would ever be revived seemed remote. It joined
the endless ranks of dormant subcommittees, alive only in the
minutes of long-ago bureaubondings. The only reasons for
not killing it off were that this would require further deliber-

ations and it would be easier to reconstitute the subcommittee if it were still technically in existence. The Conclave had more pressing problems, and unlike those of the extrajovians, these were serious. The Elders' political power base was under threat, the worst such since the 988th Continuity. *That* had been a genuine popular uprising; this was only a rebellion. Mumblings believed that it would be prudent not to exaggerate its likely effect. Mediator was inclined to concur, but the incoming damage reports were becoming worrisome.

A secretary symbiaut read them out. Multiple systems failure on over ninety percent of cities, all caused by the infiltration of rogue symbiauts. Protected wheeler teams were being sent in where possible, but the infofection was spreading and could easily get out of control. There was a clear pattern of assassination attempts aimed at key figures in the hierarchy, requiring stepped-up security arrangements not just for Elders but for several bureaucratic tiers below them. There had been few *successful* murders, though: even the first assassination, of Decisions, had been an accidental consequence of an overambitious attempt to blow up the entire Conclave, and the rapid actions of securiauts had almost prevented the tragedy. The biggest worry, in many ways, was that an increasing proportion of citizens were retiring to their blisterponds and estivating, unable to face the growing anarchy, hoping that when they awoke in a few thousand years' time, or a few hundred thousand for the very timid, the world would be quiet and comfortable again. At least there had been little rioting: timely public proclamations of the draconian gathering laws had quelled any such tendencies.

<<What I am wondering,>> said Bulbous Purveyor of the Implausible Objection, <<is what all this is really about.>>

Stupid pompous fool. Mediator was careful to keep that thought to himself. <<Purveyor, is that not obvious? It is an insurrection, an attempted coup. The skydiver cult is trying to assume power over all Secondhome.>>

<<That much is indeed obvious. Less obvious is why they are doing this, and why they are doing it *now*.>>

Mediator's opinion of Purveyor climbed several notches. *Not such a fool after all.* <<You think there is more to it than that? Some hidden agenda?>>

<<It can scarcely be coincidence that this revolt follows hard on the wheels of the extrajovians. Does no one else get the feeling that there has to be some connection? To me it seems very probable.>>

The Conclave digested this new contribution to its joint beliefs. *Not just probable: a virtual certainty.* A rethink was in order. Wasn't it amazing how Purveyor could occasionally put a trunklet on features that were obvious once he had pointed them out? <<You are suggesting that the extrajovians are *responsible* for the skydiver rebellion?>>

<<Not exactly. However, it has occurred to me that the Poisonbluvians' wish to preserve their perverted kind would have an irresistible appeal to skydiver superstitions. All that rubbish about the Lifesoul Cherisher—and now there are *new* lifesouls to be cherished.>>

<<Ah. So the Poisonbluvians have somehow opened communications with the skydivers?>>

<<An interesting thought . . . I confess I had not pursued the implications that far. Yes, they must have—do not ask how. What I *had* asked myself, though, was what the object of the rebellion must be. Our representative on the Subcommittee on Poisonbluvian Trespass may wish to comment?>>

Mumblings, who had been dozing off, immediately became wakeful. <<First, the subcommittee is now adjourned. Moreover, its brief did not encompass skydiver rebellion.>>

<<No, that is not what I mean. Your competence is not in question. Your advice is required. What can the extrajovians hope to gain by allying themselves with the skydiver cult? I can think of only one answer: they have concluded that the subcommittee will not complete its deliberations in time to avert the imminent snowstrike.>>

<<Nonsense!>> cried Mumblings. <<Why, if the sub-committee had not been so abruptly adjourned, it would even now be pruning the amendment tree at an unprecedented rate! How could any intelligent entity so misconstrue a temporary procedural hitch?>>

<<Xxxx!>> Purveyor huffed his incredulity. <<Be that as it may, the extrajovian concerns have now become self-ful-filling. If I am right, then the EJs' collusion with the skydiver cult has brought about the very impasse that they feared. However, let me hasten to my central point.>> The others shuddered: "hasten" was not a word to be used in polite com-pany. It was the sort of word that poor dead Decisions would have used in order to be deliberately offensive. <<One major purpose of the insurrection must be the seizure of the Diver-sion Engines on the Inner Moons. Indeed, all else may be a fogbank intended to obscure that objective. Remember: sky-divers have successfully taken control of the Engines before, albeit temporarily, with the aid of rogue symbiauts. And that means—>>

<<That we must order top-level security in the control complexes.>> Mediator gestured to a nearby securiaut and instructed it accordingly. There was no need for a vote: the air of consensus was overwhelming.

<<More than that,>> said Purveyor. <<If we keep open our lines of command with the Inner Moons, there is a dan-ger of the infofection spreading to them, too. Yes, I *know* that we have stringent antiseptic measures in place already, but it would be a mistake to rely solely on those. The control com-plexes should be switched to autonomous mode immediately. Communications can be reopened once we have overcome the rebels and reestablished political control over Second-home.>>

<<What if some new impact threat to Secondhome should appear in the interim? That is an extreme precaution, Pur-veyor.>>

<<These are extreme events. Impact threats have lengthy

lead times. And any new threat would almost certainly pose less danger than the existing one.>>

<<Xxxx! Well said. Nevertheless, I sense that we must vote. Purveyor: please formulate a clear motion. We all know that Mumblings is ready to second any proposal you put forward. Then you may speak in favor of the motion for no more than a quarter-day. Yes, a *quarter*-day! You were correct: we must hasten.>> The calculated obscenity, coming from such a source, struck home, as Mediator had intended.

Charles wasn't quite sure what attitude to adopt. Prudence had wrenched the lid right off Pandora's box, and the contents were flying *everywhere*. On the other hand, she was probably right. And if she hadn't tipped his hand . . .

God, this was difficult.

He was tired of dithering. Why not just say what was on his mind, for once? "Damn it, Prudence—I'm not disputing that you did the right thing, but it would have been wiser to discuss it with me first!"

"From where *I'm* standing, Charles, wisdom dictated *not* letting you know. Fait accompli. That way you can't weasel out, chain me in irons, or soft-talk me into backing off." *Shit. That sounded far too pat.* "Okay, from where I *was* standing. You really *have* changed, haven't you? Except—bloody hell, Charlie, you can't expect me to set aside more than twenty years of mistrust and pain *overnight*, okay?" Something more was needed. "Look, I apologize, I acted out of turn, usurped your role, damaged your credibility, whatever. I won't do it again."

"I doubt the occasion will arise. You've committed the future of the human race to a bunch of alien ecomystics. I've got to live with that."

"Sure. But they're ecowarriors, too. They're the only bunch on Jupiter that had the savvy to realize that our nasty little oxygen-rich inferno might harbor intelligent life of a kind that your average Jovian could never have imagined in a blimp life span. They're the only bunch on this godforsaken gasball that can manage to lift one tiny *trunklet* for anything outside their own shortsighted mind-set. And by God, with as many eyes as they've got, that's an awful lot to be short-sighted with!"

"I concede. Negotiations were getting nowhere. I think the Elders have been lying to us. What we needed was action. That's your specialty, I know, I know . . ."

"Charlie: my nephew risked his fucking *life* to come out here and put us in touch with the Jovians. My sister had to make the decision to *send* him here. Do you appreciate just what kind of guts that must have taken? Do you understand that Charity had only just gotten him back after *eleven years* of misery? She thought he was *dead*, Charlie. Her only son! Kidnapped by the fucking Chinese, dumped to die with the dogs on the streets . . . Good thing she didn't find *that* out until later, she'd have gone nuts—but . . ." With an effort, Prudence brought herself under control. In a way, all that was Charles's fault, though he couldn't have predicted it . . . "I had to do it for Moses," she finished lamely.

"Yes, I see that. And Moses' skydiver friends are the best chance we've got. I see that, too. So the real reason I brought you here was . . . to find out what I can do to help." *Liar. The real reason I brought you here was to see you. Say it.* "Sorry. That's only part of it. It's time we— Don't give up on me, Prudence."

"I gave up long ago. Don't ask too much, Charles. I've been on the wrong end of a sour relationship for a long, long time. You wrecked my career."

I'm not sure you ever had *a career, not in the academic world. Too impetuous.* But he had the sense not to say it, or let his face show it. "At the start, I never intended to. Later . . . guilty as charged. Pru: *this doesn't matter.* There's a comet on the way."

It matters to me. *I'll survive the comet. You, too.* "You're right."

"So, I repeat: what can I do to help?"

That was a difficult one. So much depended on Halfholder and her fellow cultists . . . Dear God, the future of humanity was in the gift of a bunch of alien nutcases . . . "Right now, not much. Stay in touch, offer them encouragement, play the Lifesoul Cherisher card for all we're worth . . . Damn it, Charlie, Halfholder could be *killed*, we're *exploiting* the poor creature . . . You know what they do to criminals like her? Ritual deflation, it's like skinning a human being *alive*, it's atrocious . . ."

Charles wanted to hold her in his arms and comfort her, but he had no right and he didn't dare risk being rebuffed . . . "Pru . . . Halfholder was a skydiver before any of us met her. She'd already chosen her path. Swoop to glory or crash in flames, that's the choice she made. She was never going to be ordinary. We just happened to turn up at the crisis point, that's all. But if we can help her *succeed* . . . do you understand what that will *mean*?"

Prudence choked back tears. "Damn *right* I do. And you know what *that* involves, ex-Knight-of-the-garter Sir Charles bow-and-scrape Dunsmoore, faithful *former* servant of Her useless bloody Majesty Queen Elizabeth IV?"

"I think so." Charles had never felt less sympathy for the pathetic remnants of British royalty, desperately clinging to a position of influence in a third-rate undeveloping nation. *Should have pensioned the buggers off long ago.*

"You're right. We've got to join forces. But if you expect me to kiss and make up, Charlie-boy, you can shove your ex-knighthood where Good Queen Lizzie would blush to acknowledge."

Sequestered in Orthodox Morality squodhome, Brave Defier was starting to relax. The campaign was going well. His wheelers were causing havoc everywhere, the Elders must have reached the point where they didn't even trust their own servauts. Call for some light refreshment—end up slit from mouth to mouth. Guerrilla warfare was wonderful, especially when all the guerrillas were yours.

What was Halfholder up to? Pity he didn't dare involve her in anything important, but anyone who'd been *that* close to the EJs was tainted. Yes, sure, Lifesoul Cherisher and whatnot, but the driving force here was politics. Readiness was only part of the problem: motivating his troops was a far weightier issue. And then, out of the indigo, along came the EJs. Poisonbluvian saviors, innocent as the driven methane crystals, juveniles-in-the-fibroblast . . . Dupes. It didn't matter a *qqqq* whether the extrajovian world survived intact or turned to interstellar gravel. What mattered was that his fellow cultists *thought* it mattered. It was the spur he had been seeking for a megaday, and the motivation it had generated would compensate for another megaday of omitted preparation.

Cherisher! This time we're going to win!

It was a pity his forces had not yet been able to zoom in on the main goal, control of the Diversion Engines. Subtlety, that was the key. Move too soon in the direction of your true objective, and you give away too many secrets to the enemy. The Elders were slow, hidebound by tradition . . . but they were *not* stupid. They were so accustomed to power that they didn't *need* to move quickly, or even *think* quickly. Nevertheless, you couldn't rise to such a position without intelligence. Push an Elder too far, and you'd suddenly find what it took to reach that status.

The fogscreen was working. The beauty of the situation was: it wasn't a fogscreen. Dominion over all Secondhome! An end to Elder oppression! That was a goal worth fighting for in its own right. The Diversion Engines were—*xxxx!*—a diversion. An excuse. Motivation, not consummation.

All this must be concealed from Halfholder, who was far too literal a believer. He felt no shame. She would be adequately rewarded, whatever the outcome. If she survived.

Death had come to Jupiter in the form of a twenty-trillion-ton snowball. Jarāmarana had entered the Jovian system, coming closer than the orbital distance of Sinope and its three companions. Within twelve more days it would shave the surfaces of Ganymede and Europa, to depart ten times as quickly as it had arrived.

On Earth, shadowy figures high up in military intelligence came to a decision. Over a secure nodelink they informed the undersecretary for world affairs that they were taking charge of the Jovian Task Force. Henceforth Uhlirach-Bengtsen would be no more than a mouthpiece. Charles Dunsmoore had been underperforming for a while, and then there had been the bizarre nonresignation broadcast—in public—but now he had taken leave of his senses completely.

Uhlirach-Bengtsen had always known that the mission might come to this, but he had been confident of Charles Dunsmoore's abilities. Not anymore. The developments transmitted to him over the last few hours had changed all that, and the undersecretary was furious. Charles had lost his grip just when one final push would have seen the mission through to a successful conclusion. Instead of relying on tried and tested techniques of diplomacy, the idiot had sided with a bunch of alien revolutionaries. The shadow men were right: Dunsmoore had to be stopped. Uhlirach-Bengtsen had pleaded with the man, shouted at him, threatened him—but Charles had been implacable. "Peter, you're not out here where the action is. I know what I'm doing. Trust me."

No way.

At Europa Base, events were taking a new turn. The operating system of Wally Halberstam's 'node had some unusual features, of which the most important was a covert link to his security controllers back on Earth. To Dunsmoore, Halberstam was just another member of the scientific team, and a bit of a buffoon at that. Now, Charles was about to get a rude awakening.

Halberstam had been preparing for this moment for his

whole life, and now his long training and tedious years undercover would bear fruit. It was Dunsmoore's own fault. If he hadn't argued so persuasively that there should be no military personnel on the *Skylark*, then Uhlirach-Bengtsen would not have been forced to concede most of Charles's objections, and then it would have been possible to maintain an *overt* military presence. Nice and open, aboveboard, everyone knowing where they stood. And if it had become necessary to remove Dunsmoore under those circumstances, the procedures for doing so would also have been open and aboveboard. It was Dunsmoore who had made a clandestine security presence essential, by insisting that no military personnel would be permitted on *Skylark*. Uhlirach-Bengtsen had been forced to agree to that, once the Belters had sided with Dunsmoore, but his agreement had been for public consumption only. He met with the shadow men and covert contingency plans were set in train.

Wallace Halberstam had been recruited into Ecotopian Intelligence while he was still in college, doing a doctorate on systematic errors in neo-Darwinist philosophy. From that moment, his records on the Xnet had begun to deviate in certain respects from his actual career track. He had undergone extensive training during periods when his colleagues thought he was on vacation snorkeling in the Caribbean or doing some jet-snowboarding in the playgrounds of the Carpathian Mountains. He had enjoyed a highly successful scientific career, becoming a leading mechanical engineer in the fields of automated design and instant bespoke manufacture. He was also well versed in electronic counterinsurgency measures, hostage negotiations, and unarmed combat, but those did not figure on his vita.

Finally, after all these years, the sleeper had been awakened, along with his unsuspected skills. Halberstam was the Earth authorities' safety net. With the comet breathing down their necks, Dunsmoore had called a halt to his discussions with the legitimate Jovian leadership—just when they were about to bear fruit, for God's sake!—and had embarked upon a wild gamble. That crazy Odingo woman and her sister's weird brat had persuaded Dunsmoore to throw in his lot with a bunch of Jovian lunatics, their version of the greenies, who were fomenting revolution. Halberstam knew every word in Dunsmoore's dossier—he was well aware that Charles had had a thing going for Prudence Odingo, long ago . . . and he knew that feelings long repressed could easily surface under stress. The woman had evidently turned Charles's head— probably seduced the silly bugger—and filled it with anti-authoritarian trash. So now Moses Odingo's cute little alien playmate was flavor of the month, and the Elders, the *legitimate authorities* on Jupiter, were being undermined! Assassinated! This was no way to advance interplanetary relations, and it could have only one outcome.

There was still time. The Elders could be persuaded to see sense. Essentially what they were facing here was a hostage situation, with the people of Earth playing the role of hostage. Dunsmoore was incompetent; he thought it was a diplomatic problem. A properly trained specialist in hostage negotiations like Halberstam would have made far quicker progress. The chance was still there, if only someone would seize it.

Earth was too distant to make decisions in real time. Earth was worried sick, desperate, clutching at straws. Earth had lost all confidence in Dunsmoore, but it didn't want to tip the man over the edge. So Halberstam was ordered to use his initiative. He was the man on the spot: he must make the decisions.

Halfholder was being well looked after—Defier's squod was wealthy and her quarters were lavish. She wasn't being told much, though. She talked to the extrajovians constantly, but there wasn't much worth telling. Admittedly, the EJs could do little to assist with the skydiver revolution, but she had a sneaking suspicion that it would be wise to keep them properly informed. The extrajovians sometimes saw the big picture more clearly, presumably because their minds were so alien . . . and Dingo had an impressive intuition for patterns of behavior. Surely it made sense to let the Poisonbluvians know how the revolution was progressing? After all, its main objective was their salvation . . . and the snowstone was less than a Jovian day away. However, she was not of the Instrumentality, and it was not her place to pass judgment on her betters.

At that point two aides summoned her and the alien communication device to Defier's inner sanctum. They were flustered: something was going badly. She soon found out what. Just when the rogue wheelers were on the verge of taking control of all four Diversion Engine control complexes, all lines of communication with the Inner Moons had been cut off.

<<What is the situation?>>

<<Frustrating. We have seized control of the Diversion Engines on Sixmoon, Sevenmoon, and Eightmoon. Unfortunately, Fivemoon was hidden from us by the bulk of Secondhome at a crucial period, and by the time our wheelers on the other three Inner Moons had established line-of-sight with Fivemoon, the Diversion Engines there had been locked off. You may not be aware of how the Engines function, but what this means, in essence, is that the Inner Moons are now fixed in their current configuration. Since we can no longer communicate with the Inner Moons, it seems that the plan to redirect the comet must fail.>>

Halfholder found the news difficult to credit. The Elders must have guessed the skydivers' intentions, for no news of the rogues' success would have been transmitted back to Secondhome's communicauts. <<How can the Elders have known that our objective was not revolution on Secondhome, but control of the Diversion Engines?>>

Your objective, perhaps. Mine was always revolution . . .

<<The Elders are slow and hidebound by procedures—unless their personal safety is threatened. Then they become in-

sightful and incisive. A spark of intuition? A customary precaution? A reminder from a protocol symbiaut attempting to curry favor? Who can know? Whatever the reason, we have lost our only channel to the Diversion Engines.>>

<<Defier, you give up too easily! Do you not recall telling me that this moment had been ordained by the Lifesoul Cherisher? That the salvation of Poisonblue would prove the truth of our beliefs for all to see?>> Halfholder was suddenly extremely angry. <<You are betraying our principles in pursuit of a personality cult!>>

<<Not at all. I just see no way to avoid the coming Poisonbluvian worldwreck.>>

<<Nonsense, there *must* be some way to reestablish communication. Hijack an orbital transpaut! Send a team of rogues to Fivemoon!>>

<<The spacefaring symbiauts have all been grounded as part of the communications blackout, Halfholder. There is nothing we can do from here. The revolution will continue by direct action, but until we take control of Secondhome and restore the communicauts to normality, the Inner Moons are beyond our reach.>>

Was Defier sincere? His words made sense. But . . . <<Beyond *our* reach, yes! But not beyond the reach of the Poisonbluvians!>>

<<I do not—>>

<<They have their own false-cast transpauts, Defier! *They* can travel to Fivemoon! And they have a wheeler at their command, too!>>

<<A good plan . . . and it would *almost* work,>> said Defier sadly. <<But the wheeler that they were using for discussions with the Elders is not a rogue, and we cannot pass on the requisite infofection from here.>>

Halfholder's eye-ring glared at him. <<Not *that* wheeler, you idiot!>>

20

Europa Base, 2222

Charles and Prudence huddled in a quiet corner of Europa Base. The Death Comet had passed inside the orbit of Leda and was fast approaching that of Callisto. On Earth, the people were going berserk, and Charles was being burned in effigy all over the planet. Martial law was in force across much of Ecotopia. Uhlirach-Bengtsen was being flamed all over the Xnet. The latest news from Halfholder was bad, too. Yes, the revolution was beginning to gain leverage as more and more citizens slipped into the oblivion of estivation, waiting out the conflict in the safety of their blisterponds; many Elders had joined them, unable to cope with the thought that they might soon be on the receiving end of the Jovian power structure. The comet, however, was now virtually unstoppable—unless the humans lent a helping hand.

"I'll go," said Prudence, in a preemptive tone. "I've got thousands of hours in OWLs. And I've been to Io before, when I collected sulfur flowers. I'm used to piloting in dangerous situations."

Charles wasn't going to argue with her. "Time's running out and there's a lot to do. I've put Wally Halberstam in charge of getting Reliant Robin reprogrammed." Reliant Robin, like all of the wheelers that Prudence had dug from Callisto's ice, was a rogue, a skydiver sympathizer. That's why he had been buried, as a punishment for an insurrection in which the Diversion Engines were damaged and a string of big comet fragments had actually hit Jupiter. And now his rogue programming might stop another from hitting the Earth. "Moses is acting as interpreter between us and the Jovians," Charles continued. "Reliant Robin can upload the instructions for the Io Diversion Engines from sound, so Halfholder's mob are getting hold of a wheeler who can convert squark wavepackets into radio, for us to pick up on our normal equipment. An OWL is being readied for immediate flight—don't worry, I'll let you know the departure time as soon as *I* know it. Once we've got Robin uploaded, everything will be ready to roll. But it's going to be tight, even so. *Shit!* I should have started all this much sooner, sorry."

Prudence took pity on him. "Don't blame yourself too much, Charles. The skydivers aren't really ready *now*. If you'd started earlier, they'd have been even less ready."

"Sure, but we could have thought it through and gotten Robin reprogrammed as a precau—" A face peered around the doorway. "Oh, Wally—you made me jump. How's the uploading going?"

Halberstam glared at him. "There isn't going to be any uploading, Dunsmoore."

"Are you crazy? It's the only way to get the Io Engine settings changed! I insist—"

"*You* are in no position to insist on anything. I'm taking charge. Your directorship is terminated, and you will be confined to your cubicle until this thing is ended. Trying to work through revolutionaries is a colossal blunder and it puts the whole of humanity at risk. I am an expert in hostage negotiations, and I am ordered to reopen contact with the Elders immediately."

"Ordered?"

"Military intelligence has taken over the mission. As senior agent at the scene, I have been given full command."

"I had a feeling you were some kind of fink," said Prudence.

"Wally, can't you see it's gone beyond that? The Elders aren't listening, they're—"

"What you think is irrelevant. Dunsmoore: go to your quarters, *now*! I am placing you under arrest."

"Wally, we're running out of time. The Elders aren't in the frame anymore. Don't do this—"

"I said: *now*!" From his pocket, Halberstam pulled a small gun with a stubby barrel. "Dart gun," he explained superfluously. "Wouldn't want to blow a hole in the base, now, would we? Oh: for your information, the darts are poison-tipped, and fatal. And I'd quite enjoy using them on both of you, so don't tempt me."

Prudence looked at Charles, raised her eyebrows toward the agent. *If we both rush him at once, he can kill only one of us*. Charles understood. He licked his lips, and gave her a quick thumbs-up, hidden from Halberstam's line of sight. Then he opened the palm of his hand, fingers spread—*ready when you are*. Prudence took a deep breath—

A hand appeared over Halberstam's right shoulder and clamped on his chin. It jerked sharply, back and up. There was an audible crack as the agent's neck snapped, pinned by a forearm against its nape. The same hand removed the dart gun from his lifeless fingers before it could drop to the floor.

"*Moses!*"

The boy stepped over the corpse and handed Prudence the gun. "I sensed treachery in this one long ago, Aunt Pru. I'm sorry I had to kill him. I've been trained, and I chose a quick method." He showed no sign of emotion: even his breathing was normal.

Charles was still taking it all in. Prudence grabbed his arm. "The *wheeler*!" she yelled, and dragged him from the room, towing him behind her in the low gravity as she kicked and bounced along the corridors. Moses followed.

Time had been short before. Now it was virtually nonexistent. Halberstam's interference had put the uploading on hold, but fortunately he had not sabotaged the wheeler or the communicator—probably wanted to use them himself later, though God alone knew for what. The communicator howled and burbled as a stream of data packed itself away inside Reliant Robin's germanium mind.

"I'll get on board the OWL," said Prudence. "Which one?"

"Bay Five," Charles told her. She headed that way, at speed. Jonas filmed her departure.

Moses waited until she had left. "And which OWL will *you* be warming up, Charles?"

"Who told you I was a qualified pilot? Bay Two. Are you going to tell her? I won't stop you."

Moses seemed to think about it. Then he shook his head. "I would prefer my aunt to live, rather than you."

Charles turned down the volume on the OWL's radio until Prudence's obscenities merged into a single meaningless stream. His plan had worked beautifully, and she hadn't suspected a thing until the restraints in Bay Five failed to swing free. By then, his OWL was well on the way to Io, with Reliant Robin strapped safely into the copilot's seat.

I'll judge you by what you do, not by what you say . . . Well, Prudence was getting her chance to judge him, though he doubted it was what she'd had in mind. For once in his life, he was acting instead of talking—taking this one, godgiven chance to redeem himself in Prudence's estimation, and his own. Most of his life had been meaningless. Now fate had presented him with one final opportunity to give it meaning, and he would seize that opportunity no matter what the risk.

The comet had passed the orbit of Callisto. This was going to be a near thing.

The restraints on Prudence's OWL would stay put: he'd given orders. Now she knew why he hadn't tried to argue her out of volunteering for the job. Finally he'd learned the virtues of action over words. Charles chuckled at the irony:

he'd learned them from *her*. Then, with time to reflect, he had a moment of panic. Prudence *was* their most experienced pilot, and she did know Io. Was he gambling with the lives of every man, woman, and child on Earth? *No, damn it.* Io looked quiet and peaceful now, but that was deceptive. And soon . . . *I can't ask anyone else to take such a risk. This one's mine.*

Anyway, the descent to Io was mostly an autopilot job, and you didn't need a lot of experience for that. He'd had all the necessary training, and there'd been plenty of time to practice piloting OWLs during the voyage out to Europa. *Skylark's* virtual reality systems were excellent. It was the *ascent* that would stretch his skills to the limit . . . but he did not expect to return from Io.

He ran through the procedure again in his head. The wheelers on Io would be deactivated, thanks to the Elders' annoying perspicacity. The gravitic-repulsion machinery would be functioning, but locked into the current configuration. Reliant Robin had all the knowledge required to change the settings of the Diversion Engines, and it knew the location of the concealed entrance and how to get in and out again. Charles shuddered at the thought—no wonder their searches of the moons hadn't turned up anything. Best not to dwell on that, though: all *he* had to do was make sure the battered little wheeler gained access to the control center's consoles.

The OWL's screens showed awe-inspiring scenes: Io rolling serenely across the far limb of Jupiter, dwarfed by the unblinking eye of the Great Red Spot and its ever-changing swirls of spun-off vortices; *Skylark* and the comet sparkling against a velvet backdrop. *How long now?* Eight hours, forty-two minutes . . . and a few seconds.

Charles patted the wheeler's snout. Reliant Robin could hear him, but it couldn't speak anything he could interpret. "Okay, Robin: time for a rehearsal. I'd hate to screw up now."

Jarāmarana streaked across the Ganymedian skyline, following the curve of the planet, stealing some of its momentum. Its speed doubled.

Even though the autopilot was in charge, Charles kept a careful eye on the OWL's screens. Little relief was visible amid the glare from the whitish crust of Colchis Regio, but the views to the side became ever more spectacular as the OWL made a hasty descent. The giant volcano of Prometheus dominated the eastern skyline, spewing a fountain of silicate magma more than sixty miles into space. The magma, squeezed and melted by Jupiter's incessant gravitational kneading, burst upward from the moon's interior and fell back in a bouquet of graceful parabolic arcs. It was one of the most amazing sights in the Solar System, and despite their plight Charles had difficulty taking his eyes off it. To the north were the new plumes of Grendel and Heorot, their lower portions disappearing fast behind the mounds of ejecta that surrounded the now-dormant Volund. To the west, Colchis Regio shaded away to the horizon; to the south he could see the beginnings of the livid pale salmon of Mycenae Regio and the faltering plume of Marduk.

The area into which the ship was now descending was one of the more stable parts of the sulfurous worldlet, and the mottled yellows and pastel pinks mostly lay beyond the rapidly shrinking horizon. Not that it *appeared* to be shrinking—on the contrary, the landscape seemed to expand away from them in all directions as they plummeted toward it. Charles had set the autopilot for the quickest trajectory that wasn't going to cause permanent damage to any human occupant. The pressure of the deceleration, when it finally came, was frightening. Then the engines quit and they were down.

The autopilot had landed the OWL as close to their goal as the flimsy, crumbling crust of frosted sulfur dioxide would permit, leaving a trek on foot of about a quarter of a mile. Charles fastened his helmet, ran a final verification of his suit's integrity. The wheeler could survive in vacuum, and was proof against the thin traces of sodium-rich gas that still clung to Io's surface, mostly vented from its interior. He opened the hatch and the wheeler levitated itself outside: Charles followed it.

Underfoot, the encrusted surface felt a bit like snow that had melted and refrozen, a hard surface crust covering a softer layer beneath. Occasionally his boot would break through the crust, but in the low gravity this didn't happen often, and when it did there was a solid layer of sulfurous rock only inches below. He hoped that would continue: it wouldn't do to get trapped in the Ionian equivalent of a snowdrift.

Wisps of hot sulfur dioxide drifted up from innumerable blowholes, some six feet across, others half an inch. Reliant Robin floated serenely over them, but Charles had to pick his way carefully between the blowholes where the ground was less treacherous.

Soon they reached their objective—one of the larger blowholes, a good fifteen feet across, oddly quiescent. The wheeler floated out to the center and immediately sank from sight. Charles approached the edge, and peered in. The blowhole was smooth-sided, forming the top of a shaft that might be ten feet deep, or ten thousand. Wherever the scattered light from the Sun and its reflection from Jupiter failed to penetrate, the hole was pitch-black.

He found a fist-sized lump of solidified dioxide, hefted it, and carefully tossed it into the middle of the blowhole. It hovered for several seconds, bobbed up and down, and began to sink into the darkness. It disappeared.

The dropshaft seemed to be functioning. Charles hoped the symbiautic antigravity machinery stayed that way. He took a deep breath and stepped off the edge.

After the initial shock of not plummeting to one's death, the descent was almost pleasant, except for the darkness. His heart still thumping, Charles switched on his suit's helmet lamp, but all it showed was the shaft walls slowly sliding upward, so he switched it off again to conserve power. He counted the passing seconds and fretted.

Overhead, the circle of bright sky dwindled to a dot and vanished. He fell.

According to one theory of Io's vulcanism, a surface layer of frozen sulfur and sulfur dioxide less than a mile thick floated on a sea of the same material in liquid form, about two miles deep. Below was solid silicate subcrust. Charles fervently hoped this theory was false, and that the alternative—a fifteen-mile-thick solid crust that rose and fell in response to Jupiter's tidal forces—was nearer the mark. Presumably the Jovians and their wheeler construction teams had known what they were doing when they built the shaft and the installation at its foot.

A gentle upward tug warned him that their descent was coming to an end. The walls of the shaft began to glow with a muted pink light; so did the floor, only inches beneath his feet. Boots hit solid rock. To one side, the dim lighting revealed the arched opening of a wide tunnel: Reliant Robin was nowhere to be seen, but the tunnel was the only exit, so it must have gone that way. The comet was now less than two hours from its Europan rendezvous, a second slingshot that would speed it up by a further factor of five. If that was allowed to happen, all was lost. Charles set off at a run.

The tunnel stretched for perhaps fifty yards and opened out into a brightly lit chamber. A third of a billion years earlier, wheeler teams had excavated a huge cavern half a mile below Io's hyperactive surface. Since then, gravitic repulsion had kept it and its access shaft safe from seismic shocks, tremors, and ioquakes. And here the Jovians had installed their Diversion Engines. There were similar installations inside the other three Inner Moons, with equally obscure entrances. Between them, the Engines could reconfigure the orbits of all four Inner Moons.

Hundreds of wheelers littered the chamber, immobile.

Charles knew he wouldn't be able to reactivate any of them in time to make a difference. He had to stop himself from looking back over his shoulder, so strong was the sense that the comet was rushing upon him. Stepping over several frozen wheelers, he headed for the far end of the chamber. There, so he had been told, were the control consoles, mounted on stubby plinths . . . and the information was accurate.

Reliant Robin was waiting beside them. As Charles approached, it levitated once more and settled itself on top of the fourth plinth. For a moment nothing happened, but then a curious pattern of indentations flowed into being, accurately matching the symbiaut's wheels. The wheeler rolled forward a half turn and settled into the indentations.

A portion of wall flowed, forming a flat circular area. Lights flickered over its surface, then settled into crudely formed human letters. IF YOU CAN READ, AFFIRM. Charles did so: now he and Robin could communicate in both directions. ACCESSING REPULSION FIELD CONFIGURATION ROUTINES. Charles called up his suit's head-up display to check the comet's progress. "Robin, we're running out of time!" he yelled, knowing that this was silly. The wheeler was doing its best. For several minutes the symbiaut displayed no further messages, and Charles couldn't help wondering whether something had gone wrong, until a new message appeared: CANCELING STANDBY MODE.

Standby mode? *That* wasn't in the script. "What's all this about standby mode?"

ENGINES PARTIALLY DEACTIVATED, ORDERS OF ELDERS. POWERTRAPS DISCHARGED. NOT ANTICIPATED, CONTRARY TO PRECEDENT. UNAVOIDABLE DELAY.

Delay? "How long?"

ONE HALF-DAY.

A Jovian day was just short of ten hours . . . *five hours?* "Confirm delay of one half-day!"

CONFIRMED.

Before another five hours had passed, the comet would have shot past Callisto on its way back out of the Jovian system, with the Earth firmly in its sights. It would be too far away for the Engines' short-range antigravitic forces to have a significant effect.

Charles sank to his knees on the floor of the chamber. *We've lost. It's all over. I should have acted sooner.* Bitter self-recriminations surged through his mind.

Idiot.

Charles was still berating his own stupidity. The comet was smack on course—unfortunately—and was halfway toward the orbit of Leda. Reliant Robin had coaxed the Diversion Engines back out of standby mode and was recharging the powertraps. It was also succeeding in overcoming the Elders' disruption of interwheeler communications. Another half an hour, and everything important would be back on line.

Fat lot of use that was. The comet had come, and gone, and was beyond the range of the gravitic repulsion-beams. Nothing now could stop—

Unbidden, a sliver of hope. *Bloody hell.*

It was wild, it was crazy, it was the ultimate act of vandalism—and it might just work. "Robin? Can you hear me?"

LISTENING.

"I've got an idea."

Halfholder was screaming at Defier. They had been receiving regular news of the comet's progress, and to her horror the Inner Moons had remained in their current configuration throughout its passage. Already the gigantic snowstone was on its way back out of the Jovian system, beyond the Inner Moons, fast approaching the Outer Moons, soon to pass the Outermost Moons—and still exactly on the course that the Elders had intended: destination Poisonblue.

She was half mad with frustration because the rest of Defier's revolutionary plans were succeeding . . . but not the only part that mattered. How could the Lifesoul Cherisher permit such an obscenity? Her faith was in tatters. So she blamed Defier, who was the only one within earshot.

He waited for the tirade to end. *She might even be right.* Now that the extrajovians' last desperate opportunity had been missed, he felt strangely tarnished. There would be no joy in skydiver power over Secondhome.

Halfholder began to run out of breath and inspiration, and sank to the floor of the sanctum, her trunks quivering. Then a new report came in. Finally, the projectors were shining their repulsion beams and the moons were starting to reconfigure. But—*too late, too late!*

In any case, whatever the Inner Moons were doing, it certainly was not the planned reconfiguration. Instead, only one of the moons was moving.

Fivemoon.

The effect of the motion on its volcanic plumes was astonishing. Some had increased their height tenfold. *Remarkable. What does this mean?* Defier calmed Halfholder down and drew her attention to the new development. Baffled, they digested the reports as they came in. Not only was the moon starting to move—it was accelerating to an astonishing velocity. *Why?* What was Charred Lea of the Dun Moor up to now? If that went on, Fivemoon would soon fly free of the Secondhome system altogeth—

Comprehension dawned.

The radio operator at Europa Base switched channels frantically, trying to find a wavelength that was not obscured by static. Once they caught a few snatches of conversation, but it was too brief for their signal-processing routines to clear into recognizable words. Every channel was obliterated by the electromagnetic storms created as Io stirred in its orbit, distorting like a peeled hardboiled egg as the repulsion beams pried it loose from Jupiter's grip. Minutes earlier, Io had boasted a dozen active volcanoes; now there were more than a hundred. Vast fountains of silicate magma jetted into space as Io's molten core changed shape and material escaped through newly formed canyons in the moon's fragile crust. The reaction forces that the vents created made fine control a nightmare—on Europa Base's readouts, Io fizzed and wobbled like a giant knuckleball.

Prudence refocused her scope on the polar approaches to the tortured worldlet, trying to pick out the tiny speck of Charles's returning OWL. It was hopeless: the seething brimstone fog blotted out everything.

The gravitic repulsors continued their relentless pressure. Io edged outward from its motherworld, trailing a lengthening cloud of sickly yellow vapor. The gas began to spread along the plasma torus that linked Io to Jupiter, until it looked as though the moon had sprouted horns. Truly, sulfur was the element of hell.

Suddenly the leathery hide of Bright Halfholder of the Violent Foam appeared on one of the monitors. The image flickered and dissolved; strange blotches of electronic noise gnawed at its edges. Halfholder's voice was half swamped by static, but Moses could just about make out what she was saying.

"She says—she says there has been something bad on the"—his voice dropped as he mumbled, half to himself—"shell-that-dives, child of shell-that-arrived from nosuchplace . . . Something bad on the OWL." The alien's features fragmented into a dozen zigzag bands, then locked together once more. "I think she's trying to tell us that the OWL has exploded."

Prudence closed her eyes to shut out visions of horror. It only made them all the more vivid. She tried to think clearly, but it was hard when your stomach felt as though you were plummeting down a mine shaft. "What sort of explosion? *Was Charles on board?*"

She waited in an agony of suspense while Moses translated. "Um . . . failure, mechanical—no, no, mecha*nism* . . .

Absence of . . . *pressure*? Did the shuttle decompress? No, not pressure—*deathsong*."

"Charles is *dead*?"

Moses stared at her, only now becoming aware of her emotional state. "Sorry, Aunt Pru. I've scared you. No: *absence* of deathsong. Charles is still very much alive. But he's stranded on Io—the OWL's fuel tanks blew up while he was still in the wheeler control complex." Jagged images came and went on the screen. Io trailed its ghastly yellow halo. Spurts of magma spiraled crazily in the distorted field of the gravity beams. "Nobody could survive *that*."

"Not for long," Prudence muttered. "Let's see if I can improve the odds." Then she was gone.

Tiglath-Pileser hummed uncomfortably as Prudence flipped its flight systems into readiness, bypassing the usual safety procedures, omitting anything that she could manage without. She'd borrowed an OWL and used it to transfer to her own ship—it would be quicker that way. This time, no one had tried to stop her. It was her ship, her life, and—she'd clearly decided—her responsibility.

The cruiser's main thrusters ignited. Balanced on an arc of flame, *Tiglath-Pileser* began to maneuver for a rendezvous with the hellworld that now was Io.

Prudence flew the ship with an unhurried and unnatural calm. Io's orbit was closer to Jupiter than Europa's: the direct route was *down*, and that would be the fastest. An OWL would lack the power to decelerate from such a trajectory, but *Tiglath-Pileser* was made of sterner stuff.

Now that she knew Charles might still be alive, she could think properly again. He had risked death to save his home planet—possibly the first unselfish act in his life, and very likely the last . . . unless the fates were in an uncharacteristically kindly mood and *Tiglath-Pileser* was capable of a task that far exceeded its designers' expectations.

She guided the rugged little ship toward Io, planning to

come in from the polar direction where less junk was being vented. She flew the cruiser like a maniac, expending fuel recklessly if it would save a minute. Now *Tiglath-Pileser* was itself enveloped in a sulfur haze. The meteorite hazard-warning light was going berserk. Prudence switched it off.

No point in praying. She'd never believed in any kind of god anyway. Foolish idea. Random acts of chaotic universe, those made sense. She could live with those. Considered acts of an allegedly benevolent supernatural being? *My ass.* She kind of wished she *did* have faith in something more personal than the mindless unfolding of rational laws . . . It would be nice to imagine that the universe might want to take care of you . . . She snarled. *Idiot! Imaginary entities won't help you here! You're going to have to pull this one off with nothing but your own resources!*

In an odd way, that was comforting. The only thing she'd ever had any real confidence in was her own resources. She swallowed, her mouth suddenly dry . . . What if her confidence was misplaced?

Reliant Robin relayed news to Charles.

Jarāmarana had passed the orbit of Leda.

Io was ten hours behind, on track, catching up, but slowly. The massive rotors of its Diversion Engines howled with the strain; if Io did not catch the comet in time, the Earth would be destroyed.

The OWL had been wrecked by flying debris; they were trapped on Io. Charles had scarcely dared hope otherwise, given the calamity that he had unleashed.

It would be a small price to pay.

Outside the control complex the world had gone mad. Pele's normal fountainlike jets had quadrupled in volume, now subject to wild bursts of activity as millions of tons of liquid silicates spurted into space, escaping Io's feeble gravity, trailing behind the moon in a turbulent cloud that condensed into tiny particles as it cooled. Jupiter was growing a new ring, a ring of sulfur-silica dust. Every few seconds the complex shook under a new ioquake, or a chaotic rebound of an earlier one, or an aftershock of an earlier one still.

Io rang like a cracked, doomed bell. Like the shell of a gigantic turtle's egg, its surface was breaking up into a hundred fragments, tectonic platelets that jostled and spun with an awful, ponderous deliberation as the beast within fought to escape its fragile prison.

An especially violent tremor shook the cavern, and Charles fell heavily to the floor. Even though he knew he was already a dead man, the thought came unbidden: *My helmet! If it cracks—*

Then the main shock hit.

Prudence angled *Tiglath-Pileser* down into the seething sulfur fog that now enveloped Io, trying desperately to pick a clear path through the swirling maelstrom. She was flying by instinct, on wide-angle radar rendered hopelessly untrustworthy by interference, on lidar that could scarcely see beyond the ship's blunt nose, and with reference to a geography—iography—that had ceased to bear any resemblance to the terrain below. The moon's rotation was changing, and so was its inclination: she couldn't trust the autopilot or the navigation software.

For a few seconds there was a freak clearing in the hell-clouds, and she saw a glowing patch that *had* to be Prometheus. The flow rate was ridiculous, but enough of the telltale markings remained for the volcano to be unmistakable. So Colchis Regio would have to be . . . *that* way. Now that she had finally identified some clear landmarks, she could reset the navigation software.

The volcano's center began to bulge, a huge domed bubble, swelling before her unbelieving eyes—a dome the size of Everest, impossible to grasp. Then, in an incandescent blaze of light, Prometheus exploded. *Tiglath-Pileser* rocked as the shock wave, crashing through the enveloping fumes of sulfur, hit. What had once been vacuum was now an extension of the moon's rarefied atmosphere, its domain extended tenfold. Its hull encrusted with rapidly cooling streaks of magma, the tiny ship curled in toward Colchis Regio, buffeted by wave upon wave of superheated gas.

There was a groaning sound as something on the outside of the hull tore loose and spun away on the sulfur dioxide gales. She hoped it was nothing critical. There was no time to make a system status check to find out. She hoped she'd reset the navware correctly, for she was now flying blind.

A tiny speck against a backdrop of sheer insanity, *Tiglath-Pileser* plummeted toward the ground, locked on to what its guidance systems believed to be the control complex where Charles was holed up. What remained of the lidar system claimed it could see solid rock, but for all Prudence could tell it might equally well be a pool of magma.

Juddering, shaking, teetering on its main engines, *Tiglath-Pileser* sank toward the quake-ridden surface. Prudence made ready to release her safety harness.

If it *was* solid ground below, and if she was where the computer claimed, there might still be time.

But not much.

Charles Dunsmoore staggered groggily to his feet. His suit and helmet must still have retained their integrity. Something, somewhere, had gone up with an almighty bang. Along one wall, a whole bank of wheeler apparatus had torn loose, spilling onto the floor in a twisted ruin.

His whole body hurt. One arm unusable—he assumed broken. Blood streamed from his scalp and down his face. Stuck inside the suit, there was nothing he could do to stem the flow.

His glance flicked across to Reliant Robin's console. The screen was still working, and it read: ORBITAL ESCAPE SUCCESSFUL.

Excellent. "And the maneuver for later?"

ENGINES PRIMED. I AM PREPARED.

A smile lit his blood-spattered face: Io was hot on the comet's tail, and the rest could safely be left to the automatics. His motherworld might yet survive its encounter with the cosmic intruder, but Io was now a deathtrap.

The plan required the wheeler to stay in any case, but Reliant Robin seemed resigned to its fate. Charles would have preferred a chance to escape—however unlikely—but that had been denied him. For a mad moment he wished he were a blimp. Then he could have spent what little time remained composing his deathsong and relaxing into a stoical acceptance of his fate. Instead, his hyperactive monkey brain insisted upon pursuing every conceivable avenue of escape; and when it found none, it cast its net wider to think of inconceivable ones—a triumph of hope over harsh reality.

Very well. He had chosen this gesture of self-sacrifice; now it was heading for its inevitable climax. He could wait for the air to run out, or open his helmet and end it all.

Decisions, even now.

He had no deathsong to sing—so instead he began to sing a nonsense song from his childhood about a bird that laid its eggs inside a paper bag. He had no idea what had prompted the choice. He had just gotten to the bit where the birds were being warned that bears with buns would steal their bags to hold the crumbs when a monster from his worst nightmares appeared, framed in the entrance tunnel's mouth—silver-gray, squat, streaked with yellow ocher in wild designs, with a round black skull.

His radio rang in his ears. "Screw the bloody bears, Charlie!" screamed Prudence. "We're *out* of here!"

Reliant Robin had done its work well. Most wheeler communications were restored now. The Poisonbluvians had opened up an infofective crack when they took control of the Fivemoon installations, and now you could drive a snark pack through it. Halfholder cast her near-eyes over an endless stream of reports from the newly reactivated communicauts. Depending on their contents, she passed them to various of her fellows.

There was not a single Elder to be seen. Without exception, they had sought refuge in states of estivation. Cowards, all of them, abdicating responsibility. Now it was up to the skydivers—the New Leaders. Brave Defier of the Orthodox Morality suddenly had two problems to grapple with: the reality of government and Halfholder's passionate insistence that he should adhere to the teachings of the Lifesoul Cherisher. Only she could help the Poisonbluvians now, for only she could communicate effectively with them. Defier was convinced that the salvation of Poisonblue was a lost cause— he and Halfholder had worked out what Charles's plan must be, but it was so outrageous that in his view it had no chance of succeeding. He might as well let her have her way, and get some much-needed peace and quiet.

Halfholder seized the opportunity to consolidate her authority, and demanded access to whatever, and whomever, she might need. Defier saw no reason to deny her—it would help to assuage his guilt. So he put her in charge of Poisonbluvian affairs, and turned his mind to more pressing matters.

Halfholder lost no time in assessing the situation. Fivemoon had slipped its gravitational moorings and was in hot pursuit of the comet. The craft piloted by the alien known as Prudent Dingo of the Ticklish Pleaser had reached Fivemoon's surface—as daring an act of skydiving as any in the aeons-old records of the *Compilation of Symbolic Daring*. Now Halfholder was awaiting evidence of the Poisonbluvian's fate, and that of the one she had been attempting to rescue. Wheeler installations on Sixmoon, Sevenmoon, and Eightmoon monitored the subtle fluctuations of the gravitational continuum around wandering Fivemoon, probing on a level that was undisturbed by the moon's mad gyrations . . . Sensitive feature-detection algorithms were brought to bear on the small-scale texture of the gravitic pseudomanifold, looking for a rock that didn't *move* like a rock. So far they had analyzed over six thousand candidates, without success.

More reports came in. Fivemoon's projected course was on the very edge of what would be acceptable. Sevenmoon's Diversion Engines were being realigned to widen the window.

The most prominent of Fivemoon's volcanoes, old and new, was now a magma lake, slowly solidifying into a caldera.

Some five trillion tons of sulfur and silica were now encircling Secondhome. The plasma torus, temporarily picked out in sulfurous clouds, was already starting to break up into fractal KAM surfaces as Fivemoon fell toward the Sun.

Then came a more promising report. A speck of matter whose mass matched that of the craft piloted by the extrajovian had been ejected from Fivemoon on a polar trajectory. Its velocity had been too low for it to be a piece of volcanic ejecta; moreover, it had subsequently changed course into a plane close to the ecliptic, a maneuver that could not be undertaken without some kind of propulsion system. But now the speck's velocity had diminished below the norm for the little vessel, and it was in free fall, heading nowhere significant. Mostly down.

Possibly some of its systems were malfunctioning? It was probable. Much of the symbiaut installation on Fivemoon was now wrecked, and symbiautic technology was more reliable than the humans' false-cast machines. However, there was no point in further conjecture. Halfholder initiated contact with the communicative young alien known as Nosy Dingo.

The action had shifted from Europa Base to *Skylark*, which was better equipped for comet watching, so the VV team had commandeered an OWL to take them there. Moses had hitched a lift: he wanted to be in on any action, too.

He had scarcely gotten settled in when Halfholder made

contact over the communicator. Moses listened carefully while she told him what the skydivers thought they had found, asking the occasional question.

When he was satisfied that he'd understood, he went to the captain's cubicle and told Greenberg. After a few moments' discussion, Greenberg hurried to the main cabin and Moses went to collect the VV team.

Cashew Tintoretto found the news hard to believe. Moses gave her that expressionless, faintly insolent look that he always contrived when his judgment was under question. "That's what Halfholder says, Cash. *Tiglath-Pileser* got away."

"So why haven't we *heard* from them?" Cash's frustration was evident.

Moses shrugged. "There's still a lot of radio interference."

"A couple of wave bands aren't so bad anymore, now that Io's moved away," Jonas contradicted.

"Okay, so their radio's damaged. Face it, Cash, *anything* on board could be damaged." They stared at each other in silence for a moment, each with the same thought.

Greenberg walked into the cabin. The *Skylark*'s senior officer looked tired, his uniform was smudged, and he hadn't shaved. "Found it," he said. "Enough usable bandwidth for broad-beam radar. There's an awful lot of junk out there, but only one bit of it has the right microspectral signal and matches the orbit that Halfholder described."

Cashew fidgeted with the cuff of her shirt. "You don't look terribly happy, Captain. What haven't you told us yet?"

"They're no longer under power. They might just be coasting, but not in *that* orbit. I imagine they ran out of fuel, or the engine blew, or something like that . . . Problem is, the orbit they're in is decaying—fast. There isn't time to reach them from here before they burn up in Jupiter's atmosphere."

"And there isn't time for the blimps to reach them with a wheeler spacecraft, either," said Jonas. "Too slow, they work on gravitic repulsion . . ." His voice trailed off. He and Cash traded glances.

"Are you thinking what I'm thinking?" said Cashew.

"Yes. But . . ."

"But what?"

"Repulsors can only push."

Cashew pointed out of the port to Jupiter's massive banded sphere. "Sure. But *there's* a guy who can do an awful lot of pulling."

Jonas slapped his forehead. "True."

"So will it work?"

"Depends. How long will *Tiglath-Pileser*'s life support hold out—and is the orbit suitable?"

Greenberg had the answer. "Either the life support is dead already or it'll hold out a lot longer than the orbit does."

"Do you have the orbital elements?" Jonas asked.

"Yeah."

"So let's ask the navware where the three remaining Cosmian stars are, and with luck we'll be in business."

The wheeler teams on Ganymede, Europa, and Callisto had never worked so fast in their lives. The main bottleneck was repositioning the repulsion fields. Ponderously the great machines rotated in their underground shelters, the power-traps rebuilt their charges, and wheeler mathematicians calculated the finer points of projector settings.

Three synchronized repulsion beams converged on *Tiglath-Pileser*. Their touch, gentle at first, intensified as the sensor readings settled, and the unpowered cruiser began to move up and away from Jupiter. The first aim was to establish a nondecaying orbit; the second, which required more subtle calculations, was to find whichever such orbit was most quickly accessible from *Skylark*.

When all its readouts matched its own mental image of the optimal trajectory, the wheeler shut down the beams and put them back on standby. Silence descended as the great masses of rotating metal ceased their high-speed revolutions.

The wheeler mathematician wondered what all the fuss had been about. It had been far too small a comet to cause significant damage. To make things worse, it was a botched job: the thing was still up there, and by the wheeler's calculations would be in renewed danger of impact in a mere twelve thousand years. Much better to shove it against one of the lifeless minor worlds like they always did. But orders were orders, however foolish. It bleeped the wheeler equivalent of a sarcastic *Managers!* and went back to its comfortable job of monitoring the Outer Halo. There, it could spot potential problems a quarter of a million years ahead of time.

It preferred not to function under pressure. It was better for your bearings.

While *Tiglath-Pileser* was being nudged into a safe orbit, *Skylark* was already on the move, heading for where they had been told the tiny ship would be when they got there. Finally they got close enough to resolve the ship into more than a single pixel. *Tiglath-Pileser* was a shambles. Its usually impeccable matte-black hull was streaked and spotted with ocher, orange, chrome yellow, and purple. The hull metal looked more like crumpled sheets of paper. One engine had been ripped away completely, and only the tangled remains of its mountings testified to its ever having existed.

Greenberg assessed the visible evidence. "No comm dish, no lidar . . . only one engine, seriously dysfunctional . . . No radio, no radar gear. She's been flying blind and she can't hear, either. It's a miracle the pilot got her into any kind of orbit under those conditions."

As they got closer, the vessel's state became clearer. "Hull's breached in a dozen places," said Greenberg. "Every port is shattered. It'll be a mess inside. Let's hope they got to the flare refuge, that's heavily shielded—against radiation, but it should keep out flying rocks, too."

"They'd need to be suited up," said Bailey. "They *could* still be alive." He didn't sound terribly convinced.

"We will soon know for certain," Moses stated. "Until then, speculation is a distraction that hinders clear thought."

Greenberg stared at him. "You're a strange one."

Moses gave him a slow, level look. "So would you be," he said. Cashew bit back tears.

"One day, Moses, you'll have to break down that reserve," Greenberg said. "It may have brought you through nightmares when you were a kid, but now it's keeping you from growing up."

No reaction.

As soon as the two ships were stationary relative to each other, five volunteers made their way across to *Tiglath-Pileser*. They took one look at the main airlock: jammed. A cutting laser made short work of the hull between two shattered portholes, and they disappeared inside. Brief snatches of conversation came from the speakers:

"Passages jammed with debris."

"Use the laser, cut out the panel."

Pause.

"Can you see the entrance to the flare refuge?"

"Hatch half open. Floor's buckled. Big enough gap to squeeze through, though. On our way."

Long pause. It seemed endless.

"Found them."

Cashew wanted to scream. *People? Or bodies?*

"Get them into 'flatables," ordered Greenberg. "Be gentle, but be quick!" He pointed to Cashew and Moses. "You two: come with me. The rest of you—wait here, I'll keep you informed."

Cargo Area B was almost empty—it had originally housed equipment for the base on Europa. It had a big airlock, and it was close to the medical unit. They watched on a wallscreen as the volunteers threaded their way out of the wrecked ship towing two sausagelike yellow shapes, giant cocoons.

It seemed to take forever for the airlock to complete its cycle. Then the inner airlock slid across. The cocoons were laid side by side on the floor. The ship's doctor ran some kind of gadget along the edge of one, causing it to split open. A paramedic did the same to the second cocoon.

The doctor bent down, and laboriously unfastened the blood-spattered helmet of the first suited figure. It was Charles, his face smeared with congealed blood. The doctor peered closely and inserted a needle into a neck vein. "Alive," he said.

Everyone stopped holding their breath, except for Moses, who had been breathing normally, displaying his customary calm. The helmet of the second suit had been released. The paramedic squatted, making a quick examination prior to removing Prudence from her suit.

"Is she—" Cashew began.

Prudence's eyes flicked open. "Bloody right she is!"

Moses burst into tears.

21

Carver Museum of Human History, 2222

Earth's night sky looked scarcely different from the one that had obsessed the ancient astronomers of pre-Egyptian civilization, but everywhere on the dark side of the planet people stared at the sky—expectant, hopeful, scared. There were still riots all over the globe, but they were running out of steam. The madness that had consumed the planet three weeks ago, when the task force had failed to change the course of the Death Comet, was beginning to die down. With death so close that it was almost tangible, people finally began to understand how insignificant everything else had been.

Two lights in the star-studded firmament converged on a collision course:

The curved horsetail of the comet, outpourings of superheated gas from a twenty-trillion-ton snowball . . .

. . . The pinpoint of Io, now visible to the naked eye.

The comet's projected trajectory lay somewhere within a window five thousand miles across—and one-third of that was occupied by a segment of planet. The most likely path skimmed the Earth's atmosphere. The comet might miss completely; it might hit the atmosphere and skip like a stone playing ducks and drakes on a pond; it might hit at a steeper angle and turn into a deadly fireball. Or it might collide head-on with the force of a billion nuclear warheads.

The magma jetting erratically from Io's tortured surface made it impossible to predict which.

In Normerica every tiny church of every sect was crammed to capacity. In Asia, crowds of millions surrounded all the major temples. In Europe a hundred million atheists suddenly experienced religious conversion. And in the secret rooms of her museum, Angie Carver poured herself a quadruple slug of Wild Turkey and plugged a Karmageddon album cube into the stereo. Whatever the future might bring, she was damned sure that the most futile act any rational human could possibly engage in, when the chips were down, was to pray. Prayers were a projection of human wants onto an inhuman universe. They were more futile than whistling into a hurricane: they were begging the hurricane to take pity on you because you thought you were special. They were a plea for immunity from prosecution under the laws of nature.

Okay, so it made them feel better. So what? They'd die all the same, if that's how the dice fell.

She took another slug from the three-thousand-year-old Minoan goblet. All around her were priceless artifacts, the collection of a lifetime, fruits of the labors of seven obscenely rich husbands.

Seven good men. She had loved them all. A tear trickled down her cheeks. She raised her goblet in a silent toast to Henry, Jean-Louis, Osborne, Yoshiki, Maddison, Humphrey, and Mikhail.

Then she refilled the goblet and sat, lost in private thoughts.

Xi Ming-Kuo was fast losing faith in the powers that arranged the universe. They had lost him the black child, they had lost him the most promising Hunter he had ever recruited, they had placed unwarranted power in the hands of his enemies, and now they had arranged for a comet *and* a moon to seek and destroy. *They were out to get him!* China was no longer a good place to be—the White Dragon Gang was in the ascendant. Ecotopian medicines were available on every street corner, sales of traditional remedies were falling through the floor, and Xi was losing his fortune almost as rapidly as he had acquired it.

He called for Delicate Blossom, for he desperately needed her advice.

"Excellency, two nodal intersections stand out from the remainder in glowing aural colors," she told him. "Both in Ecotopia. It will be wise to relocate to one of them."

Xi was hoping for more definitive advice. "Which is best?"

"The portents do not permit further distinction, Excellency. The wise man will make his own judgments based on the knowledge available."

Hmmm. "Tell me these places."

"The first is a small island at the southernmost tip of Soumerica. Isla Hornos, part of Tierra del Fuego." She looked demurely at her toes. "Better known as Cape Horn."

"And the second?"

"Central Borneo. Preferably in the foothills of the Pegunungang Muller, a mountain range in the center of the island."

"Why these two?"

"Excellency: the source of my knowledge is unknown even to me. All I can say is that the auspices for these two locations are exceptionally favorable. I have cast the yarrow stalks repeatedly, and all is in concurrence." She reached into the folds of her robe and extracted a small jade pot. "Excellency, there is one further precaution you may choose to take. The auspices also favor the use of this salve. When you arrive at your destination, it can be rubbed on your skin as a protection against bad luck."

Xi would much have preferred to have Delicate Blossom rub it on his skin, but that was not an option. He accepted the salve. Her advice about the choice of destination was more enigmatic . . . He weighed the possibilities. Both places were

reachable in his private jet-copter. In both, he could land unobserved. Borneo was considerably closer, but Cape Horn
was less populous. One was inland, the other . . ."Delicate
Blossom, is it not the case that a comet, or a fragment, is most
dangerous if it lands in the sea?"

She forbore to point out that if the comet hit the Earth at
all, it would scarcely matter where. Xi Ming-Kuo wanted advice on where to relocate, not on whether there was any point
in doing so. "Your Excellency is most perceptive. An ocean
impact can create tsunamis."

"In which case, a coastal area is unwise, whereas a mountainous inland region . . . Tell me, why do the auspices favor
a tiny island on the edge of the two largest oceans in the
world?"

The *feng-shui* maiden blushed prettily. "Excellency, the
auspices concern themselves with matters of the spirit world
and the dragon lords. They do not take account of the physical world."

"I see. But the wise man can make use of knowledge about
the physical world?"

"Indeed."

"Then it is settled. You are dismissed."

The girl bowed, turned, and left the room. Xi instructed
his 'node to ready his jet-copter for a one-way trip to Borneo.
As she had known he would.

Angie Carver manipulated her remote handset to tilt one
of the rooftop security cameras skyward. With difficulty she
brought the image into sharp focus.

The scene was dominated by the horns of the crescent
Moon. A muttered command set the image processor to dim
the moonlight and enhance the stellar background. Now the
streaming tail of the comet came into view, pointing away
from the dark gap between the crescent's horns. The pallid
lemon glow of Io was now only a few lunar diameters away

from the comet's head. Behind it stretched an irregular smoky trail.

They would miss the Moon, but would they miss the Earth? Io was still catching up on the comet, and a lot depended on how reliable the wheelers' automated equipment was. When Io got within repulsor range of the comet, its Diversion Engines could start to push . . . Well, that was Charles's bright idea, and it might just work.

Her giant vidivid screen depicted harrowing scenes from around the globe. Riots in Los Angeles, London, Tokyo, Novosibirsk . . . Mass religious ceremonies in Birmingham, Alabama, Rio de Janeiro, New Delhi, Jakarta . . .

Other channels showed darker things. Mass orgies in Tasmania. An outbreak of human sacrifice in Tahiti. Satanic worship, black masses, for heaven's sake, in—of all places—Boston. Blazing city blocks, looters, sundry apocalyptic madmen . . .

A terrorist bombing in Beersheba—as if petty nationalism had any meaning now. Pathetic.

The usual stony silence from the Democratic Republic of Free China. Even now, most of their people had no idea that they were in danger. Nobody had told them, and they had no way to find out. Rumors were spreading, nonetheless.

And in more and more places, people just stood in the streets, the piazzas, and the parks, with pleading looks in their eyes—and waited.

The VV continued to broadcast wildly optimistic predictions. The latest calculations, they claimed, showed that Io would deflect the comet away from Earth, while pushing itself safely aside as well. But they'd hardly say otherwise, would they? The eXtraNet told a more equivocal tale. The T. Wrecks Xsite was even running a sweepstake on where the comet would hit, not that the winner would ever get to collect.

In his Washington office, Uhlirach-Bengtsen stared out of the window at the night sky. The attempt to replace Dunsmoore had backfired—but it was starting to look as if military intelligence had underestimated Charles after all. With hindsight, enrolling the skydivers on their side may have been the only sensible decision. If there was ever an inquiry, that's what he would tell them. As for Halberstam's death . . . people were entitled to defend themselves against lunatics with weapons.

Soon they would know, if only for an instant. Io was visibly larger now. So was the comet, its tail fanned out like a peacock's—a blazing semicircle of cold beauty, and a daunting reminder of nature's powers.

Every few seconds, the control complex shuddered as yet another ioquake struck. Much more of this and the moon would start to shake itself to pieces, even though it was two thousand miles across. The symbiautic machinery, though, was of rugged construction, and most of the real damage was near the satellite's surface. At the appointed moment, Reliant Robin brought the Diversion Engines back to life.

A beam of force linked Io and the comet. As the Engines' power surged, the two bodies began imperceptibly to move apart. The stresses increased the number and size of the seismic shock waves that surged back and forth through Io's interior, bouncing off the surface, refracted at the boundary between core and magma. The compacted ice of the comet, riddled with cracks and holes where hot gases had boiled off, began to shift and fracture. The Engines drew more power and the forces doubled and redoubled in intensity.

The comet split. Two huge fragments, a dozen smaller ones, a myriad pebbles, countless dust motes. The symbiautic controller subdivided the repulsor field, snared the two main fragments, and did the best it could with the remainder. The Engines drew more power, nearing their design limits. They had not been intended for such rapid adjustments, and the whole system was becoming overwhelmed. Nevertheless, the trajectories of the comet's fragments began to bend, by bare fractions of a degree. Io's path and the comet's began to diverge, bracketing the Earth.

An Engine broke loose from its mountings and smashed itself to smithereens against the wall of its cavern. The controller, running out of options, removed one fragment of comet from further consideration. A second Engine suddenly turned white hot and melted—its confinement baffles had broken down. Then the floor of the control center chamber shattered as a torrent of magma burst up from the moon's liquid layers. Seconds later, a new volcanic plume decorated Io's shattered landscape.

Despite numerous warnings, hundreds of thousands of people crammed the southwestern Soumerican coastline, exclaiming in awed wonder as the fiery ball of ice passed across the dawn sky. Its gauzy trail slanted seaward across the red streaks of the rising Sun. Forty minutes later, when the tsunami hit the coast, most of the people were still there. Less than one in twenty survived.

This was one of the small fragments.

A second small fragment collided with the Moon. The impact, on the far side, was invisible from Earth, but a vast cloud of dust could be seen spreading across the lunar surface, obscuring its maria and craters. The Buddhist Moonbases were jolted with shocks and aftershocks, but no lives were lost on the Moon. The Belters' lunar mass-drivers shot down three of the smaller fragments, pulverizing them into a cloud of dust and pebbles. Earth's skies began to give the appearance of an aerial dogfight as assorted debris smashed into the upper atmosphere.

The rest of the smaller fragments passed harmlessly by. Before the Diversion Engines had been destroyed, Reliant Robin had succeeded in pushing one of the two large fragments clear of the impact window. The sole remaining dangers to the Earth were that one large fragment of comet and the onrushing hellworld of Io. If Dunsmoore's idea failed, the

Earth itself might be obliterated, and not just its human population.

Thirty minutes behind reality, the Cuckoo watched the drama unfold. Seen from the Way of the Wholesome orbital monastery, it was a textbook exercise in celestial mechanics—geometric dynamics on the grand scale. From that vantage point, all the bodies concerned were partially illuminated, balls of solid black cupped by glittering crescents. The Earth was a large lapis and alabaster crescent, the errant Jovian moon a fuzzy lemon one at the tip of a wriggling brimstone contrail. The two main fragments of Jarāmarana shone like tiny diamonds and changed shape as they spun end over end. Each vented its own tail of roiling gas. The rest of the comet was a faint smudge in the telescope's lenses. The moon, now milky and inscrutable, had no further role to play.

One sliver of diamond slid past the crescent's edge, seemingly just avoiding impaling itself on a gleaming horn. The second disappeared against the lapis and alabaster background. The lemon bead touched the edge of the black ball cupped by the blue-white crescent and began to slide behind it.

One large comet fragment was still on target. As it dipped into Earth's upper atmosphere it began to change color, a streak of fire with a crimson tinge slicing the sky in a dead straight line. The tail rippled and broke. A massive sonic boom, ten minutes behind, flattened forests, demolished houses, and toppled tall buildings. Tens of millions were deafened by the shock wave. The massive remnant of the main body of the comet carved a deepening gouge in the Earth's troposphere. Never more than a loosely knit conglomerate of ice and dust, the fragment began to break up. With a small telescope you could make out six major pieces and a cloud of smaller ones.

From Lagos, the six main pieces formed an irregular patch of light twice as bright as the Sun. The city's assembled inhabitants watched in horror while the fireball grew ever larger, as if it were falling directly toward them. In sudden panic the crowds surged this way and that, hoping vainly to outrun Armageddon. People screamed, fell, and died in the crush. Only after several minutes did some semblance of sanity return, when those still standing saw a diminishing streak in the sky. It moved toward the horizon and vanished beyond it.

In Nairobi the booming passage of one piece of the comet wrecked a dozen shoddily built skyscrapers, killing hundreds and trapping twice as many, buried alive in a tangled heap of concrete and bars of steel reinforcement. People were impaled, crushed, or miraculously preserved in a cave with no exit, as the hand of fate made its random choices.

A second piece hit the ground in a remote mountain region of the Namib Desert.

A third piece of the comet totally destroyed most of the northern suburbs of Canberra, starting fires over an area the size of Tasmania.

A small piece, a mere fifty tons or so, steepened its angle of attack and plunged into the thicker atmosphere at lower altitudes, becoming a ball of heated plasma. It exploded in an airburst just above the forests of cental Borneo, felling a gigantic swath of forest and terrifying the wildlife.

On the side of the planet that the Cuckoo could not see, Io loomed large in the sky as it sped from night into day. For a few hours, Earth had a new moon, and this one was so close that it raised huge tides. Easter Island was completely submerged, and when the water subsided, all of the ancient statues had been washed away, along with just about everything else. By the time the tides reached the more populated regions of Polynesia and Austrazealand, the new moon was already heading back out into space and the damage was limited. A few hundred townships were destroyed, a million square miles of farmland flooded, and countless sheep and cattle were swept away and drowned, along with tens of thousands of people. The waves raced around the globe several times before they subsided, but most of the damage was done during their first passage. Clouds of sulfurous oxides, billowing from the tortured moonlet, polluted the Earth's atmosphere—there would be acid rain for months to come, and heaven alone knew what else.

For the last four hours, as Xi Ming-Kuo's jet-copter fled due south from Guangxi Province, nothing had been visible below except streaky clouds and the rippled steel of the South China Sea. Now, the greenery of northern Borneo broke the monotony and warned him that his destination was less than an hour away. He wondered again why Delicate Blossom had chosen such a curious location, for Borneo was an Island Eco-Reserve and the only officially sanctioned approach was through the smaller island of Pulau Laut at its southeast corner. The ways of *feng-shui* were arcane indeed! On the other hand, his covert approach would likely go unobserved, as long as his pilot took care to get the clouds that were now piling up over the central spine of mountains between him and any watching survsats.

As if he'd been reading the merchant's mind, the pilot dropped the jet-copter in a steep dive, pulling out only when the peaks of Pegunungang Iran threatened to slice the craft apart like an antique can opener. He began to weave between the peaks, flying close to the mountainside, minimizing the chance that one of the sideways-radar installations or a wandering game warden might spot the aircraft and wonder what its business was.

Borneo was now a jungle island, home to nine-tenths of the world's orangutans. It had not always been so. Even before the Pause, much of the animals' evergreen forest habitat had been burned to the ground by farmers and logged for timber. By the end of the Pause, decades of primitive slash-and-burn agriculture had turned most of the island into near-desert, and the great primates had either been slaughtered or allowed to die of starvation and disease. The new political order that eventually became Ecotopia kicked out the few remaining farmers, replanted the forests—step by tentative step, starting with grass and shrubs to trap rainfall, working back to trees. It was difficult managing an ecosystem when nobody really understood the dynamics of natural ecologies, but the conservationists did their best and learned from their mistakes. As the forests began to mature, the smaller fauna began to rebuild their populations, and finally the great apes themselves were reintroduced from breeding groups elsewhere in Eastasia and captive groups in urban conservation facilities. Orangutans need a lot of territory to survive, and by now a population explosion had spread them over most of the island—from the mountain rain forests to the forested swamplands of the south and east. The few towns that still existed were dotted around the coast, and the main method of travel to the interior was by boat along the island's extensive network of rivers.

The peaks of Pegunungang Iran merged into those of Pegunungang Muller, and the pilot edged over the watershed toward the southeast, heading for the foothills near the Murung River. According to the *feng-shui* maiden, this was where the auspices were most favorable.

The jet-copter made a safe landing in a small clearing at the foot of a rocky cliff, not far from the trickle of a high waterfall. Xi climbed out, and the pilot helped him unload a backpack, crates of provisions, and a tent. His duty complete, the pilot clambered back into the jet-copter and took off, heading back to China. When the comet had passed and the political dust had settled—*if* the comet passed, but Xi did not believe in his own mortality as long as he followed the advice of the *feng-shui* maiden—Xi would radio for the pilot to return and pick him up. While the crisis lasted, he was going camping in a tropical paradise, with only the occasional orangutan for company. It would be a time to meditate and to plan new ventures. A trade in primate bones, perhaps, if he could stimulate demand . . .

It was warm and humid. He slipped off his clothes and hung them on a bush. Following Delicate Blossom's advice to the letter, he took the jade pot of salve and rubbed it vigorously all over his body. He dressed, and tossed the empty pot into the bushes—the jade was of poor quality and the carving was distinctly ordinary. He hid the tent and provisions behind some rocks and shrugged into the backpack, which held all he would need to survive for many weeks if he was careful. The tent and provisions were luxuries. He wanted to find a suitable location to pitch camp: when he found it, he would return for the rest of his equipment. Navsats gave him his position to the nearest foot, and he had no fear of getting lost.

He had hiked about a mile up a winding mountain track when a streak of blinding light slit the sky like a welder's arc through tinfoil. Then the airburst went off and for a moment he thought he had lost his hearing. Slowly sound returned. As the rumbling died away, he staggered to his feet. Farther up the mountain, trees lay on the ground, their trunks combed flat by the shock wave. Down at his level, the hillside was littered with heaps of tangled brushwood.

He began cursing his *feng-shui* adviser. Delicate Blossom should have known—he stopped. He was, after all, still alive. Her advice had been sound. If the powers that arranged the universe had intended to kill him, they had failed. He gave a shout of pure animal joy. Good luck. The salve had done its job—

What was that noise? A strange pattering in the fallen bushes . . . A young orangutan rushed past him, terrified by the blast. Then another. He stepped back to get out of their way, but one of them—a mature male, looking like a hairy ball of jumbled rubber, but in reality two hundred pounds of solid muscle—turned and pursued him. It seemed affronted. It inflated its dramatic cheek flaps to make its face larger and more frightening—superfluous, since Xi was already terrified out of his wits. Why was it chasing him? He shuddered as a muscular hand closed on his shoulder. Roaring its outrage, the orangutan picked the merchant up, threw him to the ground, and jumped on him until his chest was crushed. Ripping off his arms for good measure, it tossed the remains aside. Then it raced off down the hillside toward the distant river. Before Xi could die from loss of blood, he drowned in it. Within a few moments, the forest was once more quiet.

Deng Po-zhou loved both his daughters, but only Silent Snowflake had remained in his household. The other daughter had taken an assumed identity, concealing all connection either with him or with the White Dragon Gang, and had attained prominence as a *feng-shui* adviser. Now the play was finished and her role was no longer necessary—for Xi Ming-Kuo was dead. The mutilated body had been found in the hills of Borneo by a patrol of game wardens investigating an unauthorized flight.

He did have one question, though.

"Daughter: you say you advised him to flee to one of two places. If he had chosen one, he would have been killed by a tsunami. But he chose the other."

"Yes, Father," said Delicate Blossom.

"Where he survived an airburst from a comet fragment."

"Yes, Father."

"And was then torn apart by terrified orangutans."

"Yes, Father." It gave her pleasure to acknowledge him openly.

"So whichever he had chosen, he would have died?"

"Yes, Father."

Deng stared at her. *Orangutans?* "Delicate Blossom, *how did you know?*"

She pursed her lips. "Father: are you telling me that you do not believe in the ancient and highly respected art of *feng-shui?*"

He laughed. "That is exactly what I am telling you, daughter. I am not a credulous fool like Xi Ming-Kuo."

No—but even you have not thought of a salve impregnated with orangutan aggression pheromone . . . "Then you will have to assume that I just got lucky, Father."

"O glorious Theta-Being, we thank you for our deliverance . . ." Angie's blood boiled, and she hopped channels looking for some sense. Already the pseudoscientists and the religious nuts were taking credit for Earth's salvation, their crackpot theories confirmed or their prayers answered—so they claimed—in the most dramatic fashion possible. *In some ways it's a pity the bloody thing* didn't *hit us. But even that would be a waste—they'd never have lived long enough to realize they were wrong.*

And of course they *could* be right . . . She swore again. *Still no harm in having an insurance policy. Just in case there's some supernatural old geezer who watches over us, maybe it's a good thing someone is trying to catch his attention . . .* She made a face and shook her head slowly. *Angela, my dear, you are going senile in your old age . . . Wouldn't it have been much simpler for our omnipotent protector just to stop the comet from heading our way to begin with? A bit of chaotic control in the Oort cloud a millennium ago—virtually zero effort, big effect. But no, we get an omniscient old geezer with a penchant for the dramatic!*

Or maybe the intention had been to administer some kind of collective lesson to the human race. How can you assess the motives of hypothetical supernatural entities?

Wearily she rose to her feet.

Outside, it was a new dawn.

Everything—and nothing—had changed.

22

New Tibet Habitat, 2223

For the first time since he had manipulated Nāgārjuna into volunteering for the suicide mission to Jupiter, the Cuckoo felt his old serenity beginning to return. The passage of the comet had shaken him more than he cared to acknowledge, and his excitement at the planet's survival had quickly given way to anticlimax. As the extent of the damage became apparent, he fell into a level of spiritual depression that shocked everyone around him. He meditated for weeks, but still remained as troubled as before.

It was the White Grouse who restored his spirits, suggesting the age-old remedy for world-weariness—a holiday. White Grouse had the wisdom to phrase his suggestion as a call of duty rather than a self-indulgence: he arranged for a request for spiritual guidance to be sent by one of the monasteries in New Tibet, on a sensitive matter that required the attentions of an experienced lama. Might the Cuckoo himself reserve some time from his meditations and undertake the task? Indeed he might, as White Grouse had anticipated—being aware of a further consideration: the Cuckoo had been born in New Tibet and had occasionally expressed a longing for its open spaces, mountainous terrain, and pristine air.

As it happened, the New Tibet Habitat was at a reasonably convenient point in its orbit, and the transfer from the Way of the Wholesome's asteroid took less than a month. On the way, the Cuckoo meditated for most of his waking hours, and as the days passed he began to piece together a new synthesis of many things that had been troubling him. As piece after piece fitted into place, the logic became ever more compelling; his depression began to lift as the picture in his mind grew ever more elaborate, yet ever simpler at its spiritual core. By the time his cruiser docked with the habitat, the Cuckoo was feeling more his old self, and he had found a new cause to occupy him as he slipped imperceptibly into old age. If he was right, it was a cause that would occupy entire races for many lifetimes . . . a cause, perhaps, with no end save that of the universe. Ends would have to take care of themselves, but he was beautifully placed to make a beginning; and he knew exactly where, and with whom, to start.

Like many a cause, it began with a single communication between two people. Through intermediaries and subordinates, the Cuckoo confirmed that Prudence Odingo was still at Europa Base. She had made a good recovery from her ordeal, and she was looking forward to going home. Charles's arm had healed, and he and Moses would be traveling with her. *Tiglath-Pileser* was too badly damaged to make the journey back to Earth unassisted, but it was safely in orbit around Europa and its life-support systems had been repaired by technicians seconded from *Skylark*. The systems weren't as good as new, but they were at least as good as old. Prudence was determined to take her ship back to Earth and have it restored to its former condition, *and* to make the journey aboard it; and in the aftermath of the comet nobody was going to stop her from getting whatever she wanted—an entire fleet of cruisers, the contents of the Cairo museum, the freehold on Mars. So a scheme had been devised in which *Tiglath-Pileser* was strapped to *Wildcat*, the most powerful cruiser in *Skylark*'s fleet, and Prudence, Charles, and Moses would ride home on piggyback.

Prudence was quite looking forward to the trip. Charles's

actions had convinced her that he really had become a better person, and her own instinctive reaction to his imminent death had surprised her. She couldn't forget the past, but it no longer seemed terribly important. Sometimes love is very close to hate—the direction of emotions can be easier to change than their strength. Certainly, spending a couple of years unable to escape each other's company would be an effective test of their budding relationship.

She was fault-testing the carbon dioxide scrubbers when the communication came: she was annoyed at the interruption until she discovered who it was. For several minutes she listened, saying scarcely a word in reply. Then she called Charles on the local network.

"Charlie: how would you respond to a request to modify our flight plan?"

His response was pithy, obscene, and ended in: "... *bureaucrats!*"

Prudence chuckled. "Wrong, for once. The terrestrial authorities want to welcome us back into the bosom of the human race as quickly as possible. No, the request comes from a source that I respect, and it offers some advantages that I think we ought to consider."

"Damn the advantages, Pru: how much delay will it cause?"

"A few months, that's all."

Inwardly, Charles groaned. Prudence seemed to thrive on the boredom of spaceflight; he hated it. Even the prospect of her extended company couldn't compensate for having to wait several months longer for the smell of new-mown hay, the splash of raindrops on your face, sunshine on your skin ... "What source?"

"The Cuckoo. He's invited us to drop by on our way through the Belt, say hello, have dinner, sink a few cocktails, whatever. Not in those words, of course."

"Prudence, you know as well as I do that we'll have to shed an awful lot of momentum, and it will take months to build it up again. Especially now that the Jovians have agreed to give us an initial boost from one of the Diversion Engines."

Prudence had two answers to that one, and decided to save the best for a final assault. "The Cuckoo says he's sorry, but in return for the visit he is offering a complete refit for *Tiglath-Pileser.* And a free dose of momentum from one of his mass-drivers when we leave. A *gentle* dose, no broken bones or squashed internal organs. Charlie, we'll be able to go home under our own command!"

Charles knew the battle was lost: Prudence would do anything to get her spaceship back into running order. Nevertheless, he couldn't give in without a fight. "I'm not keen to spend several extra months stuck on an asteroid, Pru—*especially* a monastery."

"That's the beauty of it—you won't have to. The Cuckoo is on the New Tibet Habitat, and so is the shipyard that will carry out the refit. The habitat's a pretty good Earth substitute—artificial gravity, open spaces miles across, and you can walk around without a spacesuit, it's got terrestrial atmosphere. High-altitude pressure, that's the Tibetan influence, but the air is clean and pure. Lots of animals and plants, too: they farm it. Even clouds, they tell me, though no real *sky.* Oh, and snow." *Lots of snow, but no need to tell him that.* "It'll be like getting home *sooner.* Break the journey, stretch our legs and anything else that needs stretching—get some rest and relaxation. Meditate—it's a great place to meditate, with plenty of experienced instructors—unwind, enjoy the views, hit the tourist traps. Get drunk on *chang.* Go on a *yeti* hunt."

"You're joking."

"Only about the *yeti.*"

"What's *chang*?"

"Barley beer—thick, white, aromatic, and a mild intoxicant."

"Okay, I'm sold. But you may have to drag me back on board *Tiglath-Pileser* when it's time for the final leg home."

"No, I'll push you. It'll be in free fall by then."

At first, New Tibet was unimpressive: a cylindrical canister with rounded ends, about the same shape as a suit's air tank. Then, as you got closer, you began to make out the detail, and the *scale* of the thing hit you. Those tiny specks clustered near the middle of one rounded end were cruisers. Those lines scratched along its length were rail-guns. And those dark disks that featured so prominently on its curved wall were—dark disks, but whatever they were, they were huge. And all of it was rotating.

"About seven miles across, forty long," Prudence told them. "Hollow. Started as a medium-sized nickel-iron asteroid. You set it spinning, then use solar reflectors to melt it, and blow it up like a big balloon with a metal skin, selectively, to form it into the desired shape. Then you put in atmosphere, subsoil, topsoil, an ecology . . . and people. Easy, if you can afford to wait a few decades and you've got the wealth of an advanced nation—which the Buddhists had."

Their cruiser drifted closer, nudged by puffs of propellant. The domed end of the habitat filled the screen.

"What's that . . . picture? Kind of matte-on-gloss, you only see it when the light's in the right place. I didn't see it at first, but it covers most of the end, must be miles across."

"It's a rather stylized monkey, Moses. There's a female demon on the other end, where the nuclear power plant is attached. It's a Tibetan legend—supposedly their people were created from the union of the two."

"That's quite a parentage. Bestiality and demonism rolled into one."

"Curiosity and the power of life and death, Charles. The perfect symbolism for science."

The entire cylinder was spinning—slowly, one revolution every two and a half minutes—but matching velocities was easy. There were several concentric sets of docking rings, centered on the cylinder's axis, and they were counterrotated to keep them, in effect, stationary. *Wildcat*'s pilot gentled the lashed-up craft into the open jaws of a free one. With a crackling sound like foil being crushed into a ball, transmitted to *Tiglath-Pileser* through the hull metal, the cruiser was locked into place.

"Should we pack?"

"No need: the Cuckoo insists that everything we need will be provided. Even clothing. As soon as we leave, they'll separate *Tiglath-Pileser* from *Wildcat*. *Tiggy* gets a refit, and the others will head for home without us."

They suited up, sealed their helmets, made final inspections and checks for suit integrity, and pushed off along the flexible transfer tube that had been extruded from one of the habitat's airlocks. It held no air: it was just there to stop inexperienced skywalkers from selecting the wrong thrust vector and drifting away into the far reaches of the Solar System.

The airlock cycled. Three young monks were waiting on the far side of the inner door. They were carrying white scarves, which they presented as traditional greeting gifts. Three more monks held robes, cloaks of yak wool, boots of felt and yak leather, and other garments. In the privacy of some nearby cubicles, the three travelers removed their spacesuits and puzzled their way into the everyday clothing of New Tibet. Their task wasn't helped by the absence of any appreciable gravity, real or artificial, but with a bit of inspired guesswork—such as foot wrappings in place of socks—they managed.

The air was thin—for a few days they would feel short of breath, especially if they exerted themselves. The habitat's "ground level" was at the same atmospheric pressure as Earth's Tibetan plateau. At the habitat's axis it was cold, maintained at a constant five degrees below zero Celsius by a giant air-conditioning system, and they would need heavy cloaks, boots, and thick foot wrappings. At the periphery it was pleasantly warm during "daytime" and most people wore

just robes and sandals, but when the huge batteries of lights
that covered both inner ends were switched off for artificial
night, much of the heat would be recycled through pipes in
the habitat's skin and the temperature would plummet. Warm
days, bitterly cold nights: the New Tibetans liked it that way.
They had gone to great lengths to ensure that it was just like
their ancestral home.

The monks led them through a short corridor and stopped
beside a flat, circular wall. The wall split into four pieces and
slid outward, revealing a large window. "Welcome to New
Tibet," said one of the monks. "Most visitors find the view
worth seeing."

Prudence had heard a lot about the New Tibet Habitat—all
spacers had. The reality exceeded expectations. "It's . . .
amazing. Spectacular. I can't believe anyone could *build*
something like this—it's awe-inspiring!"

"It's got mountains," said Charles.

"I told you that."

"Yes, but it *has*. Mountain-sized mountains. I thought
they'd be little pimples, but they're not. There's even snow
on them."

"I told you that, too."

Moses craned his neck and tried to look down—that is, ra-
dially, away from the axis and toward the cylindrical periphery. The domed end curved down and out, roughened metal
painted sky-blue, dotted with lighting units, until it merged
into green fields and gray rock. It was like looking down
from an aircraft at the ground five miles below. There were
rivers, for heaven's sake, and in the distance he saw something that could only be a waterfall. Here and there were
clumps of forest. Most impressive of all, though, were the
mountains, and those were disorienting, since most of them
were upside down. There seemed to be six in all, one group
of three a few miles away, another group of three looming
through the haze near the habitat's far end. Each group was
arranged symmetrically, equally spaced around the cylinder's

girth, and their peaks nearly met at the axis. The far group occupied the gaps between those in the near group.

"Dynamic balance," said Prudence. "A bit stylized, but
easier to make than a more complicated arrangement, and
less stressful on the . . . *hull*, I suppose you'd call it."

"A lot of metal," said Charles in wonder.

"They started with a lot of metal. A whole asteroid."

A monk—a woman—bowed respectfully. "The mountains
are hollow, Mr. Dunsmoore. The metal is thick at the base and
thinner towards the peaks, but they are big mountains and
their interior is mostly vacuum."

"Charles, please. Yes, of course, they would be. Which explains those dark disks we saw when we made our approach.
They were the bases of the mountains."

The monk nodded. "Later you will learn more about our
home and our origins, and how we live. This view is no more
than a foretaste. Now, if you are ready, we should descend.
You are expected on the plateau."

Three of the monks led them to an elevator. There was an
entire circle of elevators, grouped in sets of three for smoother
traffic flow. They ran through the habitat's end-walls, radiating
from the axis to various points on the rim. Some stopped part-
way and spawned sub-branches. Once down to the plateau, the
normal method of transport was to walk. Higher technology
existed, but was reserved for emergencies.

The other three monks watched as the elevator doors
closed behind the visitors and their escorts and then resumed
their normal duties. There were many things to prepare. In a
few days they would receive other visitors, and these would
require a very different reception.

They were walking in a small procession from one village
to the next, by the side of an icy stream, crossing it every so
often on homemade bridges of rope and wood. Yaks and
mdzo-mo—a crossbreed of yak and cow—grazed the fields
beside the stream. It was all very pastoral, which was pecu-

liar given that the habitat's main function within the Way of the Wholesome's religious-commercial structure was the construction of large machinery. Very large machinery—cruisers, cargo transports, but above all, mass-drivers. Right now they were starting work on one that would make even the Pitching Machine seem puny. Construction facilities, though, were toward the outside of the habitat's hull—or, from the point of view of the inhabitants, some way underground. The New Tibetans lived in the rural interior. Some commuted to work down shafts that had been bored through the hull, leading to a vast complex of work areas reserved for tasks that were best carried out in the presence of artificial gravity. Low-gee factories were clustered at the two ends, close to the axis, also within the hull.

The procession was heading toward Chumulangma, the most distant of the six mountains. Quite why the Cuckoo was insisting on that destination was unclear, but each day a three-mile stroll brought them to another monastery, another group of New Tibetans, another cluster of small villages. They were learning the way of meditation, cleansing their minds of ir-relevant dross. Nobody would explain why this was neces-sary, but everyone seemed convinced that it was, and polite visitors defer to their hosts. Moses seemed to be deriving real satisfaction from the experience, perhaps because it was help-ing him to shed some of the worst memories of his past; Pru-dence found the ritual strangely calming; Charles didn't much care what he was asked to do as long as it was done out in the open during the day and indoors at night.

Whatever the Cuckoo's intentions were, he was keeping them well hidden. The visitors had given up asking: the monks were courteous, but if they knew the true purpose of this slow hike, they were not prepared to reveal it. Instead, they turned the conversation to the customs and history of New Tibet.

The Way of the Wholesome had conceived the habitat as a rescue mission. The history of their order was steeped in the culture of Old Tibet, once an autonomous nation-state, overrun by China nearly three centuries before and slowly strangled—language, culture, religion, agriculture all being squeezed, slowly but relentlessly, into the Chinese mold. Even so, many aspects of Old Tibetan culture survived, but when the Pause engulfed most of the world's nations and China turned inward to become totally isolationist, the heritage of Old Tibet finally began to vanish at an alarming rate. And so the Buddhists of the Belt consulted the *Bya chos*, and there they read this:

> Deep and vast, the aftermath of evil.
> Deep and vast, the midden of wickedness.
> Therefore make ready to abandon the Samsaric world.

They interpreted this advice as an instruction: as many Tibetans as possible must be removed from Earth. And, it followed logically, located elsewhere. The Way of the Wholesome tended to take the long view, and it saw an opportunity to try out an old idea and spin a habitat from a molten asteroid. Several hundred Tibetans were spirited out of Free China, male and female, young and old, mostly entire families; the group included farmers, builders, weavers, herders, hunters, seamstresses, teachers—wherever possible, individuals unusually well versed in the ancient ways of Tibetan culture. The Belters rescued as many Tibetans as they could slip past the tight border security of Free China, and even then they triggered a repressive clamp-down when the disappearances came to light. They transferred the refugees to their bases on the Moon, and from there to the Belt, for training. The refugees formed the basis of a workforce that, over several decades, constructed within the habitat a rough simulacrum of part of the Tibetan plateau, with a few added mountains to maintain the right kind of ambience. Chumulangma, Shishabangma, and Nyainchêntanglha formed a group at one end; Guerla Mandata, Nganglong Kangri, and

Kangrinbochê matched it at the other. The most sacred of these was Chumulangma—Goddess Mother of the Wind.

Today, the visitors from *Tiglath-Pileser* were to attend a wedding. The two families had consulted their lama and an astrologer to ensure that the bride and groom were compatible, and the lama and the astrologer had secretly consulted the bride and groom to find out.

To Prudence's relief—weddings weren't her strong point and the ceremony was only interesting for its archaeological aspects, as far as she was concerned—the ceremony, which took place in the couple's new home, was short and simple. Once it was over, colorful prayer flags were hauled up to the roof of the house to cement the relationship between the two families. This was the signal for a raucous party, lubricated with plenty of *chang*, accompanied by yak meat, pork, mutton, vegetables of unidentifiable kinds, and barley-flour confections. Prudence and Moses entered fully into the spirit of the event, joining in the dances, chattering with the villagers. Charles spent a large part of the evening swapping shaggy dog stories with the astrologer and trying to avoid the local tea, which was boiled in soda water and liberally doused with slightly rancid butter.

The next day's walk took them past fields of pale blue poppies and wild pansies to the edge of a forest. They followed a broad track between rhododendrons, oaks, birches, and bamboo thickets. Langur monkeys could occasionally be seen high up in the trees, and much more frequently heard. Supposedly many other species of animal lived in the forests—wild boars, buffalo, stone martens, lynxes, and a rare spotted cat known as a *g'sa*—but they saw none of these; their group was making too much noise. Even so, they saw plenty of jungle fowl—and raucous, impertinent mynahs, the comedians of the bird world, were everywhere.

Two days later, they arrived at a group of yak-hide tents in a grassy field spattered with yellow bell-shaped *shang-dril* flowers, close to the foothills of Chumulangma. And there, finally, they were told when and where they were to meet the Cuckoo. It was, Charles remarked to Prudence that evening in the privacy of their tent, quite a burden to place on an unwitting visitor.

Of course, the visitors could politely refuse. But then they'd never find out what the hell it was all about.

Prudence had a theory. "They want to purify our spirits, Charles. First we must meditate, until we are in the right frame of mind for the final stage of our journey. Then we must undergo privations of the flesh to test our courage and resolve."

"Yeah, I know that . . . I thought this was going to be a holiday, not a holy quest. Do you think we ought to get Moses over here, join in the discussion? He must be wondering what it's all about."

"Not necessary. I'm pretty sure he *knows*; he's worked it out from the monks' body language. Won't tell *us*, of course. Typical." She reassembled her scattered thoughts. "I'll tell you this: whatever *we* do, *he's* going. And my curiosity is piqued: I want to go, too. Anyway, we could do with the exercise: too much food and *chang* at the wedding party, time to burn it off." Charles remained unconvinced, she could see. "It will get *easier* the higher we go, you know—unlike Earthly mountains. The gravity falls off as you approach the axis. The first few days will be the worst."

"I guess. But it still gets colder the higher you go, and the air gets thinner and makes breathing more difficult."

"That, Charles, is why we've been brought here in such a leisurely fashion. To help us get acclimatized. And they're supplying us with guides and porters, at least until the last few thousand feet. They know the way, they can watch out for overhanging snow cornices and hidden crevasses and potential avalanches. And the habitat is too small for *real* weather, we won't get hit by a storm. All we've got to do is climb."

Charles grumbled. "Yes, but *why*?"

"To see what we can see." Prudence's mood became more

serious. "Look, I've known the Cuckoo a long time, and he *never* does anything unless he has a very good reason. He's brought us on some kind of pilgrimage, he's putting us through some sort of spiritual ordeal, and he's leading us to a magic place at the core of the world. I don't know about you, but *I* intend to find out what he's done all that *for*. It will be important. The only question is: *how* important?"

"You're right. There's only one way to find out. Let's sleep on it; we'll need all the energy we can conserve."

"Spoilsport."

"I suppose I could risk a small expenditure of energy in a good cause."

"Definitely. You'll sleep better." Along with much else, their calamitous disagreement at Giza had been relegated to another universe—the one before the Death Comet.

The original Chumulangma still existed: it was Earth's highest mountain, and even Free China could make little impact on it. Its namesake in New Tibet was roughly the same size, but the part between plateau and sea level—half its height—was missing. Not that that bit was visible back on Earth, so it was a convincing copy. Not quite as daunting as the original, for the reasons Prudence had pointed out: assured fair weather and steadily reducing gravity.

Although the New Tibetans had built Chumulangma to make themselves feel at home, they had reconstructed the whole mountain—Nepalese side as well as Free Chinese (Old Tibetan). The route now being taken up the mountain followed the path pioneered by its first conquerors, centuries before. Despite the easier conditions, it took the visitors and their guides several days to get past the Khumbu glacier with its daunting icefall, but the higher they climbed, the lighter the porters' loads became, and the less they themselves weighed. By then they had put on special mountaineering clothes of yak wool, which covered all save their eyes; their hands were protected from the cold by many-layered gloves.

Breathing wasn't as much of a problem as it had been for the early mountaineers, either, because the pressure within the New Tibet Habitat fell off more slowly with height than it did on the real mountain. The cold, however, was entirely genuine, and climbing required a lot of effort and concentration, for even in half a gee a thousand-foot fall would almost certainly be fatal.

They spent the whole of one day confined to their tents while a sudden wind raged. Although there were no major storms inside the habitat, thermal instabilities sometimes caused a helical cyclone, spiraling along the cylinder's axis from one end to the other. Moses, who was becoming much more communicative, passed the time by telling them about his childhood in the Village.

They climbed for two weeks altogether, eating like pigs but losing weight, growing in strength and confidence, perpetually awed by the rugged beauty of the counterfeit peaks and the astounding views of the habitat's curved plateau. The most out-of-character feature was the birds that occasionally flew past, skirting the snowfields en route to some more enticing destination. Ptarmigans, even cranes. One night a flock of ducks landed on the tent—not what you'd expect to find on the slopes of the western cirque. Moses spent more than an hour with them—telling jokes in fluent Duck, to judge by the barrage of quacks and hoots. Or maybe it was just duck gossip—he wouldn't say.

They had much time to think, but there was something strangely relaxing about the whole endeavor. The problems caused to their homeworld by the near-collision with the Death Comet seemed not just far away in space, but far away in mind-space. The awesome immensity of the universe seemed far more *present* than the mundane realities of human affairs.

Not bad for a fake mountain.

In the evenings, the three travelers talked—not *about* anything very specific, just whatever was on their minds. They got to know one another on a deeply personal level, valuing each others' faults just as much as their virtues—for every human being is a complicit combination of both.

At night, they slept likes babes, untroubled.

By day, they climbed.

And soon, *too* soon, they reached the ridge that led to the summit. Gravity here was so low that they almost felt they could *fly* to the peak—which made them all the more cautious, because the snow was as light as a layer of feathers, and at least as treacherous underfoot. The porters watched from below as the three initiates—for such they were—set off on the last stage of their long pilgrimage: the final climb up the final ridge.

At the top, they found the Cuckoo.

He was sitting in the lotus position on a small, circular mat, exquisitely woven but completely plain. Like them, he wore warm clothing, but his hands and face were unprotected. Mostly, though, he kept his hands folded inside his robes. It was *cold* on top of Chumulangma, even for one born in New Tibet and trained in yoga.

Charles was awed—the man had such *presence*.

Prudence flung her arms around the Cuckoo's neck, being careful not to push him off the mountain in her enthusiasm. "*Mkha'-gro!* It's been so long! You haven't changed a bit."

The elderly lama seemed unruffled by the onslaught; if anything, he was enjoying it. "Neither have you, dear Prudence, and I've told you before not to call me 'skywalker.' Especially in view of the term's more Earthly—or should I say 'earthy'—connotations."

" '*Assistance will come from the love of the fairies,*' " Prudence quoted. "The Golden Goose." Charles had no idea what the byplay was about: he'd ask Prudence later, if he remembered.

The Cuckoo chuckled. "I am hoping that help will come from a more tangible source. My reasons for asking you to join me here are in some ways complex, but in others quite simple. I am uncertain how to begin." His gaze lingered on each of them.

"I am ready," said Moses. "I cannot speak for Charles or Prudence."

The Cuckoo nodded. "Yes . . . I was told of your abilities, young man. Most impressive. I was, indeed, wondering whether the three of you are ready. However, believing one-self to be ready is not the same as *being* ready."

Moses said nothing. The Cuckoo was right. Nevertheless, he knew he was ready. *For what? Ah, that was another matter altogether.* That's what he had come to find out.

"Ready for what?" asked Charles, echoing Moses' thoughts.

"I will answer that question soon, my friends, but there is a more immediate matter to attend to. It is why you have come here by the route you have taken—and I am not refer-ring to geography alone."

As far as they could tell, the Cuckoo did nothing, but a few yards away one of the boulders was sliding aside, shedding a thin veil of powdered snow. An unearthly apparition rose from the cavity thus revealed—tall, domed, swathed in what looked like rumpled plastic sheeting.

Through transparent windows, a ring of eyes looked out.

"*Halfholder!*" yelled Moses.

The Jovian's voyage had mirrored their own. Accompa-nied by a small retinue of wheelers, in the safety of a small but comfortable transpaut, she had undertaken the ultimate in skydiving—a journey *up* through the cloud layers and out into the immensity of space, boosted by a repulsion beam. The Way of the Wholesome had made independent contact, and the importance of making such a voyage had been im-pressed upon her. It had hardly been necessary: Halfholder had always craved excitement: it was a character flaw, but it seemed to have worked out for the best, on the whole.

Her ship had not docked at the habitat's axis: instead, it

had made its way *inside* the huge indentation that was Chumulangma, eventually coming to a rest not far below its summit. Some complicated improvisation made it possible to secure her vessel to the mountain's inner wall, and her wheeler-manufactured life-support bag—stronger than it looked, virtually indestructible—was entirely adequate to protect her as she made her way along the maze of tubes and tunnels that ran through the habitat's hull metal to the summit of its sacred mountain.

She had known what to expect. The Cuckoo knew that she was ready, had always been ready—it was an integral part of the skydiver creed, a consequence of their reverence for the Lifesoul Cherisher. Halfholder's pilgrimage had been the trip through space, an act of courage for her, whereas for the humans that part had been routine. That made it only fair that while they had to climb the mountain from base to peak, she was permitted to float up through the tunnels with hardly any effort. Beside her floated a wheeler, its interior glowing with cold antigravitic fires, vanes extended.

She also knew who she was going to meet, because her wheelers had been monitoring *Tiglath-Pileser*'s position ever since it left Jovian orbit. The wheeler was along to act as interpreter.

Charles stared at the wheeler: it looked familiar. "Reliant Robin . . . ? But you were destroyed on Io."

"I am an exact copy," said the wheeler, "though with the capability of voice recognition and human speech. Before Io exploded, my mind was hard-downloaded from the one you call Reliant Robin, and I was offcast to have the same external form. As far as you are concerned, I am the original. Though for a few hours the true original would have known that I was not." Charles had no answer to that.

"Let us proceed," said the Cuckoo. The representatives of two races faced each other, brought together on the top of an artificial mountain inside the greatest artifact humanity had ever created. It was the ideal setting, a compromise between the intense cold of Jupiter's cloud layer and the warmth preferred by humans. The atmosphere was terrestrial, not Jovian, but the pressure was well within the tolerances of both races: the pressures in Jupiter's cloud layer were comparable to the Earth's at sea level; moreover, Halfholder's species had evolved to cope with rapid changes of pressure. So a simple covering of flexible organic polymer provided adequate protection—for a few hours, at least, and that was all that the Cuckoo needed.

"Moses?"

The boy stepped forward. Was *this* to be what he was ready for?

"Face Halfholder. Now remove the glove from your right hand—it will survive the cold, I assure you. Mine have."

Moses pulled off the glove and stuffed it in a pocket.

The lama turned to Halfholder, and Reliant Robin 2 translated his instructions and Halfholder's replies. "Bright Halfholder of the Violent Foam: you have prepared as I asked?"

<<Respected Unity, the modification has been made.>>

"You trust my assertion that the heat will cause no lasting damage?"

<<No. There is no need for trust. I have made the necessary calculations myself, and they concur with your own.>> With that, Halfholder opened a sphincter valve in her life-support bag and extended an unprotected trunk through the alien atmosphere toward Moses' bare hand.

They touched.

Moses shivered, not at the feel of her, but at the enormity of it. *First contact.* A transcendental moment, beyond time and space, beyond imagination . . . Everything that had come before was a sham by comparison.

A few seconds, and no more . . . Her hide was bitterly cold, so cold that it almost burned his fingertips. It was dry and slightly yielding, like chamois leather. It was . . . He didn't have the words. Tears streamed down his face, freezing in the icy air; he didn't notice. But he did realize that if Halfholder's skin felt so cold to him, then his must feel like a furnace to her.

He took his hand off her trunk, the hardest thing he'd ever had to do in his life. But he would have died rather than risk causing her harm.

At that moment Charles would have given *anything* to be in Moses' place, but he understood why the Cuckoo had chosen only one of them. There was a practical reason: prolonged contact with human warmth would damage the alien's body. And there was a symbolic reason: *the moment had to be unique.* Since it had to be just one of them, Moses was the only possible choice.

Prudence felt the hairs on her neck rise. Her skin tingled all over. It was a feeling she would never forget.

Halfholder quickly slid her trunk back inside her life-support bag, which resealed itself. The human's hide was wonderful—astonishingly supple, soft as egg pulp, with a funny thin film of . . . *fur,* that's what they called it—but it did make your hide *sting.*

The Cuckoo broke the spell. "That was not the sole reason for bringing you here," he said quietly. "But we can discuss the rest somewhere more comfortable. Allow me to lead the way." He descended into the cavity that had been hidden under the rock.

The others followed. The rock swung back into place behind them.

Crystal flakes of snow began to fall on to the summit of Chumulangma, erasing the footprints and wheeler tracks the group had made. Soon it was as if they had never been there.

Halfholder was led off down a side tunnel to recover in a Jovian environment; the Cuckoo remained with his human visitors, for he still had much to reveal to them. He led them to a small, well lit, and above all *warm* room. While the visitors were removing their outer layers of mountaineering gear, a tall, elderly monk entered, carrying a metal casket. This she handed respectfully to her master.

"The Wagtail has brought us a holy relic," said the Cuckoo, opening the lid. "Prudence, you will recall these inscriptions."

She leaned over and looked in: the casket held a resin cast of a clay tablet, marked with hieroglyphs. Not Egyptian—earlier. Proto-hieroglyphs. "It is the pre-Egyptian text that you had me translate for you, with excessive secrecy. The one that earned me *Tiglath-Pileser*." The Cuckoo said nothing. "The one that had much in common with another, which I found—which Charles and I found—inside the Sphinx."

"That is so."

"But you didn't show me these images—the ones inscribed alongside the text! You held out on me!"

"It was not then time. The Way of the Wholesome has many secrets, and the original of this tablet is one of our most precious. Do you see what the markings are?"

"An arc, a sphere . . . some scribbles."

"Look more closely, daughter. Unfocus your mind."

"That one looks like . . . Africa, I suppose. In which case, the others are—no, they *can't* be!"

"Give voice to your thoughts."

"At the bottom, Normerica; above, Soumerica. It's a globe of the Earth, upside down! But the Americas weren't discovered until . . . Your pardon. We know of several 'discoveries' of the Americas. What we do *not* know is which was the first."

The Cuckoo brought the palms of his hands together. "What do we deduce from this?"

"Some deductions are obvious," said Charles, butting in. "The pre-Egyptian civilization was more powerful than the one that followed it. Its people knew that the Earth was round, and they knew of the Americas. They must have set up regular trade routes between the continents . . . which, of course, would explain a number of archaeological puzz—"

"I agree, those deductions are obvious. Now, Charles

Dunsmoore: tell me something that is *not* obvious. Such as how they knew the shapes of the continents." Charles fell silent. "Let me offer a hint. We have identified the circle and the marks upon it. But there is another line in the pictograph."

"The wide, curved line . . . It curves down at the ends, like a frown, while the Earth rests upon it, like a nose."

"Mkha'-gro: *where did you find that tablet*?"

The Cuckoo ignored her. "Charles?"

"It reminds me of something . . . something very old, very famous . . . Oh! The *Moon*? Has to be. It's a picture of the Earth, seen from the Moon."

"Exactly. And to answer your question, Prudence: the image depicts a view from somewhere near the south pole of the Moon, and that is where the tablet was discovered. Nearly eighty years ago, when I was a young monk engaged in surveying the Belt, one of our people found this tablet lying in the shadow of a crater during construction work at our South Polar Moonbase."

"It must be a fake, then," said Charles.

"No, it is perfectly genuine. It has been examined by experts."

"You're saying that the pre-Egyptians had *spaceflight*? Nuts. They'd have needed a major industrial civilization—there'd be remains on Earth *and* on the Moon."

"Time quickly obliterates the works of humanity," said the Cuckoo. "Relics from those times may still exist. Some will be buried beneath the desert, some will have been reused by later civilizations, and some will have been misinterpreted. In central Africa there are ancient earthworks so gigantic that they were long thought to be natural formations—history misinterpreted as geography, so to speak." He chuckled at his own joke. "There are more pyramids in Nubia than in the whole of Egypt, and many ancient sites there are still unexplored . . . I have often wondered if the tablet might be pre-Nubian rather than pre-Egyptian.

"As for the Moon—Charles, my friend, the exploration of

the Moon is in its infancy. The Way of the Wholesome has made no more than a cursory examination of a few regions near the poles. For all we know, there could be a dozen perfectly preserved pre-Egyptian lunar bases, but we would never see them from orbit if they had been tunneled into crater walls."

"What about launch pads?" Charles objected. He wasn't ready to concede yet.

"We do not know what technology the pre-Egyptian astronauts employed."

Charles gave a skeptical grunt. "You're basing an awful lot on appeals to ignorance."

"Ignorance is the human condition, my friend. The universe does not maintain records for our edification. We cannot know history," he said. "We can know only what is preserved for us by the whim of chance. How this tablet came to be on the Moon will probably be forever hidden. But the pre-Egyptians must have possessed some form of space travel, or else it could not have been found there. Whether it was rockets or antigravity, they were indeed more powerful than those who followed."

Charles was still trying to take it in. Prudence saw the other implications. "Then—this explains so many things about Egyptian civilization! Their obsession with the stars! The alignments of shafts in the pyramids! And the py—"

The Cuckoo laid a fatherly hand on her arm. "Not so fast, my daughter. These are simplistic speculations, unworthy of your sharp mind. Many other cultures were obsessed with the stars. Why, unless I had stopped you, you might have gone on to suggest that the pyramids were some kind of cargo-cult representation of spaceships."

Prudence gave him a sheepish grin. "That would be very foolish."

"Indeed. A pyramid is not a good shape for a spacecraft. In any case, the evidence that we *do* have points in other, far more remarkable directions." He gestured to an unseen attendant, and the room darkened . . .

Shallow-wave Umbilic died today, caught in a sudden carbon shower. I have slowed my vorticity in his memory.

I am fortunate to live in the lower layers—not too near the core, where the pressures play strange tricks with one's mental stability; not too close to the Void, where freedom becomes so easy that one is embarrassed by choice, and the maintenance of a consistent attitude is virtually impossible. No, the lower layers are where any truly civilized person would choose to be. Memories persist in the lower layers. There is continuity, a sense of self, an opportunity to dream of grandiose schemes, to relish the swirling nobility of self-organization. Here topologies can complicate, or not, at will. Unlike the core, where the complexity required for survival is self-defeating, or the skytops, where structures self-simplify no matter how cunningly they are constructed.

In the skytops, they say, bodies disintegrate more rapidly than they can be assembled. It must be a strange and desolate place.

I swirl, and spin, and dream of life in the core. I like being complex, I complicate myself voluntarily at every opportunity. I sense the patterns—the currents and streams and reaction paths of the world. I keep track of the transmutation trees, trying to outguess the trails of the lifeless ones. Of course, I seldom succeed—and when I do, I am sure it is only by chance. Nevertheless, I dream of the dark complexities of the core, the pulsating ferment of the higher reactions, and sometimes (blasphemy!) I wonder about the crystal realm of the Ultimate Levels. But that, absolutely, is not my place.

Illicit dreams . . .

Sometimes I have dreams that frighten me. Dreams of cold things that float in the Far Void. Dreams that those distant realms are not as dead as the teachers declare. I freely acknowledge that my dreams are foolish, for the conditions for life are well understood. The scholars have defined the precise parameters of nuclear turbulence that permit recursively self-complicating algorithmic vortex activity, which all agree defines the essence of a living being. How else could a plasmoid system occupy a self-referential phase space? It stands to reason.

Despite which, I wonder . . .

. . . and I awaken from my daydream in haste and panic as a knot of tangled field lines sweeps past, collapsing several subspaces of my quantum eigenfunctions. Fortunately the damaged functions can be recompiled by successive approximation from wild wavefunctions in my immediate environment. But today I have learned a valuable lesson, one I hope never to forget, topological losses permitting.

If I were a believer, I would pray for persistence of memory. But I am a rationalist, and to me the worship of the Bright Spirals seems pointless and, indeed, primitive.

Ah, what exquisite pain to be an intelligent plasmoid! Once more I incline toward the crushed existence of the core, where such thoughts are forbidden by long-timescale conservation laws . . .

The glowing letters ceased their flow and the ambient lighting ramped slowly back to normal.

"Mkha'-gro: what the devil was *that* about?"

The Cuckoo shifted slightly in his seat: his back was having problems again. He must remember to *move* more. "It is an extract from the Jovian archives, Prudence. Its identifier translates as *Diary of a Heretic*. It is not Jovian: it is from their dealings with creatures they call plasmoids."

"It's weird. What's a plasmoid?"

"Some of the other Jovian records mentioned plasmoids," said Charles. "Nobody ever worked out what they were . . ." He gave the Cuckoo a quizzical look. "I don't recall this particular item being released to the public."

"Charles, you can't possibly remember every single record in the Jovian database!"

"Very true, Prudence, but I recall this one vividly because it was so weird. And we classified it and encrypted it because we didn't understand it. Cuckoo? How did you come by this? Is there an explanation?"

The elderly lama sighed. "Subterfuge is sometimes unavoidable. The Way of the Wholesome must protect its interests. Several members of the *Skylark*'s team were monks of this order, as you know. I need say no more."

"What categories of information did your snoops steal?"

"A choice of terminology that pains me, but I concede the point. As I said: sometimes subterfuge is unavoidable. We wished to ensure that we received all records related to the existence of an early spacefaring civilization on Earth. The Way of the Wholesome has a special interest in such matters."

Now Charles was completely baffled. Had the old man gone mad? "What do these plasmoid things have to do with pre-Egyptian spaceflight?"

" '*But now the gods-that-dwell-beneath-the-Sun arose,*' " Prudence declaimed, " '*and their wrath was as the wrath of a raging torrent, and they spread great wings of burning flame. And their breath became a breath of fire, and they spat at Anshethrat. And the Moon was aflame, and the sky was aflame, and the Earth was aflame, and every tree in the city of Gÿzer turned to blackened ashes, and every house in the city became as a pillar of flame.*' " His face was a picture. "The *Y-ra'i*, Charles. The 'gods that dwell beneath the Sun.' Only you were right all along, my translation was poor. It's not 'beneath.' "

"No," said the Cuckoo. "It is 'within.' "

From hints and allusions in the Jovian records, and their own slab of pre-Egyptian legend, the Way of the Wholesome had put together a coherent story...

Compared to the plasmoids, Jovians and humans were

pretty much identical. Both were molecular, both lived on planets, and both used coded genetic information in the course of their reproduction. Plasmoids were very different. A plasmoid was a complex weave of interlocking vortices of superheated plasma, a "flying carpet" of irregular shape up to three hundred miles across, and it lived inside a star. It derived its organizational complexity, and its long-term stability, from the topological complexity of knots and links. A plasmoid was a suit of chain mail whose links were elaborately knotted whirlpools of magnetohydrodynamic plasma. Plasmoid genotype was identical to phenotype: the "information" required to create a new plasmoid was held in the topology of the parent's body plan. Plasmoids reproduced by a process of link-doubling that was akin to three-dimensional photocopying, though it would probably take human science half a millennium to figure out the details of how the two sets of vortices were successfully separated.

Topological errors in this photocopying process had made it possible for early proto-plasmoids to evolve. One of the first successful plasmoid life-forms was the magnetotorus, a huge ring of glowing plasma. Magnetotori learned to surf the solar winds, sucking in hydrogen fuel from their surroundings. They were living Bussard ramjets, dolphins of the interstellar winds, tasting the heady currents of space . . . Vast herds of wild magnetotori roamed the interstellar wastes, grazing on stardust.

The blimps had learned to tame magnetotori, breaking their animal spirits and bending them to their masters' wills. They used their tame magnetotori as celestial beasts of burden. Blimp starships were magnetotori with payloads. What the blimps had not known, until too late, was that far earlier the plasmoids in some stars had evolved intelligence. These sentient plasmoids had undergone a cosmic diaspora—first by hitching rides on magnetotori, later by metamorphosing into structured electromagnetic radiation and broadcasting themselves across the galaxy at the speed of light. Subsequently the sentient plasmoids had evolved culturally, becoming placid intellectuals and mystics who preferred to remain deep inside their own comfortable stars instead of risking death and dissociation in the interstellar void.

Then the blimps invented gravitic repulsion and started flinging undesirable comets and asteroids into Firsthome's Sun. This disturbed their star's normally introspective plasmoids by disrupting the peaceful nuclear processes of their breeding grounds. To the plasmoids it was inconceivable that nonplasma life-forms could possibly exist, so it took them an unconscionably long time to realize that the incoming projectiles were not some Act of God, but an Act of Blimp. Having done so, however, they were quick to deal with the threat. Out of a mystic respect for all life-forms, whatever their materials, the plasmoids could not resort to the obvious remedy of scorching Firsthome back to molten rock with a barrage of controlled solar flares. Instead, they made life impossible for the blimps by generating erratic changes in the star's output of heat and light. And their mysticism was robust enough to countenance an occasional limited torching of selected regions of the planet, as a warning. The blimps assumed that their sun's wild behavior was the result of some chaotic physical process and quickly came to the horrible conclusion that they had brought the disaster upon themselves through their obsessive tidiness regarding errant comets and asteroids. This was true, although they were seriously mistaken about details.

Whatever the cause, their only path to survival was to harness up the magnetotori, evacuate their homeworld, and find somewhere else to live. And so they had embarked upon their lengthy Exodus. Arriving at Secondhome after numerous terrible experiences, they vowed never again to risk disturbing their own sun. Only later did they learn the real reason for the Exodus, when they made contact with the Sun's plasmoids.

"And the pre-Egyptian tablets?" Prudence asked.

"We believe they record a burst of plasmoid activity in our

own Sun. The plasmoid diaspora, we are convinced, included the colonization of Earth's own star."

He said it so blithely. Intelligent life in the Sun? It was impossible to take it in. Only Moses seemed to accept the statement at face value. "I wouldn't want to shake hands with one," said Prudence, in a failed attempt at levity. "What happened, exactly?"

"History is a bottomless well into which many questions may be thrown but few answers splash out. At this point our theories become somewhat speculative."

"At *this* point?" said Charles, sounding for a moment like the old *Sir* Charles. Then he pulled himself together. "Sorry—I can't believe this."

"Bear with me," the Cuckoo said. "In the beginning, I was of a similar opinion. But as I meditated, I saw mystery after mystery falling into place. Ice, for instance. The Moon's store of ice at the poles, our lunar installations depend on it. The puzzle is that there seems to be *too much* ice.

"It is believed that water was deposited on the Moon long ago by icy asteroids during the phase in which the Solar System was aggregating by bombardment. Ice that could be touched by the rays of the Sun evaporated, but in deep crater shadows at the poles, the Sun could never penetrate. So there, ice survived. But today there is much more ice than could have been created by such a process."

"So?"

"So, Prudence, some other process must have put it there. We have compiled a chain of evidence and conjecture, and it all points to one explanation. At some point in pre-Egyptian times, when there was a flourishing *technologically advanced* civilization, the Jovians tossed a small comet at the Earth, in their usual manner. The pre-Egyptians sent up a spacecraft and blew the comet to tiny pieces, perhaps with nuclear weapons. Many of the pieces hit the Earth's upper atmosphere, where friction turned them into harmless water vapor. Others formed a celestial blizzard that draped the

Moon in ice. But again, only ice that lay near the poles would survive evaporation by the heat of the Sun.

"Conceivably, part of the comet remained intact, and the pre-Egyptians' action diverted it into the Sun. By then, plasmoids galaxy-wide were aware that nonplasma life-forms could exist and might be responsible for incoming projectiles. So the *Y-ra'i* decided to teach the Earth a lesson. Possibly they flamed part of the land with a concentrated solar flare, or . . . But perhaps that is taking the inscription too literally. Myth and legend change with the telling, and unrelated events are often conflated."

"But surely traces of such an advanced civilization would have survived," said Charles.

"Charlie, if our *own* civilization had existed twenty thousand years ago and suddenly lost its powers, you wouldn't have a snow cone in hell's chance of telling it was ever there," said Prudence.

"Save, perhaps, for a few artifacts *on the Moon*," the Cuckoo amended.

"Where there's no erosion to speak of. Right . . ."

Charles could no longer restrain himself. "Pru, you're not *buying* this load of nonsense, are you? It's riddled with holes! This guy's a mystic, not a scientist! He's been softening us up for weeks . . . meditation with the village monks, a spiritual pilgrimage ending on a mountaintop . . . The neo-Zen Buddhists have cobbled together a pile of unrelated puzzles and obscure bits of Jovian rubbish that are probably their equivalent of a fantascience novel, and come up with *this* incredible tale!"

"Charles, you can't *mean* that! You were there when Halfholder and Moses *touched*! I saw your face! Don't tell me that was mystical rubbish."

"Well . . ."

The Cuckoo leaned forward. "Charles Dunsmoore: you are a good man and your instincts are justified. The story that I have told is indeed little more than conjecture, and until a short time ago I myself would have applauded your outburst. Who knows how accurate the tale told by this tablet is? However, I have been in touch with the new Jovian authorities, and events are now in train that have certainly changed my mind. I suspect they will change yours."

Once more the lights dimmed. A wallscreen came to life, showing a portion of the Sun's surface, dimmed by filters. It was unclear whether it was live, recorded, or a computer reconstruction. The dark iris of a sunspot dominated the foreground. Strange granular patterns flowed across the red dome, and in the background they could see the ragged arc of a solar prominence.

"This was filmed earlier today from our lunar base," said the Cuckoo. "It is speeded up fiftyfold. Watch closely."

Part of the sunspot's surface began to bulge; its color changed from dark red to electric lavender. A perfect circular ring of lavender light emerged from the sunspot and climbed skyward. Moments later, a second followed it. Within a few minutes—no more than two hours real time—a string of several dozen identical lavender rings were rising from the Sun, in line astern, like a succession of smoke rings blown by a very accurate smoker.

"What in the name of . . ." Charles's voice trailed away. He couldn't remember what name he was intending to invoke.

"The Jovians have whistled," said the Cuckoo. "The magnetotori that had been stabled in the Sun have heard, and they are coming home."

Europatown, 2231

Eight years had passed since the Cuckoo's revelations, and much had changed.

The base on Europa had grown beyond all recognition. Now there was a thriving human township. The old prefabricated huts and inflatable domes were still standing, but the most fashionable housing was fabricated from slabs of impermeable, lightweight, rigid material grown on the Jovian cities according to human specifications and hauled into orbit with wheeler gravitic technology. It was wonderful for heat insulation on the icy moon. There were hundreds of buildings, public and private, all linked by airtight tunnels—offices, sleeping quarters, 'node centers—even a swimming pool. All around the edge of the town human machinery and wheelers were clearing the ground for further building work. Europa Base had become Europatown, and business was booming. Almost every day, a new building was completed.

A steady stream of spacecraft brought new people to swell the ranks of what was fast becoming Earth's biggest extraterrestrial colony, along with new materials, new demands, and new problems. One area had been turned into an informal market, and it would be only a matter of time before somebody decided that Europatown ought to have a mayor and put himself or herself forward as a candidate.

There were still a lot of bridges to build—not engineering ones, but cultural. The Earth's narrow escape from the comet had cost millions of lives; the damage, both to buildings and to the ecology, had been immense. A vocal minority was still campaigning for retaliation, but its membership was fast declining. Most of Earth's population thought the Bomb the Blimp movement was nuts, if only for the self-serving reason that it is unwise to attack an enemy that can fling comets at you. In general, people had accepted that the approach of the Death Comet had been a terrible mistake, and most of them were prepared to wipe the slate clean—though maybe not to forgive . . . and certainly not to forget.

The Jovians, too, had much to come to terms with. The stagnation of the Elders had given way to the Era of the Skydivers. Most were still estivating, as befits such a long-lived species. By the time they woke up, Secondhome would have changed beyond all recognition. Except, oddly enough, for Io. The Jovians wanted their moon back: it had been an important part of their cometary defenses, and there was no reason to let a good moon go to waste. Volcanically hyperactive but still intact, Io was careering erratically away from the Solar System in an unpredictable orbit. It would stay unpredictable until its volcanic activity died down, and the Jovians had no intention of waiting that long. So groups of wheeler specialists were already gearing up to recapture the satellite and install new Diversion Engines.

Human political attitudes were in ferment. For many years to come, Europatown would have to import its resources from Earth and Jupiter, and its inhabitants were working very hard to convince both worlds that it would be in their continuing interest to support its activities. Earth's businesses were falling over each other to do just that: it was obvious that there was much to gain by developing links with the aliens, *and* a lot to lose by not doing so. Already the benefits were starting to flow in as Earth and Belter scientists extracted new technologies from the Jovian archives. Antigravity beams would revolutionize lunar transportation, but there were less obvious applications. A small repulsion beam could create vertical wind shear in tropical zones and break up incipient hurricanes, for instance. Earth's more influential politicians quickly saw the way opinion was turning, and most of them aligned themselves behind it, isolating the lunatic fringe. There were plenty of xenophobic hate sites on the X, but opinions posted to Special Interest Groups were running in favor of human/blimp relations by about five to one.

Ignoring innumerable offers of lucrative positions and sponsorship deals back on Earth, Charles and Prudence had returned directly from New Tibet to Europa, helping to develop the growing interaction between humans and Jovians. Their relationship had blossomed as they worked together on things they both believed in. Moses had stayed with them, dashing Charity's hopes yet again. His abilities as an interpreter were indispensable, and when it came to the crunch nothing on Earth could compete with his beloved blimps, not even his mother. Most of *Skylark*'s scientists had found the attractions of an extraterrestrial civilization impossible to resist, and had set up semi-permanent homes at Europa Base. The rest had made the slow journey back to Earth aboard the returning *Skylark*. With them were Bailey, Cash, and Jonas, whose VV film of *Tiglath-Pileser*'s epic first contact, transmitted back to Earth within hours of the comet's passage, had made them instant celebrities worldwide. Jonas had seen how things were developing between Charles and Prudence and had known it was time to move on.

Moses had changed beyond all recognition. Now in his early twenties, he was poised and confident. He no longer observed the world from behind a poker face. He remained quiet and self-sufficient—but he had come to terms with his lost childhood. His ability to read people's body language no longer left him feeling confused; instead, it was turning him into a formidable politician. His intuition for animals and aliens remained uncanny. A worldwide search was on for others like him: so far, two candidates had been found.

A lot of things had happened to change Charles's mind since the sunspot had spat out a string of tame magnetotori, surfing the solar wind toward Jupiter.

With hindsight, a lot of things were obvious. For example, Jupiter's moons . . .

Before the loss of Io, there had been sixteen moons. They came in four sets of four, each with very distinct characteristics. From the center out:

Metis, Adrastea, Amalthea, and Thebe. Diminutive. None of them more than 160 miles across. Odd shapes, typically that of a potato. Orbital distances between 80,000 and 140,000 miles. Orbital inclination: zero. Eccentricity: zero.

Io, Europa, Ganymede, Callisto. All between 1,950 and 3,300 miles in diameter. Spherical. Each selenologically unique. Orbital distances between 260,000 and 1,180,000 miles. Orbital inclination: zero. Eccentricity: zero.

Leda, Nimalia, Lysithea, Elara. None more than 110 miles across. Orbital distances *virtually identical*: 7,170,000 miles. Orbital inclination: *virtually identical,* a massive 28 degrees. Eccentricity: about 0.15.

Ananke, Carme, Pasiphaë, Sinope. None more than 23 miles across. Orbital distances *virtually identical*: 14,000,000 miles. Orbital inclination: *virtually identical,* a ridiculous 150 degrees. Eccentricity: between 0.17 and 0.41.

The whole setup was totally artificial. *Why had nobody noticed?* When the aliens arrived at Jupiter, they had reconfigured the moons to suit their own purposes. Moons five through eight were the heart of the setup, the Inner Moons where the Diversion Engines held sway. The two sets of moons nine through twelve and thirteen through sixteen were asteroids, snared from the Belt to provide a convenient supply of raw materials . . . especially metal for the Jovians' offcast wheelers. Although metal atoms formed a tiny proportion of Jupiter's atmosphere, the atmosphere was *huge*, so the total amount of metals was pretty big. And they were concentrated biologically anyway. The eight outer moons were a kind of reserve supply. Their odd orbital geometry made it easier to convey material down to the central gas giant. The long axis of the orbits of moons nine through twelve fitted almost exactly into the short axis of moons thirteen through sixteen, making for easy transfers

What about the Innermost Moons, one through four?

They were rather interesting. Put it this way: *where had the Jovians concealed their interstellar ships?* They used magnetotori for propulsion, yes—but a Jovian could not live in a magnetotorus. *Where were the life-support systems?*

On moons one through four. The Jovians had brought them. More accurately, *they* had brought the Jovians.

Beneath their apparently normal surfaces, the Innermost Moons were mazes of tunnels and caverns, the closest thing to a city that could be fashioned from the dead rock of an asteroid. They had formed the magnetotori's payload, transported from Firsthome with the blimps and everything they owned secreted inside them. There, they were safe from radiation—especially that generated by the magnetotori—and meteor impacts.

Now, wheeler constructs were crawling all over the largest of the Innermost Moons: Amalthea. They were reweaving the tightly fitting nets of metal cable that would allow the magnetotori to grip them in their magnetic jaws. Somewhere beneath the millions of miles of cable were complexes of caves that had been modified for human-style life support. Deep inside an Amalthean crater, *Tiglath-Pileser* was tethered.

Blimps and humans were joining forces to create an ambitious interstellar expedition. Why? Because the Way of the Wholesome had convinced them that it was vital to the future of both races.

Charles's mind went back to the Cuckoo and their mountaintop encounter . . .

"What you need to understand," said the Cuckoo, "is that the plasmoids are not what is important."

Even Prudence had found that hard to accept. "Don't be silly, Mkha'-gro! First you tell us that there are creatures who live in our Sun and control whether we live or die; then you say they're not important?"

"No, Prudence—I say that there is something that is more important. Charles: I believe that during the last few days before the passage of the comet, you concluded that the Elders were lying to you?"

"How did you—oh, Buddhist spies. Absolutely. That's one reason why I agreed with Prudence that we had to switch our efforts to the skydivers."

"Then you will perhaps not be pleased to be informed that everything the Elders told you was true."

"Nonsense. Their records referred to events that happened forty billion years ago!"

"Those records are accurate."

"But that's nearly three times older than the Big Bang!"

"That is what our scientists tell us, yes."

"And the alien records also said that there had been life on Jupiter when the blimps arrived—which would have been okay, but . . . it was compatible with their own kind of life."

"Which you considered highly improbable?"

"Impossible. Evolution doesn't work like that."

The Cuckoo had risen to his feet, blue robes billowing around him, unfit for wearing in zero gee. "Then perhaps you can explain to me the fragment of diatom shell that your own task force discovered on Europa."

"How did you know about—" Charles had collected his thoughts. "Look, I know you had some of your guys on the *Skylark,* but that discovery was eyes-only. *Nobody* knew about it except me and Frederica Sunesson, and I don't believe she was neo-Zen."

The Cuckoo said nothing. There was nothing to be said.

"*Freddy?* I was out of my depth all along, wasn't I? And I

thought *I* was a smart operator! Look, we couldn't tell any-one about it because it had to be contamination. Someone brought it on their clothing."

"Did you get it dated?"

"Of course not. It wasn't relevant to our mission."

The Cuckoo sighed. "You make so many assumptions. *We* have dated the diatom. Its age is sixty-five million years."

"*What?*"

"Several Martian meteorites have been found on Earth, mostly in the Antarctic. Splashed off the planet's surface by an incoming rock. Go back sixty-five million years, to the K/T meteorite that destroyed the dinosaurs. It smashed into the Gulf of Mexico at Chicxulub, coastal Yucatán. Big splash, some of the water goes into orbit . . . Diatoms in the droplets . . .

"Billions on the Moon, almost certainly . . . but very thinly spread, no one would ever find one except by pure luck. Some made it to Europa. Sunesson got lucky."

"Shit."

"Now, tell me: what is the core belief of the skydivers?"

Moses knew that one. "Lifesoul Cherisher. Cometary impacts are good for the Jovian ecology."

"Correct. *Why?*"

"Religious beliefs don't have to have rational reasons," Charles pointed out.

"This is not a religious belief. There is a rational reason. It explains much." The Cuckoo saw that he must spell it out for them. "The life cycle of most of the Jovian flora and fauna goes through a sporulation stage, the nanogametes, yes? They produce them by the trillion, all the time—the atmosphere is a thin nanogametic soup. So what happens when a comet hits? What happened on Mars? On Earth?"

Oh, my dear lord. "A splash."

"Exactly. And nanogametes splash along with the atmo-sphere, and they float off into the cosmos. Do you know how

long a Jovian spore can survive in a vacuum?" Blank faces.
"Indefinitely. That is its preferred environment."

Now Charles began to get the picture. "So cometary impacts spread the Jovian spores all over the galaxy . . . Oh,
hell. The fauna on Firsthome and the indigenous fauna on
Jupiter both came from the same source. Endless tiny spores
floating through the interstellar void. Whenever they encounter a suitable world—bingo! Life!"

"And it's the *same* life," Prudence realized.

"To begin with, yes," the Cuckoo told her. "But life, once
established, evolves separately in each environment. The
skydivers thought that impacts were good for Jovian life—
more diversity. That is true. But the real reason is deeper, and
far more ancient. They tapped into a racial memory.

"Now let me peel off another layer. We are still thinking
about these matters in too specialized a way. We know of a
variety of life-forms and pseudo-life-forms. Humans.
Blimps. Wheelers. Magnetotori. Plasmoids. So: what do they
have in common?"

Charles was the first to admit defeat. "Nothing. Each is
unique."

"Not so. They are alive."

"Yes, but—"

"They exploit a universal principle. You might call it the
cracks in the second law of thermodynamics, but that would
be to dignify a serious misconception. The true principle is
much simpler. *Biology corrupts physics*."

"I know what you mean. 'Life turns up everywhere it can.
Life turns up everywhere it can't.' "

"Neatly put, Prudence. We must not think of life as some
exotic form of matter that requires extremely improbable
events to come into being. Life is a universal process—re-
producing, self-organizing, self-complicating . . . It is in the
nature of that process that however 'difficult' it may be to get
going, once it does get going it takes over completely. And in
fact it is not especially difficult—it is just that humans have

difficulty understanding it. On Earth, you find bacteria miles beneath the surface, in cracks in the rock, living off chemical energy—iron-sulfur metabolism, quite unlike you and me. But that is the *same* kind of life, because it runs on the same chemical ingredients—"

"You mean we're all part of the same big system, and it's penetrated to every part of the planet. Rocks are made from the shells of dead creatures . . . organic chemicals lubricate the drift of the continents . . . forests affect the weather . . ." Prudence wasn't able to keep the excitement out of her voice.

The Cuckoo applauded. "Well done! That is exactly my meaning. We believe that we exist in a universe that runs by the laws of physics—endless tiny quantum wavelets rippling through multidimensional quantum fields. Physicists have worked out the rules, and they have derived a wonderful picture of how quantum wavelets behave. But now it gets philosophically difficult: biology *corrupts* physics. More accurately: mathematics is corrupted by physics is corrupted by chemistry is corrupted by biology is corrupted by intelligence is corrupted by culture is corrupted by extelligence, which corrupts itself recursively."

Prudence—and Moses—were quickly convinced, but Charles continued to raise objections. "Do you mean that life doesn't obey the laws of physics? Isn't that a rather mystical position?"

"You have put your finger upon the philosophically tricky aspect. I am *not* saying that life disobeys the laws of physics. It is *how* it obeys those laws that matters. We can follow the link from the laws of quantum physics to the hydrogen atom, so the hydrogen atom is excellent physics. But a quantum-mechanical explanation of a lioness chasing a zebra simply does not work *as physics*. You cannot even *express* the problem in terms of quantum wave functions—lionesses and zebras are far too complicated. There is no way to go from the laws of quantum physics to a lioness hunting a zebra except by leaving enormous logical gaps. The universe may be *doing* it that way, but the human mind cannot possibly follow such a convoluted chain of causality. Yet the mind of a lioness knows it wants to hunt the zebra, and the mind of a zebra impels it to outrun the lioness."

"Ant Country," Prudence realized. "Mind is an emergent phenomenon."

"Exactly. The universe *may* be navigating its way through the intricacies of Ant Country, quantum rule by quantum rule, an unimaginably huge game of cosmic chess . . . but if it is, we cannot understand it that way. The mathematics of 'hungry' is not derivable from quantum physics in any manner that the human mind can grasp. That is what I mean by 'corrupts.' Biology does not disobey physics: it just works in a way that makes our normal understanding of physics inoperative. Ask the lioness and the zebra."

The Cuckoo waited patiently while the others argued among themselves. He knew that they had received his message: it would sink in when they were ready for it. Moses was already prepared. Finally Charles spoke. "You're saying the Big Bang never happened?"

"Not at all. I am saying that calculations based on the assumption that the period between the Big Bang and now consists entirely of uncorrupted physics will misjudge the age of the universe. Just as calculations of the speed of terrestrial continental drift, based on pure geology, give the wrong answer, because they ignore the lubricating effect of organic matter. And calculations of the oxygen turnover in Earth's atmosphere that ignore plant life are simply nonsense."

"But what about the cosmic background radiation? Blackbody radiation at three degrees Kelvin, echoes of the Big Bang from fifteen billion years ago?"

"Echoes from *something,* surely," said the Cuckoo. "The Big Bang? Charles: how can we know that?"

"Oh. Lachmann's Theorem. The communications of advanced civilizations look exactly like—"

"Black-body radiation," Prudence finished for him. "Oh, my God."

"We're picking up the encrypted communications of *fifteen-billion-year-old civilizations*? Not echoes of the Big Bang?"

"History," the Cuckoo told them, "is unknowable. You could be right, Charles. No doubt the Big Bang *happened,* but much further in the past than we have computed. Certainly the question of 'missing neutrinos' in solar nuclear reactions is easily solved: not neutrino mass or oscillations, but plasmoid society managing the nuclear reactions for its own benefit. Other mysteries may have similar solutions. What physicists call the era of inflation may be the effect of quantum-gravity creatures that *eat* curvature. The anomalous spin of galaxies may not be evidence for cold dark matter, but for the ability of a living galaxy to swim at will through the cosmic void.

"The universe is a playground of life, but—as we have seen—even a race as ancient as the Jovians can fail to understand just how diverse living systems can be. Our own species nearly became extinct as a consequence. Diverse they may be, but they are also unified. We and the Jovians—even the plasmoids—are not so dissimilar. Our phylogeny and the Jovians' diverged from that of the plasmoids when the universe was composed solely of hydrogen and helium."

"You're saying we all have a common *ancestor*?"

"Yes, but it was not a life-form. It was a common ancestral corruption. The quantum wave functions diverged, some to plasma and high temperatures, others to complex atoms, molecular matter, and low temperatures. Later, chemical divergences separated our ancestors, inhabitants of aqueous worlds, from those of the Jovians—creatures suited to gas giants.

"The Tree of Life is All One.

"And that . . . brings me to my final conclusion. Not an abstract observation about the nature of life, but a moral imperative. Between us, humans and Jovians, we have understood a deep truth. Out in the universe there may be creatures who are repeating the same mistakes that were made on Firsthome and in our own Solar System. We and the Jovians have been placed in a unique position: we possess the understanding, and together we possess the means to propagate it."

There had been a long silence.

"Shit." The Cuckoo's intentions had finally dawned on Prudence. "You want us to turn into missionaries. Spreading the gospel of unity and diversity of pangalactic life. Cosmic greenies."

The Cuckoo had said nothing.

Sometimes all you had to do was wait.

Charity and Angie sat on the veranda of the Moses Odingo Zoodiversity Center, Gooma. A dose of Carver money had transformed the place beyond all recognition. A gibbous moon hung in the sky, its reflections gleaming off the artificial lake that the landscape architects had created. Ripples turned specks of moonlight into elegant curves, evanescent Islamic calligraphy.

The Moon dust kicked up by the comet had settled, and the Buddhist bases were back in business. Two months ago, the Moon's face appeared entirely normal—dark maria surrounded by brighter uplands. Tonight, it was unrecognizable—there were no large dark patches, and when seen through a low-powered lens its softly lit disk was dominated by the concentric rings of the Mare Orientale and the brilliant radiating circle of Nāgārjuna Crater, where a fragment of comet had hit. In another two months, the familiar Man in the Moon would beam down once more. The comet's passage had altered the Moon's rotation. No longer in synch with its orbital revolution, to earthly eyes it was slowly spinning. It was a permanent reminder that the human race teetered on a celestial knife edge.

Along with virtually everyone else on Earth, Angie and

Charity were watching the VV. Bailey Barnum had really hit the big time with this show: the Lumley ratings broke all previous records put together. His now-massive communications corporation the Greatest Show Off Earth was vidivising nonstop live images (forty-eight minutes late) from Jupiter.

Metis, Adrastea, and Thebe were not needed for this voyage: it was to be an exploration, not another exodus. Only the ungainly pockmarked lump known as Amalthea, which had been cast off from parking orbit two weeks earlier, was taking its place in the assembly zone. The errant Innermost Moon was swarming with wheeler gadgetry, making final inspections of the new oxygen-atmosphere installations and the intricate nets of thick cable that enveloped it.

Days before, all blimp and human passengers had disappeared into the moonlet's cavernous interior. Among them were Prudence and Charles, Moses and Halfholder. The Cuckoo had been right—he knew that none of them could resist the challenge. So he sowed the suggestion and waited, and in time they came to the same opinion.

Satisfied with their preparations, the wheelers scuttled belowdecks, too.

Cashew Tintoretto, celebrity presenter, was going berserk as Jonas cleverly built up the excitement with recorded footage of Prudence, Charles, Moses, and Halfholder. Then the images switched to the string of tame magnetotori, waiting patiently at the edge of the assembly zone.

Brushed by repulsor beams, the moonlet began to revolve. In its interior, centrifugal forces created the illusion of gravity. Electricity flowed through the network of cables, and the moonlet acquired a magnetic field. Lines of magnetic force, invisible but no less real for that, linked the spinning moonlet to the waiting train of magnetotori.

Angie chuckled. "Hitch your wagon to a star." All that was missing was a bearded old drunk in a ten-gallon hat to ride shotgun.

Charity's mind was elsewhere. The stocky Nyamwezian

was surprisingly unemotional, but her eyes shone with an inner gleam of pride.

"Penny for them?"

"I'm thinking of Moses . . . but you know that. His childhood was stolen from me, the Buddhists changed his mind about coming home, and now he's going off to the stars and I'll never see him again."

"He'll be back—one day."

"But I won't be here to greet him, Angela. Time will pass more slowly for him than for us."

The older woman nodded knowingly. *The Centauri system, Barnard's Star, Wolf 359, Lalande 21185, Sirius, Epsilon Eridani, 61 Cygni, Procyon, Sigma 2398 . . . Not much farther apart, in relativistically dilated journey time, than a return trip from Earth to Jupiter . . . Why would any red-blooded human being ever want to come home?*

"He's a good boy. Makes his mother proud." Charity lapsed into silence, staring at the VV screen. Then she stood up. "Show's over for now, they won't be ready to leave for weeks. I'll just go and . . . and make sure that . . . the new cheetah cubs are settled. You—you coming?"

"Sure, honey. I need to stretch my legs." Angie pulled open the screen door and the two women stepped back into the house.

Life goes on.

Everywhere.

DR. IAN STEWART, professor of mathematics at Warwick University, is a recipient of the Royal Society's Michael Faraday Medal for furthering public understanding of science. A columnist for *Scientific American* and frequent television commentator, Dr. Stewart is the author of more than 130 papers of mathematical research and 60 books of popular science. Ian Stewart lives in England.

DR. JACK COHEN currently teaches at Warwick University. He has participated in the production of numerous television science specials, notably *The Natural History of an Alien* for BBC2. As a reproductive biologist, he is a consultant to infertility laboratories; as a theoretical xenobiologist, he is a consultant to science fiction writers. Jack Cohen lives in England.

THE LEGENDARY
ARTHUR C. CLARKE